Remembering Miss Addie

A NOVEL BY

LAMAR WADSWORTH

© 2013

Published in the United States by Nurturing Faith Inc., Macon GA,

www.nurturingfaith.info.

ISBN 978-1-938514-32-6

About the Author

Lamar Wadsworth studied creative writing with poet, short story writer, and novelist Jesse Stuart. A Baptist minister, he has served churches in Alabama, Kentucky, Georgia, and Maryland. He is an adoptions case manager with the Polk County Department of Family and Children Services, and he and his wife are adoptive parents of three grown daughters. He enjoys old cars because he understands them and can fix them when they break. The great-grandson of a Southern Railway engineer, he has a lifelong fascination with steam locomotives and can tell you more than you want to know about valve gear, crossheads, superheaters, and Nathan chime whistles. As Jesse Stuart often did, Lamar goes to old cemeteries in search of good names for fictional characters, as well as picking some off his own family tree. He lives near Rockmart, Georgia, with his wife Marilyn and daughter Missy. *Remembering Miss Addie* is his second novel.

SPONSORS

Frieda Byrd

Mary Jane Cardwell

Dr. Patricia Ingle Gillis

Winnie V. Williams

IN MEMORIAM

Barbara Jean Clarke

Ruby Paisley

Contents

Foreword

Remembering Miss Addie honors the memory of the late Ruby Welsh Wilkins (1919-2007), pastor of Antioch Baptist Church near Wadley, Alabama, from 1971 to 1984. She was the first woman to serve as pastor of a Baptist church in Alabama. It was my pleasure to know her as a friend and as an able minister of the gospel.

The characters in *Remembering Miss Addie* are fictional, but they sometimes go to real places. A few real people find their way to fictional Harrington and Mintz County. When nineteen-year-old Cassie McWhorter is called as pastor of Peyton's Chapel Baptist Church, Ruby Welsh Wilkins makes the trip from Wadley, Alabama, to Harrington, Georgia, to help with her ordination. Ironically, Ruby was never ordained. She had no interest in formal titles or recognition. She simply delighted in doing the will of the one who called her to be a minister of the gospel. No council ever laid hands on her head, yet there was power, grace, and blessing in the touch of Ruby's small arthritic hands. Cassie can attest to that.

Remembering Miss Addie is set in 1998. At that time, my friend Bob Ballance was the editor of *Baptists Today*. In the novel, Bob and his wife, Catherine Kent Ballance, who is also a Baptist minister, travel down to Harrington to help ordain Cassie and do a story for *Baptists Today* about the little country church that called her as pastor.

Harrington has a low-power AM radio station that starts fading fast when you get about ten miles from town. The station's most popular program, next to *The Swap Shop*, is *The Obituary Column of the Air*, which 101-year-old Miss Addie refers to contemptuously as "Who's Dead Today." My cousin Perry "Bill" Bailey, who has worked in broadcasting more than forty years, graciously agreed to come over to Harrington to be the announcer for (cue the Hammond organ with too much vibrato playing "Sweet Hour of Prayer") *The Obituary Column of the Air*, brought to you by the courteous professional staff of Webster Funeral Home in Harrington, Georgia, neighbors serving neighbors in times of sorrow since 1938.

About Mintz County, Georgia

Georgia has 159 counties. Only Texas has more. We once had 161, but Campbell and Milton Counties went bankrupt in the Depression and were merged into Fulton County. There is a movement underway to revive Milton County with its original boundaries, but even if Milton County is revived, we expect to lose some counties to kudzu before it's over. When Georgia's last new county, Peach County, was created in 1924, one wag said that Georgia had run out of people to name counties for and had started naming them for fruits. I named fictional Mintz County for a delightful friend, the late H. D. "Cowboy" Mintz, a veteran Southern Railway conductor and a spellbinding storyteller, and his mother, the late Leonora Ferguson Mintz, my eighth grade English teacher and one of the people who encouraged me to write. I gave Cowboy a copy of my first novel and told him that I had named Mintz County for him and his mother, as I considered them more deserving than some of the people who had actual Georgia counties named for them. As one who knew his Georgia history, Cowboy said that he agreed with me.

Mrs. Addie Jane Peyton Aldridge, age 101, of Pine Ridge Assisted Living Center, formerly of Court Street in Harrington, died Saturday morning at her residence. Mrs. Aldridge, better known as "Miss Addie," was born July 26, 1897 in the Peyton's Crossroads community in Mintz County, daughter of the late John David Peyton and Sarah Elizabeth Nestor Peyton. She was preceded in death by her husband, Mr. Chester Aldridge, her parents, and two brothers, Rev. Lawrence Peyton and Rev. Will Peyton. She is survived by nieces, nephews, and cousins. Mrs. Aldridge graduated from LaGrange Teachers College and began teaching in 1917 at the one- room school in Freeman Valley. She moved to Harrington and began teaching at Harrington Elementary School after her marriage to Mr. Aldridge in 1922. After her retirement in 1960, she taught first grade for two years as a volunteer at the Florida Avenue Colored School. In 1962, she became the first woman elected to public office in Mintz County when she won a seat on the Board of Education. In1966, as chair of the Board of Education, she helped lead the Mintz County Schools through desegregation. Last year, on her one hundredth birthday, the Mintz County Board of Education renamed Harrington Elementary School in her honor. Miss Addie will lie in state from 6:00 p.m. to 9:00 p.m. Sunday at Addie Jane Peyton Aldridge Elementary School. The funeral service will be held Monday at 1:00 p.m. at Harrington Baptist Church, where Mrs. Aldridge was an active member for seventy-six years, with Rev. Michael Westover, Rev. Andrew Jennings, and Rev. Cassie McWhorter officiating. Pallbearers will be Aaron Stewart, Darrell Brinson, Davis Gates, Luke Groves, Ted Coleman, and Anthony McWhorter. Active and retired Mintz County educators and members of the Mintz County Board of Education will serve as honorary pallbearers. Interment will follow in the Peyton's Chapel Baptist Church cemetery. Webster Funeral Home has charge of the arrangements for Mrs. Addie Jane Peyton Aldridge.

Chapter 1

"Asalee, grab my phone," Mike Westover called out as he pulled a pan of hot biscuits from the oven. "It's on the table by the recliner."

"It's Tommy Sheridan down at Webster Funeral Home, Daddy," fourteen-year-old Asalee yawned as she handed Mike his cell. Asalee had been out until nearly 1:00 a.m. with the Harrington High School band. Mike had dozed off in the car at the high school waiting for the band buses to return from Lagrange. He and police chief Aaron Stewart, who lived across the street, had daughters in the band. Asalee Westover and Rosa Stewart had been inseparable since the first grade, so Mike and Aaron took turns on the late-night runs to meet band buses after out-of-town football games and band trips. Asalee's band uniform, trumpet case, and bra lay where they landed on the rocking chair in her room. She dimly remembered the ride home and changing into the cozy warmth of her favorite flannel gown before burrowing down under a couple of quilts. She really didn't mean to be awake this early, but the smells of breakfast cooking and coffee perking had roused her. Hungry won out over sleepy, and she was beginning to like coffee with breakfast, so she stumbled to the sofa in the den and cuddled up with her eight-year-old sister under the big afghan that Lunell Bishop crocheted for them last Christmas to watch cartoons until breakfast was on the table. Asalee was glad that Deb liked Road Runner and Wile E. Coyote, although she feared that they both had inherited their father's sense of humor. Asalee enjoyed the antics of those two now more than she did when she was Deb's age. After giving the phone to her dad, Asalee resumed the snuggle under the afghan with her little sister.

"Hey, Preacher, hope I didn't wake you up." Tommy sounded much too cheery for 8:30 a.m. on a Saturday.

"Been up a while, Tommy, cooking breakfast like I do every Saturday. Just took the biscuits out of the oven, fixing to scramble the eggs and make some gravy."

"Whooo boy, Karen's got you trained right! Be right over, sounds like some good eatin'," Tommy exclaimed with his familiar horse-whinny laugh.

"Saturday morning's Karen's time to sleep in while I cook. She likes to sleep late the one day that she can, and I like to cook, so it works for us. For what it's worth, Daddy's the one who taught me how to cook; he's a better cook than my mama is and she'd be the first one to admit that. He was the breakfast cook at our house when I was growing up, so I'm following in his footsteps." Mike had built a 350 Chevy engine for Tommy and spent last Monday helping him install it in his '46 Chevy pickup. Tommy had a spacious garage like Mike hoped to have when he got to heaven, enough mechanical aptitude to get himself in over his head, and enough tools to be dangerous, but Mike knew that Tommy wasn't calling this early on Saturday morning for mechanical advice, so he cut to the chase. "Somebody dead, Tommy?"

"It's Miss Addie, Preacher. Passed in her sleep last night. Daniel and I just got back from over't Pine Ridge, picking up the body. A hundred and one years old, born in 1897. Nurses said she seemed fine when they took her bedtime meds up to her last night, went to check on her this morning when she didn't come down to the dining room for breakfast and they couldn't get her on the phone. She was usually there by 6:30 a.m., as soon as the coffee was made, drinking coffee and talking with the dining room staff while they put breakfast out. Body was still warm, so she hadn't been dead long. They didn't try to revive her because she had a DNR order in place. Just went to sleep and didn't wake up."

"She was at church last Sunday, looked great, acted like she felt pretty good," Mike commented as the news sank in. "Couple of Sundays ago, she read one of the scripture readings in the Sunday morning service. Wouldn't have thought she was anywhere near that old just to look at her, and sharp as a tack. She knew the names of all the children at church and spoke to them by name. Always had kids lined up to hug Miss Addie when she came to church, usually had a half dozen sitting with her. You'd always see a couple of the boys walking her to and from the car, helping her with the door and the seat belt. My girls loved her to death. My eight-year-old says if she ever has a little girl, she's gonna name her Addie."

"Daniel had tears running down his face when we were over there picking up the body this morning. You know how he and Coretta loved Miss Addie, had her as matron of honor at their wedding when she was ninety-nine-years old. Made Miss Addie so happy when they asked her, said the only wedding she'd ever been in was her own back in 1922. She said she'd do it if the organist didn't play the wedding march too fast for her to walk down the aisle."

"Never will forget that wedding," Mike reminisced. "Greater New Hope's a beautiful place for a wedding, and Miss Addie stole the show. She was even more elegant than usual in that bridesmaid dress and loving every minute of it. Whole congregation was on its feet, gave her a standing ovation, bunch of people snapped pictures as she came down the aisle and took her place at the front of the church. Coretta was a beautiful bride, but she didn't have anything on Miss Addie, and she didn't even care that Miss Addie upstaged her."

"Yeah," Tommy commented, "that was the first thing I noticed when we went to her apartment out at Pine Ridge this morning. She had a nice big eight-by-ten of the whole wedding party. Staff said she showed it to everybody who came to see her. By the way, don't know if you know, I may be lettin' the cat out of the bag before I'm supposed to, but Daniel and Coretta are expecting. They just found out last week that Coretta's pregnant. Daniel came in Wednesday morning, grinning ear to ear, telling all of us at the funeral home, so I don't suppose it's any great secret. If it's a girl, wouldn't be surprised if she gets named Addie."

"Hadn't heard about Coretta being pregnant, have to congratulate them when I see them at church tomorrow. Addie would be a pretty name for a baby girl. Don't guess you know the arrangements for Miss Addie yet."

"Don't have the viewing and service times yet, but Miss Addie came in back in '91, made the arrangements with us, and paid for everything. Of course, the service'll be at Harrington Baptist and you'll be in charge. Miss Addie and Mr. Ches, I remember him, fine man, they didn't have any children. Her niece, Mrs. Kathleen Mayfield, old preacher Lawrence Peyton's daughter, she and her husband live over't Carrollton, they're coming in about 11:00 a.m., bringing the clothes for her to be laid out in. Mrs. Mayfield had power of attorney over everything while Miss Addie was living, and she's the executor of the estate. I'll know the service times after they come in; don't think there's any family that'll be traveling a long distance. We'll probably have the funeral on Monday, works out good with it being the Columbus Day holiday. I need to call Janet Baxter, principal at Miss Addie's School. Last year when they had the hundredth birthday party for Miss Addie at the school and surprised her by unveiling the new sign renaming the school in her honor, Mrs. Baxter told me that when this time came, they'd be honored to have the viewing for Miss Addie at the school. So, if that's okay with the family, we'll do that. In all my years as a funeral director, I've never had a viewing at an elementary school, but I think it's fitting in her case, considering she taught half of Harrington. She'd be pleased with that. Burial will be out at Peyton's Chapel where her husband and all of her people are buried."

"Won't have to guess about her wishes on the service," Mike noted. "She talked with me a good while back about how she wanted the service done. Got a folder at my office at the church with notes I took on our conversation. Three preachers — me, Andrew Jennings from Zion A. M. E., and Cassie McWhorter."

"Cassie McWhorter?" Tommy responded. "She's Jerry and Elaine's daughter, right? Graduated with my youngest boy."

"Right. She just turned nineteen a few days ago, graduated from Harrington High School this past June; she's in her first semester at Mercer and wants to be a pastor. We licensed her to preach, and she preached her first sermon about a year ago. She brought a good message, a lot better than I did my first time. Got ourselves kicked out of the association for that. Cassie and Miss Addie have been close since Cassie was a little girl. Miss Addie wanted Cassie to have a part in her funeral. It'll be Cassie's first funeral. I'll take care of calling everybody who's supposed to have a part in the service."

"'Preciate that, Preacher. I'll call Mrs. Baxter about having the viewing at the school and get the notices to *The Harrington Courier* and the radio station."

"Hey, Cassie, sorry to call and wake you up so early on a Saturday morning."

"It's okay, Brother Mike," Cassie yawned into the phone that her mom had handed her. "I needed to get up anyway, kept turning over and going back to sleep. What's up?"

"It's Miss Addie, Cass. Died in her sleep early this morning." Mike paused as he heard Cassie sobbing and heard her mom, Elaine, in the background trying to comfort her.

"Don't guess I should take it so hard," Cassie spoke as she regained her composure. She was one hundred and one years old, after all. So glad I went by Pine Ridge yesterday evening to see her. I'd just gotten in from Macon, hadn't been home yet, still had two laundry baskets full of dirty clothes in the back of my car. Something told me I needed to go see her. I was planning to go sometime later today, but I decided to go yesterday evening on my way in. Glad I did. I was in blue jeans and a Mercer sweatshirt, hair pulled straight back in a ponytail, and she took one look at me and told me how pretty I looked. Told me she had auburn hair, the same color as mine, when she was young, then she laughed and told me that I'd have white hair, the same color as hers, when I'm old."

"Looks like you'll be helping conduct your first funeral on Monday, Cass. Miss Addie's request — you, me, and Andy Jennings from over at Zion A. M. E."

Laughter broke through Cassie's tears. "Never will forget when I preached my first sermon and the church licensed me. Miss Addie came up and hugged me, told me how well she thought I did, and told me that she wanted me to have a part in her funeral. I told her, 'Miss Addie, I can't do that. You're not dead.' We were both cracking up, and she said, 'You know what I mean, Cassie McWhorter! I want you to have a part in my funeral after I die.' I told her that I'd do it after she died but not a day sooner. It'll be an honor. I suppose it's fitting for a young woman preacher to have a part in the funeral of the first woman to preach at Harrington Baptist Church. It was the summer before I turned eleven in October of 1990, but I remember it like it was yesterday. Miss Addie and I have had this amazing connection as far back as I can remember. I've always considered her my best friend, so you asked her to give her testimony and tell about her baptism on the Sunday that you and Daddy baptized me. She went beyond testifying and delivered a fine sermon! She was amazing as she told about being baptized in Salyers Creek below the dam at Bailey's Mill in 1908, just after her eleventh birthday. You know how she liked that quote from Harry Ironside, 'It's up to us to see that we do right and up to God to see that we come out right.' I'll always remember that and something else she said that day. She said, 'Cassie, when you come to the hard decisions in life, remember your baptism. Close your eyes and feel the water, and you'll know what you need to do.' She gave me the necklace with the gold cross that her parents gave her the day she was baptized. She wore it in the water after her mother told her not to, and so did I. I know it was made for a young girl, but I wear it every time I preach, and I'll wear it Monday. Looks like I'll be spending some time down by the creek today — need to do that anyway, but especially since I'll be getting ready for my part in Miss Addie's funeral. The place where Miss Addie was baptized is holy ground for me. I've been known to wade out in the water a few times."

"Sometime in the summer, it'd be great to go down to the creek to baptize," Mike commented. "That'd be a beautiful place to do it. I'm going to call Eric about the music and call Andy Jennings. You probably know that Miss Addie taught two years after she retired at the old Florida Avenue Colored School, without being paid a cent. She was so proud of Andrew, one of her former students she liked to brag about. Miss Addie loved to hear the quartet sing a cappella from *The Sacred Harp*. She cut her teeth on the old 'fa-sol-la' singing. She's the one who introduced Eric and Jenny to *Sacred Harp* singing, taught them and David and Cheryl to read shaped notes. So Eric can get everybody together and practice up on 'Children of the Heavenly King,' 'Hark! I Hear the Harps Eternal,' 'Wondrous Love,' and 'I Love the Lord, He Heard My Cries.' Let's plan to meet at my office about noon today to work out all of the details of the service."

Precisely at noon, as she sipped her third cup of coffee, Karen Westover turned on the kitchen radio that stayed tuned to the local AM station that you can't pick up ten miles out of town, for *The Obituary Column of the Air*, which Miss Addie referred to contemptuously as "Who's Dead Today." The program began with the familiar recording of the Hammond organ with way too much vibrato playing "Sweet Hour of Prayer." The bad organ music was mercifully turned down as Bill Bailey began the voiceover: "Welcome to *The Obituary Column of the Air*, brought to you by the courteous professional staff of the Webster Funeral Home in Harrington, Georgia, neighbors serving neighbors in times of sorrow since 1938. In today's announcements, Mrs. Addie Jane Peyton Aldridge, age 101, of Pine Ridge Assisted Living Center, formerly of Court Street in Harrington, died early this morning at her residence.

Mrs. Aldridge, better known as 'Miss Addie,' was born on July 26, 1897 in the Peyton's Crossroads community in Mintz County, daughter of the late John David Peyton and Sarah Elizabeth Nestor Peyton. She was preceded in death by her husband, Mr. Chester Aldridge, her parents, and two brothers, Rev. Lawrence Peyton and Rev. Will Peyton. She is survived by nieces, nephews, and cousins. Mrs. Aldridge graduated from LaGrange Teachers College and began teaching in 1917 at the one-room school in Freeman Valley. She moved to Harrington and began teaching at Harrington Elementary School after her marriage to Mr. Aldridge in 1922. After her retirement in 1960, she taught first grade for two years as a volunteer at the Florida Avenue Colored School. In 1962, she became the first woman elected to public office in Mintz County when she won a seat on the Board of Education. In 1966, as chair of the Board of Education, she helped lead the Mintz County Schools through desegregation. Last year, in honor of her one-hundredth birthday, Harrington Elementary School was renamed in her honor. Miss Addie will lie in state from 6:00 to 9:00 p.m. tomorrow at Addie Jane Peyton Aldridge Elementary School. The funeral service will be held Monday at 1:00 p.m. at Harrington Baptist Church, where Mrs. Aldridge was an active member for seventy-six years, with Rev. Michael Westover, Rev. Andrew Jennings, and Rev. Cassie McWhorter officiating. Interment will follow in the Peyton's Chapel Baptist Church cemetery. Webster Funeral Home has charge of the arrangements for Mrs. Addie Jane Peyton Aldridge."

Deborah Estelle Westover had been standing in the doorway from the kitchen into the dining room, tears trickling down her face, listening intently to the radio. Karen switched the radio off and took her younger daughter into her embrace. She held her close and let her cry as much as she needed to. After a while, a smile came across Deb's tear-streaked face as she said, "Y'know something, Mama?"

"What, Hon?"

"I just told Jesus that Miss Addie is really sweet and he's really gonna like having her up there in heaven with him."

Chapter 2

"Hey, Reverend Westover, anybody here?" Mike recognized the voice of Andrew Jennings, pastor of Zion African Methodist Episcopal Church in Harrington, a voice that always sounded as though it should belong to a much larger man.

"Back here in my study," Mike called out. "Come on back. I just got here and started a pot of coffee, and pulled out some notes I'd made on my conversations with Miss Addie. You're the first one here. Cassie and Eric'll be here directly." Mike stood to greet Andy Jennings, and the solid handshake turned into a hug. "Good to see you, Brother. Appreciate you coming over on such short notice."

"Glad to do it. I'm honored to have a part in Miss Addie's funeral. We've got a couple of our older members living up at Pine Ridge, so I'd always go by and see Miss Addie whenever I went up to see our folks. She loved to brag on me, tell everybody that I'm one of her former students, and that she'd taught me in the first grade. You know those two years she taught first grade after she retired from Harrington Elementary, we were so crowded down at Florida Avenue Colored School, they fixed up a classroom over't our church for Miss Addie and her children. I brought these pictures we had hanging in our church library of Miss Addie's first grade classes in '60–'61 and '61–'62 when she taught at Zion A. M. E., along with this article from *The Atlanta Journal and Constitution* Sunday paper back in '62." As Mike took the laminated newspaper article and skimmed over it, Andrew continued, "This is the article that shamed the Mintz County Board of Education into building a new addition onto our school, fixing a lot of stuff that needed fixing, buying four new buses for the black children, and hiring some more teachers. Miss Addie said the black children in Mintz County even got another planet added to their solar system. She said the books at the white schools said that there were nine planets, but thirty years after Pluto was discovered, the black children were still using worn out old books that said there were eight. Wanted you to see all of that."

"If you don't mind," Mike said, "I want to pass these on to Daniel Groves down at Webster Funeral Home, so he can display them where folks can see them at the viewing tomorrow night. Gonna have the viewing down at Miss Addie's School."

"As it should be," Andrew commented, "and I like the idea of displaying the pictures and the newspaper article. Sorry we're getting together to plan a funeral, but I've been needing to get over here and check up on you anyhow, see if you've gotten yourself in any new mischief since y'all got kicked out of the association for licensing the young lady preacher."

"Nah, figured that was enough trouble to get myself into for awhile. Can't say that I miss the associational politics. I'd pretty much reconciled myself to the fact that I'd never be elected moderator of the Mintz County Baptist Association. The ones who were my friends before we got kicked out are still my friends. The ones who never did like me, still don't. I've had some pleasant surprises, though, made some new friends. Brad Terry, new pastor out at Taylor's Crossroads, called me. Called to say that he didn't agree with what the association did. He'd only been there about a month, and I'd never met him. Bi-vocational pastor in his first church, twenty-three years old, works as a computer tech. Got him to do some upgrades on our computers at the church, did a good job and treated us right, so if you need any computer work done, he's good. Anyway, Karen and I have met him and his fiancée, long story short, once he got to know us, he asked me to preach a revival at his church this coming April. Brad's a good guy who loves anybody who loves the Lord, and doesn't think you're going to hell if you don't agree with him on everything. Most of the pastors in the association are decent guys, but you've always got a couple who think the purpose of the association is to keep the churches in line, always on the hunt for heresy — heresy meaning not agreeing with their viewpoint on everything. They're real good at whipping up a frenzy, and they keep stirring the pot 'til they get their way."

"We've got some like that in the A. M. E. Church, too," Andrew commented. "We've got a fair number of women pastors, mostly in smaller churches, but we've got some men who feel the same way as the ones who voted your church out of the association. There's been a lot of talk about nominating Reverend Vashti Mackenzie from up in Baltimore to be our bishop. If she's nominated, I'll vote for her. I've met her, heard her preach a couple of times. She's got the anointing. Powerful preacher, people who know her tell me her walk matches her talk, and she's done a fine job as pastor of her church. Church has really grown since she's been there. Still, we have some men who can't stand a woman preacher, especially one who can preach better than they can, and they'll vote against her being bishop just because she's a woman."

"Doesn't surprise me," Mike responded. "The Mintz County Baptist Association here is just like the Sanders County Association where we were up in Virginia. You've got some of the finest pastors you'll ever meet anywhere in both associations, but then you've got some who think God put them on earth to keep everybody else in line. One guy we had up in Virginia, ol' Billy Fite — spelled F-I-T-E, but he loved a F-I-G-H-T — led the charge to get my former church, Clear Springs, disfellowshipped when we ordained two women deacons in my first year as pastor. We had a fine moderator, good ol' country preacher by the name of Claude Bradley. Claude clipped Billy's wings on parliamentary grounds. Billy'd been stewing ever since, so he came loaded for bear after the church called Heather Simmons, Heather Simmons Moore she is now, as pastor after I graduated from seminary and moved to Harrington."

"Oh, yes, I remember her. She preached a revival at your church the first year you were here. I got to hear her one night. The young lady can deliver the goods, excellent preacher."

"Tell me about it," Mike concurred. "I knew her from seminary. She preached for me the Sunday that I came down to preach at my wife's home church for the pastor search committee from Harrington. Got a lot of positive feedback, so I asked her to fill in for me again when I preached the trial sermon here. When this church called me, Clear Springs called Heather on the spot without looking at any other candidates. Anyway, the second time around, when Clear Springs called Heather as pastor, they didn't have Claude Bradley as moderator, and Brother Billy was able to get enough votes to get his way. Clear Springs dates back to 1846, charter member of the Sanders County Association, and the first meeting of the association was held at Clear Springs back in 1870, but they got voted out on account of calling Heather as pastor. Split the association; seven other churches withdrew from the association because they expelled Clear Springs, pretty much the churches that carried most of the association's budget. Clear Springs and the churches that withdrew in support of Clear Springs formed the Clear Springs Association, so now there are two Baptist associations in Sanders County, Virginia. Billy Fite's counterpart here is Floyd Williams out at Freeman Valley. Floyd likes to talk about the responsibility of the association to 'police' its member churches — that's the word he likes to use, 'police,' as in sirens and flashing blue lights. Virgil Blackmon, director of missions for the association, was not in favor of kicking us out, but he's limited as to what he can say and keep his job. Virgil and I have had our differences, but we're friends. Virgil told me back when Heather preached the revival here that ol' Floyd's thermostat is stuck and it doesn't take a whole lot to get him overheated. Virgil said that Floyd's gonna end up having a stroke or heart attack the way he gets himself worked up. I hope not. If the association were to lose him, they'd have to hire an actor to play the part."

"You got that right. I've known Floyd way back," Andrew cackled. "I'm a little older than you, Reverend, so here comes the free history lesson. Floyd's daddy was one of the grand exalted nincompoops, or whatever they call them, in the Ku Klux. Floyd was one of the few white kids who tried to make trouble when the schools were desegregated in '66. Most of the kids, black and white, acted decent and civilized. Ol' Floyd was one of the exceptions. Old Prof Robinette was principal at Florida Avenue Colored School for years, only principal in the Mintz

County school system with an earned doctorate. They brought him over to Harrington High School as assistant principal, finally promoted him to principal a few years before he retired. Now Prof's a kind, gracious man, as fine a Christian gentleman as I've ever known, member of my church, but he doesn't suffer fools gladly. His customary way of dealing with discipline problems was not to have them. Mrs. Mamie Porter, math teacher, one of our best, came over to Harrington High School the same time as Prof. Mrs. Porter was accustomed to being in charge of her classroom. Floyd took exception to Mrs. Porter telling him what to do and called her a nigger. Mrs. Porter didn't get upset or raise her voice. Just as calm as could be, she looked over at me and said, 'Andrew, would you be so kind as to go down to the office and ask Professor Robinette to come down here for a minute?' Well, ol' Prof suspended Floyd for five days, told him that should give him enough time to write a sincere letter of apology to Mrs. Porter. Floyd quit school in his senior year rather than do it. Now that the Ku Klux has pretty much died out in Mintz County, I guess Floyd had to find another outlet for his meanness, so he took up mean religion. As you've no doubt discovered, there's some mean, angry people in the ministry. Religion's just an outlet for their natural meanness. Like I said, we've got them, too. They come in all colors and denominations. Did y'all get any backlash in the church when you licensed the young lady to preach?"

"We had two families who left," Mike responded. "They'd been threatening to leave pretty much from the time I got here, especially after Heather preached the revival back in '91. After years of threats, they decided that licensing Cassie was the straw that broke the camel's back. Miss Addie said she didn't think she was going to live long enough to see them leave. We've had eleven families join since those two left. The association just gave us some free publicity when they kicked us out. We've had letters, phone calls, and e-mails from all over, most of them supportive. We started seeing a lot more visitors in our services. Ted Coleman even gave us some good ink on the editorial page of *The Harrington Courier*.

"Yeah, I saw that, cut it out and saved it. Good stuff. Never will forget what he said in that editorial: 'This long after Pentecost, a woman preaching the gospel should be controversial only insofar as the gospel itself is controversial. If the gospel message is true, it is not more true when it is proclaimed by a man or less true when it is proclaimed by a woman.'"

"Ted writes some mighty fine editorials for a little small town weekly paper," Mike concurred. "Speaking of the young lady preacher, I can't wait for you to meet her. She'll be here any minute, and Eric Latham's coming as soon as he can get here."

"Eric Latham, the band director at the high school?

"Right," Mike replied. "He leads the music here, does a fine job. We're blessed. Some bigger churches that could pay him more would like to have him. He's had some offers and turned them down because he's happy where he is. He and I work together well, good man as well as a good musician. Eric's from up at Villa Rica, wife grew up in this church. Two children, almost said 'kids,' but I caught myself. I could just hear Miss Addie saying, 'Kids are baby goats, and I have seen no young goats in church recently. I'm sure you mean children.' So, yes, two children, one who is eight, same age as my Deborah Estelle, and a four-year-old. His wife Jenny is the pianist for our Sunday morning service. Both of them fine musicians, both sing well, Eric plays trombone and baritone, too. Talked to Jenny this morning. She said that Eric was out with her father's truck and splitter getting a load of firewood. I called him on his cell and told him about Miss Addie. He said he'd be here as soon as he can, provided we don't mind him looking like a man who just came out of the woods. So, you might say he's not out of the woods yet."

"I'll have to do the same thing he's doing in about three or four years," Andrew laughed. "We had those two big ol' hickory trees next to the church building we were needing to take out anyway. They were overhanging the roof and doing damage, and the roots were cracking the sidewalks and parking lot. Storm last spring took 'em down for us. We were blessed the way they fell that they didn't hit the building. Couple of our men that had chain saws and splitters busted them up for firewood. That old hard hickory's some fine firewood, burns slow and hot. Cooks some good barbeque, too. They brought Hoyt Barton's big ol' F-350 dually loaded to the top of the cab with firewood to my house, and we still gave away a lot more to folks we knew who would be struggling to buy firewood in the winter."

Andrew was groaning over Mike's bad pun about a "windfall" coming right on the heels of the one about Eric Latham not being out of the woods yet, and they were reminiscing about Miss Addie's love of puns, which she said was her one guilty pleasure other than fine chocolates, when they heard the door open at the other end of the hall. "Is that you, Cassie?" Mike called out.

"Hey, Brother Mike," a young feminine voice responded.

"Back here in my study. Come on back. Coffee's ready. Andrew's here and Eric's on his way." As Cassie came in, Mike continued, "Andrew, I want you to meet Cassie McWhorter, the other preacher who'll be having a part in Miss Addie's service. This'll be her first funeral."

"Pleased to meet you, Reverend," Andrew said as he stood and took Cassie's outstretched hand. "I've heard good things about you. Went to high school with your mama and daddy, played football with your daddy, but that's been a few years. I look forward to hearing you."

"Thank you," Cassie replied and then hesitated before adding, "You're the first person who ever addressed me as 'Reverend.'"

"Well, I'm honored to be the first," Andrew smiled. "I won't be the last. When you were growing up, your mama bought your school clothes big on you at the beginning of the year because she knew you'd grow into them. Now, 'Reverend' feels like it's one or two sizes too big for you right now, but you go on and wear it like you wore those school clothes that fit long and loose on you. From what Reverend Westover and Miss Addie told me about you, you'll grow into it. It'll fit you just fine in due time."

"You have Miss Addie's gift of encouragement," Cassie commented. I feel so overwhelmed being asked to have a part in her funeral. I've preached a grand total of four times and attended one Baptist Women in Ministry conference this past summer. That conference was so good! I felt like I'd been up on the Mount of Transfiguration, spending time with Julie Pennington Russell, Molly Marshall, Sarah Shelton, and Heather Simmons Moore. Heather sent me a graduation card with a flyer about the conference, told me that she'd reserved a room for two and that I was the second person, told me that my registration was paid, graduation present from her and Joel. Of course, I talked Heather's ears off, got to talk at length with Molly Marshall, too. Both of them told me all about their experiences of being called to ministry. When you're an eighteen-year-old girl and God's called you to preach, it helps to have some people who'll believe you and tell you that you're not crazy, just like Elizabeth told Mary she wasn't crazy and that really was the angel of the Lord and not some weird dream. Lord knows I didn't want to come down off that mountaintop. I was all for building some tabernacles and staying. Now here I am, just turned nineteen on October 2. I've never done a funeral before, and I'm being given the honor of a lifetime to have a part in Miss Addie's funeral. I know she made that request to encourage me, to tell me one more time that I can do what God's called me to do."

"That, too," Mike observed. "No doubt she wanted to encourage you. She's been doing that pretty much all of your life, but it was more than that. She saw God's hand on you when you were a little girl. Miss Addie was gifted in that way, able to discern when God was speaking to a young person. She had confidence in you as a minister. When you were eleven, not long after you were baptized, when Heather preached the revival here, Miss Addie saw how excited you were, how attentive you were when Heather was preaching, and how much you talked to Heather that week. Miss Addie was the first person you told that God was calling you to preach, back when you were fifteen, before you told me or the church. She told me about it at the time, told me that she'd been expecting it, so it was no great surprise to me when you came forward and told the church. That Sunday evening after you preached your first sermon, Miss Addie called me and told me that she really meant it when she told you that she wanted you to have a part in her funeral."

"I went down to the creek at Bailey's Mill for about an hour before I came over here," Cassie began. "Plan to go back this afternoon. I've just been sitting on the rocks with my Bible, a note pad, and my memories of Miss Addie. I remember when you and Daddy baptized me, and Miss Addie told about her baptism at my holy place on the creek. Ninety-three years old at the time, never been behind a pulpit before, and she did the most skillful thing I ever witnessed. She made the water below the dam at Bailey's Mill and the water in the church baptistery flow together into one stream, and she brought the people on the creek bank in 1908 and the people in church that Sunday together into one cloud of witnesses, all to make ready for my baptism. She and I were baptized in the same water before the same cloud of witnesses. I know that someone born in 1979 should not remember something that happened in 1908, but I do. My memory of my own baptism and Miss Addie's memory of her baptism are all blended together in my mind. I've been going to Bailey's Mill to think, pray, and meditate ever since I got my driver's license. Before that, I'd get up ridiculously early to go with Daddy when he went fishing down there. Doesn't take much imagination to visualize how it looked ninety years ago. When I told Miss Addie that I'd been going down there and told her that it was my holy place, she gave me a picture she had of a baptismal service there in the 1920s, when the mill and the old covered bridge were still there. The big stone piers of the old bridge are still there, they just built the new bridge beside it. The dam and the foundation of the mill are still there. Not much of a stretch to see Miss Addie's uncle, Preacher Tim Nestor, standing out there in the water between the piers of the old bridge. I've seen Miss Addie's daddy out there in the water, coming up to the bank, taking his little girl's hand, and wading with her out to where Uncle Tim's standing, and I've witnessed her baptism. I'm a little apprehensive about my first funeral, but what I feel more than anything is an overwhelming sense of gratitude to God for bringing this amazing woman into my life and letting her live so long. We've always had this connection I can't explain. Mom and Dad always sang in the choir, so my earliest memory of being in church is sitting with Miss Addie. As far back as I can remember, I could look into her eyes and see a little girl my age looking back at me. So, yeah, I can do this for Miss Addie. I've already flagged more scripture and written down more thoughts than I can use in the time I'll have. I've picked out what I'm going to wear. In honor of Miss Addie, no drab colors! You remember how she challenged people to show her where it said anywhere in the Bible that old women were supposed to wear dull, drab colors?"

"She's going to be buried in the bridesmaid's dress she wore at Daniel and Coretta's wedding," Mike noted as he opened the file folder with notes he had made on conversations with Miss Addie about her wishes for her funeral. "She said it was the prettiest thing she'd ever worn in her life."

"Got here as quick as I could," Eric apologized as he poured himself a cup of coffee and joined Mike, Andrew, and Cassie. "Hope you don't mind me looking and smelling like a man who's been cutting firewood all morning. Haven't been home yet, got Carl's truck out there loaded down with wood. Dropped his splitter off at the barn and came on over here."

"Not a problem, Eric," Mike responded. "I figure you'll be cleaned up before church tomorrow. We haven't done a whole lot other than reminisce and swap stories about Miss Addie."

"Which is probably the most important thing any of us could be doing right now," Eric observed. "It's what I've been doing up in the woods this morning after I got word about Miss Addie — remembering and giving thanks. Tried to pray, and the only prayer I could manage was, 'Thank you, Lord!'"

"Nothing wrong with that prayer," Andrew commented. "It's pretty much all you can say when you've been overwhelmed with the goodness of the Lord. I expect the Lord would like to hear that from us more often, considering what he's done for us."

"So, 'Thank you, Lord!' it's been, along with singing through some of the old songs from *The Sacred Harp* that she loved so much. I knew nothing about that whole tradition until I got to know Miss Addie. She cut her teeth on it, back when the churches had singing schools in the summer like they have Vacation Bible School now. Miss Addie taught Jenny and me to read shaped notes, and she could still sing quite well for an old woman. Never will forget how much fun Jenny and I had when we took Miss Addie to the big Sacred Harp singing up at Henegar, Alabama, when she was in her early nineties. She was right in there, singing with them, having the time of her life, didn't even need to look at the book on most of the songs. We went back the next year and went to the one up at Bremen, too. David and Cheryl Groves went with us. Miss Addie talked our ears off all the way up there and back. We brought her home dog-tired and ready to fall into bed, but I think it was about the happiest I ever saw her. David and Cheryl learned to read shaped notes, too. We bought us some copies of *The Sacred Harp* and started singing some of that music at church. It's some beautiful music — some really rich, theologically meaty hymn texts. Jenny's already called David and Cheryl. We're going to get together and practice some tomorrow afternoon after church. I know her favorites — 'Hark! I Hear the Harps Eternal,' 'Wondrous Love, The Christian's Hope,' and 'I Love the Lord, He Heard My Cries.' We're going to sing them all."

"And she wanted y'all to sing 'God Be With You 'Til We Meet Again' at the graveside," Mike added.

"We'll do it, and Jenny's practicing those really good piano arrangements she plays of 'All Hail the Power of Jesus' Name' and 'For All the Saints.'"

"Brenda Coleman has the invocation," Mike noted as he began making a rough draft of the order of service on a yellow legal pad. "Asalee, Molly Coleman, and Karen are reading scripture. Congregation sings 'The Solid Rock.' I asked Miss Addie what she wanted said about her at her funeral. She said, 'Tell them that I had a secure hope in Jesus Christ. Tell them that I tried to do right because I loved the Lord, though I did acquire a reputation for knocking down the occasional hornet's nest. Tell them that I invested my life in children and prayed that I did them some good.'"

"Three preachers," Cassie thought out loud, "and three things she wanted said about her. I think she gave us a good outline. Let me take that last part, about Miss Addie investing her life in children."

Andrew Jennings picked up the thread, "Doing right because she loved the Lord — I could start talking about that right now. I can tell about some of those hornet's nests she knocked down, strongholds of the devil is what they were, needed to be knocked down. I liked the way Miss Addie put it, 'speaking the truth in love with both barrels.' Kept on teaching her first graders down at Zion A. M. E. after the Ku Klux burned a cross in front of her house and one in front of the church. Standing up to people who said ugly things about Daniel Groves marrying Coretta Brinkley, telling how a lot of white folks and black folks in Mintz County have common ancestors much more recent than Adam and Eve and how *all*, and I do mean *all* of the Brinkleys around here are kin, and her being matron of honor at their wedding when she was ninety-nine years old. Yes, siree, let me talk about that."

"Y'all left me the part I wanted, talking about her secure hope in the Lord. Plenty to talk about there," Mike added. "Good thinking, Cass. Let's take our parts in the order Miss Addie gave them. Coretta has the benediction at the church, singing 'Take the Name of Jesus With You.' And Cass, Miss Addie asked that you do the committal out at Peyton's Chapel."

Chapter 3

Mike was pleased, but not surprised by any of the responses to the invitation at the end of the Sunday morning service. When Miss Addie moved to Pine Ridge Assisted Living four years ago, Darrell and Rhonda Brinson, or Rhonda Gates as she was at the time, bought the house that had been her home since her marriage to Chester Aldridge in 1922. Miss Addie had invited them to Harrington Baptist Church, as had Cheryl Groves. Cheryl's company, Red Carpet Realty, had handled the sale of the house. Darrell worked at Southwire in Carrollton. Rhonda, who worked at Phillips County DFCS, had jumped at the chance to transfer to Mintz County when the Child Protective Services supervisor position came open with Susan McKnight's retirement. Both of them had been burned by the infidelity of former spouses, failed marriages, and painful experiences in church. Each had a child from the previous marriage, and they struggled with all of the shared custody and blended family issues.

Rhonda's ex had been a pastor. In fact, he still was. The church in Hansonville fired him when the extramarital affair and a DUI charge came to light in the same week, but he was a charmer and, she had to admit, "one hell of a pulpiteer." The church ended up splitting over firing him and, within a month, he and his followers had started a new church on the other side of Hansonville, two miles from his former pastorate. By the time the ink was dry on the divorce decree, he had married the woman with whom he had the affair, and it made him livid that Davis wouldn't call her "Mom" when he came to visit on alternate weekends. Davis stood his ground and refused to go along with his father's demands. Rhonda told Davis not to be mean or disrespectful to his stepmother, but he didn't have to call her anything other than Denise or "Hey, you." Rhonda's ex was even more irate because Davis had almost unconsciously fallen into calling Darrell "Dad." It was all so natural that it didn't even register with Darrell until about ten minutes later. "He just up and called me 'Dad' like that was my name," he explained to Rhonda after the fact. "I don't think he realized he did it at first." Rhonda told Davis that it was all right if he wanted to call Darrell 'Dad,' because Darrell had earned it by not demanding it, but by spending time with him, treating him right, and loving him like his own flesh and blood. Rhonda told Davis that one of the reasons she loved Darrell was because he was so good to him. Davis enjoyed church a lot more on the weekends he didn't have to go to his father's church. Davis said that Brother Mike was a lot better preacher than his father, and you could tell he loved Miss Karen and didn't put her down and make her the butt of jokes. Davis used to cringe when his father put his mother down or made crude jokes about her. Davis said that the way Brother Mike treated Miss Karen was more like the way Darrell treated his mom.

Darrell was a pastor's son. Before his death five years ago, Ed Brinson served a series of small churches in Phillips and Mintz Counties while working during the week as a route salesman for R.L. Clark and Sons Wholesale Grocers in Hansonville. Darrell remembered his father as "just a good ol' country preacher who loved the Lord and loved people, never met a stranger, and had a photographic memory for people's names. Wad'n nothin' fancy about him, and he could talk to anybody. He had friends with doctorate degrees and friends who couldn't read or write." Darrell's memories of church were a mixed bag. His most delightful and most painful memories were connected with churches. He recalled how some churches blossomed under his father's leadership. "Never will forget," Darrell reminisced, "Gilberton Baptist Church was talking about closing its doors and disbanding. Daddy went down there, preached a revival for 'em, baptized twenty-two people in Hooper Creek at the end of the revival, most he ever baptized at one time. They called him as pastor, stayed there about four years, church was running about a hundred every Sunday when he left." He recalled how a couple of churches "like to have killed him and probably did shorten his life." Darrell said that his most painful memory of church was the rejection and abandonment he felt when his first marriage ended. He said that some of the people who cared for him the most and stuck by him the closest were some guys he worked with at Southwire who didn't even profess to be Christians. "People I thought were my friends," he said, "acted like I had some kind of contagious disease or something."

Thus, Darrell and Rhonda had tested the waters cautiously with regard to both marriage and church. They attended Harrington Baptist Church sporadically, along with occasional visits to other churches, in the first year they lived there. About a year after they bought Miss Addie's house, Darrell told Rhonda that he knew they'd both been through a lot of hurt, but he figured if they could trust each other enough to buy a house and commit to a thirty-year mortgage together, they could trust each other enough to commit to marriage. The next Sunday, Rhonda asked Mike to stop by and see them one evening after Darrell got home from work. At their home, Rhonda told Mike that she and Darrell had been living together two and a half years. Darrell said that he had not made any sort of romantic marriage proposal. It was more of an off-hand comment, more like an observation than a proposal, after writing the check for the mortgage. Rhonda said that she thought about it and decided that he was right, especially after her twelve-year-old, Davis, told her that he wished she would marry Darrell. They asked Mike to marry them. Darrell added, "Now, let's keep it real simple, Preacher. No suits or ties. If you see me wearing a suit and tie, you'll know I'm dead and the undertaker put it on me." They invited Mike and his family to their home for a cookout the following Saturday evening. They brought Miss Addie, too, so she could see how they had decorated the house and see the gazebo that Darrell had built as a wedding present for Rhonda. Darrell put the hamburgers and hot dogs on the grill along with some marinated chicken breasts that Rhonda had prepared. Then, they walked to the gazebo. Miss Addie liked the gazebo and the flowers that Rhonda had planted around it. Before Chester Aldridge died in 1964, they had talked about building a gazebo on that very spot. Under the gazebo,

Darrell and Rhonda joined hands. Darrell Wayne Brinson and Rhonda Faith Davis Gates pledged life and love to each other, pledged to love and honor each other's children as their own, and exchanged rings. Davis Daniel Gates and Laura Elizabeth Brinson pledged in their own words to love and honor their stepparents and to love and honor each other as siblings. Mike pronounced a blessing on marriage and blended family before they ate.

Laura and Davis were involved in the youth choir and other youth activities, and Darrell and Rhonda enjoyed the couples' Bible study class. They had been in church almost every Sunday since Mike baptized Laura last year. They were among those who took turns driving out to Pine Ridge to bring Miss Addie to church. This morning, when Davis came forward on the invitation to present himself for baptism, Darrell and Rhonda exchanged a look that said, "We need to go ahead and do this. Now." With tears trickling down their faces, they came forward not only to support Davis in his commitment, but also to join Harrington Baptist Church. Davis was a big twelve-year-old, easily the tallest seventh grader at Harrington Middle School. He and Darrell would be among Miss Addie's pallbearers, and the Brinsons said that they would meet Daniel Groves and Tommy Sheridan from the funeral home at Miss Addie's School at 4:30 p.m. to help them set up for the viewing.

Mike and Karen's younger daughter, Deborah Estelle, had also come down the aisle, accompanied by her mom, to make her public profession of faith and present herself for baptism. Her decision was the culmination of many conversations dating back to Vacation Bible School last summer. Last Sunday night, they'd talked with her about why she had decided to partake of the Lord's Supper that morning, mostly to assure her that she had not done anything wrong. Last night, they had talked long past her regular bedtime. The conversation was mixed with generous amounts of cuddling, silence, tears, and prayer, until she fell asleep in Mike's arms, talking about Miss Addie's death. Miss Addie was at church last Sunday morning, and Deb had sat cuddled up between her and Cassie McWhorter while Karen was in the choir. Miss Addie said that she couldn't help being a hundred and one years old, but she was not required to sit with the old people in church. It was not that she objected to sitting with old people. She enjoyed the company of some of them, but she had ample opportunity to sit with old people six days a week out at Pine Ridge. Last Sunday, the first Sunday of the month, was communion. When the trays were passed, Miss Addie offered them to Deb instead of passing them over her to Cassie. Deb looked at the communion trays and looked up at Miss Addie. Miss Addie saw the question on her mind. She answered it with a nod, a smile, and a gentle hug. With pounding heart, trembling hands, and tears coursing down her face, Deb broke off a piece of the communion bread and took one of the little cups of grape juice.

Until Karen told him about it at home after dinner, Mike didn't know about the brush fire that Doris Lawhorn tried to start over Deborah Estelle taking communion before she was baptized. Karen said that Doris tried to climb down her throat about it after the service, told her she needed to supervise Asalee better and tell her not to be taking the Lord's Supper until after she's baptized and she's old enough to understand what it means. Karen told Doris that Asalee was baptized five years ago when she was nine and that her younger daughter's name was Deborah Estelle. At that point, Miss Addie waded into the conversation, thumping the floor with her cane for emphasis and punctuation. Miss Addie had not tolerated Doris' smart mouth and bossiness during the 1936–37 school year, and she saw no need to tolerate it now. "Doris," (thump) Miss Addie's cane struck the floor about an inch and a half from the toe of Doris' left shoe, "the Westovers have been here since 1990, that's eight years (thump), long enough for you to know the names of their children (THUMP)." Then, speaking as one having authority and not as the Scribes and Pharisees, she added, "You know what Jesus said (thump), 'suffer the little children to come to me and forbid them not, for such is the kingdom of heaven (thump).' He told the disciples that it would be better to be cast into the depths of the sea with millstones around their necks (thump) than to have to answer for hindering a child coming to him (thump). I know that you know that because I taught you in Sunday School, too. I don't think Jesus would object to an eight-year-old child deciding to partake of the Lord's Supper (thump). He'd give the child a hug and tell her that she did the right thing, so that's what I did (THUMP). He'd rebuke the ones who got upset over her taking it, so I'm doing that, too (thump). Doris (thump), we ought *never* hinder a child coming to Jesus (thump). Taking the Lord's Supper was Deborah Estelle's way of accepting Jesus (THUMP). She'll be baptized soon enough, mark my words (THUMP)! Now, as for supervising the child adequately (thump Thump THUMP), I taught school in Mintz County for forty-five years (THUMP). Surely I can supervise one eight-year-old child, especially one as well-behaved as Deborah Estelle, while her mother is in the choir (thump). By the time Mike found out about the brush fire, Miss Addie had already extinguished it, beating out every last ember with her cane before Karen had a chance to say anything she would regret to Doris Lawhorn.

Daniel Groves eased the hearse to a stop in front of the main entrance of Addie Jane Peyton Aldridge Elementary School, where the Brinsons and principal Janet Baxter were waiting. Tommy Sheridan pulled up behind him in the funeral home's van, bringing the guest book stand, easels for displaying photos and newspaper clippings, adult-size chairs, and all of the other things they would need to set up for the viewing. It was the first time Daniel had been there since the end of fifth grade. Janet had taught Daniel in the fifth grade before she became principal. By the time Daniel got out and walked to the back of the hearse, Janet was there to meet him. "Lord, have mercy! Daniel Groves, you're making me feel old. Old and short!" she exclaimed as she stretched, even in her high heels, to hug Daniel. "Seems only yesterday that I had you in fifth grade. It sure is good to see you. I love that sweet wife of yours! So glad she's teaching here. The children in her kindergarten class love her to death. She's a good teacher. Of course, I taught her, too. Miss Addie taught me, and I taught you and Coretta. I hope something of Miss Addie got passed down through me to the children I taught."

"I think it did, Mrs. Baxter," Daniel commented as he opened the back door of the hearse.

"Please, call me Janet."

"Janet it is. So thanks, Janet, for offering to let us have the viewing at the school. You have a lot more parking than we have at the funeral home, and I think we'll need it. I expect that there'll be a big crowd here tonight."

"You're welcome. Yesterday morning when I heard that she had died, I called the superintendent to make sure he was okay with me offering to have the viewing here. Got a busy signal the first time I tried to call him. When I finally reached Dr. Melton, I found out that we'd both been getting busy signals because we were trying to call each other at the same time. He was trying to call me to suggest that we offer to have the viewing at the school. So, he was fine with that, and it's an honor for us. Ever since they renamed the school for her last year, I love the way that most people just call it 'Miss Addie's School.' I can't wait for you to see our banner. We have a half-dozen or so retired teachers who are into quilting. They quilted this beautiful patchwork banner, that hangs next to the office, that says 'Welcome to Miss Addie's School.' It's the first thing you see when you walk in the door. Wish you could've seen the look on Miss Addie's face the day they unveiled our new sign and renamed the school. Lunell Bishop unrolled that banner and presented it on behalf of the retired teachers. Anyway, I'm thinking if we set up here in the big open area in front of the office where the hallways converge, that'll give us the most space. Plenty of room for people to mill around and talk to each other, we'll have room for flowers and displaying pictures and newspaper clippings, and the rest rooms will be accessible. You can put the stand with the guest book right by the office door, under the banner where everybody will see it."

"That'll work, Janet." Daniel unfolded the portable bier, released the stop on the floor of the hearse, and grasped the handle on the end of the casket to roll it out. Without prompting, Darrell, Davis, and Tommy took hold of the handles on one side of the casket, and Rhonda, Laura, and Janet took hold of the other side of the budget-priced metallic silver casket and gently lifted it onto the bier. Tommy remembered years ago when Miss Addie came in to make her funeral arrangements. She told him that she didn't see any need for an expensive casket. 'I can't think of anyone who is remembered for the cost of his casket. No matter what you do, our bodies will go back to the dust from whence they came,' was the way she put it. Janet held the door open as the others wheeled Miss Addie's casket into the school that bore her name.

Mike Westover had not taken it upon himself to call off the Sunday night service at Harrington Baptist Church because of the viewing for Miss Addie, but he found no objection when he called around to the members of the administrative council. Deacon chair Brenda Coleman, who taught fourth grade at Miss Addie's School, observed, "We're all going to be over there at the school. No point in you preaching to an empty house."

Mike liked Brenda's idea of setting up an open mic at the viewing for anyone who wanted to share a story or favorite memory about Miss Addie, so he asked her to make the announcement about that and the cancellation of the evening service on Sunday morning. When she came to the pulpit to make the announcement, she said, "I'm supposed to announce that we will not have our Sunday night worship service due to the viewing for Miss Addie, but that's really not true. We will simply have it at a different place, at Miss Addie's School. Brother Mike reminded us not long ago that, in the theology of the Old Testament, sin begins not with doing bad things but forgetting what God has done for us. Sin and spiritual death start with forgetting. Repentance, renewal, and restoration start with remembering. So, we will gather at 6:00 p.m. this evening at Miss Addie's School for a time of remembering. As we remember Miss Addie tonight, we'll have some open mics set up for anyone who has a Miss Addie story to tell. This is going to be good! As we remember Miss Addie, we will be refreshed in our faith and refocused on the gracious God who brought Miss Addie into our lives."

Over breakfast yesterday morning, as they were all absorbing the news of Miss Addie's death, Asalee had commented, "I loved Miss Addie. She was for real." On Sunday afternoon, as Mike sat alone in his office working on his part in tomorrow's service, he thought about what Asalee said and began writing on the blank legal pad that had been staring him in the face. "Yesterday morning over breakfast," he wrote, "our daughter Asalee said, 'I loved Miss Addie. She was for real.' Asalee got it right. That's why we all loved her. One 'for real' saint is a more compelling argument for the Christian way than all of the volumes of apologetics ever written." After he had written those words, it all began to flow easily. Mike was putting the finishing touches on his part in the service when the phone on his desk rang.

"Daddy," Deborah Estelle said, "Mom says it's time to get ready for us to go to church over at Miss Addie's School. I'm going to tell my Miss Addie story from last Sunday. Mom said I could. I'm kinda scared, but I really want to. Mom said she'd stand beside me and help me."

Chapter 4

"Deb, honey, I'm really proud of you wanting to tell your Miss Addie story," Mike commented to his youngest as she held his hand walking across the parking lot of Miss Addie's School, where she was in Mrs. Jennings' third grade class. A half hour before time for the viewing to start, the close-in spaces in the faculty parking lot and the bus lanes were starting to fill up, and people were beginning to park along the curbs in the car rider lanes. The hearse from Webster Funeral Home was parked in front of the main entrance, ahead of the van from Flowers by Natasha. The van's back and side doors were open, and Natasha Ware and her oldest son were unloading dozens of floral arrangements with help from people arriving for the viewing.

"I need to tell my Miss Addie story, Daddy. I'll never forget her and I don't want anybody else to. If people forget Miss Addie, they might forget Jesus and God. You know what Mrs. Coleman said at church this morning."

"Yeah, Deb, you have a point there," Mike concurred, "and I'm glad you were paying attention in church even during the announcements."

"Daddy, you know how Mom's always teaching me new big words, making me learn how to spell them and tell what they mean?"

"Hmmhmm," Mike acknowledged.

"Well, she taught me another one right before we came over here. In-ter-view, I-N-T-E-R-V-I-E-W. She's gonna interview me, just like Mr. Coleman interviews people so he can write about it in the paper. That means she's gonna ask me some questions to help me tell my story."

"Sounds like a good plan," Mike observed, "and you have an awesome Mommy. I can't wait to hear this. It's going to be good."

"Hey, Preacher Man," Tommy Sheridan called Mike aside as soon as the Westovers made it inside the door. "Never did a viewing at a school before, so Daniel and I are winging it on this one. Daniel's got some advantage because he went to school here. We were still in the old building, where the Board of Education offices and the Senior Center are, when I was in elementary school. Don't have any viewings going on at the funeral home tonight, so Mr. and Mrs. Webster are coming over to help us. They're supposedly retired, but they help us out when we have a big crowd, and we're expecting a slew of people tonight. We got that part covered all right, but then y'all surprise me with this open mic thing. Never did anything like that before."

"Miss Addie would say that everything that's ever been done had to be done for the first time," Mike reminded Tommy, who had undoubtedly heard Miss Addie say those exact words when she taught him in fourth grade the last year she taught at Harrington Elementary. "Relax, Tommy. It's being handled. We have two of Miss Addie's understudies, Janet Baxter and Brenda Coleman, in charge of that, which is nearly as good as Miss Addie herself being in charge. Brenda talked with me after church this morning. She has it all figured out, so I told her to take the ball and run with it. We'll have the viewing for the first hour, then at 7:00 p.m., Janet is going to step up to the mic and welcome everybody to Miss Addie's School. She wants me to say a few words and then call on Reverend Conway from Greater New Hope to pray. Coretta's going to start it off, telling about Miss Addie being matron of honor at her wedding when she was ninety-nine years old, and she's going to sing 'Hold to God's Unchanging Hand.' Brenda's already talked to Lunell

Bishop. Lunell's eight-seven years old, another one of Miss Addie's protégés. Lunell's got a great story I want you to hear from back in the 1920s when Miss Addie was teaching in the one-room school out in Freeman Valley before she married and moved to Harrington. Lunell started the first grade there in 1917, the first year that Miss Addie taught. My eight-year-old, Deborah Estelle, has a great Miss Addie story from just this past Sunday. It's going to be good, Tommy. All you have to do is look sharp in your undertaker suit as you smile and greet people, unless you have a Miss Addie story you want to tell."

With Tommy Sheridan no longer in panic mode over doing something he had never done before, Mike joined his family in the line waiting to file past the open casket. "What did Tommy want?" Karen asked.

"He was about to go into panic mode over the open mic thing, so I had to talk him down off the ceiling. Told him that Janet and Brenda were running the show on that, which is nearly as good as Miss Addie herself being in charge, so we didn't need to worry about it."

"Way to go, Miss Addie," Karen laughed, "even in death getting people to do things they've never tried to do before. I just wish that Tommy had put up a little more resistance and said that people weren't ready for that. Then you could've quoted Miss Addie on where the children of Israel would be if Moses had waited until everybody was ready."

"Yeah, they'd still be in Egypt," Deb added dryly. "Moses should've had some grown-ups like Miss Addie to help him with the children of Israel."

"You're right, Deb," Karen commented as she tried to choke back the laughter and keep a straight face since her daughter had not meant to be funny. "Miss Addie would've lined those children of Israel up and marched them straight to the Promised Land. There would have been none of that forty years of wandering in the wilderness."

"Mom, Dad, look! The bridesmaid dress!" Asalee exclaimed as soon as the line moved enough for her to see into the casket. "She was serious about being buried in her bridesmaid dress. She looks so pretty with her snow-white hair against all the bright blues and yellows! Mom, I'll never forget us going out to Pine Ridge to bring her to the wedding," Asalee babbled excitedly as she recounted the wedding of Daniel Groves and Coretta Brinkley two years ago at Greater New Hope Progressive Missionary Baptist Church. "We got out there way early thinking we'd need to help her get ready. We walked in, and there she sat in the lobby in all her glory waiting for us, the whitest little white lady you ever saw dressed up like an African princess! One of the aides who's from Senegal came in early before her shift started to help Miss Addie with her hair and help her fix everything just right. Miss Addie was absolutely delighted with herself, and there was her niece, the one who was always trying to get her to act old, having a dying duck fit, saying, 'Aunt Addie, have you lost your ever-loving mind?' Miss Addie said, 'No, Kathleen, I've lost some of my hearing, and I have these gadgets in my ears to help with that, but I still have my ever-loving mind.' So then, her niece starts in on her about the dress. What was it she called it, Mom?"

"A ridiculous costume," Karen replied as they moved past the casket.

"Yeah, she said, 'What is this ridiculous costume you're wearing?' and Miss Addie acted like she didn't hear a blessed thing her niece said. She just hugged us and took on over how good we looked, and she said, 'Kathleen, I'd like you to meet our pastor's wife, Karen Westover, and their daughters, Asalee and Deborah. They've come to take me to the wedding. It was so kind of them to come for me. I must go now so as not to be late. I shall return after the reception. Then her niece said, 'Aunt Addie, you'll wear yourself out.'"

"Ooooh yeah, that was the best part," Karen picked up the thread. It was all I could do to keep from cracking up, laughing in her face, and saying, 'Tell her, Miss Addie!' Miss Addie just looked at her, shook her head, and said, 'Kathleen, I am ninety-nine years old. I am worn out, but if a nice young couple wants me to be the matron of honor for their wedding, I shall grant their request. This is likely to be my last opportunity to be a bridesmaid. Besides, I feel better when I wear bright colors, and I sleep better if I'm tired when I go to bed. If I die tonight, I'll be in heaven, you'll know I died happy, and you can bury me in this dress."

"You'd never think she was a hundred and one years old just looking at her," Mike commented.

"I hope I look that good at eighty, if I make it to eighty," Karen concurred.

Mike gave Karen a gentle hug and told her, "You're looking mighty good for thirty-six."

It was precisely 7:00 p.m. — punctuality being a thing that Miss Addie valued — when the principal, Janet Baxter, came up to the microphone and adjusted the gooseneck to her height. "On behalf of the Mintz County Public Schools, Superintendent Melton, and the faculty, staff, and students of Addie Jane Peyton Aldridge Elementary School, it is my honor to welcome you here tonight. If this is your first time here, let me call your attention to the beautiful quilted banner that says 'Welcome to Miss Addie's School,' hand-quilted by some of our retired teachers when the school was renamed in honor of Miss Addie's one hundredth birthday, and the portrait of Miss Addie that normally hangs in our office, painted by Jonathan Chance, who was a student of Miss Addie's in the early fifties. Let me see a show of hands — how many of you here tonight are former students of Miss Addie's? I see a lot of hands going up! I was one of her students, too. I was in her fourth grade class in 1958–59, and I decided then that I wanted to become a teacher. I was thirteen years old in 1962 when Miss Addie ran for a seat on the Board of Education. I couldn't vote, but I certainly campaigned for her and helped get out the vote! I brought in that 1962 campaign poster that is displayed here tonight. I am here to honor her, and I want to thank Miss Addie's family for accepting our invitation to host the viewing. Miss Addie was a member of Harrington Baptist Church for seventy-six years, and her funeral service will be held there tomorrow at 1:00 p.m. Now, Miss Addie's pastor, Reverend Michael Westover, will come and tell us how we'll go about sharing our memories of Miss Addie tonight."

"Thank you, Mrs. Baxter," Mike began. "Our deacon chair, Brenda Coleman, teaches fourth grade here at Miss Addie's School. She suggested a good old-fashioned testimony meeting, where we set up some mics and give people the opportunity to share their stories about Miss Addie and how God worked in their lives through her. That's what we're going to do. We have four mics set up around the room, and we look forward to hearing some great stories about Miss Addie. As my family and I were walking in from the parking lot, our daughter Deborah Estelle, who is a third grade student here in Mrs. Jennings' class, told me that she wants to tell a Miss Addie story that happened at church just this past Sunday. Deborah said that she doesn't want anybody to forget Miss Addie, because then they might forget Jesus and God. A real saint has lived among us. Deborah Estelle got it right. If we forget Miss Addie, we are in great danger of forgetting Jesus and God, too. May it be said of us, when we come to the end of our lives, that remembering us will help people remember Jesus and God! Let us remember Miss Addie as we hear each other's stories about her, and let us build on the legacy she has left us, a legacy of faith, hope, justice, courage, and goodness. We need more people with the spirit of Miss Addie for today and for future generations. Now, my friend Reverend Henry Conway, pastor of the Greater New Hope Progressive Missionary Baptist Church, will come to lead us in prayer, giving thanks for the life and witness of Miss Addie."

Conway almost fell into his call-and-response preaching cadence, with each pause in his prayer filled by voices calling out, "Yes, Lord," "My, My," and "Help us, Lord." As eyes opened, heads lifted, and voices echoing Conway's "Amen" faded into silence, Coretta Brinkley Groves, who was standing with her husband Daniel, stepped confidently up to the nearest microphone. Gifted with absolute perfect pitch, she needed no instrument to give her the key of F, and she really had little need for the microphone as she began singing in her rich, powerful mezzo-soprano voice,

> Time is filled with swift transition,
> Naught on earth unmoved can stand.
> Build your hopes on things eternal,
> Hold to God's unchanging hand!
>
> Hold to God's unchanging hand,
> Hold to God's unchanging hand!
> Build your hopes on things eternal,
> Hold to God's unchanging hand!

"Miss Addie taught me that song," Coretta began her story. "Miss Addie liked the story Reverend Conway tells about the one hundred-year-old man who said that he'd seen a lot of changes in his lifetime, and he'd been opposed to every one of them. Miss Addie wasn't like that. She helped bring about many changes for the better. She didn't live in the past or fear the future. Miss Addie prayed for God's will to be done on earth as it is in heaven, and that is a prayer for change! She witnessed more of 'time's swift transition' than any other person I've known, and she held to God's unchanging hand in a changing world. She welcomed changes that were for the better, and she did not fear uncovering the secrets of the past. My husband and I have known each other since kindergarten, but we didn't date until 1991, the summer before our senior year of high school. Neither of us had dated much before then. We really got to know each other and found ourselves attracted to each other when our church, Greater New Hope, and Harrington Baptist Church held a combined Vacation Bible School, and the high school youth from both churches worked together on some mission projects. Even though our churches had done some things together, I can't begin to tell you how nervous I was the first time Daniel and I came to church together at Harrington Baptist. My heart was pounding so hard that I was sure everybody could hear it, me being the only black person there, when this tiny white-haired little lady came up, hugged me, and said, 'Welcome to Harrington Baptist Church. You're Arthur and Louise Brinkley's daughter, aren't you?' I said, 'Yes, ma'am.' She said, 'I'm Addie Jane Aldridge, most people call me Miss Addie. I don't know whether you know it, but you have some relatives in this church.' She sat with us in church, and after church, she told us how all of the Brinkleys, and I do mean *all* of the Brinkleys in Harrington and Mintz County are related. She told us that she had known my great-great-great grandfather — my *white* great-great-great grandfather — Reverend Joshua Higgins Brinkley. Daniel and I dated from that summer until I graduated from West Georgia. Miss Addie invited us to her home many times, and she told us many things I didn't know, things my parents didn't know, about our family history. When Miss Addie decided to sell her house and move to Pine Ridge Assisted Living, when she was ninety-eight, Daniel and I helped her pack and sort out what to keep and what to sell or give away. Daniel had just given me an engagement ring, although we had not set the date. He had just graduated from Gupton-Jones College of Mortuary Science and started working for Webster Funeral Home. I still had one more semester at West Georgia. Miss Addie said, 'I'd like to go ahead and give you your wedding present. You won't need to register china and silver patterns, because I'm giving you mine. Take it home with you and put it in your hope chest. I'll have no need for it at Pine Ridge." I wish you could've seen how happy Miss Addie was when Daniel and I went to see her, told her about our wedding plans, and asked her to be our matron of honor. She laughed and told us that she'd never been in a wedding other than her own, and if we wanted a ninety-nine-year-old matron of honor, she would do it with pleasure. The matron of honor got a standing ovation when she came down the aisle at Greater New Hope, and it didn't hurt the bride's feelings one bit! She showed off the pictures from our wedding for the rest of her life."

Daniel stepped up beside Coretta, put his arm around her, and whispered to her — loud enough for the mic to pick it up — "Let's go ahead and tell everybody."

"We just found out that I'm pregnant, six weeks along," Coretta announced proudly. "We had only told a few people, but I suppose the whole world knows now. The jury is still out on boys' names, but if we have a girl, her name will be Addie Jane Groves. Boy or girl, our little one will be sung to sleep with an old song Miss Addie taught me,

> Remember thy creator, God,
> For him, thy pow'r employ.
> Make him thy fear, thy love, thy hope,
> Thy portion and thy joy!

"Oh, Lord!" Lunell Bishop laughed as she steadied herself on her four-prong cane and made her way up to the mic. "I don't know where to start with the stories about Miss Addie! We go back a long way, and I could tell Miss Addie stories all night if I could stand up that long. I'm eighty-seven years old, grew up out in Freeman Valley, the valley is named for my family. The building that is now the sanctuary of Freeman Valley United Methodist Church is the old Freeman Valley School. The church bought the building when the county closed all of the little rural schools and started busing children to the consolidated school in town. Miss Addie began her teaching career there in 1917, the year that I started the first grade. Miss Addie taught me from the first through the fifth grade, until she married Chester Aldridge and moved to Harrington. I became a teacher, and Addie and I taught together at Harrington Elementary for twenty-seven years. I taught second grade and Addie taught fourth.

She was my teacher, my colleague, and my dear friend. My story dates back to 1920, the first day of school, when I started the fourth grade and my little brother Oliver started the first."

"I was the sixth of nine children," Lunell continued. "My sister Grace was the oldest. When Grace was sixteen and headstrong, she and her boyfriend ran off to Alabama and got married. It lasted just long enough for her to get pregnant. Mother and Daddy took her back in, and she was living at home with us when her baby was born. She named him Oliver, Oliver Martin. Oliver grew up with the rest of us. We always thought of him as a brother, treated him like a brother, fussed and fought with him the same as I did with my other siblings. Oliver turned six in May of 1920. The first day of school in September, Oliver walked to school with me. Hugh Woodson, rest his soul, was in the sixth grade. I see some of Hugh's children and grandchildren here tonight. Hugh started teasing me before school, saying that Oliver couldn't be my brother because he had a different last name. Come recess, he started it up again, and I'd had my fill of it. I was big for my age, used to helping around the farm, and strong for a girl, so I tore into him. As I took him down and started pounding him into the dirt, I explained to him, 'Just 'cause my sister had him instead of my momma don't mean he's not my brother!' About the time I said those words, here came Miss Addie! She saw and heard everything. Addie waded right in, pulled me off Hugh and separated us. Then, she looked at me and said, 'Lunell Freeman, you know better than that! Did I not teach you anything about subject-verb agreement last year? You should've said 'it doesn't mean,' not 'it don't mean.' Then she turned to Hugh and told him, 'Other than the grammatical error, Lunell is absolutely right. Oliver is Lunell's brother, no matter who gave birth to him or what his last name is. While the rest of us enjoy recess, march yourself inside up to the board and write twenty times, 'Oliver Martin is Lunell Freeman's brother.' In 1934, when I arrived as a new teacher at Harrington Elementary School, as soon as Addie saw me, she came up, hugged me, and said, 'Well, if it isn't Lunell Freeman! How is your little brother Oliver?'"

Lunell shuffled slowly back to her seat and steadied herself with her cane as she sat down. As the laughter subsided, a tall, slender man of regal bearing rose to his feet, and a hush came over the room as he strode up to the mic. "Silas Robinette is my name," he began in a strong, clear voice. "Most people in Harrington know me as 'Prof.' I'm eighty-six years old. I started teaching at Florida Avenue Colored School in 1935 after I graduated from Morehouse. We had all twelve grades under one roof, one leaky roof. I taught civics and history, junior high and high school. I coached the basketball team, too, so I also answer to Coach Robinette. If I'd been a musician, they'd have given me a baton and made me band director, too. I became principal in 1947, continued as principal and basketball coach until I moved over to Harrington High School as assistant principal when the schools were desegregated in 1966. I didn't have to coach basketball any more, which I actually missed because I was a good athlete in my younger days. I had some fine teams over the years, and two state championships. In 1965, when we knew that desegregation was coming, we played an exhibition game against Harrington and won. After Mr. Mattingly retired in 1971, I became the principal at Harrington High School until my retirement in 1977.

"Like Mrs. Bishop, I could tell my share of stories about Miss Addie," Prof segued into his story. "I will never forget August of 1960, when our teachers reported for pre-planning and getting their classrooms ready for the first day of school. The first day the teachers reported, Miss Addie walked into my office at 8:00 a.m. sharp. As I stood to greet her and welcome her to our school, not knowing why she was there, she said, 'Dr. Robinette, I retired from Harrington Elementary School at the end of last school year. Now, it's time for school to start back, and I don't know what to do with myself! I just turned sixty-three, and I am far too healthy to sit around, be old, and practice being dead. If I ever start watching those inane soap operas and game shows, I shall lose my mind and have to be carted off to Milledgeville. You've never had enough teachers or enough of anything for that matter, and I need to be useful instead of ornamental, so I came to see where you need me and what I can do to help.' I remembered Jesus saying, 'You have not because you ask not,' so I decided to aim high, shoot for the moon, and tell her what my greatest need was, all the time thinking she'd say that it was more than she could do. I said, 'Mrs. Aldridge, I have two first grade teachers and ninety-one children starting first grade on Monday.' Big tears welled up in Miss Addie's eyes. She said, 'No, Dr. Robinette, you have three first grade teachers. Take fifteen children out of each class and give them to me.' That gave me another first grade teacher, but I didn't have a classroom for her. Zion A. M. E. Church, across the street from the school, made space available and let us set up another classroom at the church. People from Zion A. M. E., Greater New Hope Baptist, Miracle Temple Church of God in Christ, Miss Addie and her husband Mr. Ches Aldridge, and Reverend Seals from Harrington Baptist, all came and helped get that classroom ready for us. Miss Addie taught first grade there for two years without being paid a cent. Some of our finest citizens — our police chief, the pastor at Zion A. M. E., three business owners including one who is on the school board, four teachers in the Mintz County Schools, plus a lawyer, a physician, and a colonel in the United States Army, all came from among the first grade students Miss Addie taught those two years. Somehow, *The Atlanta Journal and Constitution* heard about what Miss Addie was doing, and they sent a reporter and photographer down to Harrington. There was a big feature article in the Sunday paper about the conditions at our school and what Miss Addie and her husband and some of the churches in town were doing to make things better. That article upset a lot of people, but it was the truth, and it led to a lot of improvements at Florida Avenue Colored School. They hauled in some surplus Quonset huts from Fort Benning and put them up for temporary classrooms until they could build an addition onto the school. They painted our school inside and out and put on a new roof. They fixed things that had needed fixing for years. They hired five more teachers. All of our buses were old ones that had been retired from hauling white children, the newest and best one was a '49 model GMC. All of a sudden, we had four shiny new 1961 Ford sixty passenger buses. Now, there were people who didn't think that Miss Addie should have been doing what she was doing, a white woman teaching black children. Right after that piece came out in the Atlanta paper, the KKK boys came and burned a cross in front of her house and burned another one in front of Zion A. M. E. All of us were afraid that someone would kill her, or burn her out of her home, or burn the church down, but we kept on praying and she kept on teaching. Come 1962, Miss Addie went down to the courthouse on the first day of qualifying for the Democratic primary and paid her qualifying fee. She was the first woman to run for public office in Mintz County, ran against Roland Millican for his seat on the school board, and won by thirty-four votes. Once she got on the school board, she took the bull by the horns! Two of her former students were on the board, and they minded her just like they did when they were in the fourth grade, so she had herself a majority. She was re-elected by a wide margin in 1966 and became chair of the board." There were smiles and ripples of laughter around the room as Prof added, "They knew they might as well make her chair because she was going to be in charge anyway." Tears welled up in Prof's eyes, and his voice broke with emotion as he continued, "Nobody did more than Miss Addie to bring about equal educational opportunities for black children and accomplish the peaceful desegregation of the Mintz County Schools. Now, as Miss Addie has done, and as I shall do before long, we must all come to the end of our lives on this earth. Miss Addie lived longer than most people. She was blessed with clarity of mind and the ability to get around until the very end of her days. Now she has finished her course and received her eternal reward. Most of us won't live as long as Miss Addie did. We know not how long we will live, or what kind of shape we will be in, or whether we will still have our mental faculties at the last. None of us will live forever in these mortal bodies. Let us all resolve, as Miss Addie did, to do all the good we can in whatever time we have left." As Prof pushed up his wire-rim glasses to dab away the tears, he concluded, "Thanks be to God for one who did so much lasting good!"

As Prof sat down, Deborah Estelle squeezed her mother's hand and said, "Now, Mom. I have to tell my Miss Addie story."

With Deb at her side, Karen made her way to the nearest microphone. "I'm Karen Westover," she began. "My husband Mike is the pastor at Harrington Baptist Church. The little girl beside me is our younger daughter, Deborah Estelle, and she has a Miss Addie story to tell. Every week, in addition to the vocabulary words she learns at school, I teach her a new big word and make sure she learns to pronounce it, spell it, and use it correctly. What's our new big word for this week, Deb?"

"Interview."

"Very good. When you told your dad and me last night that you wanted to tell your Miss Addie story, I decided right then that our new big word for this week would be 'interview.' I told you that I would interview you to help you tell your Miss Addie story. Tell me, Deb, what is an interview?"

"That's where you ask me questions and I answer them to help tell my story, the way Mr. Coleman interviews people and then writes about it in the paper."

"That's right. So, let's start our interview. Tell me your name and how old you are."

"My name is Deborah Estelle Westover, and I am eight years old."

"Where do you go to school, Deborah, and what grade are you in?"

"I'm in the third grade at Miss Addie's School, in Mrs. Jennings' class."

"I understand that you knew Miss Addie very well. Where did you sit in church when your dad was in the pulpit and I was in the choir?'

"I sat with Miss Addie. She always had children sitting with her. Miss Addie didn't want to sit with the old people in church because she liked children. She said that she could sit with old people all she wanted to out at Pine Ridge."

"Anything else you'd like to tell us about Miss Addie?"

"She told me that she remembered being eight years old and riding to church in a wagon pulled by a horse. She really listened when I talked to her, and she knew the names of all of the children at church. She never called me by my sister's name."

"Something very special happened last Sunday when you sat with Miss Addie. Can you tell me about that?"

"We had the Lord's Supper and I took it for the first time."

"Deb, do you know why we have the Lord's Supper?"

"We do it to help us remember Jesus and how much he loves us and how he died for us on the cross."

"You know, Deb, that some people think that children shouldn't take the Lord's Supper until after they are baptized. How did you know it was okay for you to take it?"

"Miss Addie offered it to me."

"She offered it to you?"

"She could see I wanted to take it. She smiled at me and gave me a little hug to tell me it was okay. She held the trays while I broke off a piece of bread and took one of the little cups of grape juice."

"Dad and I told you at home that Miss Addie was right, and that you had done the right thing. Miss Addie told me that your decision to take the Lord's Supper was your way of accepting Jesus, and she said that no one should ever get in the way of children coming to Jesus. It sounds as though Miss Addie was one of the people who helped you come to Jesus. What very important decision did you make at church this morning?"

"I came down the aisle and told Daddy that I'm ready to be baptized."

"Your dad, your sister, and I are very happy about the choice you made, and we thank God that you knew Miss Addie and that she helped you so much, even when she was a hundred and one years old. What did you tell Jesus when we told you that Miss Addie had died?"

"I told him that Miss Addie was really sweet and he is going to enjoy having her up there in heaven with him."

"Would you like for more adults to try to be like Miss Addie?"

"Yes, ma'am. Moses needed some more adults like Miss Addie to help him with the children of Israel."

As the laughter died down, Karen continued. "I think you're right. Miss Addie would have lined them up and marched them straight to the Promised Land. There would have been none of that forty years of wandering in the wilderness. Why do you want everyone to remember Miss Addie?"

"Because remembering Miss Addie helps us remember Jesus and God."

Chapter 5

It was about 7:45 when Mike walked through the empty, silent sanctuary of Harrington Baptist Church and unlocked the front doors. It would be another three hours or so before the florists or the funeral home staff would need to get in, but he had told them last night at the viewing that he would have the front doors open ahead of time. Miss Addie once told Mike that she could remember when none of the churches in Harrington locked their doors. The house of God was left unlocked day and night for the benefit of anyone who needed a place of solitude in which to pray, think, or take a nap, or perhaps simply take shelter until the rain slacked up. In her honor, at least for a couple of hours, it would be so again.

In the quiet solitude, Mike caught himself singing softly the words that Coretta sang last night, "Time is filled with swift transition, naught on earth unmoved can stand..." A quick glance around the sanctuary reminded him of just how much had changed in the eight years and five months that he had been the pastor of this church.

The ugly gold carpet that had been put down in 1971, when earth tones were all the rage, was finally where it needed to be, buried deep under the earth-tone dirt of the Mintz County landfill. The dirt-color tile floors under the pews had been covered over with hardwood laminate flooring. Mike rode with Carl Baxter up to Dalton to pick up the carpet. Carl was able to get the church an excellent price from somebody he knew up there on premium quality Berber carpet in a bluish-gray color that came as a welcome relief from that awful gold. The two guys who did the flooring work on all of the houses Carl built gave the church a break on the installation when the older youth group volunteered to unbolt the pews, lug them out to the parking lot, rip up the old carpet, and put everything back in place after the new flooring was installed. The flooring guys didn't have to move a single stick of furniture. Later today, Cassie McWhorter would look elegant as she helped conduct Miss Addie's funeral, but Mike remembered her two years ago, at seventeen, in grungy jeans and a faded Camp Pinnacle T-shirt, pouring sweat, working as hard as any man ever did, helping rip up the old carpet and load it onto Carl's dump truck for its final ride to its eternal destination. The girl could handle a carpet knife. The matching ugly gold choir robes met the same fate as the carpet after a year of trying to give them away. Nobody wanted them locally. Eric put them on *The Swap Shop*, which came on every morning right before *The Obituary Column of the Air*, free, come and get them, with no takers. The cost of shipping them to some distant mission field would have been prohibitive even if somebody there had wanted them.

Franklin A. Brinkley, former Chairman of the Board of Deacons of Harrington Baptist Church, probably knew to the penny what those choir robes cost in 1971 and how much that would be in today's money. He would have died in a fit of apoplexy had he known about those robes joining the matching carpet, together forever, or for however long it takes polyester to decompose, deep under the earth-tone dirt at the landfill. That was one of those need-to-know things that Frank didn't need to know.

The estate of Roland and Geneva Millican had paid for the renovation of the sanctuary without touching budgeted funds. The irony of that was not lost on Mike. They had already done a few things piecemeal as the church had the money, such as painting throughout the sanctuary and educational building and installing a new sound system with wireless headphones for the hard of hearing. It had taken lots of the pale ivory to smother the last gasps of the gold color on the walls, but it was now six coats under, never to rise again. Roland had been Miss Addie's political nemesis thirty-six years ago when she bumped him off the school board, and he and Geneva had opposed pretty much everything Mike had done in his tenure as pastor. They were constantly talking of their discontent as members of Harrington Baptist Church and threatening to leave. They eventually did, feet first in top of the line Batesville caskets, Roland in March of 1995 and Geneva in November of the same year.

Not wanting their two daughters killing or suing each other, Roland and Geneva named their niece, Jean Brinkley, wife of Franklin A., as executor of their estate. According to the terms of their will, when the Millicans' house sold, twenty-five percent of the proceeds went to each of the daughters and fifty percent to Harrington Baptist Church to be used as the church saw fit.

Susan Barrington, Roland and Geneva's younger daughter, told her Aunt Jean that her mother always liked the song "Precious Lord, Take My Hand," and that she would like for someone to sing it at her mother's funeral. Jean told her that she'd never heard anybody who could sing that song better than Coretta Brinkley, then added, "Coretta is black if that makes any difference, although she's kin to your Uncle Frank." Susan and her sister Gail said it didn't make any difference to them. At the funeral of one who had been unkind and unwelcoming to her, Coretta sang as beautifully as if she had been singing for a close friend or a beloved family member. Not ordinarily one to show emotion, Frank Brinkley had tears running down his face when Coretta sang that song. The same man who had ranted about "miscegenation" in that deacons meeting when Daniel Groves started dating Coretta, went up to her after the funeral, hugged her, and thanked her for singing so beautifully and for being so kind to their family.

The day after Geneva's funeral, Frank took down the photograph of his great-grandfather Reverend Joshua Higgins Brinkley that hung in his living room, carefully removed it from the frame, and took it down to *The Harrington Courier* office. Five or six years ago, Ted Coleman had opened his photography studio as a sideline to the newspaper business. Frank asked Ted whether he could make him two more eight-by-ten prints of that picture. Ted said that he could, and that he would like to run the picture in the paper as the weekly Historic Mintz County feature. Frank gave Ted a caption for the picture in the paper, "Rev. Joshua Higgins Brinkley,

1832–1919, Confederate soldier, state senator, and Baptist minister, was the ancestor of all of the Brinkleys in Harrington and Mintz County. Photo courtesy of great-grandson Franklin A. Brinkley. Ted made the prints for Frank, who took them and had them mounted in identical matting and frames. The following Sunday night, he called Daniel and Coretta over to his car out in the parking lot after church and gave her one of the pictures. The next morning, he stopped by Arthur Brinkley's garage and gave him the other one. Frank told Arthur that he remembered playing with his father Cleon Brinkley when they were both little kids but that all of that stopped abruptly when they got to be school age. Frank said that he'd known growing up that they were related somehow or other but that such things, white folks and black folks who were kin to each other, weren't talked about back then. Frank acknowledged to Arthur, "You could tell by looking at your daddy that he was a Brinkley." Arthur said that one of his daddy's sisters was so light-skinned she could pass for white, which she did after she moved to Atlanta and worked thirty years as a legal secretary at a big law firm there.

Frank told Arthur that he'd heard two different stories about how Grandpa Brinkley lost his right arm. In one story, the one that got passed down in the family, he got it shot off reaching up to reload when his company was in a heated engagement with some New Hampshire sharpshooters at Chickamauga. The other story, which Miss Addie heard from her grandfather Elmer Peyton, who had been a first sergeant in the same company with Joshua Brinkley, was that Private Brinkley only lost one finger at Chickamauga — his trigger finger — which he "accidentally" shot off in camp before the battle began. As for the rest of the arm, Grandpa Peyton told Miss Addie that was a sawmill accident shortly after the war and a lesson for all on the dangers of running a sawmill while intoxicated. Arthur told Frank that, if it wouldn't hurt his feelings, he'd be more inclined to believe the version Miss Addie heard from her Grandpa Peyton, since the more embarrassing version of a family story is usually closer to the truth.

Arthur said that he clearly remembered his great-grandmother Lizella Harbin, who was ninety-eight years old when she died in 1956. Her parents, he said, had been slaves on the Brinkley farm when she was born in 1858, and she had lived on the Brinkley place most of her life. The Brinkleys had never charged her any rent to live in the house she was born in. She stayed there until 1944 or '45 when she fell and broke her hip and had to be in a rolling chair the rest of her life, so she moved in with Arthur's parents. Frank told Arthur that he remembered her from when he was a kid, only name he'd ever heard was Lizella, never heard a last name, and he and his three sisters all knew her as Aunt Lizella. Frank said that the thing he remembered most clearly about Aunt Lizella was that she always had the prettiest flowers growing around that old shack and that she was a sweet old lady as long as you didn't mess with her flowerbeds. He recounted her warning that she'd tear up a white hide the same as a black one if anybody messed with her flowers.

Arthur asked Frank if he and Jean would join his family for dinner at his house Sunday afternoon. "We generally eat about 2:00 p.m. or 2:15 p.m. since we don't get out of church as early as y'all do," Arthur added. "Reverend Conway'll just be announcing his text and buildin' up a good head of steam 'bout the time Reverend Westover pronounces the benediction. Y'all can do a whole service in the time it takes us to get warmed up good." Frank accepted the invitation.

Frank admitted to Mike after the fact that he hadn't meant for it to go that far, that he'd just meant to drop off the picture and be done with it. He accepted the invitation because he saw no polite way to decline since he couldn't think of any previous engagement, and he knew that Jean, who had been declared cancer-free following her surgery but was not back to full strength yet, would be in favor of any Sunday dinner she didn't have to cook or clean up after. Frank said that the last time he'd been to a black person's house was when he and Cleon Brinkley played together as kids and they went to Aunt Lizella's house. Frank said that it felt awkward at first, but Arthur and Eloise put him and Jean at ease and across the table from Daniel and Coretta. Over dinner, Frank recounted how Aunt Lizella had put hog wire up all around her porch and planted grape vines mostly for shade with the grapes being a bonus. She also planted the little cherry tomatoes by the front steps. Frank said that he and Cleon had often taken refuge from the summer heat on her porch, sitting in the swing eating her grapes and cherry tomatoes. Arthur said that the grapes were not just for shade, because his great-grandmother used to make the communion wine for church. Before they left, Arthur told Frank that he wanted to give him something. The same day that Frank brought Arthur the picture of their common ancestor Joshua Brinkley, Arthur stopped by Ted Coleman's studio with a picture of Lizella Harbin at age ninety-seven, sitting in a rocking chair crocheting. Ted ran the picture in the paper as a Historic Mintz County feature, with the caption, "Lizella Harbin, 1858–1956, was born the daughter of slaves on the Brinkley Farm in Mintz County. She was ninety-seven when this picture was made in 1955. Photo courtesy of her great-grandson Arthur Brinkley." The beautifully framed picture, identical to the one in Arthur and Louise's living room, now hung in Frank and Jean's living room.

Frank told Arthur about the Brinkley family reunion the first Saturday in August under the big pavilion out at Salyers Creek Park and told him that the announcement that his cousin puts in *The Harrington Courier* every year always says, "All descendants of Reverend Joshua Higgins Brinkley are cordially invited to come and bring a covered dish." Frank told Arthur and Eloise that all means all, and that if all of them showed up, they'd really have a crowd. Frank said that he and his oldest sister counted it up one time, all the children Josh Brinkley had with two wives plus the four he fathered by Aunt Lizella. Ever obedient to the divine mandate to be fruitful and multiply, the man fathered at least seventeen children, all of whom lived to be grown and had descendants. The last one, Aunt Lizella's daughter Annie Mae, was born in 1896 when Joshua Brinkley was sixty-four years old. Frank concurred with Arthur's assessment that God alone knows how many descendants of Josh Brinkley are walking around out there.

Although Mike rejoiced in the demise of earth-tone walls, carpet, and choir robes, he rejoiced more in the kinds of change that delighted Miss Addie, changes that require a theological explanation, such as Frank Brinkley and Coretta Brinkley Groves hugging each other the way you hug kinfolks. Other changes came to mind. Mike had become so used to women serving as deacons at Harrington that it seemed bizarre now that anyone got upset when he asked Deacon Carol Richardson, who was visiting one Sunday from Mike's former pastorate at Clear Springs, to help serve communion, or that it was such an issue when the church learned that Brenda Coleman had been ordained at her former church in Macon. Now Brenda was the deacon chair. Over the past eight years, the church had ordained other capable women as deacons. The church had selected Joyce Baxter, Elaine McWhorter, Lori Pettit, Cheryl Groves, Jenny Latham, and Laura Cason, not because of any shortage of eligible men but because they recognized the giftedness of these women. Six women and three men now served as active deacons. Mike remembered the late Royce Green saying that no woman would ever serve as a deacon at Harrington Baptist Church as long as he was living. Royce was right about that, but he probably would have lived to be wrong had he not been too cheap to fix the brakes on his truck.

It was no longer an issue for a woman to preach at Harrington Baptist Church. Back in his study now, Mike retrieved a treasured cassette from his desk drawer. In1990, when ten-year-old Cassie McWhorter was baptized, Mike asked Miss Addie to tell about her baptism. From the beginning of his pastorate at Harrington, Mike had been amazed at the friendship of those two, a friendship that completely transcended the age difference of more than eight decades. They were, all at the same time, like two little girls and two little old ladies. Miss Addie's testimony had ended up being more of a sermon — some said the best sermon ever preached at Harrington Baptist Church. Mike's assignment today was to "tell them that I had a secure hope in the Lord Jesus Christ." Nothing could better prepare him for that task than putting that cassette in the tape deck and hearing Miss Addie's sermon in her own voice.

The essence of that message was that such assurance comes not from being able to remember one's response to an invitation in a brush arbor meeting or one's baptism in the creek eighty-two years ago — although she remembered and recounted those things vividly — but from living in an ongoing conversation with God and making many daily choices to do what one knows to be the will of God. Mike listened again as Miss Addie told about times throughout her life that she had to face the same fears she faced as she walked down the aisle at that brush arbor meeting and as she waded out into the baptismal water under the covered bridge below the dam at Bailey's Mill, the times when she had to choose whether to shrink back in fear or to trust God not knowing fully where God might be leading. "I've learned," Miss Addie said, "that all fear feels pretty much the same. The fear of being killed or burned out of your home at sixty-four feels about the same as the fear of being embarrassed to death when you are eleven." The message, which was good for the whole church, went straight to the heart of the little girl being baptized that day. Cassie had always loved to hear Miss Addie tell about things that had happened when she was her age. The message was on target, and the messenger had credibility.

Mike recounted the conversation with Cassie McWhorter in his office on the Friday afternoon before she told the church that God had called her to preach. "Brother Mike," the tall slender eighteen-year-old told him, "I'm terrified at the thought of preaching, but I can't get away from it, and I'm more afraid not to obey God. I am very sure about this or I would not be sitting here having this conversation with you. I told you about our vacation last summer. I asked Mom and Dad to arrange our trip so we could go to church at Clear Springs one Sunday, and they did. We dropped in and surprised Heather and I got to hear her preach again. It just confirmed everything for me. I've known since she preached the revival here when I was eleven that God was calling me to preach. I'm glad that you had her preach that revival. Heather and I have been e-mailing back and forth a lot, and she's been a big help. If I knew I could be as good as she is, I wouldn't be so scared. I don't know that. All I know is that this is what I have to do to be obedient to God, even if I fall flat on my face. I still remember something Miss Addie said the day I was baptized, 'Cassie, when you come to the hard decisions in life, remember your baptism. Close your eyes and feel the water, and you'll know what you need to do.' I'll always remember what she said, and in my mind, I still hear her voice saying it. So far, God's response to all of my fears and objections has been, 'You've felt the water. You know what you need to do. Trust me and do it.'"

In the cool, quiet, deserted sanctuary, Mike paused to pray. He prayed for all who would have a part in today's service for Miss Addie and for all who would attend, but he prayed especially for the barely nineteen-year-old girl who was both grieving the death of her best friend since childhood and preparing to conduct her first funeral. It was a simple prayer for Cassie, that she would feel the water that engulfed her in baptism, that she would be strengthened and encouraged by Miss Addie's powerful blessing, and that she would experience a surprising anointing by the Spirit engulfing her like baptismal water.

Miss Addie's closest relatives were nieces, nephews, and cousins, so the bereavement ministry work group was not having to prepare a meal for a large group. The family was coming for lunch at 11:30 a.m., which would give them time to eat before the funeral service at 1:00 p.m. At the family's request, they were keeping the meal simple with a couple of different kinds of bread, a tray of sandwich meats and cheeses, Cole slaw, and potato salad. Karen was bringing a Crock Pot of homemade bean and ham soup. Rhonda Brinson was bringing vegetable soup, and a couple of people were bringing desserts. With his office door open, Mike heard people bumping around in the kitchen and fellowship hall and getting set up for the meal, and he heard the quartet out in the sanctuary practicing their "fa-sol-la" harmonies. As they sang through "I Love the Lord, He Heard My Cries," an Isaac Watts hymn text based on Psalm 116, Mike wondered how one man could be so prolific, composing hundreds of hymn texts including at least one based on each of the one hundred and fifty psalms, along with writing textbooks on mathematics and astronomy.

Mike was looking over the order of service and his notes for his part in the funeral one more time when Deborah Estelle stuck her head in his study. "Daddy, Mom said for me to come and get you. They want you to say the blessing and Mom said there's plenty of food and we're invited to eat with the family."

Mike and Karen found themselves across the table from Kathleen and Houston Mayfield, which was awkward at best, since the last time Karen and the girls had seen Kathleen was out at Pine Ridge two years ago when Kathleen made a "special trip" down from Carrollton the day of Daniel and Coretta's wedding because she suspected that Aunt Addie had finally lost her ever-loving mind. Miss Addie had waited until 9:00 p.m. the night before the wedding to call Kathleen and Houston to tell them that she was going to be the matron of honor at the wedding. Miss Addie had not wanted Kathleen to have an excessive amount of time to worry about it, and Kathleen had not realized that, in her later years, Miss Addie's favorite form of amusement was putting her into a dying duck fit over concerns that she had lost her ever-loving mind. Marvalene Thomas, the activities director at Pine Ridge, had been at the viewing for Miss Addie last night, and she told Karen about Miss Addie showing her the bridesmaid dress the week before the wedding. She said that Miss Addie was taking on over all the pretty bright colors and then added with a laugh, "Kathleen's going to put on a very entertaining show for us when she sees me in this dress. It might be worth your time to come over here on Saturday just to watch her. I'll call her the night before the wedding and let her know about it, tell her about the dress and everything. Kathleen'll get up about 5:00 a.m. Saturday morning and come rushing down here to see whether I have finally lost my ever-loving mind, and I shall tell her that I've lost some of my hearing, which is the reason I wear those gadgets in my ears, but I still have my ever-loving mind." Kathleen had made other "special trips" down to Harrington for the same reason, such as when Aunt Addie made the decision to sell her house and move to Pine Ridge Assisted Living, something Kathleen had been pushing her to do since Pine Ridge opened in 1985, without consulting her. Kathleen and Houston subscribed to *The Harrington Courier*, but being out of town, the paper was usually a week or more old when they got it. When they got the issue with the Red Carpet Realty ad listing her aunt's house for sale, Kathleen came down there in a tizzy to confirm that Aunt Addie had finally lost her ever-loving mind. By then, the Brinsons had put a contract on the house and Miss Addie had already sold or given away her excess furniture on The Swap Shop, which comes on right before The Obituary Column of the Air, and she had already signed the contract on the apartment at Pine Ridge, called the phone company to have them move her phone service, and made arrangements with the movers.

Today, the only thing Karen could think of to say to Kathleen to break the awkward silence was, "You know, Mrs. Mayfield, your Aunt Addie was very blessed to be past a hundred years old and still have all of her mental faculties. I hope that you and I do as well, but we'll probably lose our ever-loving minds before we're that old."

Chapter 6

"Blessed are the dead who die in the Lord from henceforth, yea, saith the Spirit, that they may rest from their labors, and their works do follow after them," Mike shouted from the back of the sanctuary precisely at 1:00 p.m. This was Jenny's cue to start the processional, the CORONATION tune of "All Hail the Power of Jesus' Name," "loud and majestic," Mike had noted Miss Addie's wishes when they planned this service, and that was how Jenny was playing it now. The congregation would have stood as one on the downbeat of the first measure even if they had not known that they were supposed to. The sheer power of the new Baldwin grand piano — another legacy from the estate of Roland and Geneva Millican — unleashed by the skilled hands of Jenny Latham, would have lifted them out of their seats. Jenny always played well, and she was at her best today. Mike, Andrew, and Cassie walked slowly ahead of the casket as Tommy Sheridan and Daniel Groves rolled it down the center aisle. Six pallbearers — Darrell Brinson, Davis Gates, Ted Coleman, Aaron Stewart, Luke Groves, and Anthony McWhorter — walked behind the casket and ahead of the honorary pallbearers, members of the Mintz County Retired Teachers Association, teachers in the Mintz County schools, the superintendent and staff of the superintendent's office, members of the board of education, and their spouses. After they positioned the casket in front of the pulpit, Daniel and Tommy took their places at the ends of the casket as Mike, Andrew, and Cassie stepped up to the pulpit platform where they were joined by deacon chair Brenda Coleman. They all remained standing as Paul Webster escorted the handful of relatives to their seats before announcing, "Everyone, please be seated."

"Blessed be the God and Father of our Lord Jesus Christ, the father of mercies and God of all comfort, who comforts us in all of our affliction so that we may be able to comfort those who are in any affliction with the comfort with which we ourselves are comforted by God," Brenda began as she stepped up to the pulpit. "As chair of our deacon ministry, it is my privilege to welcome each of you to Harrington Baptist Church, which was Miss Addie's spiritual home for seventy-six years. We are here to worship the Lord, to remember Miss Addie with joy and thanksgiving, to receive comfort from God, and to comfort one another with the comfort we have received. Our amazing God who reconciles us to himself and gives us the ministry of reconciliation also comforts us and gives us the ministry of comforting others with the comfort we have received. We would have counted ourselves blessed if Miss Addie had only lived to be seventy-five or eighty. To have enjoyed her presence among us, to have had her among us to the age of a hundred and one, to the very end of her life teaching, mentoring, loving, and encouraging us has been a phenomenal blessing. Miss Addie's delight in doing the will of God and being a blessing to all of us may have contributed to the length of her life. Certainly it contributed to the joyfulness of her life. May all of our lives be as well-lived, rich, and blessed as hers, and may we all receive and give comfort. That is our prayer in Jesus' name. Amen."

From his vantage point on the pulpit platform, Mike looked out on the largest crowd assembled in the sanctuary of Harrington Baptist Church during his tenure as pastor. He noted that there were some good singers among them, as he could hear all four parts distinctly when the congregation sang Edward Mote's hymn "The Solid Rock." Now he breathed a prayer for his older daughter Asalee as she came to the pulpit to present the first scripture reading, Psalm 103, although he was confident that she would do well. Asalee read scripture in church for the first time when she was eleven, and she had done it many times since. Miss Addie had hugged her after church the first time she read scripture and told her what a delight it was for her to hear children who read well, and her particular delight in hearing the words of scripture read by one who reads expressively with good enunciation in a strong, clear voice. Miss Addie would have been pleased today as Asalee made good eye contact, projected well, and read with flawless enunciation, "Bless the Lord, O my soul, and all that is within me, bless his holy name. Bless the Lord, O my soul, and forget none of his benefits..."

"As a musician," Eric Latham began his introduction of the Sacred Harp Singers, "I am grateful to Miss Addie for introducing Jenny and me to *The Sacred Harp*. This is a tradition we knew nothing about until one rainy Sunday afternoon when we visited her at her home. She was ninety-four and recovering from a knee replacement. I noticed that she had a large collection of old hymn books. One in particular caught my eye. It was *The Sacred Harp*, first published in 1844, with many reprints and revised editions that added newer songs. I noticed the odd-shaped notes and how the melody line was woven through all of the parts instead of being carried in the soprano line all the time. Miss Addie noticed my fascination. Before time for the Sunday evening service, she had taught us to read shaped notes, and Jenny and I were sight-singing this fascinating old music as Miss Addie sang along with us. To be as old as she was, she still had a good clear singing voice, and she thoroughly enjoyed having someone who could sing along with her on songs that had been a part of her childhood, songs that employ no musical instruments other than the human voice. That visit led to some delightful times taking Miss Addie to the big Sacred Harp singings up at Bremen and over at Henegar, Alabama. David and Cheryl took an interest in it, too, and before long, we were sharing some of this wonderful music with our church family. Miss Addie requested that we sing today, so we will sing some of her favorites from *The Sacred Harp*. On each song, we'll sing it through once singing the notes — the 'fa sol la's' — and then go back and sing the words. When we sang Sacred Harp with Miss Addie, we noticed that she didn't have to look at the book very much. Sit back, relax, and listen as we share some of the songs that helped form the foundation of Miss Addie's faith."

"Miss Addie was among the most considerate people I've ever known," Mike began his remarks. "So considerate that she tried to make it as easy as possible for those who would have a part in her funeral. She did that in two ways, first by living in such a way that there could be no doubt about her spiritual condition. When we heard the news of Miss Addie's death Saturday morning, our daughter Asalee said, "I loved Miss Addie. She was for real." Asalee got it right. One 'for real' saint is a more compelling argument for the Christian way than all of the volumes of apologetics ever written. The second way that Miss Addie tried to make it easier for us was by sitting down with me in my study several years ago to plan this service. I wrote down three things that she wanted to have said about herself. She said, 'Tell them that I had a secure hope in Jesus Christ our Lord. Tell them that I tried to do right because I loved the Lord. Tell them that I invested my life in children and prayed that I did them some good.' When Andrew, Cassie, and I met Saturday to talk about our parts in this service, Cassie came up with a good idea. She suggested that, with three preachers, each of us could talk about one of the three things Miss Addie wanted us to say. My assignment is to tell you that Miss Addie had a secure hope in Jesus Christ our Lord. If you knew her very well at all, you know that she possessed that assurance, and you know that hope informed every aspect of her life.

"I've often conducted funerals for people who provided little if any evidence of such a hope. I've often been called by the funeral home to conduct a service when a family had no connection to a local church and did not know a minister to call. I have conducted services for people I knew barely or not at all. Perhaps the person had been baptized and joined a church at some point in the distant past, but sadly, there seemed to be a total disconnect between that long-ago commitment and the rest of the person's life. Not so with Miss Addie! She was deeply rooted in church with her presence, her prayers, her time, and her resources. It was my pleasure to be her pastor and enjoy a delightful friendship with her. The surest evidence of salvation is that one delights in doing what is pleasing to God. The better you knew Miss Addie, the more you realized how fully her relationship with God permeated her whole consciousness, her whole way of thinking and acting. We have not only Miss Addie's testimony of her conversion in a brush arbor meeting and her baptism in Salyers Creek below the dam at Bailey's Mill in 1908, we have the testimony of ninety more years of living consistent with that long-ago commitment.

"I've always been an early morning person. This morning, I left Karen and the girls asleep at home since they had the day off from school and work because of the holiday, and I walked over to the church about 7:30 a.m. I'm so glad we recorded Miss Addie's testimony — Miss Addie's sermon — on the Sunday that Cassie McWhorter was baptized. Because Cassie and Miss Addie have had this amazing connection since Cassie was a little girl, I asked Miss Addie to share her testimony on the Sunday we baptized Cassie. I knew that it would be good. I had no idea just how good. I listened in awe as a ninety-three-year-old woman who had never stood behind a pulpit before did the most homiletically skillful thing I ever witnessed. Miss Addie gathered the people on that creek bank in 1908 and the people in church that morning together into one cloud of witnesses for the baptism of her ten-year-old best friend. She painted the picture so vividly that she had all of us standing on that creek bank watching a little girl in a white dress take her father's hand and wade out to where her uncle, Preacher Tim Nestor, was waiting to baptize her, and she brought all of the people who were on that creek bank in 1908 here to witness as Jerry McWhorter took his daughter's hand as she came down the steps into the baptistery and Jerry and I baptized her. Cassie told me on Saturday, 'I know that someone born in 1979 should not remember something that happened in 1908, but I do. Miss Addie's baptism in 1908 was the beginning of her life of faith, not her entire testimony. My former New Testament professor, Dr. Paul Kerns, was once asked to tell about his Christian experience. He responded, 'Which one? I've had many.' Miss Addie had many experiences with the Lord and knew him as one who was always with her. The main point of Miss Addie's message was that her long-ago commitment in a brush arbor meeting and her baptism in Salyers Creek under the old bridge at Bailey's Mill on the first Sunday of September 1908 informed her thinking and the choices that she made throughout her life. The many bold and courageous things she did were the only choices consistent with her baptismal vow to live as a follower of Jesus. She gave some superb advice to ten-year-old Cassie: 'When you come to the hard decisions in life, remember your baptism. Close your eyes and feel the water, and you'll know what you need to do.' She quoted the wise words of Harry Ironside, 'It is up to us to see that we do right and up to God to see that we come out right.' You never know when something you say to a child may have lasting if not eternal significance. Miss Addie's message that day was a good word for all of us, but it was especially tailored to the little girl being baptized that day. It made a lasting impression on her. The little girl baptized that day is one of our preachers today. Miss Addie had a secure hope, not only because she 'got saved' a long time ago, but because she lived out what it means to be a saved person, one who delights in doing the will of God, guiding and encouraging others walking in the way that leads to everlasting life. There is no worse distortion of the gospel message than to make the conversion experience the sum total of what it means to be a Christian, to reduce a way of life, a journey with God and God's people, to a mere transaction.

"Miss Addie knew God as the one who reconciles people to himself. One who experiences God as forgiving and gracious must of necessity become forgiving and gracious. The end result of grace is gracious people. How can people know God is gracious if they never encounter people like Miss Addie who treat them with grace?

"Miss Addie took God seriously but took herself and everyone else with a grain of salt. She had a rich sense of humor. Grady Nutt got it right when he said that there is a profound relationship between humor and faith. Miss Addie relished a good pun and referred to puns as her one guilty pleasure other than fine chocolates. She had no patience with people who were self-important or self-righteous. She could and did use her sharp wit to let a few pounds of air out of dangerously over-inflated egos. Every pastor needs at least one Miss Addie to keep him humble and keep him real. She could spot egomaniacs, phonies, and charlatans a mile away. She had no patience with bumper sticker theology and glib, easy answers to questions that are unanswerable or require serious thought. She challenged me to be at my best in sermon preparation and not try to slide by with halfhearted efforts. She made me a better preacher.

"Miss Addie enjoyed remarkably good health, clarity of mind, and mobility to the end of her life. Seeing people much younger than her, including some of her former students, in wheelchairs, bedfast, or suffering from dementia, she realized how blessed she was. Unusual longevity did not run in her family. Her two brothers died in their early eighties, and both of her parents died in their seventies. She told me once that she didn't do anything different from what they did, she just kept doing it longer. Miss Addie once told me, 'I assume that God is keeping me here for some good reason. I am ready to go when he is ready to take me. I've no fear of life or death.' She liked to quote Paul's words, 'for me to live is Christ, and to die is gain.'

"I thoroughly enjoyed the viewing last night when we shared so many wonderful stories about Miss Addie. She stood all of four-feet-ten-inches tall and never topped a hundred pounds, but she was larger than life! We'll be telling Miss Addie stories for a long time to come, and we should. To be alive forever in the presence of God and also to live on here in so many good memories and in the sharing of so many great stories — that's as good as it gets. We celebrate Miss Addie's clear Christian witness and her secure hope in Christ. Let us all embrace that same blessed hope! Thanks be to God! Amen."

"I am honored to be here today," Andrew Jennings began in slow, measured cadence, "to celebrate the life and home going of one of God's saints, Sister Addie Jane Peyton Aldridge. Old Mother Phillips over at Zion A. M. E. used to say, 'I'm not going to be at my funeral. I'm going to a big family reunion that day.' Now, Miss Addie's gone to the reunion, as we all shall in God's good time. This service is for those who remain, to talk about how shall we live in light of Miss Addie's faithful witness, the life of a saint in our midst? I am also honored to stand behind the pulpit of my dear friend and fellow minister of the gospel, Reverend Michael Westover. My wife and I met Reverend and Mrs. Westover and their daughter Asalee shortly after their arrival in Harrington, and we celebrated with them the birth of their daughter Deborah Estelle. My wife teaches at Miss Addie's School, and Deborah Estelle is in her third grade class. We count the Westovers as dear friends, and I hold Reverend Westover in the highest esteem as my fellow minister of the gospel.

"Today is not my first time to take an assignment from Miss Addie, for she was my first grade teacher. Today's assignment is to 'tell them that I tried to do right because I loved the Lord.' Although her passing saddens me, the assignment is the easiest one she ever gave me! Miss Addie believed that Christians ought to do what Jesus said to do. She heeded the admonition of the prophet Micah to 'love justice, do mercy, and walk humbly with your God.'

"Sister Coretta Groves and Sister Molly Coleman laid a good foundation for what I am going to say. Sister Groves sang two fine songs about the Lord as one who takes our hands, guides us day by day, and keeps us going when we'd otherwise be discouraged. Then Sister Coleman read that beautiful passage in I Corinthians that makes a perfect bridge from all that Reverend Westover said about Miss Addie's secure hope in Christ to me talking about how one lives in light of that hope. The apostle Paul talks about the certain hope of the resurrection, freedom from the fear of death, and death as the last enemy going down in defeat. All of that leads up to verse 58: 'Therefore, my beloved brethren' — the Greek there includes women as well as men, brothers and sisters — 'be stead-fast, immovable, always abounding in the work of the Lord, knowing that your labor is not in vain in the Lord.' Reverend Westover spoke ably about Miss Addie's secure hope in Christ. Because she possessed this hope — this confidence in the resurrection — she was able to be firm in her faith, bold and courageous in her obedience to God, fruitful in God's service, and confident that what she did was not a wasted effort.

"Miss Addie was a devoted worker in the church, but she knew that the work of the Lord entails much more than church work. Just as the main work of the fire department is not done in the fire station, the main work of the church is not done in the church building. It's out there where many people don't know Jesus and haven't encountered very many people motivated by the love of Jesus. It's out there where there are acts of mercy that need to be done. It's out there where injustice and oppression need to be confronted and where the righteousness and justice of God need to be established.

"Miss Addie found many opportunities to do God's work as a teacher. Over her long career, she made an indelible imprint upon almost thirteen hundred children. She taught so long that she even taught grandchildren of some of her first students. When she retired at sixty-two still in good health, she took that as God's way of reminding her that 'the fields are white unto harvest but the laborers are few, and you're too healthy to be sitting in a rocking chair in front of the TV. There's some work for you down at Florida Avenue Colored School.' She went down there to see what she could do to help, and she ended up teaching first grade there for two years without being paid a cent. I was in her class the first year, and she taught my sister Gloria the next year. Early this morning, I went and sat for a while in the room at our church that was Miss Addie's classroom for those two years. I thought about how much we enjoyed going to school every day. If we ever had to stay home sick, we cried because we couldn't go to school. We didn't care about Miss Addie being white and us being black. I don't think we ever thought about it at the time. Little children don't think about race unless someone teaches them to think about it. If you love children and treat them right, they'll love you back, doesn't matter what color you are or what color the children are. We loved Miss Addie because she first loved us! We knew we were smart enough to learn anything we put our minds to because Miss Addie told us so every day. We learned because we were taught well, because she knew how to connect with a child's natural desire to learn, and because we were expected to learn. It went beyond the classroom. We saw how Miss Addie treated our parents. She addressed them as Mr. and Mrs. and sir and ma'am. She did that, not only when our parents came to the school, but if she met them on the street or in the grocery store. If she saw us outside of school, she called us by name and gave us a hug. We knew that she loved us and delighted in us.

"Miss Addie did right because she loved the Lord, and she didn't quit when she met opposition. Not long after she started teaching the black children, the Ku Klux came and burned a cross in front of her house one night, burned another one in front of Zion A. M. E. Now, a lot of folks would have shrunk back in fear when that happened. Not Miss Addie! Miss Addie's husband, Mr. Ches Aldridge, I was just ten years old when he died but I remember him well, fine man. Knew his wife well enough to know that she was going to obey God no matter what, and he supported her all the way.

"Miss Addie and Mr. Ches joined our local chapter of the NAACP. They joined because it made them furious that the children Miss Addie taught and their parents and siblings were not allowed to use the public library. Reverend Arthur Stewart, pastor at Greater New Hope Progressive Missionary Baptist Church, was president of the Mintz County NAACP.

Miss Addie and Mr. Ches went with him to a meeting of the library board to demand that all residents of Mintz County, regardless of race, be allowed to use the library and check out books. Miss Addie's students and the other first graders at Florida Avenue Colored School had already read what books the school library had on their grade level, and their parents needed to be able to check out books and read with them at home, too. The Aldridges knew that the librarian, Mrs. Violet Garmond, agreed with them and wanted the library open to everyone, knew how Mrs. Garmond hated that White Only sign on the library door, and she had expressed that to the board. The board said 'no' to the Aldridges and Reverend Stewart just like they'd said 'no' to Mrs. Garmond. The NAACP decided to demonstrate in front of the library. Daddy carried a sign that said 'My taxes support this library. Let my children use it!' Mama carried one that said 'I just want to read.' Miss Addie and Mr. Ches were right there with us every Saturday, rain or shine, picketing the library. The library board wouldn't budge, so the state chapter sent us a lawyer and helped us prepare to file suit against the library board in federal court. Lawyer told the library board that he was going to make them think their name was 'the defendant' and that they would have a hard time defending their position and actions in federal court. Library board backed down and opened the library to everybody because they didn't have the money to fight a case in federal court, and the county attorney told them that they'd lose if they spent their last nickel trying to fight it. They opened the library, but they closed the restrooms because they didn't have separate restrooms for white and colored. They did put in a separate colored water fountain. Every time Miss Addie came in the library, which was pretty often because she loved to read and she and Mrs. Garmond were friends for years, she'd stop and take a drink from the colored water fountain. She said that one of her great-grandmothers was a Creek Indian, so she wasn't sure that she was white enough to drink from the white fountain. Mrs. Garmond was a fine Christian lady, too, first woman to serve as an elder at Harrington Presbyterian Church. Mrs. Garmond said that most of the people who tried to keep us out of the library had never checked out a

book in the whole thirty years that she had been the librarian. Then in
'62, the same year that Miss Addie was elected to the school board, Mr.
Ches won a seat on the library board. They re-opened the restrooms at
the library and hired Gloria Hammondtree, a senior at Florida Avenue
Colored School, member at Greater New Hope Baptist Church, Lennox
and Miriam Hammondtree's daughter, to help Mrs. Garmond after
school and on Saturdays. Dr. Gloria Hammondtree Robbins, professor
at Morehouse, delivered the eulogy at Mrs. Garmond's funeral.

"Miss Addie was, as some would say, stubborn, or as the apostle Paul
would say, steadfast and immovable. When it came to a clear-cut matter
of right and wrong, Miss Addie wouldn't back down from anybody, especially if it involved what was right for children. I remember her telling me
— with the sweetest smile — 'I've been known to knock down my share
of hornet nests. Most of them needed to be knocked down. I also have a
reputation for speaking the truth in love with both barrels.'

"As long as she lived, Miss Addie found ways to abound in the work
of the Lord. She continued to make the connection between loving the
Lord and doing right. She did it in her service on the school board. She
did it as she continued to substitute teach and tutor children who needed
extra help well into her eighties. She did it in her faithful service in this
church. She helped in Vacation Bible School when she was ninety-four.
All that she did, she did gladly because she loved the Lord. Love that
doesn't act is like wind that doesn't blow or current that doesn't flow. You
may have a mass of air, but you don't have wind unless it's in motion,
blowing. You may have an electrical charge, but you don't have current,
don't have electricity, unless it's flowing through a conductor. You may
have a sentimental feeling about God or people, but you don't have love
unless that is translated into action. Love, like wind and electricity, exists
only when it is active.

"How shall we honor Miss Addie? By making a connection between
what we believe and how we live, doing right because we love the Lord,
like Miss Addie did. A saint has lived among us and shown us the way.
Let us study and follow her example! As the hymn writer put it, 'Trust

and obey, for there's no other way, to be happy in Jesus, but to trust and obey.' Thanks be to God! Amen."

"I'm wearing my most cherished possession today, as I do every time I preach," Cassie began, "this gold chain with a simple unadorned gold cross. Miss Addie's parents gave it to her in 1908 on the Sunday that she was baptized. She gave it to me in 1990 on the Sunday that I was baptized. I wear it to honor her. I wear it as a visible reminder of her powerful blessing on my life and ministry. Most little girls have a best friend. I was no different, except that my best friend was a white-haired little old lady. Even if I live as long as Miss Addie, I shall never have a greater honor than the one I have today. Like my colleagues, I have an assignment from Miss Addie: 'Tell them that I invested my life in children and I hope that I did them some good.' Speaking as one of those children — yes, Miss Addie, you did us some good, more good than you could have possibly known in your lifetime. It will take eternity to calculate the return on Miss Addie's investment.

"I am glad that we sang 'Jesus Loves Me' and 'Jesus Loves the Little Children.' The tune of 'Jesus Loves the Little Children' is an old Civil War song, 'Tramp, Tramp, Tramp, the Boys Are Marching,' a song about soldiers marching off to war. It was written by George Root, who wrote many gospel songs. With the growth of the Sunday School movement following the Civil War, many new songs were written for children, songs with lively tunes that appealed to the energy of children. Herbert Woolston took that tune, written by his friend George Root, and gave it the words we know so well, 'Jesus loves the little children, all the children of the world, red and yellow, black and white, they are precious in his sight, Jesus loves the little children of the world.' The songs we sing often shape our theology more than the sermons we hear. Those Sunday School songs like 'Jesus Loves the Little Children' took their place alongside the beautiful old songs of *The Sacred Harp* in shaping little Addie Jane Peyton's understanding of God and helping to lead her to become a follower of Jesus. She learned how Jesus rebuked his disciples for keeping children away from him. She was attracted to Jesus who loved all children and loved her individually. She was baptized as a follower of Jesus just after her eleventh birthday. Miss Addie's love for children was rooted deeply in her Christian experience. For her, being a follower of Jesus meant learning to love children as Jesus did.

"At the Baptist Women in Ministry conference I attended this past summer, I got to meet and hear some powerful preachers, women who not only preach, but preach very well. For me, the best part of the conference was the informal time we had for conversations with the people who were on the program. I talked at length with Dr. Molly Marshall from Central Baptist Seminary about her spiritual journey, as well as mine. She is warm and genuine. Within minutes, we were on first-name basis. We talked about people who led us toward faith and nurtured us in the faith. I told Molly about Miss Addie. Molly said something I'll never forget: 'Cassie, before we trusted Jesus, we trusted the people who told us about Jesus.' Even as a small child, I knew that Miss Addie loved me, and Miss Addie was one of the people who taught me about Jesus, so for me it was a very small step from 'Miss Addie loves me' to 'Jesus loves me.' The first year our church did Vacation Bible School jointly with Greater New Hope, I was in elementary school. Miss Addie came to teach the Bible lesson. I learned that Jesus loves 'red and yellow, black and white' as I watched Miss Addie show the same love toward black children and white children. The children responded to that. The color of a child's skin made no more difference to Miss Addie than the color of her hair or eyes. I learned that God loves each of us as unique individuals, not just humanity in general, because Miss Addie took a personal interest in each of us. She learned our names and called us all by name.

"Now I love my sister Emily, but I don't want to be called by her name. It's a beautiful name, a good name, but it's not my name. Didn't you hate it when you were a child and someone called you by the wrong name, called you by your brother's or sister's name? It probably carried over from all of Miss Addie's years as a teacher, but it was more than that. Miss Addie knew the names of all of the children in Harrington Baptist Church and any other children she saw on a regular basis. When we were children, some adults ignored us and acted as though we were invisible unless we did something bad. Then, there were those adults who, as far back as we can remember, knew our names, engaged us in conversation, listened to our thoughts and ideas, and showed a personal interest in us. They made us feel important and valued. Miss Addie helped prepare me to encounter the living God who knows my name and has never once called me by my sister's name, the one who 'walks with me, talks with me, and tells me that I am his own,' the God who hears my prayers, the God who calls me to repentance and faith, the God who throws me a curve ball every time I think I have him and his ways figured out, the God who called me to preach the gospel.

"Miss Addie was the first person I told that God was calling me to preach. I was fifteen. She was ninety-seven. Miss Addie talked with me about Mary's encounter with the angel who told her that she was going to give birth to the Messiah, and Mary taking refuge with her cousin Elizabeth — the one person on earth best prepared to believe her story about the encounter with the angel and the angel's message. She laughed and said, 'So that's why God has kept me around so long, to be like Elizabeth and tell you that you're not crazy for thinking God called you to preach.' Miss Addie said she wasn't surprised because the Lord had already told her, and she had been praying that I'd get around to telling her before she died. When Heather Simmons preached the revival here, Miss Addie noticed me on the edge of my seat listening to every word she said. She remembered how much I had talked to Heather that week. She said that she'd been praying for me, that I would say 'yes' to the call. Then, she held me close and prayed for me. I know what Paul meant when he wrote to Timothy about 'the gift that is in you through the laying on of my hands.' I have such a gift in me, courtesy of Miss Addie.

"The gospel lesson that Karen read includes words of our Lord that we cherish at such a time as this: 'Let not your hearts be troubled, you believe in God, believe also in me. In my Father's house, there are many dwelling places. If it were not so, I would have told you. I go to prepare a place for you, and if I go, I will come again and receive you to myself so that, where I am, there you may be also.' These are wonderful promises, assuring us that the one we love is with the Lord, and that we too shall join her in the Lord's presence forever. But there's more to it than that. Jesus was concerned with more than giving his disciples a hope beyond this life. It was to give them hope within this life. He was preparing them to go on living after he was no longer physically present with them.

"That's what Miss Addie did. She was keenly aware that few people lived as long as she did. The last time I talked with her, this past Friday evening, she told me, 'Cassie, I rarely see an obituary for someone my age, but these younger people in their seventies and eighties are dropping like flies! All of the obituaries in *The Harrington Courier* are for people younger than I. Almost every week, I see the obituary for at least one of my former students.' Miss Addie had long since come to terms with her mortality. She fully believed the promises of Jesus recorded in today's gospel lesson, and she looked forward to being with the Lord forever.

"Miss Addie had no concerns about her own death or what would happen to her. Her concern was the concern Jesus had for his disciples, how they would fare when he was no longer with them. That's why Miss Addie poured her life into the lives of the children she taught and the young adults she encouraged and mentored. She invested her life in this church. Just a few Sundays ago, she read the gospel lesson at the Sunday morning service.

"I'm blessed to be one of those taken under Miss Addie's wing. Her powerful blessing will go with me the rest of my life. There will be something of Miss Addie in every sermon I preach. Paul told Timothy to take what he had taught him and teach it to other faithful people who will in turn teach others. He was saying, 'If you value the gift, pay it forward!' That's how we can best honor Miss Addie. Take the gift and pay it forward!

"I started to say Miss Addie never realized how much good she did for me and so many others, but that's not true. Early Saturday morning, when she awoke in the presence of the Lord, she got to see the full measure of all of the good she did for all of us. Thanks be to God! Amen."

"Coretta will come now to offer our benediction," Mike announced, "after which we shall adjourn to the cemetery at Peyton's Chapel Baptist Church for the service of Christian burial."

As David and Tommy loaded the casket into the hearse and as people found their way to their cars, Coretta came up to Cassie and hugged her. "Excellent message, Cass. Nobody would have thought it was your first funeral."

"Thank you, and you sang beautifully as always," Cassie replied. "Miss Addie would have been pleased. It's easier to preach after you sing. I thought I was going to be nervous and shaking like a leaf, but I wasn't. I've never felt more calm and confident in my life."

Coretta laughed, hugged Cassie, and explained, "It's the anointing, Honey. Takes the fear out of you."

Chapter 7

Tommy Sheridan had lined up the cars for the procession out to the cemetery at Peyton's Chapel, with the church van first in line behind the Harrington Police patrol car and ahead of the hearse. Andrew and Monica Jennings, Cassie, and Coretta rode with Mike, Karen, and the girls in the van to cut down on the number of vehicles. Police chief Aaron Stewart, who had been one of Miss Addie's first graders at Florida Avenue Colored School, had served as one of the pallbearers. Now he sat behind the wheel of the Ford Crown Victoria at the head of the procession. Normally, the Mintz County Sheriff's Department would have provided the escort since the cemetery was out in the county, nine miles from the Harrington city limits, but Aaron wanted to escort this procession himself. When Daniel called Aaron on his cell to tell him that they were ready to proceed, Aaron started the car, turned on the blue lights, and started the procession on its way out toward Martin Luther King Boulevard, which most people in Harrington still call Monument Avenue. He sounded a short blip on the siren to stop traffic before pulling out into the intersection and turning right onto MLK, leading the procession through town and out onto the Hansonville highway. Three and a half miles outside the city limits, the highway curves sharply to the left and Bailey's Mill Road angles off to the right, with Pulliam's Store, or what used to be Pulliam's Store, sitting in the fork of the road. The store closed after Mr. Pulliam died back when Aaron was in elementary school. Over the years, several others had leased the building and tried to make a go of it with a general store and gas pumps, with varying degrees of success. The building had stood empty for several years at a time. Now short stubs of pipe and wire stuck out of the concrete island where gas pumps had been, and a small

steeple topped by a cross was perched almost but not quite plumb on top
of the 12/12 roof. The sign atop the porch roof read,

Gloryland Way Missionary Baptist Church
Independent — Fundamental — Premillennial —
Soul-Winning — KJV Bible
Sunday School 10:00 a.m.
Preaching 11:00 a.m. & 6:00 p.m.
Wednesday 7:00 p.m.
Bro. Milford Braswell, Pastor

Still, the sign on the door said "Colonial is Good Bread," which is
the gospel truth, and anyone who asked for directions to Bailey's Mill
Road would be told to go like you're going to Hansonville and bear right
at Pulliam's Store. The newer sign atop the porch said "Gloryland Way
Missionary Baptist Church;" the older lettering above the fading hand-
painted Coca-Cola signs on the sides of the building still said "Geo. C.
Pulliam Gen. Mdse." They might as well have named it Pulliam's Store
Missionary Baptist Church.

Like the Red Sea parting for the Israelites, traffic — what little
there was on Bailey's Mill Road — pulled off onto the shoulder and
waited for the long procession to pass. Four miles out Bailey's Mill Road,
Aaron sounded another short blip on the siren to stop oncoming traffic
before making the sharp left onto Peyton's Chapel Road, beside a weathered sign reading "Peyton's Chapel Baptist Church 1½ miles" with an
arrow pointing left and a smaller sign suspended under it reading, "Bro.
Bobby Simpson, Pastor." At the intersection of Peyton's Chapel Road
and Freeman Valley Road, where Peyton's Chapel Baptist Church stands
on the northeast corner, crusher run gravel crunched under the tires as
Aaron guided the procession through the church parking lot and onto
the narrow road that winds up the hill behind the church and through
the cemetery, as close as he could get to the Webster Funeral Home

tent spread over an open grave in the Peyton-Aldridge family plot. The Wilbert Vault truck, a truck and trailer from Freeman's Grave Service, and a small Bobcat backhoe waited at a respectful distance on the other side of the road as cars filled the road through the cemetery and the church parking lot. Aaron, the other pallbearers, and the ones who had ridden in the church van were milling around, waiting for the last of the cars in the procession to file in and for people to walk from their cars up the hill to the funeral home tent.

"Mr. Sheridan!" the fifty-something, short, chubby, balding man in an ill-fitting suit called out as he approached Tommy Sheridan. Tommy recognized him as Bobby Simpson, having had a half dozen or so funerals with him. After thirty years with the same funeral home, there weren't many preachers in Mintz County and Phillips County that Tommy didn't know. Some, like Brother Bobby, he knew better than he really wanted to. Tommy had known Brother Bobby when he was at Pleasant Grove over in Phillips County before he came to Peyton's Chapel. "Who's the preacher doing the committal?" Brother Bobby demanded.

"I am," Cassie spoke firmly before Tommy could get his mouth open, "And you are...?"

Ignoring Cassie, Brother Bobby spoke to Tommy, "You did'n say nothin' about no woman preacher when you called about buryin' in our cemetery."

"You didn't ask, and I didn't see any need to tell you," Tommy responded calmly. "You weren't the one I called. Peyton's Chapel set up a cemetery association separate from the church about twenty years ago, back when Brother Gordon Harris was pastor, and deeded the cemetery over to Peyton's Chapel Cemetery Association. Brother Gordon's son, who was a lawyer, drew up the paperwork for them. The cemetery association's incorporated. They own the cemetery, not the church. The sign at the entrance says to call Mrs. Josie Bailey, president of Peyton's Chapel Cemetery Association, before opening a grave, so that's who I called, just like I do every time we have a burial in this cemetery. Mrs. Bailey gave us permission to open the grave, and she never asked who was doing the committal. Brother Bobby, you're in charge of who preaches at the church, but it's not up to you to say who can conduct services in this cemetery. Reverend McWhorter is going to do the committal, as Mrs. Aldridge requested."

"No she's not, and I don't care what you say some dead woman requested," Brother Bobby spoke in a more agitated tone, "as long as I'm pastor of this church, we ain't havin' no women preachers 'round here! And don't be callin' that girl 'Reverend' 'cause she ain't no preacher! God don't call women to preach! Any woman that thinks she's called to preach is sadly mistaken!"

"Brother Bobby," Cassie spoke firmly but courteously, "there are some things you can't control, like who God calls to preach and who conducts services in this cemetery. Miss Addie was my best friend as far back as I can remember. She asked me to do this service, and I intend to honor her request."

Brother Bobby was now seething with rage, his face and even his ears and the top of his bald head getting redder and redder, looking like his blood pressure was high enough to blow the top of his head off. He stepped toward Cassie and tried to snatch her Bible out of her hands. Cassie instinctively turned away from him to keep her Bible out of his grasp. Brother Bobby's hand missed Cassie's Bible and landed squarely on her left breast. Cassie stumbled backward as she jerked away from him and yelled, "Get your filthy paws off of me!" Mike, Tommy, and Daniel caught Cassie and helped her back on her feet. As they did, they heard a solid *WHOOMP*. Aaron Stewart and Andrew Jennings had Brother Bobby face down on the hood of the hearse as Aaron grabbed Brother Bobby's wrists, clicked the handcuffs on him behind his back, and told him that he was under arrest. He advised him of his right to remain silent, strongly recommended that he exercise that right since anything he said could and would be used against him in court, and advised him of his right to have an attorney. Aaron felt a sense of utter disgust as he escorted Brother Bobby to the patrol car. "I was brought up to respect preachers," Aaron told Brother Bobby, "My grandfather pastored Greater

New Hope in Harrington for thirty-seven years. I've been in law enforcement twenty-six years, first time I ever put handcuffs on a preacher. Didn't want to do it, but you didn't give me any choice. There's a fine line between acting a fool and breaking the law. You just had to cross it." As he put Brother Bobby in the back seat of the patrol car, Aaron added, "Now you're gonna sit right here in my car while we have this service and you're gonna be here until a county officer can get out here and get you out of my sight. You make me sick at my stomach; supposed to be a man of God!" After he slammed the door shut on Brother Bobby, Aaron leaned against the car and took a few slow, deep breaths to calm himself before he radioed for a county officer. After explaining the situation to the 911 dispatcher, Aaron added, "Tell him to take his time, Cathy, no lights or siren, tell him he's got time to go through the drive-through at Mickey D's on his way, and give us time to finish the graveside service for Miss Addie. I got him handcuffed and shackled in the back of my patrol car, so he's not going anywhere, we'll be here when he gets here."

With Brother Bobby secure and in no position to cause further trouble, Aaron walked back to the church van where Cassie sat between her parents, tightly embraced by Jerry and sobbing on his shoulder as Elaine gently rubbed her back.

"You gonna be all right, Preacher?" Aaron asked.

"Yeah, I'm okay, just shaken up," Cassie said as she struggled to regain her composure. "I wasn't expecting this. Only time I ever saw that guy was last year at the associational meeting when our church got voted out. He creeps me out, just having him touch me makes me want to go home and take a really long shower. Thanks for putting the handcuffs on him."

"Yeah, I appreciate what you did, Aaron," Jerry added.

"You're welcome. Hate to arrest a preacher, but he crossed the line from being stupid to breaking the law right in front of my eyes. No way I'm gonna let him get by with such as that. Got a county officer on the way out here to give Brother Bobby a ride to jail after we finish the graveside. Preacher, you don't have to worry about pressing charges. That's out of your hands, though you'll be called as a witness if it goes to trial. I saw what he did, so I'll be charging him. He's looking at disorderly conduct, simple assault, and sexual battery. There's a statute against preventing or disrupting a lawful assembly, and I'll charge him on that, too. People have a right to bury their dead in peace without having to deal with such as that."

Cassie was using her mother's compact to touch up her makeup as best she could when Daniel Groves stuck his head in the van. "Are you going to be all right to do the service, Cass? Or do you need me to ask Mike or Andrew to do it?"

"I'll do it," Cassie answered resolutely. "Miss Addie wouldn't let something like this stop her, and she dealt with worse than this. Jesus dealt with way worse than this. I'm good. Mostly just embarrassed that I lost my balance and fell backwards before I could get in a good swift kick. These shoes could've caused Brother Bobby a lot of pain if I'd kicked him in the right place. I'm not hurt, just embarrassed and mad. I'd've landed on my butt if Mike, Tommy, and Daniel hadn't caught me. I'm okay. This is for Miss Addie. I can do it for her. Let's get started." Cassie stepped out of the van and, flanked by her parents, walked to the rear of the hearse, Bible in hand.

"Ladies and gentlemen, we regret the delay in starting the service because of events beyond our control," Tommy announced. "Gentlemen who are serving as pallbearers, please take your places three on each side of the hearse and be ready to take hold of the handles as Daniel pulls the casket out. Reverend McWhorter will walk ahead of us to the gravesite. Be careful and watch your step, gentlemen, as we'll be carrying the casket over uneven ground. When we reach the gravesite, I'll help you guide the casket into position." It must not have occurred to the people who built walls around their family burial plots with little or no space to walk between them that someone someday might need to get in there to bury somebody or just mow the grass.

"Proud of you, honey," a tearful Jerry McWhorter said as he and Elaine gave their daughter a quick hug and kiss before she took her place ahead of the casket. "Miss Addie would be proud of you, too."

"Remember, you're long-legged like your daddy," Elaine added. "Don't walk too fast." Another time, Cassie might have rolled her eyes as only an adolescent girl can, like an odometer turning over 100,000 miles, and replied with "Mo-therrrrr, puh-lease..." Today, she appreciated her mom's gentle humor, indeed welcomed it as a relief from the tension of a few minutes ago, as Elaine refocused her mind on something utterly practical, reminding her not to go off and leave six pallbearers and two funeral directors carrying a casket over the obstacle course of a country church cemetery. It was the kind of practical thing that Miss Addie would think of. Elaine's point was well taken. The long legs had served Cassie well in high school when she played basketball and ran track, and they could have caused Brother Bobby a lot of pain if she had not lost her balance. They might yet help her impress the socks off of a church youth group when she shows them that the lady preacher can shoot hoops with the best of them. Her mom once told Cassie that, as a toddler, she disproved the conventional wisdom that you have to walk before you can run. Cassie had to work at it, but she made herself walk slowly ahead of the casket, occasionally glancing back to be sure the pallbearers were still with her. When they reached the tent, she took her place at the head of the grave as Daniel helped the pallbearers position the casket on the lowering device and Tommy directed the handful of relatives to their seats under the tent. As they gathered in, Cassie silently prayed the psalmist's words, "Let the words of my mouth and the meditations of my heart be acceptable in thy sight, O Lord, my strength and my redeemer." Coretta and the Sacred Harp Singers stood beside Cassie. When Tommy had gathered everyone as close in as he could get them, Daniel turned to Cassie and whispered, "We're ready, Preacher."

"Grace to you and peace from God our Father and the Lord Jesus Christ," Cassie began. She expected her voice to sound shaky, but it did not. "This is the first time I have done a committal, but it is a privilege for me to honor the request of my delightful friend, mentor, counselor, and encourager, Miss Addie, who liked to remind us that everything that has ever been done had to be done for the first time by somebody. I loved her and would have done anything for her. Giving me this privilege of committing her body to the earth in confident hope of the resurrection was an expression of her love for me and the final gift she could give me to encourage me as a young minister of the gospel. I hope to live a long and full life as Miss Addie did and pay forward the gift I received from her. When I come to the end of my journey, I pray that the one who commits my body to the earth will be a young preacher I have mentored and encouraged.

"Miss Addie's maiden name was Peyton. The land for Peyton's Chapel Baptist Church and Cemetery was deeded to the church by Miss Addie's great-grandfather Nathaniel Peyton in 1846. Her husband, parents, brothers, grandparents, great-grandparents, and numerous aunts, uncles, nieces, nephews, and cousins are buried here. Miss Addie is the fourth generation of her family to be laid to rest here. Her resting place is beside her husband of forty-one years, Mr. Chester Aldridge, with whom she shared her life and love from 1922 until his death in 1964, and within a few yards of her parents who brought her into this world and brought her up in the nurture and admonition of the Lord.

"Scripture describes the deaths of Moses and Aaron in terms of them being 'gathered to their kin.' Miss Addie has been gathered to her kin, and we lay her to rest among them. Being gathered to one's kin is the oldest biblical image of reunion beyond this life. God is all about bring-ing people together — into families, into friendships, into communities of faith, and ultimately to gather us to each other and to himself forever. We meet this God in Jesus the good shepherd who leaves the ninety-nine sheep safe in the fold and goes out to find the one straggler.

"I experienced this even in the unpleasant incident that happened a few minutes ago. I was drawn into the embrace of a community that protected me, comforted me, and helped me back on my feet. When I was afraid, wise, strong, older brothers in Christ stepped in to protect me. When I lost my balance and fell backward, I fell into the arms of dear friends who caught me and stood me back on my feet. When I needed to cry, I was pulled into the tight embrace of my parents. I heard familiar voices of people who love me and felt familiar hands rubbing my back as I cried. Now I feel the prayers of a community praying for me as I speak.

"Scripture reminds us that the Lord God formed us from the dust of the earth, and that we will return to dust. It reminds us that this perishable body must put on the imperishable, and that this mortal must put on immortality. Let us hear the word of the Lord from I Thessalonians chapter 4: '...we do not want you to be uninformed, brothers and sisters, about those who have died so you may not grieve as others do who have no hope. For since we believe that Jesus died and rose again, even so, through Jesus, God will bring with him those who have died. For this we declare to you by the word of the Lord, that we who are alive, who are left until the coming of the Lord, will by no means precede those who have died. For the Lord himself, with a cry of command, with the archangel's call and the sound of God's trumpet, will descend from heaven, and the dead in Christ will rise first. Then we who are alive, who are left, will be caught up in the clouds together with them to meet the Lord in the air, and so we will be with the Lord forever. Therefore, encourage one another with these words.'

"Let us remember Miss Addie. Our pastor's younger daughter, Deborah Estelle, was profoundly right when she said that, if we forget Miss Addie, we might just forget Jesus and God. Let us give thanks for her amazing, long, rich, good life and for having her as a part of our lives. Let us take hold of the faith and hope that sustained her. Let us live worthy of our calling from death to eternal life. Let us take care of each other and comfort each other with the comfort we have received from God. In Jesus' name, Amen."

Coretta joined with the Sacred Harp Singers as they sang the benediction,

> God be with you 'til we meet again,
> By his counsel guide, uphold you,
>   With his sheep secure enfold you,
> God be with you 'til we meet again.

'Til we meet, 'til we meet,
'Til we meet at Jesus' feet
'Til we meet, 'til we meet,
God be with you 'til we meet again.

"This concludes the service here at the graveside," Daniel announced as a Mintz County Sheriff's patrol car squeezed into the church parking lot.

Aaron recognized the county officer, Tamika Barrentine, as soon as she got out of the patrol car. He drove the rest of the way around the circle through the cemetery and pulled his car up alongside hers. "Hey, thanks for coming out, Tamika."

"Not a problem, Aaron, it's been a slow day. I came on duty at 7:00 a.m., and this is the first one I've hauled in all day. What's this bad boy done to win a free ride in my patrol car?"

"Caught 'im red-handed, first degree stupid. Had words with the funeral director about a woman preacher doing the service, then he goes off on the preacher, tries to snatch her Bible out of her hands, and ends up putting his hand on her breast. Kind of a nice touch to have a female officer take him in, have to tell Reverend McWhorter about that. I'll follow you in, sign the warrants for disorderly conduct, simple assault, sexual battery, and preventing or disrupting a lawful assembly."

"Preacher, I'm Josie Bailey," the kind-faced woman who looked to be in her seventies introduced herself to Cassie as she was about to get in the back seat of her parents' Buick Century. "Addie was my cousin, she and my daddy were first cousins, my maiden name was Peyton." Turning to the tall, slender man with dark deep-set eyes, olive complexion, and hair that remained coal black despite his age, she added, "And this is my husband, J. T. Bailey."

"Pleased to meet both of you."

"It's a pleasure for us to finally meet you," Josie replied. "Addie talked about you a lot, has for years. I'm glad you had a part in the funeral and that you did the graveside. You did such a good job. Today's the first time I ever heard a woman preach. Never really thought much about a woman being a preacher before today, but I could listen to you every Sunday."

"Speaking of which," the quiet, soft-spoken J. T. commented, "I could, too. I'm chairman of deacons at Peyton's Chapel, and I've already talked to our other two deacons. Josie and I saw what Brother Bobby did to you and how he treated you and Tommy Sheridan. I'm glad the Harrington police chief saw it happen and locked him up. He needed to be locked up for what he did to you. The other deacons see it the same way I do. We're embarrassed for the church to have our pastor do what he did and treat people the way he did. Don't know if he'll be out of jail before Sunday, but I've got news for him, if he is, he's not gonna preach at Peyton's Chapel. He's preached here for the last time. What he did was uncalled for, and to tell you the truth, I'm tired of being screamed and yelled at and made to feel sorrier than gully dirt every time I go to church. If I'm not doing right, show me where I'm wrong and teach me how to do better. Don't just tell me how sorry I am."

"You and me both!" Josie concurred. "His wife is sweet. The way Brother Bobby talks to her in public, I hate to think how he treats her when it's just the two of them. I worry about her. They live in Hansonville. J. T. and I are going to go see her this evening before Brother Bobby gets out of jail, see if she needs anything. He's gonna be madder'n an old wet hen when he gets out, and I worry about him taking it out on her."

"I know we'll get an ear full when we go see him and ask for his resignation. Anyway, Preacher, what I'm getting at is to ask you if you'll come and preach for us this Sunday morning. Probably won't be more than twenty people, twenty-five on a good Sunday. Sunday School's at 10:00 a.m., preaching at 11:00 a.m."

Cassie's mind was racing as she thought about getting back to Macon tonight, classes all the rest of this week, assignments to be completed and turned in, and now preparing a sermon, then some time at her holy place down by the creek on Saturday to prepare the preacher. She was aware of her heart pounding as hard as it ever did when she ran track, and she was still getting her mind wrapped around what J.T. had just asked her, when she heard herself say, "Yes, I'll be happy to."

Chapter 8

The phone was ringing as the McWhorters came in the door, and Elaine grabbed it just as the answering machine picked up, saying "Hello" about the time the recorded message started announcing that nobody was there to take the call. "Excuse me," Elaine tried to talk over the recording, "let me turn off this answering machine so I can hear you. There!"

"Hey, Elaine, this is Aaron Stewart. I need to get a little information from Reverend McWhorter for the police report before she heads back to Macon, and I've got some news she'll want to hear."

"She's here, Aaron. We just walked in the door, stopped and ate at The Lonesome Whistle on the way home, since she's got to get on the road directly. I'll get her for you." Holding the receiver at arm's length, she called out, "Cass, honey, it's for you. Aaron Stewart needs to talk with you."

"Hey, Chief," Cassie answered, "what's up?

"Couple of things, Preacher. I need your date of birth and Social Security Number for my report on this afternoon's unpleasantness, along with a number where the D.A. can reach you during the week while you're at school. Somebody from the D.A.'s office will want to talk with you in the next few days." After Cassie gave him the requested information, Aaron continued, "First, I want to tell you that you did a beautiful job with your part in the funeral. I know it was hard for you because you and Miss Addie were so close. You had a good message and you delivered it well. I was proud of the way you stood up to that fool and pulled yourself together and did the committal after he attacked you. I still can't believe what he did. I don't care what he thinks about women preachers. The law's concerned with actions, not opinions, and his actions broke the law. He committed a crime, actually a couple of crimes, right in front of my eyes, so I didn't have a choice about arresting him. Anyway, you handled a bad situation as well as anybody could. The Lord's got his hand on you. Miss Addie sure would've been proud of you."

"Thanks. I could feel the people praying for me. I appreciate what you did. I'm still processing what went down, still can't believe he tried to snatch my Bible out of my hands and put his hands on me. The whole thing's so bizarre, I'm glad you and some others saw it, too, so I know I'm not crazy. I keep thinking this whole long weekend is some kind of weird dream and I'm going to wake up, go see Miss Addie, and tell her, 'you won't believe this strange dream I had last night.' I just wish I hadn't lost my balance and fell backwards before I could kick him. The shoes I had on could've caused Brother Bobby some serious pain."

"Well, you had plenty of witnesses, including me, to testify that he deserved it. You'd have been within your rights to kick him as hard as you wanted to. That brings me to the other thing I called to tell you. The law's fixing to cause Brother Bobby more pain than a swift kick in the groin."

"How's that?" Cassie asked, wondering what Aaron was getting to. "I was thinking they probably wouldn't do much to him, maybe keep him overnight, let him bond out tomorrow."

"That's what I was thinking when I followed the county officer over to the Harrington Hilton to book him in. Oh yeah, one other thing you'll appreciate. The county sent a female deputy to take him in, thought that was a nice touch."

"Sweet," Cassie laughed. "I bet Brother Bobby loved that."

"Yeah, and of all the female officers, they sent Tamika Barrentine. You'd have to know Tamika to appreciate this, she gets out of the car and walks over to my car where Brother Bobby's sitting in the back, looks at him through the window, and says, 'Hey, Aaron. What's this bad boy done to win a free ride in my patrol car?' I told her, 'first degree criminal stupidity.' Anyway, all the way over there, I'm expecting the magistrate to set a property bond for this walking powder keg, put him back in circulation, acting a fool before lunchtime tomorrow. Come to find out, today's not the first time Brother Bobby's temper got him in trouble. Now he's got violation of probation on top of the stuff I charged him with. Probation put a hold on him, so he's not going anywhere real soon. I know his probation officer, Marla Houston, just talked to her. Made my day when I found out who his probation officer is. She's good."

"Yeah, and I bet he loves having a female probation officer," Cassie commented. "What's he on probation for?"

"Assault, battery, terroristic threats, third degree cruelty to children under the Family Violence Act, plus interfering with a 911 call. Hansonville P.D. arrested him. He was going off on his wife, yelling at her, threatening to kill her, escalated to the point that he shoved her, made her fall and hit her head on the edge of the kitchen counter, put a gash on her head. They were foster parents for Phillips County DFCS at the time, had two brothers ages six and ten placed in their home. The children witnessed everything. Even a little scalp wound bleeds something awful, kids were terrified, thought she was bleeding to death. The older boy picked up the phone and called 911, which was the right thing to do. Mr. Simpson took the phone away from him and hung it up before the child could say anything. He should've known that when 911 gets a hang-up like that, they know where it is but not what it is, so they send the whole works, police, fire, and ambulance, pretty much everything but the game warden and the forestry service. 911 dispatcher heard one of the children crying and heard our friend yelling at the child to hang up the phone. She knew there were kids present so she paged the on-call DFCS worker while the police were en route. DFCS shut them down as a foster home and moved the children that night. Hansonville Police and DFCS interviewed the children separately and got the same story from both of them. Sad thing about it, the kids were in foster care because of the same kind of stuff going on at home with their parents, and they get placed with a foster parent who treats his wife the same way their daddy treated their mama. Doyle Sumner, the Hansonville officer that put the cuffs on him, is a good friend of mine and a good officer. Whatever Doyle tells you, you can take it to the bank."

"Wow," Cassie responded dumbfounded. "How did he get to pastor a church with that kind of record?"

"Well, the church where he was, Pleasant Grove, little country church over in Phillips County, between Hansonville and the Alabama line, fired him after all of that went down, so he didn't pastor for about a year. He had some that supported him no matter what. They footed the bill for him to have a Sunday afternoon radio program on the Hansonville station. Peyton's Chapel was down to about fifteen or twenty people and didn't have a pastor. Old Preacher Willard Glenn was filling in for them, he's a good man, but he was about eighty-five years old and not in the best of health. He passed away not long after they called Brother Bobby; that was back in November of '96, not quite two years ago. Brother Bobby has his own business, puts in septic tanks and does backhoe work, so he doesn't depend on the church for his livelihood. Some of the people at Peyton's Chapel heard him on the radio and heard him conduct a funeral, and he'd done septic tank work for some of them. They thought he was a good enough preacher, as good as they could afford. He was available and cheap, only question they asked was could he afford to take the church for what they were able to pay, and he said he could, so they called him without asking too many questions. They thought Brother Bobby was the answer to their prayers. They're good country people who think everybody else is as honest and decent as they are, want to believe the best about everybody, trust people until they have a reason not to, so they didn't ask the questions they needed to ask."

"Speaking of not asking questions," Cassie began, "you're not going to believe this. I'm not sure I believe it."

"What's that?"

"I've been invited to preach at Peyton's Chapel this coming Sunday."

"Well, Brother Bobby's sure not gonna be out of jail in time to preach Sunday, so he's not gonna be there to give you any trouble. That's great."

"Yeah, the church only has three deacons, and they were all at the cemetery this afternoon and saw what Brother Bobby did. Right after you left to get Brother Bobby a room at the Harrington Hilton, Mrs. Josie

Bailey, the one who's in charge of the cemetery, and her husband Mr. J. T. Bailey, who's chairman of deacons, came up and talked to me as I was about to get in the car with Mother and Daddy to go home. Found out that Mrs. Bailey is Miss Addie's cousin, her grandfather and Miss Addie's father were brothers. She told me they were glad to finally meet me since they'd heard Miss Addie talk about me so much. They told me how much they appreciated my part in the funeral and the graveside. Said they'd never thought much about a woman being a preacher before today, but they'd like to hear me again. Mr. Bailey apologized to me on behalf of the church for the way Brother Bobby treated me, said they didn't know what to think about a woman preacher, but they did know what they thought about the way Brother Bobby went off on me. They'd already about had it with him before this happened, and what he did today was the last straw. Mr. and Mrs. Bailey were going to go see Brother Bobby's wife, see what they could do to help her, see if she needed anything, and let her know they didn't hold anything against her. Mr. Bailey said that after they see Mrs. Simpson, he and the other deacons were going to pay Brother Bobby a visit at the jail, ask for his resignation, and let him know that he's preached at Peyton's Chapel for the last time. Then he asked me if I'd come and preach for them next Sunday."

"I hope you said 'yes.'"

"I did," Cassie replied, "but there are a couple of things that bother me."

"Such as...?"

"Well, for one thing, they ended up with that turkey Brother Bobby by not asking the questions they needed to ask, not finding out stuff they could have found out if they'd just asked around. They invited me to come and preach without checking me out. For all they know, I could be just as crazy as Brother Bobby. I could be a pleasant, well-mannered ax murderer. Of course, you know I'm not crazy, mean, or violent, but they don't. All they know is that I seem like a nice person and they heard me at one funeral."

"You're forgetting something important," Aaron observed. "Miss Addie recommended you. They knew Miss Addie, and they knew you wouldn't have had a part in her funeral if she hadn't thought highly of you. In light of Miss Addie's recommendation, they didn't need to ask any other questions. On top of that, with what went down at the cemetery today, they learned a lot about Brother Bobby, but they also learned a lot about you. They saw that you have the backbone to stand up to a bully, and they saw how you act when somebody mistreats you. Those are things you want to know about a preacher. I'd say they already know you better than they knew Brother Bobby when they called him. They've seen you under fire, and they liked what they saw. They've checked you out pretty well, I think, and it's pretty easy to check out somebody who's not hiding anything. I think all of their surprises will be pleasant ones."

"Never thought about that," Cassie responded. "I guess I was recommended by Miss Addie. And as far as how I handled the situation at the cemetery, Miss Addie prepared me for that. When I told her that God was calling me to preach, the first thing she told me after she hugged me was that I'd better be ready to stand up to some bullies. I heard all of her stories about the ones she stood up to..."

"And the training kicked in," Aaron added. "Just like my law enforcement training kicked in when I saw what Brother Bobby did. Reverend Jennings is former Military Police, and it was the same for him. Lord knows I hate having to arrest a preacher, only time I've ever had to do that, but when I saw what he did, I couldn't just let it go because he was a preacher. I didn't have to think about whether I needed to arrest him. Reverend Jennings didn't have to think about whether he ought to help me take him down, either. Reverend Jennings is not a big man, but he's fast and strong as an ox. I know, we played football and wrestled together in high school. Have to think to call him Reverend Jennings, still want to call him Snake, that's what we called him in high school, got that nickname from a guy that wrestled against him in a state championship match, said that wrestling him was like trying to wrestle a snake, you'd think you had him pinned and he'd slide right out of your arms.

I could've taken Brother Bobby by myself, but it was nice to have ol' Snake's help. We pinned that clown down on the hood of that hearse and got the cuffs on him before he had a chance to put up a fight. We did what we were trained to do. You did what Miss Addie trained you to do."

"I did the only thing I could do," Cassie responded thoughtfully, "but I do remember a thought flashing through my mind, I could just see Miss Addie handling Brother Bobby, and I followed her lead."

It was about 8:30 when Cassie guided her faded silver '80 Chevy Citation into a vacant parking space in front of Porter Hall on the Mercer campus. She normally hated the drive from Harrington to Macon, two hours and fifteen minutes any way you go. Pick any one of three equally bad routes, it's two-lane roads and small towns all the way. You could go over to Forsyth and pick up I-75 south to Macon. Jerry McWhorter tried to convince his daughter that would be the best way, but you'd still have to drive miles of two-lane roads through small towns and open country to get to Forsyth so you could have a short stretch of Interstate into Macon, so you really don't gain anything or save any time. Every possible route has its drawbacks including ample opportunities to get stuck behind farm equipment, pulpwood trucks, slow drivers, and people making left turns. Cassie had tried every possible way, including the route her father recommended. Tonight, she chose her usual route, going over to Greenville and picking up Georgia Route 18 into Macon. She did bear off the Hansonville Highway at Pulliam's Store as Miss Addie suggested to her, following Bailey's Mill Road to where it comes out about two miles east of Hansonville on the highway that takes you into Greenville. That cut off about five miles and saved a little time.

Cassie had actually enjoyed the drive, passing her holy place at Bailey's Mill and the turn-off for Peyton's Chapel Road, where she noticed that Brother Bobby's name had already been removed from the Peyton's Chapel church sign. She welcomed the solitude that the trip afforded her. Normally, she would have had the radio blasting, but it never occurred to her until she was parking the car on campus that she had never turned it on. Tonight, the quiet solitude had been conducive to meditation and prayer. While Baptists have not been known for venerating saints, Cassie thought of that line in Samuel Stone's hymn, "The Church's One Foundation," that speaks of "blissful sweet communion with those whose rest is won," and she felt sure that the Lord wouldn't mind her thanking Saint Addie for having her back today.

It felt good to be driving Miss Addie's old car. When Miss Addie decided to give up driving about ten years ago, Jerry McWhorter bought her car for Cassie's older sister. Emily, seven years older than Cassie, drove it all through high school and college before passing it down to Cassie. The car had a little less than 8,000 miles on it when Jerry bought it in 1988. Emily had lived at home and commuted to West Georgia, so she had put most of the miles on it. The metallic silver paint had faded and dulled beyond any possibility of being buffed out, thus Emily had dubbed it "the Old Gray Mare." It still had the softball-size dent in the rear bumper that Miss Addie herself put there when she backed into a lamp post in the Food World parking lot, her first accident and the incident that made her decide to give up driving. Still, the OGM, despite being roughly the same age as its current driver, had only 71,000 miles on the odometer. Early Saturday morning, before Cassie got up, Jerry took it and had new tires put on it and had the front end aligned. It was far from the coolest thing on campus, but it was rock-solid reliable. It had never left Emily or Cassie stranded, and it drove like a new car.

"Hey, Mary Grace," Cassie spoke to her roommate who was propped up in bed reading with stereo headphones on her head. Mary Grace was in a flannel housecoat, and the room was dark except for the reading lamp beside her bed. "How was your weekend?"

"Okay. It's a long haul up to Elberton, probably wouldn't have tried to go home if we hadn't had the extra day with the holiday today, that and a fiftieth wedding anniversary reception for my grandparents Sunday afternoon. Most of the time, seems like by the time I get up there, it's just about time to head back. Nice to get some home-cooked meals and sleep in while Momma washes my clothes, dries them, folds them, and packs them for me. Got some of my grandmama's fudge brownies and pecan divinity that I brought back, help yourself to it, I don't need to eat it all. It's in the Tupperware thingies on my dresser."

"Don't need the calories, but I'll take you up on some of Grandmama's goodies, thanks."

"So how was your weekend down in Harrington?"

"Let's see. I went to see my 101-year-old friend, Miss Addie, on the way into Harrington. Pine Ridge Assisted Living is about two miles out from Harrington, go right past it on my way in, so I stopped by there before I went home, just felt like I needed to see her, can't explain it. She looked great, we had a wonderful visit, stayed about an hour, got my hug from her, and went home. I almost didn't stop, my hair looked awful, I was tired, and I had two baskets of dirty clothes in the back seat. Saturday morning about 9:30, I woke up to a phone call from the pastor of our church telling me that Miss Addie had died in her sleep. She had requested that I have a part in her funeral and that I conduct the committal at the graveside. So, I spent most of Saturday getting ready for my part in the funeral. Mom took me Saturday afternoon to get my hair done, and my older sister Emily and her husband took me out to eat Saturday evening and took me to Belk's in Carrollton and told me to pick out a new outfit to wear for Miss Addie's funeral. Went to church Sunday morning, Sunday night we had the viewing. Last year, on her one-hundredth birthday, they renamed Harrington Elementary School, where she taught so long, in her honor, and we had the viewing at the school. Huge crowd for the viewing and the funeral. We buried her out at Peyton's Chapel, little church way out in the sticks where she grew up. I got assaulted at the cemetery by the pastor at Peyton's Chapel because he's against women preachers in addition to being a jerk in general. Now he's in jail, his name's off the church sign, and I'm supposed to preach this Sunday at Peyton's Chapel. Other than that, it was a quiet weekend in Lake Wobegon."

It was about 11:30 when Cassie finished the reading she needed to do for tomorrow's classes and pondered where sermon preparation might fit into this week's schedule. It would not be tonight, when all she could pray for was for the whirlwind of thoughts to die down and for her mind to settle enough for her to go to sleep. Mary Grace's reading lamp was off, and she was sound asleep over on her side of the room, when Cassie logged onto her computer and checked her e-mail.

After she waded through all of the campus announcements, Cassie recognized Coretta Brinkley Groves' e-mail address with a subject line of "Sunday at Peyton's Chapel" and clicked it open.

Hey, Cass—

I just ran into Latisha Stewart in Food World. She told me you're preaching Sunday out at Peyton's Chapel. Daniel and I plan to come. We're praying for you, glad you're getting an opportunity to preach, know you'll do fine. Be glad to sing if you want me to.

Coretta

Cassie clicked on "Reply" and typed,

Coretta—

At the risk of sounding like a Bartles and Jaymes commercial, thank you for your support! Always glad to see you and Daniel, and you know I'd love for you to sing. How about singing "How Sweet the Name of Jesus Sounds?"

Love you both, Cassie

Cassie felt the service next Sunday starting to take shape already. Yes, that would be the song for Coretta to sing. Cassie had been thinking about what Mr. Bailey said about feeling sorrier than gully dirt after going to church, and she knew the people needed to hear a message of grace. They needed to hear it from someone who loves them. She remembered hearing Reverend Conway at Greater New Hope tell about the sign on the pulpit at Thankful Baptist Church in Rome, "Sir, we would see Jesus." Coretta would sing "How Sweet the Name of Jesus Sounds." A preacher who had been assaulted would preach to people accustomed to being beaten up every Sunday, and she would preach the pure, sweet, healing message of Jesus.

She needed to be in bed, but she needed to send one more e-mail. Cassie pulled up Heather Simmons Moore's e-mail address from her address book and typed a subject line, "First Funeral/Preaching next Sunday."

Heather—

We need to talk — I've got so much to tell you! I had a part in my first funeral today. My 101-year-old friend, Miss Addie, died early Saturday morning. She wanted me to have a part in her funeral and to do the committal at the graveside, so I did. We buried her at Peyton's Chapel Baptist Church, little country church where she grew up and where all of her family is buried. Long story short, I've been invited to preach at Peyton's Chapel this Sunday. This will be my first time to preach anywhere other than Harrington. Don't know where God is going with this, but I'm excited about it. There is a lot more to this story. I'll call you Saturday morning.

Hugs, Cassie

Cassie was drifting into twilight sleep when a very groggy Mary Grace asked, "Cassie, did you say what I think you said?"

"Huh?"

"You whispered, "Saint Addie, pray for us."

"I knew I was thinking it, didn't know I said it," Cassie laughed. "Just some blissful sweet communion with those whose rest is won."

Chapter 9

Six weeks into her first semester as a college freshman living on campus, Cassie had perfected sleeping until the last minute to an art form. She could sleep until 7:00 a.m., shower, dress, hit the cafeteria for a bowl of cereal, a piece of fruit, and coffee, and make it to her 8:00 a.m. class with seconds to spare. On this Tuesday morning, at 5:30 a.m., she was wide awake, already showered, dressed in jeans and Harrington Hornets sweatshirt, hair pulled back in a pony tail, an hour before the cafeteria opened for breakfast. Just enough light shone through the blinds from the security lights outside for her to see her way around. Mary Grace was sound asleep in her bed, turned over on her right side, covers pulled up to her chin. Careful not to disturb her, Cassie turned the computer monitor to the side so the light would not shine on her before logging on and opening her e-mail.

The first message was from Brother Mike, sent at 11:30 p.m.:

> Hey, Cassie,
>
> Karen talked to your mom earlier tonight, and found out that you'll be preaching this Sunday out at Peyton's Chapel. Only other time I ever saw the preacher at Peyton's Chapel was at the associational meeting when we got kicked out, so I'm not overly impressed with him. I saw what went down at the cemetery, glad Aaron was there to arrest him. Didn't know until Karen talked to Elaine that you got an invitation to preach out of it. I'm thankful that you're getting this opportunity. I know how you've struggled with your calling, knowing

the opposition you'd face. Two of my prayers just got answered: I've prayed that you'd have more opportunities to preach at other churches, and I've prayed that you wouldn't become beaten down and discouraged by those who oppose you. Remember what I told you when you said you were ready to preach your first sermon and be licensed. I told you that you'd have people—good people who love the Lord and love you—telling you that you can't do what God's called you to do. Should've told you that you'd run into some jerks who show no sign of loving the Lord or anybody else, guess you've figured that out by now :-). Glad your parents are supportive. Your dad had a hard time with it. He wasn't against women preachers. He grew up Church of God, so he'd heard women preach, and he really enjoyed Heather the times that he heard her. He said he'd be fine with a woman as his pastor, but he wanted to be sure you were following God's call and not just your own desires. He knew what you'd be up against and he didn't want to see you get hurt. He's seen how serious you are about this, and he's totally on board now. I'll be praying for you as you prepare to preach on Sunday. I have a lot of respect for you. You have no illusion that your path will be easy, but you've chosen to obey God anyway. You'll do well Sunday. I'll always remember Miss Addie saying the Lord let her live as long as he did so she could tell you that you were not crazy for thinking that God was calling you to preach.

MW

The second was from her father, sent at 1:10 a.m.:

Cassie,

Too wound up from yesterday to go to sleep, won't be much good to anybody at work in the morning. Can't stop replaying everything that happened yesterday. Your mom and I love you and we're proud of you. You did such a good job with Miss Addie's service. No doubt in my mind that God called you to preach. A lot of people at that funeral had never heard a woman preach before. I heard a few women preachers growing up in the Church of God, but I'd never thought much about women preachers until Preacher Simmons preached the revival here when you were a little girl. She's one of the best preachers I ever heard. I remember how excited you were, wanting to go every night of that revival, how you talked her ears off asking a million questions the night she ate dinner with us, and how you paid attention when she was preaching. Your mom and I were in the choir, and we could see you sitting with Miss Addie, on the edge of your seat listening to every word Preacher Simmons said. I thank the Lord that you and Preacher Simmons are so close now. I'm glad we have the pastor we've got. Brother Mike's been good for our church, and I appreciate the way he's encouraged you and helped you. Every young minister needs an older and more experienced minister to look to for guidance, and you have two of the best with Preacher Simmons and Brother Mike. Not many will encourage a girl who's called to preach like they have. A lot of preachers would try to shoot you down and tell you that you're wrong to think you're called to preach. I see it the way Brother

Mike does. God wouldn't give you the gift and tell you not to use it, and he wouldn't stir up the desire to preach just to make you miserable and frustrated. I still can't believe that nut out at Peyton's Chapel. Most preachers are good men who love the Lord and love people. That goes for most of the ones who are against women preachers. There are a few sorry and mean-spirited preachers out there. You ran into one of the bad ones, but you handled yourself well. You stood up to him and didn't let him intimidate you. He didn't know what to do with a woman he couldn't bully. Never will forget seeing him sprawled out on the hood of that hearse while Aaron cuffed him. The look on his face was priceless. As Brother Mike said, it was a great moment in church history. It's a good thing Aaron and Preacher Jennings got to him before I could, or I'd be in jail, too. You said "Daddy, hold me," and I realized that holding you was way more important than beating up some jerk. You kept me out of trouble. Your mom and I are coming to Peyton's Chapel Sunday to hear you. You'll be a big improvement over what they're used to.

Love you, Girl—
Daddy

The last was from Heather Simmons Moore, sent at 4:50 a.m.:

Hey, Cass,

Being a pastor and a mommy has taught me to multi-task, so I checked my e-mail while I nursed Olivia. She's three months old today and growing like a weed. She woke up at 4:30 a.m. ready for breakfast, just finished nursing her and put her down. Joel's a sweet guy, helps a lot with the kids, but when my little Olivia's hungry, she's gotta have her mommy. Got about ten or fifteen minutes before time to put on the coffee and start breakfast. It'll be time for Joel to get up to get ready for work, and then I'll be getting Wallace ready to get on the school bus. Can't believe Wallace is already five and in kindergarten! He acts so grown up standing with me at the front of the church and shaking hands with everybody. He'll look you in the eye and shake your hand like a grown man. Once I get the guys out the door, I'll get myself ready and Miss Olivia and I will go over to the church office. The church is fine with me keeping her at the office with me. You'd think every pastor had a baby bed and changing table in her study. She goes with me on some of my pastoral visits, especially when I visit the nursing home and our homebound folks. There's a lady in the nursing home over at Ledford, ninety-nine years old, doesn't know her own family half the time, but she lights up anytime anybody brings babies or small children in, really takes on over them. I took a picture of her holding Olivia, put it in a frame from Dollar General and brought it to her. Her son called me after he saw the picture and one of the staff told him whose baby it was. He was in tears telling me how much he appreciated me letting his mom hold my baby and taking that picture, said that was the happiest he'd seen his mother in a long time. He and his wife have visited Clear Springs the past two Sundays, and they invited us to have dinner with them tonight. They'll be joining Clear Springs this Sunday. When Olivia can't go with me, I've got lots of grandmas and aunts in the church. If Clear Springs ever splits, it'll be over whose turn it is to watch Olivia.

I was sorry to hear about Miss Addie's death. She had a long and blessed life. I ate lunch with her one day when I preached the revival at Harrington in '91. She was amazing, and not just because she lived a long time. She was one of the most fascinating people I've ever had the opportunity to talk with. I'm thankful that she was there for you like Granny Becker and Olivia Harris were for me. I preached my first sermon when I was eighteen at the little church Olivia started in Pendleton. The first funeral I conducted was Olivia's. The second was Wallace Coggins' here at Clear Springs. You can tell from the names of my children how much Olivia and Wallace meant to me, so I understand how honored you were to have a part in Miss Addie's funeral.

Can't wait to talk to you Saturday, and you can expect a call from me Sunday afternoon to find out how it went. Something tells me that there's a lot more to this story of how you got invited to preach at Peyton's Chapel. Harrington Baptist and Clear Springs will have your back in prayer. So will Miss Addie, my Granny Becker, Olivia Harris, and Wallace and Estelle Coggins.

Love you, little sister!
Heather

Cassie clicked on "reply" and typed,

Hey, Heather,

So sweet of you to e-mail me so early in the morning. You know how to give hugs from 400 miles away. Love the pics you sent of Olivia last week, can't wait to see her and hold her. She's a beautiful baby.

I went to sleep thinking and praying about a sermon for next Sunday and woke up this morning thinking and praying about it. I heard from Coretta Groves last night, David and Cheryl's daughter-in-law. Miss Addie was the matron of honor for Daniel and Coretta's wedding when she was ninety-nine years old. Coretta said that she and Daniel were coming to Peyton's Chapel on Sunday to hear me and asked me if I'd like for her to sing. She sings beautifully, wish you could hear her, so I told her you know I want you to sing and asked her to sing "How Sweet the Name of Jesus Sounds," That will fit well with my sermon. Not going to recycle anything I've preached before. I've turned over a lot of ideas in my mind, but I keep coming back to Luke 4 where Jesus reads "The Spirit of the Lord is upon me..." passage from Isaiah 61 at the synagogue in Nazareth. When I told Miss Addie that God was calling me to preach, she held me tight and prayed for me, then she quoted that passage to me. Last year when I told Brother Mike that I was ready to try to preach my first sermon, he opened his Bible to that same passage. The more I think and pray about it, the more sure I am that this is the direction I need to go.

Hugs,
Cassie

Cassie shut down her computer, slipped the burgundy leather-bound New Revised Standard Version Bible into her backpack along with the textbooks and notebooks she would need for her morning classes, and closed the door gently so as not to wake Mary Grace before making her way across campus to Jesse Mercer Plaza where the life-size statue of Jesse Mercer sitting on a park bench perpetually beckons Mercer students and faculty to sit down for a while and take a load off their feet. The top of Mercer's bald head was slicker and shinier than Mercer's head had been in real life, worn smoother than the sculptor had made it, by thousands of Mercer students rubbing and patting it, and Brother Jesse's shiny dome had often been adorned with Georgia, Georgia Tech, and Atlanta Braves caps, along with black conical hats at Halloween and Santa Claus toboggans at Christmas. Cassie McWhorter had been far from the first Mercer coed to have her picture taken as she planted a big kiss on Old Brother Jesse. No kiss or Harrington Hornets baseball cap for Brother Jesse today, but she did sit down beside him, feeling his outstretched arm on the back of the bench embracing her shoulders. She didn't know what Mercer might have thought about women preachers, but if he was against them in his lifetime, he was in heaven now and he knew better. Judging by what she had read about Mercer, he probably would have been glad that the gospel was being preached, as she planned to do, and he wouldn't have been too worried about the gender of the preacher. She knew for sure that Mercer believed that those called to preach should have the best possible academic preparation, and she was six weeks into that long journey. As the sun came up over the horizon, sitting in the welcoming embrace of Jesse Mercer, Cassie again read the text for Sunday's sermon. She closed her Bible, returned it to her backpack, and spent a few moments in prayer. As she got up to walk to the cafeteria, she whispered, "Saint Jesse, pray for us. You and Saint Addie can handle this."

"Kinnebrew and Ellis, Attorneys at Law, this is Elaine. How may I help you?" Elaine McWhorter took the first call of the day after unlocking the office door.

"Hey, Elaine. Ted over at *The Harrington Courier*. Just found out that Cassie's preaching Sunday out at Peyton's Chapel. Mr. Bailey, chairman of deacons, just stopped by first thing this morning, said that Bobby Simpson was no longer pastor at Peyton's Chapel. He asked us to take his name out of the church listing in the paper and run an announcement in the paper that Cassie would be preaching for them this Sunday. Told him we'd be glad to do that for them. I told him that my family and I are members of Harrington Baptist and that we'd known Cassie since she was a little girl, told him that she's a good preacher to be barely nineteen years old. I'm calling you to see if we could get a photo of Cassie to run with the announcement. Can you bring me one on your lunch hour today?"

"Sure, be glad to. Mr. Kinnebrew and Mr. Ellis are both in Phillips County in court all day, and we close from noon to 1:00 for lunch. I'll run home at lunch, get you a good picture of her, and get it to you by 12:30."

"Great. Mr. Bailey said he was going by the radio station and give them the announcement to put on the church news program. I know you get the paper, but I'll bring you a few extra copies to church Wednesday night."

"Thanks, Ted. See you about 12:30."

Ted sat down at his computer and composed the announcement for the paper,

REV. McWHORTER TO PREACH
AT PEYTON'S CHAPEL BAPTIST

Rev. Cassie McWhorter, recently licensed to preach by Harrington Baptist Church, will preach this Sunday at 11:00 a.m. at Peyton's Chapel Baptist Church. The church is located at the intersection of Peyton's Chapel Road and Freeman Valley Road. Rev. McWhorter is the daughter of Mr. and Mrs. Jerry McWhorter of

Harrington. A 1998 honor graduate of Harrington High School, she is a ministerial student at Mercer University. Everyone is cordially invited.

Ted had not really planned it that way, it was just the way it worked out. The arrest report, with the names and charges of all who had been lodged at the Harrington Hilton in the past week, would be on the page facing the page with the church announcements. The last entry on the arrest report, barely making the deadline, read:

> Simpson, Bobby Lee, 56, of Hansonville, arrested October 12 by Harrington Police, charged with disorderly conduct, simple assault, sexual battery, preventing or disrupting a lawful assembly, and probation violation. Simpson remains in jail on a probation hold from Phillips County.

This was J. T. and Josie Bailey's week to clean the church building at Peyton's Chapel, a chore they rotated among four retired couples who lived within a mile of the church. J. T., at eighty, kept a few head of cattle and put in a big garden every year as he had done all through the forty-two years he worked with the State Highway Department. Since retirement, he had taken on a few more head of cattle and made the garden a little bigger. He had found a deal on a good running old 9N Ford tractor and gang plow in the *Farm and Market Bulletin*, so he bought it and gave their son-in-law the garden tiller he had. A couple of months later, J. T. bought an old bread truck with a bad engine for $400, way cheaper than he could build a building of comparable size, had it towed to his house, took off the wheels and leveled it up on concrete blocks, sold the transmission out of it for nearly as much as he paid for the whole truck, and fitted it with shelves all around plus a double row of shelves down the middle to hold hundreds of quart Mason jars full of good things from the garden. Josie told J. T. after they finished canning this year that they'd have enough quarts of Kentucky Wonder beans, Italian green beans, sweet corn, yellow squash, tomato juice, vegetable soup, okra, pickled okra, watermelon rind pickles, dill pickles, sweet crunchy bread and butter pickles, mild chow-chow, hot chow-chow, and eight varieties of jellies and preserves to last until Jesus comes again even if they give away half of it. The kids and grandkids debated where one draws the line between a large garden and a small farm. J. T. said he didn't see how he ever had time to work a regular job. Josie, in 1943 when J. T. was overseas, had been the first woman hired to drive a school bus in Mintz County. She quit when the first of their three children was born but started driving again when the youngest got to be school age and drove until she retired in 1985. The spot that J. T. leveled off for her to park her bus was now the permanent home of J. T.'s old bread truck and the lean-to he attached to the side of it for the tractor. Josie said she didn't see how she ever had time to drive a fifty-four mile bus route twice a day either. J. T. was just telling Josie how he needed to take the tractor and blade this afternoon and go spread that gravel they'd had put on the church parking lot when they heard the phone ringing as they walked in the door. They were on a party line with the Meadows who lived across the road, but it was their ring. "Hello," Josie answered, a bit out of breath.

"Hey, Miss Josie. Floyd Williams, pastor over't Freeman Valley and moderator of the Mintz County Baptist Association. Is Brother J. T. where I could speak with him?"

"He is. We just walked in the door from cleaning the church this morning and I was about to fix us some lunch. I'll get him for you." Covering the mouthpiece of the phone with her free hand, she called out, "J. T., honey, it's for you. It's Floyd Williams, the pastor over't Freeman Valley."

"Hey, Brother Floyd," J. T. answered as Josie handed him the receiver. "Beautiful day the Lord made for us today." It was in fact a spectacularly beautiful fall day, although J. T. would have said the same thing if it had been thundering, lightning, and pouring down rain. "How are things over't Freeman Valley?"

"The Lord's blessing us like he blesses all who are obedient to his word," Floyd answered coolly, his tone of voice indicating that he was not calling just to talk about the goodness of the Lord in the land of the living. "And," he continued, "speaking of being obedient to the word, I was a lot happier before I got my Harrington paper this morning and saw that y'all've got a girl comin' to preach to y'all this Sunday. We just got through turning Harrington Baptist out of the association on account'a them licensing that girl to preach, and I seen where she had part in the funeral of that crazy old Aldridge woman that stirred up so much trouble with the coloreds, didn't surprise me that she had a colored preacher have part in her funeral, too. Now, I don't doubt that girl means well, but the word's mighty plain that God don't call no woman to preach, so y'all'd best uninvite her 'fore Sunday or y'all're gonna have some problems with the association."

"Brother Floyd," J. T. spoke firmly but courteously, "I thought you called for us to have a conversation, but it sounds like you called to threaten and lay down the law to me and Peyton's Chapel Baptist Church. Funny thing, the association didn't say a word when we had a pastor that abused his wife and talked to her worse'n a dog, your church was the one that ordained him and you didn't say a word when we called him as pastor, but we invite a young lady to preach one Sunday, and you're having a dying duck fit. You telling me how it's gotta be is not a conversation. You've been stirring up trouble all of your life, bet you've still got your Klan robe hanging in your closet, so if you don't like what we're doing over't Peyton's Chapel, why don't you round up some of your boys and come burn a cross in front of the church tonight, just for old times' sake. If you're determined to stir up trouble in the association, go right ahead. If you didn't have this, you'd find something else to make trouble over. And, by the way, that crazy old Aldridge woman was my wife's cousin. Josie was a Peyton, her daddy and Miss Addie were first cousins. You got to be careful talking about people 'round here, Brother Floyd, 'cause chances are you're talking about people's kinfolks. Now, I'm going to hang up before I say something I'll regret."

J. T. sat down at the table, and Josie said grace over their lunch of homemade vegetable soup and grilled cheese sandwiches. "J. T., Honey, you don't need to let Floyd Williams get you that upset. You're gonna run your blood pressure up."

"No, I'm not. I'm gonna stay nice and calm and let Brother Floyd run his blood pressure up. He can run his up as high as he wants to, no reason for me to run mine up." J. T. burst out laughing.

"What's so funny, J. T.?"

"I forgot to tell Brother Floyd something. You remember Preacher McWhorter called last night and asked if it'd be okay if she asked one of her friends to come and sing the Sunday she preaches, and I told her to go right ahead. Should've told Brother Floyd that we got a colored girl singing the same Sunday as the woman preacher."

Chapter 10

"Cassie," Mary Grace asked as she finished studying for the night on Thursday evening and got a diet Sam's Choice cola from the small refrigerator in their dorm room, "I know it's short notice and all but do you think your folks would care if I come home with you this weekend? It's a long hike up to Elberton and there's no good way to get there. I don't want to spend the weekend on campus. I can't believe I'm about to say this because you know I've never been to church much. Don't know much about the Bible, couldn't tell you the difference between a Baptist and a Buddhist, but I really want to hear you preach."

"You'd be welcome. I love to preach. I'm a little nervous because this'll be my first time to preach anywhere other than the church I grew up in, but I'd love to have you tag along to hear me. It'll be good to see some friendly faces in the congregation. My folks've been wanting to meet you anyway. You'll like the Baileys out at Peyton's Chapel. The little bit of contact I've had with them, they seem to be really good people. He's the deacon chairman, the one who invited me to preach, and she's a cousin to Miss Addie. They know I've got some family and friends coming to hear me, you'll be one of the friends, and they'll make you feel welcome. It's a little bitty church, only been having about twenty-five people on Sunday morning, so my family and friends may outnumber the Peyton's Chapel folks. I'll introduce you to people but I won't do anything to put you on the spot. Mom and Dad've always been good about me having friends over. My older sister moved out on her own and got married two years ago, so there's an extra bed in my room. I'll e-mail Mom right now, and let her know you're coming. She'll be fine with it."

Cassie logged onto her computer and opened her e-mail. She was about to type an e-mail to her mom when she saw a message from her waiting in her inbox and opened it.

Cass—

We're really excited about Sunday! Why don't you invite your roommate Mary Grace to come home with you if she wants to? We want to meet her. I was going to fix a big dinner at home, but Mrs. Bailey from out at Peyton's Chapel called us this evening and said they were all bringing food and we were going to eat at church, so they hoped we were all coming. She said they put in a big garden this year and she never canned so much in her life, and they've got two freezers full of beef, so they need us to help them eat some of it. We'd love to have Mary Grace if she can come. If she needs to wash clothes this weekend, she's welcome to wash them here. See you and Mary Grace in time for supper tomorrow evening.

Love you,
Mom

"Well, I don't guess I need to ask permission," Cassie commented to Mary Grace after reading her mom's e-mail aloud.

"Tell Mom I'm coming," Mary Grace responded with a laugh, "hungry for some good home cooking and carrying a big basket of dirty clothes. She's gonna treat me like family, I'm gonna act like family."

As Cassie typed her reply to her mother's e-mail, she wasn't sure why she felt the need to tell Mary Grace about this, but she added, "When I was in ninth grade, one of my friends spent the night with me and ended up staying with us about a month."

"A month? What happened?" Mary Grace sounded puzzled.

"Her stepfather, that's how she referred to him, actually he was just her mom's live-in boyfriend, was an alcoholic, he and her mom were all the time at each other's throats, fighting, lots of bad stuff going on at home. When she told us she was afraid to go home, Mom called her sister-in-law, my Aunt Susan, who works for DFCS, or did until she retired last year. Aunt Susan was the supervisor over investigations. Mom called her at home about 10:00 p.m., and she came over along with the worker who was on call. After they talked to Alicia, that was my friend's name, they went to check out the home situation. They safety planned her out of the home right then and there. They didn't have any family close by who were willing to help or able to offer any better than what she had at home. My parents said she could stay with us as long as she needed to, and her mom was okay with that until things got sorted out. Her mom's boyfriend ended up going to jail. She eventually went back home with her mom after he was out of the house for good. If she hadn't been able to go back to her mom, my parents would've adopted her. Alicia asked me after she'd been with us about a week, 'Cassie, are your folks this nice to each other all the time?' 'Yeah,' I told her, 'they are.' I'd never thought about it, didn't think it was anything unusual, just assumed everybody's parents got along as well as mine did. First couple of days Alicia was with us, she tiptoed around like she was afraid she'd step on a land mine, just waiting for Mom and Dad to yell or cuss or throw things at each other or at her or tell her to get out. She kept thinking every night would be the night that Daddy would come home drunk and there'd be a big knock-down drag-out fight. She kept waiting for it to happen, never did. I kept telling her I'd never seen either one of my parents drunk, never saw them have a fight, and never heard them raise their voices at each other. She finally realized there weren't any land mines under the carpet, and she started to relax a little bit. My parents stayed on an even keel and actually looked forward to coming home to each other at the end of the day. They didn't act any different because Alicia was there, didn't treat her any different than they treated me. By the time she was with us a few days, she had chores like everybody else, and she did them without complaining. Both of my parents grew up in Harrington, knew each other since first grade, neither one of them ever dated anybody else. Their families had all known each other forever and liked each other. I'm pretty much kin to half of Harrington one way or another. Mom's a legal secretary and office manager for Kinnebrew and Ellis, small law firm in Harrington. Jack Kinnebrew, Uncle Jack, married my dad's sister Joyce. Dad is the public works director for the city. I've got a younger brother, Anthony, still at home, he's fifteen and in tenth grade, sweet guy, even if he is my brother. We fussed and argued when we were younger, but we're close now. I still call him 'Little Brat' even though he's six feet tall, but it's a term of affection now. He's kinda quiet and shy, the opposite of me, you won't hear much out of him, computer whiz, and I hear he now has a girlfriend he talks to on the phone all the time. So, the short answer is, yes, you'll be welcome, my folks'll treat you like you were born into the family. If you were staying longer than the weekend, you'd get your very own chores. It'll be nice to have some company driving to Harrington and back, makes the trip go faster. Hope you don't mind riding in the Old Gray Mare, not much to look at but it's never left me stranded."

"That's all that matters, not being stuck on the side of the road or stuck here over the weekend." Mary Grace hesitated a moment, not sure whether she ought to say what she was about to say. "Distance is not the only reason I don't want to go back to Elberton this weekend." Mary Grace tried to stop herself, afraid she'd already divulged too much, but in defiance of all the inner voices telling her not to say any more because you don't want people thinking bad of your family or telling your business all over town, she continued haltingly, "Your friend Alicia sounds a lot like me. Never had DFCS involved, guess we flew under the radar because the police never got called. House sits in the middle of nine acres, so our neighbors weren't close enough to hear the fussing and fighting. We live in a nice house, never went hungry, always had nice clothes and nice cars. Dad worked, now that I'm in college, Mom's started working, which is good just to get her out of the house, meet some sane people.

I've done my share of spending the night with friends and sleeping on couches when Mom and Dad were fighting or it got too crazy at home. One of the friends who used to let me spend the night whenever I needed to lives in the projects, but I envied him because nobody was fussing and fighting, getting drunk, or zoning out on Xanax at his place. My dad went ballistic because my friend was Hispanic. He and mom both accused me of sleeping with him. Never did. He and his mom just let me crash on their couch where it was quiet enough for me to sleep. I helped him with English and he helped me with Spanish, so my Spanish sounds like a country girl from Chiapas. That's where he was from. His mom's the one who taught me to cook, so I know how to cook up some good down-home Mexican food. Pretty sad that I had to walk out of this big elegant house and go over to the projects to find someplace quiet enough to get a good night's sleep."

"You'll find it pretty quiet and relaxed at my house," Cassie commented, "and you'll be welcome the way my friends always have been."

"Cassie, I'm eighteen, almost nineteen, and I've never had anybody spend the night at my house. It's not that my parents wouldn't let me, they probably would. Hell, I could've done it, snuck guys in or whatever without them knowing it when Dad's passed out and Mom's floating above the clouds on her Xanax. It's not that I couldn't, I wouldn't do it because I'd be ashamed for anybody else to be around the craziness, not like my folks could straighten up and behave while I had company. Besides, somebody who wasn't used to what goes on might pick up the phone and call 911. Dad's a functioning alcoholic. During the week, he stays sober enough to work, travels a lot on his job, pharmaceutical sales, makes real good money. He's paying for me to go to school, and I'm thankful for that, but if something was really bothering me and I needed to talk to somebody, he and Mom would be the last people I could talk to. Dad would rather give me a hundred dollars, tell me to go spend it on myself and see if that makes me feel better, instead of having a real conversation with me. He thinks the solution to any problem is to throw money at it. Thinks he's God's gift to women, so I may have some half-brothers or half-sisters out there. That'd be awful, wouldn't it, to like some guy and find out after you've been making out with him that he's your half brother."

"Ewww, Yuck!" Cassie acknowledged. "Some of the guys I dated in high school wanted to run the other way when they realized I had a brain and wasn't afraid to use it, or they acted like I was a different species because I want to be a pastor. As for making out, my experience is limited, a few kisses, but yeah, I never worried that some guy might end up being my half-brother."

"Know what you mean about the brain thing," Mary Grace commented. "It tends to scare off the guys who just want to play with my boobs and get between my legs as fast as they can. That's an extra benefit of being a girl with a brain, along with being able to get into a good school and get some scholarships, the brain scares away all but the most persistent Neanderthals. Speaking of the yuck factor and Neanderthals, the way my dad looks at me and some of his comments about how I look, you'd think he had the hots for me like some high school knuckle-dragger, especially when he's been drinking enough to be obnoxious but not enough to be snoring. He's my dad and he's forty-six years old, for God's sake! You know I'm pretty reserved. I don't dress like a hooker, don't wear anything too low-cut or tight, but I still get the looks, the comments, and the pats on the butt. God, I hate it when he slaps me on the butt! I'll never take you home with me because I wouldn't want him doing that to you. My folks would treat you like family for sure, but being treated like family means something entirely different at my house than it does at yours. Dad starts drinking heavy on Friday night, by Monday morning he's sobered up enough to go at it again. Last weekend was awful because he had to stay reasonably sober for my grandparents' fiftieth anniversary reception. Mom's parents don't drink, reception was at their church over at Royston, so there was no alcohol at the reception, and he was miserable. I hate to say this, but it would've been better if he'd been drinking more. If I could've slipped some vodka into his punch, I would have. He can drink his way past obnoxious, stupid, belligerent, and creepy to just plain sleepy by one or two o'clock on Sunday afternoon, then it gets quiet. Until then, Mom nags him about his drinking and takes Xanax for her nerves. He drinks to cope with her nagging and the stress of his job. My brother's solution was to join the Marines right out of high school, mine was not to go to school too close to home, so I could say it's too far to go home every weekend. I got accepted at the University of Georgia, could've been close enough to have an easy drive home every weekend, but I needed to get further away. Once I graduate from Mercer, I plan to get myself even further away. My family's easier to love from a distance, but it's hard not to have anybody close."

"I'm sorry," was all Cassie could think to say. Mary Grace and Cassie had gotten along all right so far. She was pleasant, considerate, and quiet, not a party animal, and focused on her studies. Yet, their conversations had thus far been pretty superficial for two people living in the same room. Cassie knew that Mary Grace Tillison was from Elberton and that she had one brother who was in the Marines, beyond that, she had been circumspect with regard to talking about home and family. Mary Grace didn't get mail or phone calls from home, and if she got e-mails from home, she said nothing about them. Now, she had just blurted out more in two minutes than she had in the previous six weeks.

Cassie did the only thing she knew to do as she sat down on the bed beside Mary Grace, put her arm around her shoulders, and tried to give her a hug. That's what her mother would do, what her grandmother McWhorter would do, what Grandma Whitmire would have done, and what Miss Addie would have done. Mary Grace initially protested, "It's okay, I'm used to it," but the tears starting to trickle down her face contradicted her words. Her whole body began to tremble with pent-up emotion. Mary Grace stiffened herself against Cassie's effort to hug her before collapsing into her embrace, burying her face against Cassie's chest, and weeping, hard, racking sobs, the way a small child cries when the only thing that will help is to cry out the hurt. Cassie held her room-mate tightly, the way her daddy held her at the cemetery after Brother Bobby put his hands on her, the way her mom held Alicia that awful night four years ago when Alicia disclosed that her mom's boyfriend had been molesting her, the way a parent is supposed to hold a child who just needs to be held and made to feel safe while she cries. Cassie held Mary Grace close, gently rubbed her back, and whispered softly to her, "Jesus said, 'Blessed are those who mourn, for they shall be comforted.' Jesus was a man of sorrows, acquainted with grief. My God is the Father of mercies and God of all comfort. He understands and cares, Mary Grace." Then she prayed silently for her. They stayed like that a long time, until the tears ran out, until Mary Grace's sobs faded into the quiet, slow breathing of one completely at rest, until Mary Grace was quiet enough to hear Cassie's soft breathing and slow, steady heartbeat.

As Mary Grace sat up and started to apologize for losing her composure, Cassie cut off the apology with another quick hug and said, "You don't have anything to apologize for. You didn't do anything wrong. Yeah, you're going home with me this weekend. You need to." Mary Grace was clearly embarrassed for Cassie to have witnessed her emotional train wreck, embarrassed that Cassie had seen her Like That. As roommates, they had seen each other in various stages of undress, no big deal, but Cassie seeing her Like That was a big deal. She had learned not to let anybody see her Like That. That was one thing her family had taught her and taught her well. Spilling her guts the way she did, telling all the secrets, was like taking Cassie home with her to see what goes on inside the big pretty house that everybody admires from the road. Mary Grace was embarrassed that she had broken down in front of Cassie, further embarrassed that she had found comfort in Cassie's embrace — she certainly didn't want Cassie to get The Wrong Idea, embarrassed that she had needed and had permitted someone to just hold her while she cried, and that she, like a small child, had found it so soothing to be held close enough to hear the heartbeat of the one holding her. Still, she appreciated Cassie's kindness, and her embarrassment subsided as she realized that Cassie did not think any less of her because she had seen her Like That, wounded, hurting, and needing to be held. She was intrigued by the words Cassie had whispered to her and by how naturally Cassie had stepped into the role of comforter. It was too much to process right now. Mary Grace did not know the scripture about another Mary a long time ago who "pondered in her heart" things she did not yet understand. She only knew that she needed to hold those thoughts and come back to them because she was beginning to believe in something she did not yet understand or know much about. Mary Grace did not know the beautiful imagery in Psalm 131, "I have calmed and quieted myself, like a weaned child with its mother...," nor did she know that line in "Leaning On the Everlasting Arms" that describes the awareness that one is "safe and secure from all alarms." All she knew was that it was something more than the promise of being treated like family this weekend that made her feel accepted and loved, something more than Cassie's tight embrace that had caused her to know that she was safe, and something more than the rhythm of Cassie's heartbeat that had soothed her spirit. All of these earthly things had served as parables — *the Kingdom of Heaven is like a home where guests are treated like family, the Kingdom of Heaven is like the embrace of a friend who holds you securely when you need to cry, the Kingdom of Heaven is like a crying child being soothed by the sound of her mother's heartbeat* — down-to-earth images to help her begin to wrap her mind around things of eternal significance. Mary Grace Tillison trusted Cassie Elise McWhorter, and she realized that trusting Cassie was somehow connected with trusting the one who sent her. That was as much gospel as she knew or understood, but it was enough for now. She needed and wanted to know more, but she believed in and trusted as much as she knew. She was composed now, more so than she ever remembered being. The composure she felt was completely unlike the appearance of composure that she had tried to project as a superficially nice person who didn't need anything.

Cassie and Mary Grace both had their class schedules arranged so that they had no late afternoon classes on Fridays. A few minutes before 3:00 p.m., Cassie had the OGM rolling west on University Drive, which is Georgia Route 74 and takes you to Thomaston where you pick up Route 18 through Woodbury to Greenville. They made good time, somehow getting behind only one school bus, which they followed about a mile before it turned off onto a county road. At Greenville, she picked up 297. Just past the sign reading "Hansonville 3 miles," Cassie put on her left turn signal and made the turn onto Bailey's Mill Road. "You could stay on 297 through Hansonville all the way to Harrington," Cassie commented to Mary Grace, who had the passenger seat leaned back and was half asleep, "but the highway dog-legs to go through Hansonville, Bailey's Mill Road brings you back out on 297 between Hansonville and Harrington, cuts off a good five miles, straight shot. Besides, I can take you by and show you the church where I'll be preaching Sunday."

"Glad you know where you are," Mary Grace replied sleepily, "'cause I sure don't. Riding with you is kind of like this whole religion and faith thing. I don't know the way to your house, but I know you know how to get there, so I don't worry about you getting us lost. I'm just as clueless about the religion and faith thing as I am about how to get to your house. I don't know where I'm going, but you seem to know where you're going. I trust you probably more than I've ever trusted anybody, and I'm riding with you on that, too. I'm not afraid of you getting me lost there, either."

"I appreciate you trusting me that much," Cassie spoke haltingly, taken aback at what Mary Grace had just said, "and I'll try not to do anything to violate that trust. I'm the same age as you, still got a lot to learn, but I've been blessed to have some good people showing me the way. Miss Addie's the one who showed me that I could cut off five miles using Bailey's Mill Road, don't know when or if I would have discovered that on my own. Faith is pretty much the same way, I don't think I would have discovered it on my own either."

"I was so afraid last night when I started spilling my guts and couldn't stop that you'd be like 'what is wrong with this girl, take her to the looney bin, get her out of here,' and you'd want to push me away, probably try to get yourself a different roommate next semester — God, Cassie, this is hard for me to talk about without getting all emotional again..."

"It's all right if you do get all emotional again, keep talking."

"Instead of being put off and pushing me away, you held me so close I could hear your heart, and the things you said about Jesus and God..."

"Jesus said, 'Blessed are those who mourn for they shall be comforted.' Jesus is a man of sorrows, acquainted with grief. My God is the father of mercies and God of all comfort?"

"Yeah," Mary Grace was again fumbling for words to describe something she knew so little about, "I don't know how to say this, but it was like you taking me home with you in more ways than one, kinda like you were saying, 'Jesus, this is my roommate Mary Grace,' and like he gave me a big hug just like he gave you, it was like you weren't the only one with your arms around me."

Cassie prayed silently as she listened, prayed for the right words to respond to Mary Grace, prayed that she would not say too much but that she would say enough. "I wasn't the only one holding you, Mary Grace. Jesus wants to hold you close. All the sin, all the hurt, everything you are ashamed of, everything you think would make him reject you, he wants to take on himself. Just like I saw how bad you were hurting and put my arms around you, that's what he wants to do, too. Yeah, that's a good way to describe it — me taking you home with me in more ways than one. I was praying for you as I held you. 'Jesus, this is my roommate Mary Grace. You know how to help her.' That was pretty much the prayer I prayed for you."

The girls rode in silence broken only by the hum of the tires on the coarse tar and gravel pavement as Mary Grace tried to absorb the things Cassie had told her. Cassie turned off Bailey's Mill Road onto Peyton's Chapel Road, the silence remaining unbroken until Cassie eased the car to a stop in the graveled parking lot of Peyton's Chapel Baptist Church, moved the shifter to park, and shut off the engine. "Well, Mary Grace, this is it. Want to get out and walk around, stretch our legs a little? It'll be about a half hour before Mom and Dad get home anyway."

"This place is so pretty. It feels peaceful." Mary Grace was again searching for words as she took in the elegantly simple, neatly land-scaped, steep-roofed white clapboard sanctuary with clear old wavy-glass windows, the much later addition to the back of the building for Sunday School classrooms, all surrounded by towering oaks, a couple of hickory trees, overlooked by a large old cemetery up on the hill behind the church building. "I love this place already. Can't wait to come out here Sunday and hear you. Now take me and show me where Miss Addie is buried. I love her just from hearing you talk about her, and I feel like I need to pay my respects."

"It's up at the top of the hill. You want to get in the car and drive up closer or you want to walk up there?"

"Walk. Back when I was in high school, after I got my driver's license, I used to go for walks in this old country church cemetery about a mile from my house out from Elberton. I didn't know any of the people buried there, I just went there for the quiet sometimes to get away from the craziness. They had the big concrete tables outside where they had dinners, just like the ones here, used to sit there to study and do my homework when the weather was nice. But mostly, I just took sanity walks in the cemetery. So, yeah, let's walk. You've given me a whole lot to think about. Walking helps me think."

"Me too," Cassie concurred, "and I'm not worried about getting assaulted like I did the last time I was out here. With my connection to Miss Addie, I may be taking lots of walks up this hill. This is a peaceful place in spite of what happened here when we buried Miss Addie."

Cassie and Mary Grace stood silently at the foot of Miss Addie's grave. The reddish brown dirt was still loose and mounded up. Cassie noticed that the people from the monument place had been out and added Miss Addie's death date to the double marker. The little aluminum temporary marker with the name of the funeral home, Miss Addie's name, and her birth and death dates on a card inserted under a clear plastic window was stuck in the dirt between the stone monument and the head of the grave. Mary Grace noticed the tears making their way slowly down Cassie's cheeks, put her arm around her shoulder, and drew her into her embrace. Although she did not know the scripture that talks about "bearing one another's burdens and thus fulfilling the law of Christ," Mary Grace had learned the concept last night in Cassie's strong embrace. Cassie reciprocated the hug, and they held each other tightly. Mary Grace finally broke the silence, speaking haltingly, "I don't know how to say this. I mean, I don't want you to get the wrong idea because I don't mean it like *that*, but I...I...I love you, Cassie. I mean, the way I'd love a sister if I had one."

"I love you, too, Mary Grace. And I know what you mean, I love you the same way."

"You remember the other night as you were drifting off to sleep and you whispered, 'Saint Addie, pray for us?'"

"Mmmhmm."

"Well, I've never asked anybody to pray for me before, but you think Saint Addie would pray for me, too?"

"I think she already has been. Would you like for me to pray for you, too?"

Mary Grace answered the question, "Yes, please do," as she and Cassie embraced each other, and Cassie offered a prayer of thanksgiving for her sister Mary Grace and her new-found faith, for the love that would never let go of either of them, and for Mary Grace's love for her as a sister in Christ.

They walked silently back down the hill and got in the car. Cassie made the right turn back onto Bailey's Mill Road. As they approached the bridge over Salyers Creek, Cassie slowed down. "Mary Grace, if you look off to your right, you'll see the old dam, what's left of the foundation of Bailey's Mill, and the stone piers of the old covered bridge that used to be there. Down below the dam, close to the old bridge, is where Miss Addie was baptized in 1908. It's a special place for me. I love to come out here when I just need to be by myself, be quiet, think and pray. Once in a while somebody'll be fishing down there, but most of the time I have it all to myself. I call it my holy place."

"So stop, Cassie. I need to see this place."

Cassie pulled the OGM off the road onto a well-worn, hard-packed dirt road just beyond the bridge that led down into a flat clearing up near the foundation of the old mill. It was where she parked when she came here for solitude, where others parked when they came here to fish in the creek or hunt in the surrounding woods, where many of the people buried at Peyton's Chapel had tied up their wagons when they brought a load of corn to the mill or a wagon load of people down to the creek for a baptismal service. Mary Grace got out of the car, and Cassie followed. "I've got a picture at home I'll show you that Miss Addie gave me," Cassie told Mary Grace, "of a baptism here back in the '20s. The covered bridge and the mill were still standing. There was a line of people in the water waiting to be baptized, and the preacher was baptizing right over there in the deeper water between the piers of the old bridge. Miss Addie said that's where she was baptized."

Without saying anything, Mary Grace took off her shoes and anklet socks, stepped over the rocks, and waded out into the water. "Whoa, this water's cold!" she exclaimed over the steady roar of water cascading over the old dam. "I don't care. I want to be baptized. Come on out in the water, Cass, you need to baptize me. Right here, right now. Let's do it before I'm dead from hypothermia standing in this water!" Mary Grace waded in deeper as she spoke, walking cautiously, testing the bottom as she went, until she stood in chest-deep water about where Miss Addie was baptized.

Cassie started to protest that she wasn't ordained and that she'd never baptized anybody before, and she started laughing because she knew full well what Miss Addie would say to shoot down those objections. All she could say, as she took off her shoes and socks and waded in, was "Saint Addie, look what you got me into!" Cassie waded out to where Mary Grace was waiting for her. After giving Mary Grace a hug, she said, "I can't believe we're doing this. You know I've never baptized anybody before."

"I know, Cass. I want to be the first one you baptize." Cassie did it like she'd seen Brother Mike do it, putting her left arm behind Mary Grace's back, extending her right arm, and asking Mary Grace to put her hands on her forearm. "In obedience to our Lord Jesus Christ, following the example he gave when he was baptized by John in the Jordan River, and upon your confession of faith in him, I baptize you, my sister Mary Grace Tillison, in the name of the Father, the Son, and the Holy Spirit." As she held Mary Grace's nose and lowered her beneath the cold, dark water, Cassie said, "Buried with him in baptism," and as she brought her back up and embraced her, "raised to walk in the newness of life in Christ Jesus. The Spirit of glory and of God be upon you, Mary Grace. Because of you, may others come to know the Lord. Amen."

As they walked back to the car, sopping wet and dripping Salyers Creek baptismal water, Mary Grace said, "I can't wait to see the look on your parents' faces when we show up at their door dripping water all over the place. Should make for a memorable first meeting."

Cassie parked the OGM in the driveway behind her dad's red Silverado pickup. They were both laughing hysterically when Cassie opened the front door and called out, "Mom! Dad! Little Brat! We're home! We've got to change into some dry clothes real quick and we'll be right with you!"

Chapter 11

"Today's been such a perfect fall day," Elaine told Cassie and Mary Grace," and you know how your dad loves to grill out. He took off early today, about 2:00 p.m., got his big grill all fired up, got some ribeyes and boneless chicken breasts ready to go on the grill, got some potatoes that've already been on the top rack of the grill about two hours, crock pot full of baked beans that he started before he left for work this morning, plus he's got a big pork roast on the grill for barbeque tomorrow. When Jerry McWhorter fires up his grill, I stay out of the way. He knows what he's doing, and everything always turns out good. I enjoy cooking out more this time of the year when it's not so hot and humid and you're not having to swat mosquitoes."

"Sounds wonderful," Mary Grace commented. "I really appreciate you inviting me to come home with Cassie this weekend."

"Our pleasure, honey, glad you could come. We'd've been disappointed if you hadn't. Hope you're hungry. You made Jerry's heart glad, giving him a reason to fire up his grill. It's what he lives for, Mary Grace. He'll probably get up off his deathbed to fire it up one more time."

"Yeah, Mary Grace," Cassie added, "you gotta see Daddy's grill. You thought I was exaggerating when I told you about it, big ol' honkin' thing about six feet long mounted on a trailer so he can pull it behind his truck, that's the only way you could move it, it's so big and heavy. He and one of the guys that works for him worked after hours and a couple of Saturdays over at the city maintenance barn building it. Of course, one thing led to another, he had to have the trailer part and the fenders painted to match his truck, and he got some fancy wheels for it to match the ones on his truck, wouldn't do just to get some wheels from the junkyard, got the same kind of tires on it he has on his truck. The crowning touch, he had a sign painter he knows over at Hansonville letter the back of the thing 'Jerry McWhorter, King of the Grill.' He fires it up every year for the McWhorter and Whitmire family reunions, and the church has a couple of big cookouts a year. Daddy, Darrell Brinson, and a couple of other guys with these monster grills do the cooking."

"Cassie's not exaggerating about the grill, Mary Grace," Elaine continued. "Jerry loves to cook for a crowd. You've heard Cassie talk about Coretta and Daniel Groves, Coretta's singing Sunday out at Peyton's Chapel, they're coming, should be here directly, and our pastor Mike Westover and his wife Karen are coming in a few minutes. When Jerry grills out, we have to have help to eat it all. I look forward to you meeting everybody. Karen just called right before you got here. They've got to drop their older daughter Asalee off at the high school on their way over. She's got an out-of-town trip with the band tonight, football game over't Centralhatchee, probably won't be back before 11:00 p.m. Their younger daughter, Deborah Estelle, is spending the night with the Stewarts. Aaron Stewart, our police chief, he and his family live across the street from our pastor and his family. Talked with Coretta, she said they'd be here about 6:30 p.m."

"Yeah, Aaron Stewart's the one who slammed Brother Bobby down on the hood of the hearse and put the cuffs on him after he put his hands on me out at Peyton's Chapel," Cassie commented.

"Of course, Brother Mike wants to talk with Cassie about Sunday out at Peyton's Chapel, and he and Karen want to meet you, Mary Grace. Daniel and Coretta are eager to meet you, too. By Harrington standards, you're a celebrity. Just one more thing, though. I'm dying to know, and I'm sure there's a perfectly logical explanation." Elaine was choking back the laughter, thinking about the sight of Cassie and Mary Grace coming in as though it was perfectly normal for people to show up at the door soaked to the bone when there had been no rain for over a week. "There's got to be a really good story to explain you girls showing up at the door sopping wet and leaving a trail of water all the way from the front door to the bathroom and laundry room, followed by the sound of soaking wet clothes and towels landing in the washer. Things like that arouse my curiosity. I can't help it, it goes with being a mother, I guess, to wonder about things like that."

"Yeah, I saw the wet seats in the Old Gray Mare and the trail of water up the sidewalk, kinda wondered the same thing," Cassie's brother Anthony added as he came in from the patio where he had been helping Jerry with the grill. "This is sure to be one of your more memorable escapades, Cass, the sort of thing I'll want to tell your children and grandchildren. Let's hear it."

"Mary Grace, this is my brother Anthony, lovingly and otherwise known as Little Brat. He'll answer to either name. Stand still, Little Brat, and you can hear the story the same time Mom does."

To Cassie's surprise, Mary Grace took the lead in explaining what happened. "Hey, Little Brat! Pleasure to meet you. Now, where was I? Oh, yes. There was a baptism about thirty minutes ago down at Bailey's Mill where Miss Addie was baptized..."

"Excuse me just a minute," Elaine cut in, "Anthony, quick, go get your dad and bring him in here to hear this so Mary Grace doesn't have to tell it twice..."

"Hey, you must be Mary Grace," Jerry McWhorter spoke cheerfully as he hugged her. "Welcome to our home, sorry I smell like charcoal, glad you could come and, by the way, your hair's soaking wet like you just got baptized or something."

"That's sort of what happened, Jerry. That's what Mary Grace was starting to explain," Elaine said, "and I told Anthony to get you in here to hear this 'cause it's gonna be good."

A hush came over the room, and all eyes were on Mary Grace as she continued, "Cassie and I have been talking a lot about things I don't know much about, you know, religion, God, Jesus, the Bible, faith, spiritual things. This is all so new to me...bear with me, I may not make a lot of sense or use the right words..." Mary Grace dabbed away tears with her shirt sleeve.

"Keep going," Cassie encouraged her, "we all love you, we know what you're talking about, and you're doing great so far." Cassie moved closer to Mary Grace and put her arm around her shoulders.

"I told Cassie last night that I've never been to church much and couldn't tell you the difference between a Baptist and a Buddhist, but I wanted to come and hear her preach. She was about to e-mail you and ask if it was okay to bring me home with her and there was this e-mail from you saying 'why don't you invite Mary Grace to come home with you this weekend?' So, here I am. Anyway, I don't know why I ended up pouring out all of this stuff. I started and I couldn't stop, told Cassie that the distance wasn't the only reason I didn't want to go back up to Elberton this weekend. I broke down and cried, talking about all the stuff I've been holding in. I was so afraid Cassie would be put off seeing me like that, afraid she'd be saying, 'get this crazy girl out of here,' but instead she pulled me close, wrapped her arms around me, and held me while I cried. As she held me, she rubbed my back and whispered things about Jesus and God, and somewhere in all of that I realized that Cassie was not the only one holding me and making me feel safe and loved. Somewhere in all of that, I went beyond trusting Cassie to trusting Jesus. You might say Cassie brought me home with her in more ways than one, home to her family and home to Jesus. I don't know if any of this makes any sense..." Mary Grace's voice trailed off.

"It makes perfect sense, honey," Elaine spoke soothingly as she took Mary Grace's right hand and caressed it with her hands. "I can't think of a more beautiful way to describe what you've experienced."

"Y'all're just like Cassie said you'd be." Mary Grace was visibly relieved.

"I told you they'd understand, didn't I?" Cassie smiled as she blotted tears. "They didn't look at you like you were speaking Chinese, did they?"

"I believe in Jesus with all my heart even though I don't know much and I've got a lot to learn," Mary Grace continued. "On the way in, Cassie took me by and showed me the church where she's preaching Sunday, then we visited Miss Addie's grave. After we left there, as we were going over the bridge on Bailey's Mill Road, Cassie pointed out the dam and the ruins of the old mill, and told me that Miss Addie was baptized there below the dam at Bailey's Mill. I asked her to stop the car, and she did. We got out and walked over the rocks down to where the old bridge used to be, and Cassie told me that Miss Addie said her uncle baptized her out in the deeper water between those big stone piers of the old bridge. I took off my shoes, socks, and watch and started wading out there. Cassie looked at me like, 'what in the world are you doing,' and I told her I needed to be baptized and wanted to be baptized more than I've ever wanted anything in my life, and I wanted her to baptize me."

"Mary Grace! Cassie! That's wonderful!" Elaine exclaimed, tears running down her face.

Jerry was not even trying to hide his tears as he moved toward Cassie and Mary Grace and embraced them both simultaneously. He was so overcome with emotion that the only words he could get out were, "Praise God! Thank you, Jesus!"

Even Anthony/Little Brat, not ordinarily one to show much emotion, had tears welling up in his eyes. "That is so cool, Cassie. You and Mary Grace have got to tell Brother Mike about this!"

"I told Mary Grace I'd never baptized anybody before," Cassie added. "I started to tell her I wasn't ordained and I didn't know if it was okay for me to be baptizing just yet, but she was already too far out in the water to hear me over the roar of the water coming over the dam, only thing I could do was wade in after her. If I'd told her that I wasn't ordained, I'd've had to explain ordination while we were standing chest-deep in ice water, so I didn't go there. All I could think was Miss Addie would've loved this and she probably had something to do with it. I already knew what she would've said to any objections I could have raised, so I didn't bother to raise them."

"You just said, 'Saint Addie, look what you got me into.' I told Cassie I knew she'd never baptized anybody before," Mary Grace continued, "and I said I wanted to be her first one. I told her she needed to go ahead and do it before we both died from hypothermia standing in that water."

"Brand new Christian, and you're already starting to sound like Miss Addie," Cassie quipped. "That water was cold, all right, like Heather says about baptizing in that creek up at Clear Springs, all you have to do is put them under, you don't have to worry about bringing them back up."

"The baptism was the most serious and solemn thing I've ever done, and I think it was for Cassie, too," Mary Grace continued the story, "but once it was done, we felt so free and joyful we were plumb giddy, we couldn't look at each other without busting out laughing. We were laughing so hard on our way over here, Cassie could barely see to drive, just thinking about the absurdity of us showing up sopping wet and what a memorable first meeting that was going to be. Then Cassie said that getting hypothermia at your baptism would be an embarrassing way to go to be with the Lord. She said she wants to hear, 'Well done, good and faithful servant,' not 'we never got one in that way before,' and I said, 'Yeah, we'd be known for all eternity as those crazy girls from Georgia who got hypothermia baptizing at Bailey's Mill in October.'"

"Yeah," Cassie commented, "and I said I gotta tell Daddy and Uncle Jack about that big ol' large mouth bass that swam within an inch of my legs as I was wading in. They'll be down there at sunrise in the morning trying to catch it."

"Jerry," Elaine spoke up, "I think some of our folks are here, I heard car doors open and close. Look out there and see who it is."

As Jerry opened the front door, he told Elaine, "It's Mike and Karen," and then called out, "Hey, Brother Mike, Karen, y'all come on in the house!" Jerry called out as he held the storm door open. "Y'all must've smelled the steaks cooking. Speaking of steaks, I'd better check on them in a minute so I don't burn 'em."

"Yeah, Jerry," Mike commented as they exchanged a Vise-Grip handshake, "I heard the Wal-Mart in Hansonville was sold out of charcoal, they said some tall skinny guy driving a red Chevy Silverado with a Mintz County tag bought every last bag they had."

"Thanks for inviting us over, Elaine," Karen said as they hugged. "Always good to be in your home, and I think I hear another car in the driveway, must be Daniel and Coretta."

"It is," Jerry confirmed as he held the door open again and greeted Daniel and Coretta as they came up the sidewalk. "Hey, Dan, Coretta. Glad you could come. Mike and Karen are here, and Cassie and her roommate, Mary Grace, are already here. Dan, I've gotten so used to seeing you in the undertaker suit, almost didn't recognize you in blue jeans."

"Took the day off, got some things done around the house," Daniel responded. "We had six funerals from Sunday to Wednesday, then nothing since Wednesday, that's how it is when you're in a dying business."

"Bad pun, Daniel," Coretta groaned, "but I know Jerry would've said it if you hadn't, right before he said that you'll be the last man to let a person down. Beat you to the draw this time, Jerry! I asked Elaine if we needed to bring anything, and she said just bring ourselves and our appetites."

"Mary Grace," Elaine made the introduction, "I want you to meet our pastor, Mike Westover, his wife Karen, and Daniel and Coretta Groves. Coretta's going to be singing out at Peyton's Chapel on Sunday when Cassie preaches. Can't wait for you to hear her awesome voice. Everybody, this is Cassie's roommate at Mercer, Mary Grace Tillison. She's spending the weekend with us so she can hear Cassie preach on Sunday..."

"and her hair's still a little wet 'cause she just got baptized in the creek out at Bailey's Mill about forty-five minutes ago," Cassie added to her mother's introduction of Mary Grace. "She's a new believer, wanted to be baptized right then and there, and asked me to baptize her. She was like, here's the water, let's do it."

"Pleasure to meet you," Mike said as they all hugged Mary Grace and Cassie. "Congratulations and blessings on your baptism, Mary Grace.

"Sounds like a good story we need to hear," Karen added.

"It is, and I'm glad to tell it," Mary Grace responded confidently. "Cassie's the one who baptized me. In the creek, below the dam at Bailey's Mill, same place where Miss Addie was baptized in 1908. Cassie showed me the place on our way home today. I've never been to church much, but I told Cassie I wanted to hear her preach. We've been talking a lot, I know she's been praying for me, and she's helped me with some hard stuff I've been dealing with, when I broke down and cried talking about it, she held me instead of pushing me away, somewhere in all of that I went beyond trusting Cassie to trusting Jesus. On our way down here today, I told Cassie I was glad she was driving 'cause I had no idea where we were going, and that I'm pretty much riding with her on the whole religion and faith thing, too. Cassie brought me home with her in more ways than one, home to her family and home to Jesus, so I can say 'here I am' in more ways than one. Cassie showed me the place down by the creek, she calls it her holy place, where she likes to go to think and pray, where Miss Addie was baptized. It seemed real important to me to be baptized right then and there, so I took off my shoes, socks, and watch, laid them there on the rocks, and started wading out there to the deeper water between the piers of the old bridge, and I told Cass I wanted her to baptize me. Cass said she'd never baptized anybody before, I told her I knew that and I wanted to be the first one, so she waded in after me and baptized me. We showed up here dripping wet, made for a memorable first meeting."

Mike and Karen embraced Mary Grace. "That's wonderful," Karen spoke in a voice breaking with emotion.

"Hope I didn't do anything I wasn't supposed to do, baptizing when I haven't been ordained," Cassie commented, "but it's done now, and we all know what Miss Addie would've said, that it's easier to get forgiveness than permission."

"I know a lot of Baptists would say you shouldn't have done it, but they're basically the same ones who would say that a woman shouldn't be preaching in the first place," Mike observed. "The way I look at it, you don't need forgiveness and you didn't need my permission because you already cleared it with God. I'd say the Lord put you in that situation, what else were you supposed to do? Kinda like when Coach Sawyer used to yell, 'Ball's in your court, Girlfriend!' And, Mary Grace, there's good precedent for a new believer wanting to be baptized immediately. In the Bible, in the book of Acts, a man named Philip catches a ride in a chariot with a man from Ethiopia, a high-ranking official of the queen. Philip notices that he's reading from a scroll of the prophet Isaiah, asks him if he understands what he's reading, the guy has a million questions, and Philip uses the same scripture the man had been reading to tell him about Jesus. They come to a place where there is some water, and the man says to Philip, 'Here's the water, what's to keep me from being baptized?' Just like you did. Philip tells him if he believes with all of his heart he can be, and Philip baptizes him right then and there. Just like Cassie baptized you. Nobody else around. Philip won that man's trust, just like Cassie earned yours. He wanted to be baptized, and he wanted Philip to be the one to baptize him, just like you wanted to be baptized and wanted Cassie to do the honors. As for ordination, looks like God beat us to the draw on that, Cassie. That's a God thing anyway. God's the only one who can make anybody a minister. God's already set you apart. Whenever the time comes for the church to ordain you, we'll just be giving formal recognition to what God's already done and giving you our blessing. It'll be our way of saying you're ours and we're proud of you. Y'all did the right thing, and don't ever let anybody tell you that you didn't."

"Amen, Preacher," Daniel concurred.

"And, Mary Grace, your eagerness to be baptized says something about the sincerity of your faith," Coretta added. "You're a new believer, but the Lord's already given you the discernment to know that Cassie is somebody you can trust to lead you the right way. I've known her a long time. She's the real deal."

"Take your time visiting with everybody, Daddy, I just turned all of the steaks and took up the potatoes," Anthony/Little Brat called out as he came back in the den. "Everything's getting pretty close to done."

"Thanks, Son. You want to go ahead and get those marinated chicken breasts your mom fixed out of the cooler and put them on the grill? Those won't take but a couple of minutes on each side as hot as that grill is, time they're done, the steaks'll be good and done."

"As you can see," Cassie commented, "Daddy's grooming Little Brat for the day he will inherit the grill and the big ol' two-foot-long stainless steel burger flipper. Then, someday, Little Brat will have a son of his own, and Little Brat's son will get his own little grilling apron, and Little Brat will start grooming him for the day that he inherits the grill and the big long burger flipper. A hundred years from now, we'll look down from the portals of heaven and see future generations of McWhorter men and their sons wearing their aprons and sacrificing Black Angus cattle on the grill."

"We're going to eat out on the patio," Elaine announced. "Jerry and Anthony finished screening it in a couple of weeks ago, so it ought to be real pleasant out there. By the time we get situated, everything should be ready to eat."

"Honey, let's go ahead and have the blessing in here," Jerry suggested. Then, he called outside, "Anthony, come in here a second while we have the blessing." After that, he put an arm around Cassie's shoulders, gave her a gentle squeeze, and said, "Preacher McWhorter, say grace for us."

"So, how are you feeling about Sunday, Cassie?" Mike asked as he cut another bite from his ribeye. "Pretty good, I hope."

"I feel good about it," Cassie answered. "Glad that Coretta volunteered to come and sing. I know they'll be inviting her back to sing whether they invite me back to preach or not. It'll be easier to preach after she sings. I believe the Lord gave me last night and today with Mary Grace, being able to see her come to faith in Christ and getting to baptize her, to help get me ready for Sunday. I need to spend some time tomorrow down at my holy place where Miss Addie and Mary Grace were baptized, putting the finishing touches on my sermon, thinking, resting, praying. Expecting a phone call tomorrow night from Heather Simmons Moore up at Clear Springs. I love her. We were already friends, but we really got close at the Baptist Women in Ministry conference I went to with her last summer. She can give you a hug from four hundred miles away, so positive and encouraging. Of course, I am thankful for you and Karen, too. I've been blessed to have you as my pastor since I was ten years old, and I never would have met Heather if you hadn't invited her down to preach a revival here. Not many pastors in this neck of the woods would've encouraged me and given me opportunities to preach like you have."

"That's part of the reason I do it, Cass, because I know there are not many others who will. That, and I know it's the right thing to do," Mike commented. "God's up to something good with you, and I want to be part of it, want to be on board with what God's doing. Like ol' Conway over at Greater New Hope says, 'When God's ready to roll, you'd best be on board or you'll get left standing at the station.' I don't want God to take off and leave me. I believe that mentoring others with a call to ministry is among the most important things I can do, and I've found it to be among the most enjoyable. I'm glad you've got Heather as another good mentor, too. Most of the people doing what you're called to do are men, so I'm glad you have Heather as a role model, a woman who does what you're called to do and does it well, been doing it eight years now up at Clear Springs. If I had to make my short list of the half-dozen or so best preachers I ever heard, she'd be on it."

"I told you about our family vacation summer before last," Cassie reminisced. "I persuaded Mom and Dad to plan our trip so we could just show up on Sunday morning at Clear Springs, visit the church, and hear Heather preach. Never felt more welcome in my life, Daddy said if we lived up there, he'd be ready to join Clear Springs. You can tell they really love Heather and her family, you can feel it when you walk in the door. And, oh my Lord, did she preach that day!"

"It's like ol' Wallace Coggins used to say," Mike noted. "Wallace was chairman of deacons up at Clear Springs for years, he's the one our dog, Wallace, and Heather's little boy, Wallace, are named after. Wallace said that a lot of preachers are against women in the pulpit 'cause they're afraid a woman might be able to preach better than they can. In Heather's case and in yours, I think Wallace nailed it. When you preached your first sermon, you were already better than that clown they had out at Peyton's Chapel. I'm still shaking my head over that nasty run-in you had with him at the cemetery on Monday."

"So anyway," Cassie continued, "I'm thankful for any opportunity to preach, but I won't make more of it than it is. I've only been asked to fill in one Sunday. I'm going to do that and do it the best that I can, and thank them for inviting me."

"One Sunday that you know of," Mike responded. "Ask Heather about where a one-shot pulpit supply can lead. I asked her to fill in for me the Sunday I preached at Karen's home church over at Williston, Alabama, for the pastor search committee from Harrington. She was well received, so I asked her to fill in again the Sunday that I preached the trial sermon here. They ended up calling her without even looking at anybody else. She started her pastorate at Clear Springs the same Sunday I started here in Harrington. Not saying that's what'll happen with you at Peyton's Chapel. Don't know if you'll consider taking it if they offer it to you. I'm just saying it happened with Heather, she came as a pulpit supply, been there eight years and counting. Don't mean to scare you. Anyway, enjoy this Sunday for what it is, and if that's all it is, it'll be good."

Chapter 12

Cassie woke up and looked at the clock. 6:12 a.m. Still pitch dark outside. She had gone to bed a little after 11:00 p.m., thinking that she'd be too wound up to sleep, but neither she nor Mary Grace knew when their heads hit their pillows. There was just enough light from the street light outside and the night light in the hall outside her room for Cassie to see Mary Grace in a deep, peaceful sleep in the other bed. She noted her stillness, the slight, almost imperceptible rise and fall of her chest, and the slowness of her breathing. Mary Grace usually slept in fits and spurts, up and down several times a night. By the time she got up most mornings, her cover would be tossed and twisted every which way. This morning, her cover was barely disturbed, no more than had been necessary for her to get under it, as though someone had made the bed up with her in it. Cassie had never seen Mary Grace sleep like this before, like a little child "leaning on Jesus, safe and secure from all alarms." Cassie breathed a silent prayer, giving thanks for Mary Grace's peaceful spirit and restful sleep. Seeing Mary Grace sleep like this reminded her of that line in "My Shepherd Will Supply My Need," which she had heard Coretta sing a few weeks ago, "No more a stranger or a guest, but like a child at home."

Cassie had slept well herself. She felt rested, but at 6:12 a.m., she was as wide awake as she would ever be, and she knew that her dad would already be up. He always got up early to make coffee and pray for the safety of Juan Valdez and his sure-footed little burro bringing more coffee beans down from that mountaintop in Colombia. She smelled the aroma wafting down the hall, coffee brewed from the finest freshly ground Colombian beans, and she heard the gurgling sounds of the big percolator. Perhaps that is what roused her two or three hours earlier than she had meant to get up, she didn't know. Her father was as serious about his coffee as he was about his reputation as King of the Grill. Having a guest in the house for the weekend gave him the excuse he was looking for to get out the big twenty-four cup urn instead of the twelve-cup drip coffee maker. Cassie put on her favorite pink chenille housecoat over her gown and stopped by the bathroom where she ran a cold wet washcloth over her face before walking toward the source of the aroma and the gurgling sounds. "Hey, Daddy, didn't think I'd be up this early," Cassie yawned as she spoke to Jerry, who was sitting on the big overstuffed sofa in the den, sipping from a big mug of steaming black coffee and watching CNN. She got one of the big mugs her dad had set out on the counter— there were no dinky-dainty little coffee cups in the McWhorter house other than the purely ornamental ones in the china cabinet—poured it about a third full with milk, topped it off with coffee, and stirred in a spoonful of sugar before snuggling up next to Jerry on the sofa.

"Mixed you up some little girl coffee, I see," Jerry said as he gave his daughter a gentle squeeze. "You still like to pretend you're drinking coffee with Daddy?"

"I am drinking coffee, Daddy Longlegs!"

"Whoa! Been a long time since you called me Daddy Longlegs! Brings back good memories. Did you sleep good?"

"Never knew when my head hit the pillow, last thing I remember was telling Mary Grace good night about 11:00 p.m., next thing I knew, the clock said 6:12 a.m. You know me, once I wake up, doesn't matter what time it is, I might as well get on up, can't just turn over and go back to sleep like normal people, can't stay in bed once I'm awake. Guess I needed my Saturday morning Daddy Longlegs time. I remember when I was a little kid, I always woke up before Emily or Anthony on Saturday mornings. You were always up drinking your coffee and watching the news or something dumb. I'd snatch your remote control, switch it to cartoons, then I'd snuggle up with you, and we'd watch cartoons together until everybody else got up." As she said those words, Cassie reached across her dad, snatched the remote from the armrest of the sofa, announced gleefully, "Got your 'mote, Daddy Longlegs!," switched the TV to the

Cartoon Network, stuffed the remote down between the sofa cushions, and giggled like she did when she was six years old.

"Mary Grace still asleep?" Jerry asked the little girl cuddled up next to him.

"She is. I've never seen her in such a deep sleep, glad to see her sleeping like that. She usually tosses and turns a lot, mumbles in her sleep, up and down several times a night. I don't think she's moved since her head hit the pillow. You can barely tell she's breathing."

"Good," Jerry commented. "Glad she's that comfortable here. We want her to be. I noticed last night while you were cleaning up out on the patio and Anthony and I were taking care of the grill, Mary Grace helped your mom put up the food, load the dishwasher, and clean up the kitchen. I know the two of them talked a lot, don't know what they talked about, don't need to know, got the feeling it was mom-daughter stuff, but I could tell Mary Grace was talking with her like she'd known her all of her life. Your mom gave her a good night hug and kiss, told her that she loved her, just like she did you and Anthony. Glad all of that led up to a real good night's sleep for her. That's the way your mom's always been when you had friends over. That's just how she is, most maternal creature I ever saw."

"I'm glad she's that way," Cassie replied thoughtfully, "and I'm glad you're the way you are, all of the teasing and corny jokes included. I'll never forget Mary Grace saying last night, 'y'all are just like Cassie said you'd be.' That's how y'all have always been with my friends, Emily's and Anthony's friends, too. I'll never forget the way y'all took Alicia in back when I was in ninth grade, talked about adopting her if she couldn't go back home, and I know you would've done it. I told Mary Grace about Alicia, how you and Mom took her in and took care of her, all the time I'm asking myself 'why am I telling her this, this is too much information.' When Mary Grace started getting teary-eyed and said she could relate to Alicia a lot, I knew why I all of a sudden felt the urge to tell her about Alicia. She told me what it was like growing up in her family, broke down and cried, and I just held her close, rubbed her back, and told her

about the Lord and how much he cares for her. That's what led to everything else, the baptism and all. I like the way she described it, saying she
came home with me in more ways than one."

"Cass, it sounds like we need to get ol' Benny the street sign guy to
fix us up a big yellow sign that says 'God Working.' There are a lot of
kids out there like Alicia and Mary Grace, which brings me to something
I want to ask you about, see what you think about it. I know you've got
a lot on your mind with preaching tomorrow out at Peyton's Chapel,
and I don't want to pile too much else on your plate, but this seems like
a good time to talk about it. Your mom and I want to run the idea by
you and see how you feel about it, something we've talked about off and
on ever since Alicia stayed with us four years ago. We've talked with your
Aunt Susan about it, she thinks we'd be good at it and she's really encouraged us to do it. She said they never have enough good foster parents,
especially ones who'll take older kids, so we want to take the classes, get
our home approved, and become foster parents. Emily's out on her own.
You're at school during the week. We've got the room. Your mom said
she'd move her sewing machine and all her sewing and craft stuff and her
computer down to the basement, set it all up down there, so we can set
that room up as another bedroom. We've both got some flexibility with
our work schedules and the ability to work from home some. Gets too
quiet around here with Anthony being the only kid at home. How would
you feel about it?"

"Wow." Cassie was choking back tears as she hugged her father. "I
think it's great. You and Mom would be awesome foster parents. All of
my friends love you and Mom. You're in a position to do it, and like you
said, there are a lot like Alicia and Mary Grace who need what you have
to offer. As for my sermon tomorrow, what you're talking about is right
in line with it."

"Hadn't got around to asking you, Cassie, meant to last night. What
are you preaching on tomorrow?"

"The passage in Luke 4 where Jesus preaches in the synagogue in
Nazareth, quoting from Isaiah 61. Back when I was fifteen and I told

Miss Addie that I was called to preach, she held me close and quoted that passage to me from memory. The first time I talked with Brother Mike about my calling, he opened his Bible to that same passage and talked with me about it. One of the things that passage talks about is "proclaiming release to the captives." I think taking children out of abusive and dangerous situations and giving them a place of refuge where they are safe, nurtured, and well cared for is an excellent example of what it means to "proclaim release to the captives." You just helped me with a sermon illustration. Thanks, Daddy Longlegs!"

"You're welcome. Want me to warm up your little girl pretend coffee?"

"Sounds good. Daddy, I don't know if I ever told you in so many words, meant to if I didn't, but I really appreciate what you and Mom did for Alicia. I appreciate you doing it because she was one of my friends, but I also appreciate what you taught me in the process of helping her, about thinking of others and sharing my blessings. One of my happiest memories growing up is when I went clothes shopping with Mom and Alicia. We were just buying for her, didn't buy anything for me, 'cause I had plenty and didn't need anything right then. I had so much fun helping her pick out some nice new stuff that fit her and looked cute on her, more fun than I ever had buying for myself. You know how Mom can smell a bargain a mile away. We spent a lot, but Alicia had a ton of nice clothes to show for it, more than she'd ever had at one time. I realize now that y'all didn't get any money for taking care of Alicia, and you spent a lot on her because you wanted her to have as nice as the rest of us. Emily always liked to do hair, and she could fix Alicia's hair so pretty. You and Mom were always good to Emily, me, and the Little Brat. When Alicia came to live with us, you and Mom didn't do anything different from what you'd always done, and you didn't treat her any different than the rest of us. You gave her chores like everybody else, but she ate as well as we did, dressed as nice, and got as much attention as the rest of us. She had to get used to how quiet it was most of the time, nobody yelling, cussing, or fighting, people just talking in normal conversational tones.

The only time it got loud was if we were all laughing, cutting up, and carrying on foolishness, or if we got wrapped up in a football or basketball game on TV. Alicia learned to go to sleep at night and not be afraid some creep who smelled like beer, cigarettes, and sweat would try to crawl in bed with her and mess with her."

"Yeah," Jerry commented. "I thank the Lord she told your mom and me what was going on. I had a gut feeling that there was more going on than the fussing and fighting, that's bad enough, but it didn't surprise me when we found out that he was molesting her."

"She told me first, Daddy, and told me I had to keep it a secret. I told her I couldn't keep a secret like that because what he was doing to her was wrong. I told her that you and Mom would help her and she wouldn't be in trouble because she hadn't done anything wrong. I told her that either I'd tell Mom what she told me, or I'd be with her when she told Mom. I was with her when she told Mom."

"Your mom hugged her," Jerry reminisced, "and we both told her that she was a very courageous young woman for speaking up. Your mom told her that her mom's boyfriend had molested her for the last time, and that we were going to call some people who could put a stop to it. Your mom called your Aunt Susan, Alicia told Susan and the other DFCS worker the same thing she told us. Aaron Stewart came out, wanted a female officer to talk to Alicia and didn't have one on duty. He called the Sheriff's Department, and they sent Tamika Barrentine, the same one who hauled Brother Bobby to jail. She's had advanced training in interviewing sexually abused children. She was so good with Alicia, and Alicia told Tamika and Aaron the same thing. Your mom held Alicia all night long that night. When I got up at 5:00 the next morning to get ready for work, your mom was still right here where I'm sitting, holding Alicia, Alicia's head on her chest, both of them sound asleep. We both went to court with Alicia for moral support when she testified against her mom's boyfriend. It helped her a lot to see him brought into the courtroom in shackles and handcuffs, to know he couldn't hurt her any more, and have a jury convict him and the judge send him to prison on the strength of her testimony. It broke our hearts to hear her tell what he had done to her and how long it had been going on, but she was such a good witness, a lot of the jurors were in tears just like we were hearing her testimony. We were so proud of her, the way she stood her ground when the public defender cross-examined her. He knew she was telling the truth, couldn't trip her up, realized he was wasting his time, and gave it up after a couple of minutes. The public defender's a good guy, he was just doing his job trying to defend his client, but he knew his client was toast after Alicia testified. Never will forget the D. A. telling the jury, 'Alicia's testimony is my closing argument. I can add nothing to it. If you believe, as I do, that she is telling the truth, you need to find the defendant guilty on all counts. I rest my case.' The jury returned with a verdict in less than an hour, and Judge Briscoe gave him the maximum sentence on every count. Never will forget us running into Judge Briscoe in the hallway after court. He had tears running down his face, hugged Alicia and said he was proud of her for telling the truth and being such a good witness. We were as proud of her as we are of you when you preach. Both things, Alicia testifying in court and you preaching, come down to the same thing, a young lady who looks people in the eye and tells them the truth."

"Daddy, there's no telling how long that creep would have kept on molesting her if you and Mom hadn't believed Alicia and called DFCS and the police, and she might not have had the courage to testify against him if y'all hadn't been there for her. It didn't take her long to figure out that you were not like her mom's boyfriend. You won her trust and made her feel safe. When she told you what was happening, you believed her and protected her. She got so comfortable with you that she joined us watching Saturday morning cartoons and started calling you Daddy Longlegs just like I did."

"Talking about Alicia, you'll never guess who I ran into this past Thursday. Had to go up to Carrollton to take delivery on a new dump truck the city just bought. They'd just gotten it back from having the dump bed and hydraulics installed. I took Hoyt Barton up there to drive it back to Harrington. Lo and behold, Alicia's mom works in the office at the International truck dealership. She talked to me, seemed really glad to see me. She said nearly losing her only child was a wake-up call for her, helped her realize she didn't need to put up with sorry men drinking and drugging while she worked and mistreating her and her daughter. She got her GED, and she's been working at the truck dealership about two years. She recently got married to a good guy, diesel mechanic who works at the same place, been there about fifteen years, guy lost his first wife to cancer about a year and a half ago. He's got two boys, twelve and fourteen. They live in Carrollton. Alicia lives at home and goes to West Georgia, all of them doing good. I told her that you were going to be preaching this Sunday at Peyton's Chapel. She was so excited, said she couldn't wait to tell Alicia. She knows where the church is, said some of her mother's people are buried there, and they're planning to come to hear you."

"That's great, Daddy. I remember how I cried when Alicia and her mom moved away, and I felt so bad that I lost touch with her and didn't know where she was. I couldn't tell you how many times I've thought about them, wondered whether they were safe, and prayed for them over the past four years. Her mom was sweet, just a good person who had a hard life. I remember Alicia telling me that her mom's dad skipped out when Alicia's mom was eleven or twelve. Alicia's mom quit school as soon as she turned sixteen to help out at home and take care of the younger kids while her mom worked. Got hooked up with a series of men who used and abused her. Alicia had no memory of her father, said as far as she was concerned he was just a name on a piece of paper, the name of a guy who got a seventeen-year-old girl pregnant and flew the coop, only thing he ever contributed was one sperm cell. Talking with Mary Grace, and her identifying with Alicia so much, reminded me how blessed I am. I never wondered who my daddy was. You were always there, and I always knew I could count on you. Never will forget falling off my bike and breaking my arm when I was eight. You took me to the ER in Carrollton while Mom stayed home with Emily and the Little Brat. I remember you holding me and reassuring me while the doctor set my arm and put the cast on it. It was about 2:00 a.m. when we got out of there. We went to

Krystal 'cause it was the first thing we saw open and we were both starving in a pile. We pigged out on Krystal burgers and fries, think I ate about six of those little burgers. I ate a lot to be as little and skinny as I was. You kidded me, said I must have a hollow leg to be able to hold that much. I thought you were serious, you had me thinking one of my legs really was hollow and all of those burgers had settled somewhere down around my ankle. All the people who were working there and most of the customers who came in signed my cast, bunch of law enforcement people, four or five Carrollton police, couple of state troopers, plus assorted creatures of the night. That's my favorite memory of just me and you, eating Krystals at 2:00 a.m. with my Daddy Longlegs."

"Figured you'd forgotten about that," Jerry laughed. "I still think about that, too. You were tough as a little pine knot, I was thankful that you only broke your arm and not your neck or your skull. Still, I've always wanted to protect you and not let anybody hurt you. It's what a daddy longlegs does. Now if somebody outran you in track, scored more points than you on the basketball court, or bumped you down to second place in your class by having a higher grade point average, no problem with that. I'd congratulate them for coming in first and congratulate you for doing your best, still be just as proud of you. No problem with somebody who plays by the rules and comes in ahead of you, but I do have a problem with anybody who's mean to you and deliberately mistreats you or sets out to hurt you. I don't look for fights to get into, pretty easygoing guy, but I wanted to take ol' Brother Bobby down and stomp the living daylights out of him for the way he treated you at the cemetery on Monday."

"I know you did, Daddy, but you don't have to worry about him for a while. I talked to Robert Lanning from the D. A.'s office on Thursday. I told him all about what happened, he said it's a strong case, plenty of witnesses including me, Aaron Stewart, two other ministers, two funeral directors, and three deacons and their wives from Peyton's Chapel. He's going to prosecute him. Said that even if the sexual battery gets plea bargained down to simple battery, he's still looking at some time behind bars, what with the violation of probation for the stuff he already got convicted on in Phillips County. Magistrate set a pretty high bond for him and ordered him to stay away from me. Mr. Lanning said to call 911 if he comes within sight."

"That's good, Cass. I'd still like to have a little fist-to-face meeting with him, though. I'd be more inclined to forgive him after breaking his jaw."

"I don't want you to do that, Daddy, don't want you to get in trouble."

"I know, Cass. I'm not going to fight him. It's just that I don't like people who hurt you or anybody else in our family. I felt that way about Alicia, too, wanted to beat her mom's boyfriend to a bloody pulp for what he did to that child, of course your mom wanted to scratch his eyeballs out first, so he wouldn't have been able to put up much of a fight what with being blind and all after your mom got through with him. Starting to feel protective like that toward Mary Grace, just the nature of a daddy longlegs. Brother Mike and I have had some long conversations about this, several lunches together at the Lonesome Whistle and Uncle Lease's Barbeque around the time you announced your call to preach and the church licensed you. I was raised Church of God, so you know I'm not against women preachers. I think the world of Preacher Simmons from up at Clear Springs, really appreciate the way she's helped and encouraged you. Eleanor Basden, Joyce Baxter's sister, did a fine job as pastor of the Methodist church here in Harrington. She still gets calls to come back to Harrington to do funerals. Everybody I know at the Methodist church always spoke well of her. I got to hear her preach several times, Easter sunrise service, community Thanksgiving service, couple of funerals, very good preacher. I've known her and Ben as far back as I can remember, good people. The few women preachers I know are some of the best. I'd put Preacher Simmons and Eleanor Basden on my short list of the best I ever heard anywhere. You're mighty good to be barely nineteen years old. I've had at least a dozen people who've commented to me this week about how good you did at Miss Addie's funeral. Like I said, I don't have any problems with a woman preacher, wouldn't have any problem with a woman being my pastor, don't have any doubts about your ability to do it and do it well. It's always been your nature to do it well if you do it at all. What I'm concerned about, like I told Brother Mike, I know some people and some churches can be awful mean to preachers, chew 'em up and spit 'em out, then send a pulpit committee out to bring in another one to do the same thing to. Our church has been mighty hard on preachers in years past. It was awful what our church and this town put Franklin Seals and his family through. Your mom and I were in junior high school when all of that went down. You'll have a rougher row to hoe because you're a woman and so many people are against a woman preacher no matter how good she is. You'll have to be twice as good to get anywhere, and you'll still have a lot of doors closed in your face if you stay Baptist 'cause most Baptist churches will only consider men. I know you and Brother Mike have talked about all of that, and you don't have any illusions that it's going to be easy for you. You're going to get hurt along the way and you're going to have to deal with some meanness. Brother Mike helped me work through that. He talked about Romans 8:32 where Paul says that God did not spare his own son, but freely delivered him up for us all, and he asked me, 'Jerry, what if God's greatest concern had been keeping his son from getting hurt?' That's when I realized that, whether you're in the ministry or whatever you do, you're going to get hurt along the way. You're going to encounter meanness and ugliness like you did with Brother Bobby, and I can't always intervene to protect you from it, but you're also going to encounter people like Mary Grace who will accept you, love you, and welcome your ministry. It took me a while to get there, your mom struggled with it, too, for all of the same reasons. We realized we had to let go, trust God to take care of you, and be glad that you're investing your life in something that matters."

"Daddy, you remember out at the cemetery on Monday, Aaron telling me that it was not up to me about pressing charges against Brother Bobby, 'cause he saw what went down and he was going to charge him?"

"Mmmhmm."

"You know what a control freak I can be, thinking I have to orchestrate every little detail on every little thing. It helped me to have a good person I trust tell me that something was out of my hands, beyond my control, and being taken care of by someone else who can handle it better than I can. It's funny to me now that I think about it, Cassie Elise McWhorter, world-class control freak, telling Brother Bobby there are some things he can't control, like who God calls to preach and who conducts services in the cemetery at Peyton's Chapel. Then, the angel of the Lord, wearing a Harrington Police uniform and looking an awful lot like Aaron Stewart, tells me there's something I can't control. You're struggling with the same thing. You want to control what happens to me, keep me from ever getting hurt, and as much as you love me and want to, you can't."

"Good breakfast, Mrs. McWhorter. That was one of the best omelets I've ever had anywhere," Mary Grace commented as she put her plate and silverware in the dishwasher.

"Thanks, glad you enjoyed it, Mary Grace, and please call me Elaine."

"Yeah, there are omelets and then there are momelets," Anthony added. "Momelets are the best."

"Bad pun, Little Brat," Cassie shot back. "You're gonna turn into a daddy longlegs if you keep making corny puns like that. Of course, Miss Addie would have loved it. She said that bad puns and fine chocolates were her two guilty pleasures."

"We haven't made any big plans for today," Elaine spoke to Mary Grace. "Figured you and Cass could hang loose and do what you want or need to do today. Give me whatever clothes you and Cassie need washed, and I'll wash, dry, and fold them for you."

"That's sweet of you to offer, and I'll take you up on it. Everything of mine is in that blue laundry basket in Cassie's room except for the soaking wet stuff of hers and mine that's already in the washer. I've got to do some reading for a couple of my classes this weekend, so I'll probably do that today."

"Yeah, I need to do some of that, too," Cassie added, "and I need to go to my holy place for a while today. The sermon's prepared, but I need to do some praying and meditating to prepare the preacher, preach through it in my mind, probably do that this afternoon. I promised Heather I'd call her sometime this morning, she wants to talk with me before Sunday."

"Call her whenever you want to," Jerry spoke up. "You know where the phone is. Talk as long as you like. That's the reason we got that flat rate long distance plan, so we can call anybody we want and talk as long as we want. The longer you talk, the more we're getting for our money. Anthony and I are going to rake some leaves, do a little yard work this morning, then we're gonna watch the Georgia-Vanderbilt game this afternoon."

"I think I'll go on in a few minutes after I put the clothes in to wash," Elaine said, "and let Martha fix my hair, catch her before she gets too busy."

Cassie pulled up her e-mail on her mom's computer. She had three new messages. The first was from Brother Mike, sent at 12:05 a.m.:

Hey, Cassie,

Karen and I really enjoyed last night with your family and getting to meet Mary Grace. I can't wait to tell our church tomorrow morning about you leading Mary Grace to faith in Christ and baptizing her out at Bailey's Mill where Miss Addie was baptized. Wish I could be out at Peyton's Chapel to hear you. You know our church will be praying for you. You've got as much preaching experience as I had the first time I preached at Clear Springs. Don't know whether this will turn into more than a one-Sunday pulpit supply, but if that's all you get to do, that will be good and we'll be thankful. You will do well. I've heard so many positive comments about your part in Miss Addie's funeral. I am proud to be your pastor and now your fellow minister of the gospel. It has been a pleasure to know you since you were ten years old, and I'll tell anybody that I baptized you! The church is proud of you, and I know Miss Addie would be. Now you've got Deborah Estelle talking about becoming a preacher. Can't wait to talk with you after church tomorrow.

Blessings,
Mike

The second was from Coretta, sent at 6:40 a.m.:

Cassie,

Been up since about 6:00 a.m., Dan got a call from the funeral home answering service, had to go to a nursing home in Carrollton to pick up a body. Dan has tomorrow off, Tommy and his son who's been helping some at the funeral home said they would cover if they got any calls on Sunday. I thought I would go back to sleep after Dan left, but I'm wide awake, so I've been making good use of the time, praying for you and for the service tomorrow at Peyton's Chapel. As Reverend Conway likes to say, "I been wallowing in blessings this morning," just thinking about how good my life is and how richly blessed I am—being married to such a good man, being pregnant, doing something I love for a living, having the friendship of you and your family, meeting Mary Grace and hearing her faith story. The more I sit here and think, the longer my blessing list gets. I'm so excited about singing tomorrow at Peyton's Chapel and getting to hear you preach! Last night with your family and Mary Grace was so good. I'm glad we all had that time together. Your dad's reputation as King of the Grill remains intact.

Love you,
Coretta

The last was from Heather, sent at 8:07 a.m.:

Hey, Cass—

Wide awake here, ready for you to call me anytime, can't wait to talk with you. Olivia likes her breakfast early, got up about 6:00 a.m. to nurse her. Every time I nurse my baby, I think about what Paul wrote in I Thessalonians 2 about his ministry in Thessalonica, being as gentle as a nursing mother. After I put Olivia back down, I sat out on the porch and watched the sun come up over the mountains while Joel cooked breakfast. I love this part of Virginia and our front porch that faces due east. The Lord and I have some good conversations on our front porch. I love living in Wallace and Estelle Coggins' old house. Estelle died before I came here, but I feel like I knew her from hearing Wallace and others in the church talk about her. Not saying this house is haunted or anything, but it's like their spirits linger here in a pleasant sort of way. They were such good people, it's like they sanctified this house for all who live here after them. I'm still in my nightgown and housecoat. My little Wallace is watching cartoons. Joel plans to do some yard work today, rake the leaves, and change the oil on my car and his truck. Call me, I'll be here. Nothing on my agenda this morning but cuddling with my kids and talking with you. I will talk your ears off.

Love you, Little Sister!
Heather

Cassie was about to pick up the phone to call Heather when it rang. "Hello," she answered.

"This is Floyd Williams, pastor at Freeman Valley Baptist Church and moderator of the Mintz County Baptist Association. I need to speak with Cassie McWhorter."

"Speaking. How can I help you?"

"Miss McWhorter, I need to know if you're still planning to preach at Peyton's Chapel tomorrow, 'cause if you are, Peyton's Chapel's gonna have some serious problems with the association."

"Yes, Brother Williams, I still plan to preach there tomorrow. The church invited me, and they have not withdrawn the invitation. Harrington Baptist Church licensed me to preach whenever and wherever I have the opportunity. I get an invitation to preach, I accept it if at all possible."

"And the association withdrew fellowship from Harrington Baptist on account of them licensing you to preach, and we'll do the same with any other church in this association that has you or any other woman in its pulpit."

"So it's okay for a preacher to be a total jerk, beat up on his wife, attack another preacher in the cemetery at a funeral, and have a criminal record in the next county, just as long as the preacher's not a woman?"

"Miss McWhorter, the Bible is clear that God does not call women to preach, and the Southern Baptist Convention spoke very clearly on that a few years ago, said that women should not serve in 'leadership roles entailing ordination.' There is going to be trouble in the association if you go ahead and preach at Peyton's Chapel tomorrow."

"Brother Williams, there's going to be trouble in the association because you're bound and determined to make trouble. If you don't make it over this, you'll make it over something else. You just love a fuss. I agree with Brother Mike, I don't think God pays that much attention to SBC resolutions. As for what the Bible's clear on, Brother Williams, it's pretty clear about preachers not being the kind of people who always want to start a fight or join one in progress. Go ahead and do what you're going to do, I'll go ahead and do what I'm going to do, and Peyton's Chapel is going to go ahead and do what it's going to do. Now, I'm going to end this conversation before I say something I regret." With those words, Cassie hung up the phone, took some slow deep breaths, pondered the question raised by the psalmist in Psalm 94, "How long shall the wicked triumph?" and dialed Heather's number.

Chapter 13

"You look nice in that outfit," Mary Grace commented as Cassie headed the Old Gray Mare north on the Hansonville Highway about 8:30 a.m., an hour and a half before they needed to be at Peyton's Chapel.

"Thanks. You look good, too. I like those colors on you. I wore this dress when I preached my first sermon. Mom made it for the occasion. I'm sentimental about it, and I like the way it fits me. Hard to find things that fit me being so long legged. It's easy to find stuff that would be just right if I were, say, 5' 4" instead of 5' 10". I'm wearing the necklace with the gold cross Miss Addie gave me the Sunday I was baptized, the one her parents gave her when she was baptized in 1908. I think you're as excited about this morning as I am. I know we both woke up before the clock went off. This'll be my first time to preach anywhere other than our church, unless you count preaching to the rocks and trees around Bailey's Mill."

"I'd count that, Cass. You gotta practice somewhere," Mary Grace observed as her hands caressed a new burgundy leather Bible, just like Cassie's, with her name embossed on the cover. "I love my new Bible. I was overwhelmed when your mom came back from getting her hair done and gave it to me. After what's happened the past couple of days, and seeing how much your Bible means to you, I was thinking I need to get one. I meant to buy one if we got out anywhere. Then your mom came in with this beautiful Bible with my name on it. Couldn't believe she'd do that for somebody she just met two days ago. I mean, your folks are sweet, and they've made me feel so welcome, but still, I couldn't believe this. I tried to thank her, but all I could do was hug her and cry."

"She took that as a thank you," Cassie laughed. "You know she's pretty much adopted you."

"Tell me about it. I couldn't believe how comfortable I felt with her and how much we talked while we were cleaning up after the cookout Friday night. You know how guarded I am most of the time, and there I was telling this woman I just met pretty much everything there is to know about me and my family, my whole life story, way more than I meant to tell her. After she'd heard it all, the good, the bad, and the ugly, she gave me a good night hug and kiss, told me she loved me, just like she did with you and Anthony, said she was so glad I came home with you. Then she laughed, gave me another hug, and said, 'I'm glad Cassie brought you home in more ways than one.'"

"I told Mom how much I appreciated her buying you a Bible," Cassie commented, "and she said, 'Well, Cass, she needed one. God's up to something good with Mary Grace. I want to do all I can to encourage her.'"

As Cassie bore right onto Bailey's Mill Road at Pulliam's Store/ Gloryland Way Missionary Baptist Church, Mary Grace exclaimed, "Stop the car, Cassie! I've got to get a picture of that sign!"

"What sign?" Cassie asked as she braked hard and pulled the OGM off onto the side of the road. "Give me a minute here, Mary Grace, let me see if I can get my heart restarted. You scared the living daylights out of me."

"Sorry, Cass. See the sign for the church that's in that old store building? They put it up just for you." Mary Grace quickly retrieved the camera she kept in her purse and started to get out of the car. "Check it out. It says, 'No women preachers.'"

"Gotta see this," Cassie said as she shook her head in disbelief, got out of the car, and followed Mary Grace across the road. She remembered seeing the sign Monday on the way out to Peyton's Chapel describing the church's doctrinal stances, "Independent, Fundamental, Premillennial, Soul-Winning, King James Version Bible." Now, someone, obviously not a professional sign painter, had climbed up there and added, "No Women Preachers." All Cassie could do was laugh and tell Mary Grace to get some good pictures.

"Cass, on our way back to Mercer tonight, you've got to bring me up to speed on what all that other stuff means, but 'No Women Preachers' is pretty damn clear. I'd say you won't get invited to preach here any time soon," Mary Grace commented as they got back in the car. "We need to make them a sign that says 'No Girls Allowed' and post it on the door."

"You wouldn't dare." Cassie paused. "Or would you?"

"Why wouldn't I? I've got some bright red lipstick in my purse. You got a sheet of paper? Hey, instead of A-L-L- O-W-E-D, I'm gonna make it A-L-O-U-D!"

"Oh, wow, Mary Grace, that's good! No Girls Aloud! I love it! That's way better than Dad's and Brother Mike's corny puns. Miss Addie would like that one. I hope they get it, be a shame if it goes over their heads and somebody has to explain it to them. You're really gonna do this, aren't you? Look in that green binder in the back seat, just remember, I didn't see this and I know nothing about it." Cassie was about to hyperventilate from laughing so hard as Mary Grace printed "NO GIRLS ALOUD!" in blood-red lipstick on a sheet of notebook paper. She rummaged around in the glove box of the OGM, discovered the big roll of duct tape that Jerry put there in case Cassie had some emergency on the road that could be fixed with duct tape, looked around to be sure there were no witnesses, and then, like a latter-day Martin Luther, sprinted across the road, duct-taped her handmade sign to the door of Pulliam's Store/Gloryland Way Missionary Baptist Church, just above the metal sign proclaiming the gospel truth that "Colonial is Good Bread," and snapped a picture of her handiwork. Mary Grace was breathless as she jumped back in the car and clicked the seat belt. Cassie moved the shifter down to drive, whispered "Saint Addie, you didn't see this," pulled back out onto Bailey's Mill Road, giving it a little more gas than she needed to, way more than Miss Addie ever gave it, enough to kick up some dust and bark the tires a little as the front wheels came off the dirt and gripped pavement. "You know," Cassie mused, "I always wondered how it felt to drive the getaway car and speed away from the scene of the crime. Thank you for giving me that opportunity."

"You're welcome, Cass." Mary Grace's voice took a more deliberate, serious tone as she continued, "I know I'm new to all of this and I've still got a lot to learn, but it sounds like some people think it'd be better for me not to learn about Jesus at all than to have me learn about him from a woman."

"It looks that way to me, too, Mary Grace. I don't understand it either. And they'd rather see a little church like Peyton's Chapel close its doors and die than to see it do well with a woman preacher. It's like the time Jesus healed a woman on the Sabbath. She'd suffered for years, so you'd think everybody could just be glad the poor woman was healed, but if that's what you're thinking, you haven't had many dealings with legalistic religion. Some of them stirred up a stink because Jesus went against their rules and healed her on the Sabbath. So, yeah, you'd think all Christians could just be glad people are hearing about Jesus, but noooo, it can't be that simple. You know our church got kicked out of the Mintz County Association about this time last year after they licensed me to preach. Same thing happened up there in Virginia when Heather's church called her as pastor. Sanders County Association gave them the boot. I went to the associational meeting when they had the vote on kicking us out, only day I missed school my senior year. I couldn't stop them from doing it, but at least I made them say all of the hateful, ugly stuff about me to my face. They'd been gunning for us ever since Heather preached the revival here seven years ago, more so since we elected some women deacons. I guess licensing me was the last straw."

"Now, explain to me what licensing means," Mary Grace asked. "Remember, I'm not fluent in churchspeak."

"I'll show you the certificate when we get back home. It's hanging in my bedroom. It's like a letter of recommendation from Harrington Baptist Church to other churches saying, 'she's ours, we know her, we believe God called her to preach, and she has our blessing to preach whenever and wherever she has the opportunity.'"

"But it's up to other churches whether to invite you and give you a chance to preach, and each individual church does pretty much what it wants to?"

"You got it. If you heard me being a little short with somebody on the phone yesterday, I got an unpleasant phone call from Floyd Williams, pastor at Freeman Valley and moderator of the Mintz County Baptist Association, warning me there'd be trouble in the association if I go ahead and preach today. He led the charge against us after I was licensed, so I told that turkey there'd always be trouble in the association as long as he was in it, because he was determined to stir it up. Miss Addie would call that 'speaking the truth in love with both barrels.'"

"Proud of you for standing up to him."

"Thanks, Mary Grace. Most preachers, including the ones who are not in favor of women preachers, are good people, but there are some bullies, some mean people, in the ministry. I could just see the news story in *Baptists Today*, 'Female Preacher Stomps Living Daylights Out of Associational Bully.' I was so furious after I got off the phone with that clown. I wanted to go after him so bad I could taste it. It helped me a lot to talk with Heather after that. She calmed me down, talked me down off the ceiling. Heather's good at that. She agreed ol' Floyd could benefit from an attitude adjustment, said she hopes somebody gives him one sooner rather than later, and she agreed that it'd be nice to see him get stomped by a girl, but she said she didn't think it'd look good on my resume for me to do it. I want you to meet Heather. You know how much she's encouraged me and how close we are. She's one of the best preachers I've ever heard, excellent pastor, everything I want to be. Brother Mike's been great, couldn't have been more supportive, but it's helped me to know a woman who does what I'm called to do and does it well. Right after I talked with Heather and she prayed with me on the phone, I had a pleasant surprise. Brad Terry, new pastor at Taylor's Crossroads, called. I've never met him, heard Brother Mike speak of him, seems like a good guy. He called to say he was praying for me and for Peyton's Chapel, said he didn't agree with what the association did when they kicked us out.

Said he's thankful for anybody, man or woman, who preaches the gospel. As for the unpleasant call from Floyd Williams, it helps to know some history," Cassie observed. "Andrew Jennings, pastor over at Zion A. M. E."

"What's A. M.E.?" Mary Grace asked.

"African Methodist Episcopal. Andy's a good guy, played football with my dad in high school, had part in Miss Addie's funeral. Miss Addie was his first grade teacher. He's known Floyd since high school, told me Floyd's daddy was real big in the KKK and that Floyd was one of the few white students who tried to make trouble when the schools were integrated back in the '60s. Andy said, by the time Floyd was grown, the Klan had pretty much died out, so he turned to religion as an outlet for his meanness."

"Glad I met you and your family and all of the folks who came over Friday night before I ran into any of the mean ones," Mary Grace observed. "If I'd met the mean and angry ones first, or the ones who want to lay a long list of rules on me, I'd've run the other way. I hope Peyton's Chapel's not like that."

"Don't think it is. The Baileys, the older couple I told you about, she's a cousin to Miss Addie, she and her husband impress me as good, decent, kindhearted people. My impression of the church is based on my impression of them, that and knowing a lot of them are kin to Miss Addie. They had a mean, crazy preacher for a while, doesn't mean the church is like that. I think they're glad to be rid of him because they're better than that. I'm going into this believing the best about them."

"Are we stopping at our holy place?" Mary Grace asked. "It's not just your holy place now. It's mine, too."

"That's one reason I wanted to come this early, figured we'd both want to stop there and have time to visit Miss Addie's grave before church." Cassie put on her left turn signal and guided the car onto the dirt road leading to the level clearing up near the ruins of the mill. After she parked the car, Cassie took off her dress shoes and put on the old ragged pair of sneakers she kept in the car behind her seat. Mary Grace watched silently as Cassie nimbly scampered over the rocks, down to the edge of the water, where she bent over, cupped her hands, scooped up some Salyers Creek baptismal water, and let the Baptist holy water run through her fingers. After a while, despite terrain that was not friendly to the shoes she was wearing, Mary Grace cautiously made her way down to where Cassie stood, put an arm around her shoulders, and hugged her.

"Cass," Mary Grace began, searching for words, "you remember telling me God hears my prayers because he loves me, not because I'm good at praying? You said you'd as soon have me praying for you as anybody you know?"

"Yeah, Mary Grace, I do. It's the truth. I meant every word of it."

"And I believe it. I love you, Cass, and I want to pray for you now."

Cassie reciprocated the embrace. "I love you, too, Mary Grace. Please do pray for me. I can't think of anything that would help me more."

"Dear God," Mary Grace began deliberately, "you know I just got baptized two days ago and this is all new to me. I'm going to pray anyway and trust you to hear me and answer my prayer. Thank you for bringing Cassie into my life. God, most of what I know about you is what I've learned from Cassie, her family, and her friends. I don't know much about the Bible, but I want to learn. Thank you for my new Bible. Thank you for giving Cassie a chance to preach today. I've got so much to learn about this whole religion and faith thing. Help Cassie make it clear for me. Lord, help Peyton's Chapel. They're so discouraged. They don't have many people or much money, and they've been beaten down by a preacher who was mean and didn't love them. Help them know how much Cassie loves them and how much you love them and want to help them. Let Cassie's sermon today encourage them and give them hope. In Jesus' name. Amen."

It was a while before Cassie composed herself enough to form the words, "Amen. Thank you, Mary Grace. Thank you, Lord." They slowly released their embrace, and Cassie helped Mary Grace steady herself as she made her way back over the rocks in her dress shoes. Cassie told Mary Grace, "God's going to grant all you asked for and more." Then, they walked silently back to the car, and Cassie headed the OGM back out onto Bailey's Mill Road. They were the first ones to arrive at Peyton's Chapel. It was about 9:30 a.m., a half hour before Sunday School time, so Cassie drove on through the church parking lot, onto the road through the cemetery, and up to the top of the hill, parking as close as she could to the Peyton-Aldridge cemetery plot. She adjusted the rear view mirror to look at herself and retrieved her compact from her purse. "I'm glad we're early, and glad I don't use a whole lot of makeup. You can tell I've been crying, can't you? Need to take a minute and redo my makeup—or war paint as Daddy and the Little Brat call it."

"You and me both," Mary Grace acknowledged as she rummaged for the compact in her purse. "At least it was happy tears. Soon as we fix our faces, we can visit Miss Addie's grave before people start getting here. I want to do that. I'm starting to feel like I knew her. This sounds crazy, but I remember when she was baptized at our holy place."

"Mary Grace, I'd say it sounds crazy, but you and I are about the same age, and I remember it, too. Sounds as crazy as a nineteen-year-old girl thinking God's calling her to preach, doesn't it? Miss Addie said one reason God let her live so long was so she could tell me I'm not crazy for thinking God called me to preach."

Cassie and Mary Grace stood silently at the foot of Miss Addie's grave for a few minutes before Mary Grace spoke, "Saint Addie, you've already been praying for us. Keep up the good work!"

"Amen," Cassie concurred. Then, they got back in the car, and Cassie drove back down to the freshly graveled church parking lot and found a shady parking place. J. T. and Josie Bailey pulled in and parked beside them on Cassie's side.

"Mornin', Preacher," Josie greeted Cassie as they got out simultaneously and hugged each other. "Sure is good to see you, hon. Everybody that was at Addie's funeral's been talking about how good you did, especially being as close as you were to her and it being your first funeral. If all the people who told me they're coming show up, we'll have more people than we've had in a long time. Can't wait to hear you. And who is your friend here with you?"

"Mary Grace Tillison, my roommate at Mercer," Cassie replied. "She came home with me this weekend so she could hear me preach. This is Josie and J. T. Bailey."

"Good to meet you, Mary Grace," Josie replied.

"Welcome to Peyton's Chapel, hope you feel at home with us."

"Glad you're here with us, Mary Grace. J. T. stands for Jedediah Tumlin, named for my Grandpa Tumlin," J. T. added, "so you see why I've always gone by my initials." J. T. and Josie hugged Mary Grace as though they had known her all of her life. "So where are you from, Mary Grace?"

"Elberton, up on the South Carolina line."

"Know where Elberton is. I retired from the State Highway Department, big quarry up there's where we got a lot of our gravel. No telling how many tons of Elbert County rock are under the roads you've been riding on." As they spoke, J. T. opened the trunk of their car, and Cassie and Mary Grace helped them carry all the food they brought for the dinner into the kitchen and fellowship hall.

As they made their way from the fellowship hall up to the sanctuary, J. T. commented to Cassie, "I'm looking forward to Sunday School this morning. All of the adults are going to meet together for Sunday School in the sanctuary, like we did for years. For the past two years, I've been teaching the men, and Myrtle Hill's been teaching the women because our former pastor had a dying duck fit over a woman teaching men, had to set us straight about it. I asked him, what about Priscilla teaching Apollos over there in Acts? He got all flustered, said she might'a done it but she didn't have any business doing it, so we divided the class, separated the men and women, just to pacify him. We shouldn't have done it. It just made him worse, just made him look for more things to set us straight about. If you disagreed with him about anything, you didn't believe the Bible and you probably weren't saved, to hear him tell it. Last year when the association kicked Harrington Baptist out for licensing you to preach, Brother Bobby got so worked up I thought he was gonna have a stroke 'cause he voted in favor of kicking y'all out, and all the rest of our messengers, including Josie and me, voted against it. Made him furious that we didn't vote like he did. That's all he preached about for five or six weeks after that, women keeping silent in church and not allowing a woman to usurp authority over a man. Didn't matter what text he started with, he could start with John 3:16 or the twenty-third Psalm and end up on that subject. Now he's gone, so we're bringing all the adults back together in one class like it used to be. I look forward to hearing Myrtle teach again about as much as I look forward to hearing you preach. She was our teacher for years before Brother Bobby came, lot better teacher than I am. She knows the Bible and knows how to teach, taught history at Phillips County High School about forty years. We figured a woman preacher wouldn't object to a woman teaching men. I don't mind filling in once in a while, but Myrtle's the best Bible teacher I ever sat under. She loves to teach, and it shows."

"Look forward to hearing her," Mary Grace commented.

"Me, too," Cassie added, "and yeah, I'm okay with a woman teaching men."

"And we're looking forward to hearing a preacher who'll preach the gospel and try to build us up instead of beating us up," Josie replied as she began introducing Cassie and Mary Grace to people who were arriving for Sunday School.

"Two young women made a big impression on me this past Monday at the funeral for my wife's cousin, Addie Jane Peyton Aldridge, one with her singing and one with her preaching," J. T. began the introduction. "Both of them impressed me as people who love the Lord Jesus Christ.

We're blessed to have them here today. Coretta Brinkley Groves, who sang so beautifully at Addie's funeral, will come in just a moment to sing, and then another gifted young woman, Cassie McWhorter, will come to preach. Until Monday at Addie's funeral, I'd never heard a woman preach. This young lady's only nineteen years old, but God's got his hand on her. No doubt in my mind that God called her to preach, and I don't think there'll be any doubt in your mind after you hear her. She brought a fine message at Addie's funeral, but something else impressed me as much as her preaching, and that was the way she handled herself after our former pastor attacked her in the cemetery Monday, the way she pulled herself together and did the committal after that. I'd've understood if she'd asked one of the other ministers to do it after what happened, but she did it and did it well. Sister Cassie was licensed about a year ago by Harrington Baptist Church, where Brother Mike Westover is pastor. She's a student at Mercer, preparing herself for the work God called her to. I talked with our other two deacons, they felt the same way I did, so we asked her to preach today, and we're thankful she accepted the invitation. We're pleased to have so many of Sister Cassie's family and friends with us today. Sister Coretta Groves will come to sing for us now. She's a kindergarten teacher at Miss Addie's School, where she makes good use of her musical gifts with the children she teaches. After she sings, Sister Cassie McWhorter will bring us the word of God."

"Thank you, Deacon Bailey," Coretta began. "My husband and I loved Miss Addie. She was the matron of honor at our wedding when she was ninety-nine years old. Cassie and her family are dear friends of ours. When Cassie told me that she'd been invited to preach today, I asked her if she'd like for me to sing, because I was going to be there anyway to hear her. I was already thinking of this song when Cassie asked that I sing it. It's one of my favorites that I've sung many times, written by John Newton, who wrote "Amazing Grace." I learned it from Miss Addie. She learned it as a little girl here at Peyton's Chapel." Coretta closed her eyes for a second and took a deep breath. Needing no instrument to give her the key of G, she began singing *a capella* in her powerful mezzo-soprano voice,

> How sweet the name of Jesus sounds,
> In a believer's ear.
> It soothes her sorrows, heals her hurts,
> And drives away her fears,
>
> It makes the wounded spirit whole,
> And soothes the troubled breast,
> 'Tis manna to the hungry soul,
> And to the weary, rest.
>
> Dear Name, the rock on which I build,
> My shield and hiding place,
> My never-failing treasury filled
> With boundless stores of grace!
>
> Jesus, my Husband, Shepherd, Friend,
> O Prophet, Priest, and King,
> My Lord, my Life, my Way, my End!
> Accept the praise I bring.

"I'm delighted to be here today," Cassie began. "I love to preach! Proclaiming the gospel is the greatest privilege ever given to anyone, and God gave it to me! Wow, I get to do what angels only wish they could do! It overwhelms me when I try to think about it. I don't deserve it, I did nothing to earn this privilege, but it's all about grace, not what any of us might deserve. The apostle Paul, in II Corinthians, reminds us that 'we have this treasure in earthen vessels, that the surpassing greatness of the power may be of God and not from ourselves.' This is my first time to preach anywhere other than my home church, unless you count preaching to the rocks and trees around Bailey's Mill. My roommate, Mary Grace, said we should count that because one has to practice somewhere! I appreciate all of you coming today. I have a lot of family and friends here today, including some friends I haven't seen in a long time. Bless your heart, Alicia Givens! Today's the first time I've seen you since you moved away when we were in the ninth grade. Love you, Alicia! So glad we connected again, appreciate you and your family coming down from Carrollton. It's an honor to preach at this good place. Thank you for singing, Coretta. I love you, love the song, and love the way you sing it!

"In addition to the people here today, we have brothers and sisters in other places praying for us. I've received messages of prayerful support and encouragement for us from my pastor, Mike Westover, at Harrington Baptist Church, Pastor Brad Terry at Taylor's Crossroads Baptist Church, Pastor Andrew Jennings at Zion A. M. E. Church, Pastor Henry Conway at Greater New Hope Progressive Missionary Baptist Church, Pastor Janice Hall at Harrington United Methodist Church, and Pastor Heather Simmons Moore at Clear Springs Baptist Church at Ledford, Virginia. We're all immersed in the love of God and the love of brothers and sisters in Christ. The Spirit of the living God is in and among us! You're hungry to hear the gospel, and I'm eager to preach it!" With self-effacing humor, Cassie added, "So eager, in fact, that I forgot to change back into my good shoes when Mary Grace and I got here this morning. I put on these old sneakers when Mary Grace and I stopped on our way here this morning at our holy place below the dam at Bailey's Mill, where Miss Addie was baptized in 1908, where I often go to think, meditate, and pray, and where Mary Grace gave me the honor of baptizing her this past Friday evening. I mostly keep these grungy old things in the car for when I'm out at Bailey's Mill. I just noticed while Coretta was singing that I still had them on!" Cassie was relieved that the congregation was laughing with her, not at her. "Can't believe I did that! Too late to worry about it now. I really do have a good pair of shoes in my car. At least my feet will be comfortable while I'm preaching." As the laughter died out, Cassie continued, "So, you know your preacher is a flawed, very human nineteen-year-old girl who makes a very audacious claim: The Spirit of the Lord is upon me. He has anointed me to proclaim the good news of Jesus Christ.

"I know. It may be hard for you to believe. I had a hard time believing it myself. Every time we think we've got God figured out, he throws us a curve ball, like choosing a teenage girl from Nazareth to give birth to the Messiah, or calling a teenage girl from Harrington, Georgia, to preach the gospel. You may have grown up thinking God can't call girls to preach. Miss Addie was the first person I told that God was calling me to preach. I was fifteen at the time. I told her, 'Miss Addie, you're probably going to think I'm crazy when I tell you this, but God is calling me to preach.' She said, 'Cassie, I don't think you're crazy. I've known a long time that you were called to preach. I've been praying that you'd get around to telling me before I die.' She held me close and quoted the passage that Mrs. Bailey read a few minutes ago, my text for today, from the fourth chapter of Luke's gospel. She said, 'That's why the Lord's let me live so long, so I could be here to tell you that you're not crazy for thinking you're called to preach.' She had a gift of discernment that enabled her to know that the Spirit of the Lord is indeed upon the little girl who used to ride her bike over to her house almost every day. Her powerful blessing will go with me for the rest of my life.

"Perhaps you never met me prior to Miss Addie's funeral, but you know of me. You've seen my picture many times in the sports section of *The Harrington Courier* when I was in high school. You may know my parents, or you may have known my grandparents. You at least know my people if you've been in Mintz County very long. The McWhorters and my mother's people, the Whitmires, have been in this county since before the Civil War when it was called Ferguson County. Captain Cicero Mintz, for whom the county was renamed after the war, was one of my three-times-great grandfathers on my mother's side. You may be among the many who were baptized in Salyers Creek. My grandmother McWhorter was a Salyers. Between the McWhorters, the Whitmires, the Salyers, and the Mintzes, I'm probably some kind of kin to a pretty high percentage of the people in this county, including some of you here today. My parents have known each other since they were little children. I have to trace back five generations to get out of Mintz and Phillips Counties. I'm as connected to this place as a person can be.

"That's how it was for Jesus in the synagogue in Nazareth. That synagogue in Nazareth was like any small town or rural church today, with lots of family connections and families that had been there for generations. When Jesus read those familiar words from Isaiah 61 and then declared, 'Today, this scripture has been fulfilled in your hearing,' his words fell on the ears of people who had known him all of his life—siblings, cousins, aunts and uncles, classmates, and childhood playmates. They knew him, or thought they did. Some of them lived in houses that he had helped build. They'd seen him up high, walking the top of a wall, guiding rafters into place. They knew him as Joseph's son. They assumed that he'd follow Joseph's trade the way Joseph followed his father's trade.

"They were so proud of him when he stood and read that familiar, beloved passage of scripture! Don't you love to hear scripture read well, read by someone who makes good eye contact, enunciates clearly, and speaks in a strong, confident voice, as Mrs. Bailey did when she read our text today? All language was spoken before it was written, and all scripture was written before the printing press was invented and long before it was possible for everyone to have his or her own copy. That's why all scripture was written to be read aloud and read publicly. At the time the scriptures were written, one who could read well was a valued member of the synagogue or church! All who love the scriptures love to hear scripture read well.

"But then, Jesus went beyond a beautiful reading of the text. He declared, 'Today this scripture is fulfilled in your hearing.' Today. This scripture. In your hearing.

"All of us believe that God did great things in the past. Time and again, God went beyond what was humanly possible to deliver his people. Over and over, God made a way out of no way. In the Old Testament, the exodus is the central event in the story of redemption. In the New Testament, the cross and the resurrection are the central events in the story of redemption. The Jewish observance of Passover, and our observances of Holy Week, Easter, and the Lord's Supper are all about remembering what God did for us in the past. And we need to remember. When we take the bread and the cup together at Harrington Baptist Church, my pastor, Brother Mike Westover, often speaks a single word— Remember—as we eat the bread and drink the cup. Remembering is important. That's why we have rituals that are all about helping us remember.

"Our faith is also informed and sustained by the hope that God will do more great things in the future. Hope is a word that we often use loosely to mean roughly the same thing as 'wish.' That's not how the New Testament writers use the word. When Paul writes to Titus and speaks about our 'blessed hope,' in the next phrase he defines that hope as, 'the appearing of the glory of our great God and Savior, Jesus Christ.' Hope in the New Testament means a specific promise of God upon which we base our faith, or the confident expectation that God will do as he has promised. That hope is especially comforting to us when we go through difficult times, when we lay our loved ones to rest, and when you come to the place of realizing that you're not going to live much longer. Miss Addie said that she reached the point that she rarely saw an obituary for someone her age; all of them were for younger people. We are right to expect God to act in the future, and to trust Jesus' promise, 'I go to prepare a place for you, and if I go, I will come again to receive you unto myself, that where I am, there you may be also.'

"We can be comfortable with a God who has done great things in the past and will do great things in the future, or does great things somewhere else, but we are often terrified by the prospect of God acting in the present and in this place. God wouldn't let me preach this without first experiencing it. Thursday evening and again Friday evening, I had an encounter with this God who refuses to stay in the past or future or some other place and insists on taking over the present time and place. I have the permission of my friend Mary Grace Tillison to share this with you. Thursday evening, God let it be known that he was in charge of the present moment and place, and I got to be on holy ground with Mary Grace in our dorm room at Mercer as she began believing in and following Jesus. Friday evening, on our way into Harrington, I took the short cut through Bailey's Mill Road instead of going through Hansonville. I brought Mary Grace by here and showed her the church where I'd been invited to preach. Then, as we crossed the bridge over Salyers Creek, I pointed out my holy place at Bailey's Mill where Miss Addie was baptized ninety years ago. Mary Grace asked that we stop, so we did. We got out and walked around, and we made our way down to the edge of the water. I told her that Miss Addie's uncle, Preacher Tim Nestor, baptized her between the piers of the old bridge. Without saying anything, Mary Grace took off her shoes and socks and started to wade out toward the deeper water between the old bridge piers. I asked her what she was doing, and she said she needed to be baptized and wanted me to do it. I told her I'd never baptized anybody before. She said she knew that and she wanted to be my first one. I started to tell her I wasn't ordained yet and didn't know whether I could do that, but I knew what Miss Addie would say to those objections. By then, we were chest deep in ice water, and we'd've both been dead from hypothermia by the time I explained ordination to her. There you go, God! You just won't stay in the past or future or somewhere else, will you? You have to take over the here and now! So I had the privilege of baptizing Mary Grace. Did we break the rules? Maybe we did, but we serve a God who delights in playing havoc with the rules! Mary Grace, you may be a new Christian, but I am learning from you. You and God taught me what Jesus tried to teach the people in the synagogue in Nazareth—this present moment belongs to 'the year of God's favor.'

"In this present moment, in the year of God's favor, I proclaim a message that is good news to the poor. A gospel that is not good news for poor people is not the gospel of Jesus Christ. Last summer, my church, along with Greater New Hope Baptist, Zion A. M. E., Harrington United Methodist, and Miracle Temple Church of God in Christ, partnered with Habitat for Humanity and a family in Harrington to build a house. The family has a house payment that is no more than they were paying in rent on a run-down leaky trailer that was impossible to heat or cool, and they have a path out of poverty. Now the body of Christ is stronger because some of us learned that the gospel must be good news for poor people or it is no gospel at all. Now the body of Christ is stronger because that whole family we partnered with is part of it—they are now faithful members of Zion A. M. E. They believed the gospel when they saw people acting out the gospel. We who live comfortably often think of the poor in terms of them and us. At the heart of the gospel is the truth that God came in Jesus Christ, took on our humanity, and walked among us. When we enter the world of poor people and walk among them, when we learn that there is more to them than their socioeconomic status, when we come to know poor people as brothers and sisters in Christ, they are no longer 'them.' They are part of 'us,' and we see them differently and treat them differently! We find that the giving goes both ways, and we find that they have some things to offer that we need. We learn that we need poor people in our fellowship to have a healthy church. They receive a new dignity, a new hope, and a place of belonging. They have the opportunity to discover and exercise their spiritual gifts and to become assets to the church. Someone who can play a guitar and sing with the children or be an effective deacon or Sunday School teacher can build up the church as much, possibly more, than someone who can drop big checks in the offering plate. And that is good news for all of us!

"In this year of God's favor, I proclaim a gospel that is about recovery of sight to the blind. In the time and place of Jesus' public ministry, it was very common for people to lose their sight due to eye infections that are now preventable or treatable, and blindness usually translated directly into abject poverty. To compound the problem, people who were blind or had some other impairment were commonly believed to be under some punishment from God. In John 9, when Jesus and his disciples encounter a man who was blind from birth, the disciples wanted to know who sinned, this man or his parents, for him to be born blind. As Jesus healed this man's physical blindness, he revealed far worse spiritual blindness. To this day, only Jesus can cure that kind of blindness! In healing this man's physical blindness, Jesus reveals the sort of blindness that is able to see problems but not people—the blindness that sees the irrelevant questions of who to blame for the man's condition, but is totally unable to focus on the man himself, unable to focus on what Jesus focuses on and see what Jesus sees. Jesus reveals the sort of blindness that can spot a violation of rules or tradition a mile away, but can't see the obvious work of God at point-blank range! When Jesus healed the man who was blind from birth, some people actually got upset because he was working on the Sabbath! Talk about blindness! They could zero in on the Sabbath violation with hawk-eye precision, but they couldn't see and celebrate the blatantly obvious work of God—a once-blind man who can now see—standing squarely in front of them! In this year of God's favor, Jesus is healing us of the inability to see what is really important and see people the way God sees them!

"In this year of God's favor, I proclaim a gospel that is about releasing captives and liberating the oppressed. I'm not just saying this because they're here today. I am blessed to have two awesome parents who love and follow the Lord Jesus Christ! I just learned this weekend that my parents are acting on this part of the gospel. So many children are captive and oppressed in situations where they are deprived of basic needs, lacking the nurture they need to thrive, being physically abused, or being sexually abused. My sister is married and out on her own, and I'm away at school during the week. My fifteen-year-old brother is the only child still at home all the time. Mom and Dad are taking the classes and doing what they need to do to be approved as DFCS foster parents! Some children and teenagers who are in home environments that threaten to destroy them are going to find refuge in the home that nurtured me, my sister, and my brother, the home that has been a place of grace for so many of my friends. For some of those children, the entire direction of their lives will be changed! In offering their home as a place of safety and nurture, they are exemplifying the power of the gospel. In the safety of their home, some of those children will find the ultimate safety and nurture that is found in Jesus Christ our Lord. I anticipate that my pastor, Mike Westover, will get to baptize some of those children! My parents want to be a part of releasing the captives and liberating the oppressed because Jesus has set them free. They have long since been freed from the bondage of living only for themselves and they have discovered the joy of living for the one who loved us and gave himself for us!

"Whoa! This gospel is powerful stuff! So powerful that people are terrified by the prospect of its raw power being unleashed here and now. That's why some of the people in Nazareth wanted to throw Jesus off a cliff! That's why we're more comfortable with a God who will keep his mighty works in the past or the future or do them somewhere else. The gospel Jesus announced, the gospel that I have the privilege of proclaiming, is that God is taking charge of here and now. This gospel is the power of God unto salvation for all who believe! When this gospel is proclaimed and lived full-strength, poor people who are now nameless and faceless become our brothers and sisters and we who think we have so much are enriched and amazed by what those who have less can bring to the table! When this gospel is proclaimed and lived full-strength, our eyes are opened to see people as God sees them. We are able to recognize the activity of God in our midst, and upholding people becomes more important than upholding the rules. When this gospel is proclaimed and lived full-strength, people are freed from bondage and oppression so they can enter into the liberty of the children of God!

"Today. This scripture. Fulfilled. In your hearing. Thanks be to God! Amen."

J. T.'s voice was choked with emotion as he announced, "It sure is good to see a crowd in God's house this morning. Sister Coretta, thank you for singing so beautifully!" Cassie had taken a seat on the front pew. J. T. motioned for her to come and stand with him. As he put his arm around her shoulders and hugged her, he continued, "Sister Cassie, God bless you! Thank you! Excellent message! I guess I'm putting you on the spot, but as you were concluding your message, I turned around and asked Brother Arnie and Brother Henry, our other two deacons, if they were thinking the same thing I was thinking. I knew I'd heard 'amens' from both of them while you were preaching, and they both said 'yes.' Our bylaws for calling a pastor call for us to hear the candidate three Sundays and vote on the third Sunday. Sister Cassie, will you come and preach for us the next two Sundays and then let us vote after the service on Sunday, November 1, on calling you as pastor of Peyton's Chapel Baptist Church?"

"Somebody got some Kleenex handy?" Cassie asked, fighting back tears. "I wasn't expecting anything like this. I thought at the most I might supply a Sunday or two until you found somebody."

"We found somebody," J. T. laughed, "and she's standing right here beside me."

Cassie took the pack of Kleenex that Josie Bailey handed her, dried her tears, and took a deep breath. "I accept your invitation."

"Thank you, Sister Cassie. I want to invite all of our visitors to stay and eat with us. Plenty of food, and we appreciate all of you who have helped prepare such a delicious meal. Preacher, I'll ask you and your family, Sister Mary Grace, Sister Coretta, and Brother Daniel to move to the head of the line so you'll have a chance to eat before everybody starts talking to you. I'm going to ask Sister Cassie's father, Deacon Jerry McWhorter, to pronounce our benediction and offer our thanksgiving for the food. Brother Jerry..."

Chapter 14

"Excellent sermon, Preacher. Big improvement over what we've been used to. I'm glad you're coming back next Sunday," Myrtle Hill commented as she hugged Cassie between bites of banana pudding. "I'm going to vote in favor of calling you."

"Thank you, and I enjoyed the Sunday School class. You were well prepared, and we had some good discussion. I can tell that you love teaching."

"Lord knows I did it long enough," Myrtle laughed. "Don't know how to stop. I'm glad to have all the adults back together instead of having the men and women separated. I call it the 'Eighteen to Glory Class,' men and women, all ages. Some of our younger members who haven't been in a while are here this morning, glad they were in Sunday School. Mary Grace, you brought up some good questions about the lesson, some I hadn't anticipated, stirred up some good discussion. That means there's some thinking and learning going on. I want you to come back. You're good for us."

"I'll definitely be back," Mary Grace responded. "This is all new to me, don't know much about the Bible but I want to learn. I feel at home here, and Cassie's folks treat me like one of their own. Won't be able to be here every Sunday, have to go up and see my folks at Elberton once in a while, but I'll be back as much as I can."

"You young ladies are at a fine school," Myrtle continued. "I graduated from Tift down at Forsyth, which closed a few years ago and merged with Mercer. My late husband, J. B. Hill, John Bunyan Hill, was a Mercer alumnus, class of '49, taught at Hansonville Junior High thirty-two years, principal there when he died. I'm from up at Rome, we met when I took a teaching job in Phillips County. I was Myrtle Davey before

I married. All of my friends and family teased me when I married a Hill, because Myrtle Hill's the name of the big cemetery down at the south end of Broad Street in Rome. President Woodrow Wilson's first wife was from Rome, and she's buried there. Anyway, my mother-in-law was a Nestor, she and Addie were first cousins on her mother's side. As long as your people've been in Mintz County, you're bound to be kin to some of us one way or another."

"Wouldn't doubt it," Cassie acknowledged. "My grandmother Whitmire was working on the Whitmires and Mintzes when she died, and Uncle Dan Whitmire, lives in Columbus, he's worked on it some. One of my cousins has done some research on the McWhorters and Salyers. I want to learn more about all of that one of these days. Right now, I've got to get myself through four years at Mercer and then three years of seminary. The genealogy will have to wait, but we're kindred spirits. It felt good to preach here, look forward to coming back next Sunday. I'm still kind of overwhelmed, didn't expect anything more than filling in a Sunday or two, still trying to get my mind around this."

"I'd never thought about a woman being a preacher 'til I got to know Eleanor Basden, who used to be at the Methodist church in Harrington," Ruth Peyton observed. My brother and his wife were members there 'til they died. They thought the world of Preacher Eleanor. Myra went through a long ordeal with cancer. Preacher Eleanor was a nurse for years before she became a preacher. She was their pastor all through the time Myra was sick, couldn't have been more kind and helpful. She conducted her funeral. She's pastoring a church up at Carrollton now, but she came back to have part in Ray's funeral last year. Our whole family thinks the world of Preacher Eleanor, and she can preach. I never was dead-set against a woman preacher like some people are; it's just something I never thought much about until Eleanor came along. She wouldn't be able to do what she does as well as she does if God hadn't given her the gift. I feel the same way about you."

"I appreciate the vote of confidence," Cassie commented. "It felt good to preach here today. I could tell everybody was with me, listening and praying for me. I'm excited about coming back."

"Way I see it," Arnie Peyton began, "God's called you to preach, and maybe helping a young preacher get off to a good start's about the most important thing a little church like Peyton's Chapel can do. You're gonna make mistakes, like forgetting to change shoes this morning. We're gonna kid you about that as long as you're here or as long as we're living. We're gonna check your feet first thing when we see you every Sunday. You'll never live that down if we can help it, but that wad'n the end of the world, you forgetting to take off them ragged old sneakers and put on your good shoes. We all had a good laugh about it, then you went right on and brought a fine message. We've got a perfect savior, Amen? We don't have to have a perfect preacher, which is a good thing since there's not any. As long as you love the Lord, love us, and preach the gospel, you'll do all right. Only preacher we ever ran off in my lifetime was Bobby Simpson. What he done wad'n a mistake, it was willful meanness. Ought to've sent him packin' long time 'fore we did, if you ask me. Ought not to've called him in the first place. It's not a sin to make mistakes. You forgettin' to change shoes is a mistake but it's not a sin. Pencils wouldn't have erasers if sin had never entered the world. It's a sin to be mean and try to hurt people. If you put Moses on the ark and Noah on Mount Sinai, nobody's gonna miss going to heaven because of it."

"Cassie's been fascinated with the Bible since she was elementary school age, read it all the way through when she was in the sixth grade," Jerry commented. "Elaine and I have prayed for Cassie and our other two children to follow Jesus and honor him in whatever they do. We haven't tried to steer her toward the ministry. Of course, we're mighty pleased that the Lord called one of ours to preach. Got to admit I worried about all the resistance she's going to meet and people hurting her, but our pastor, Brother Mike Westover, helped me work through that. Brother Mike's stretched my thinking, expanded my horizons a lot. One thing I appreciate a lot is him inviting Heather Simmons, pastor up in Virginia at the church he served when he was in seminary, to preach a revival at Harrington when Cassie was eleven. Cassie got to hear a woman who not only preaches, but preaches very well. She's preached at Harrington a couple more times since then. Her husband's got some family up at Bremen, so they try to get down to Harrington when they come down to visit his folks. Heather's really taken an interest in Cassie and encouraged her a lot."

"I'm thankful she's got people like that encouraging her and has the support of her parents and family," Josie commented. "It would be a lot harder if she didn't." With a hearty laugh, Josie added, "As for resistance, she doesn't seem to be meeting much here. Y'all raised her to love the Lord, and she grew up singing 'Wherever He Leads, I'll Go.' You just didn't know that this is where the Lord would lead. That's okay. God is full of surprises."

"Preacher," J. T. spoke up, "you mentioned Bailey's Mill this morning. I was baptized there in 1931, when I was thirteen years old. Josie was, too, both of us baptized the same Sunday. She was twelve at the time. We've known each other all of our lives, both grew up in this church. My daddy, Arthur Bailey, was the last one to operate the mill. I've always been fascinated with machinery, guess that comes from helping Daddy keep all that old machinery in the mill running when I was a kid. I'm one of the few men left that knows how to run an old grist mill. My great-grandfather Daniel Bailey built the mill in 1853. It was the middle of the Depression when it burnt down, 1933 or '34, lightning struck it and caught it on fire one night. Daddy said the mill wad'n making enough money to justify rebuilding it. I was fourteen or fifteen when the mill burned. I cried like a baby, cried because it burned and cried more when Daddy said he wad'n going to rebuild it. I loved helping Daddy at the mill, but he said 'Son, it's simple arithmetic. The only reason I was able to keep the mill running as long as I did was because I inherited it free and clear, didn't owe anything on it. If I went in debt to build it back, I'd be past a hundred years old by the time we made the money back if we ever did. If there was money to be made running old-timey grist mills, people'd be damming up creeks and building new ones. The big factory mills can produce a ten-pound bag of cornmeal and sell it for a lot less than I can. They can grind more corn in a day than we could grind in a month. The old grist mills like the one we had are a thing of the past.' I saved both of the millstones. It amazed me they didn't break. They fell a good twelve feet when the floor burned out from under them. I put 'em on either side of my driveway, buried halfway in the ground, when we built our house in 1939. They're not going anywhere. Those rascals are heavy! Daddy had a one-ton Model A Ford truck. Those two millstones were all the weight it could haul up that steep hill right before you turn onto Peyton's Chapel Road. I was in granny gear all the way from the mill to the top of that hill, never did get past second. Had to put a new clutch in the truck not long after that. Our mailbox post is a piece of the jack-shaft from the mill. Henry and Minnie Ree have another piece of it for their mailbox post. Minnie Ree's my sister. We all grew up playing around that old mill. All of us learned to swim there between the dam and the bridge. That's where most of the people in this church got baptized, so a lot of us had tears running down our faces when you talked about baptizing Mary Grace there. You did the right thing, baptizing her right then and there, just like Philip did with the Ethiopian eunuch. Mill's named for my people, and the creek's named for some of your people. I liked you calling it your holy place. Last few times we baptized somebody, we used the baptistery over't Freeman Valley. Doubt we'd be welcome there now. Might finish Brother Floyd off if we asked to use their baptistery after we call you as pastor. We'd at least get to see him run his blood pressure up and make himself turn red in the face, get to see all his veins pop out. Might be worth asking him just to see his reaction. I'd like for us to go back to baptizing at our holy place. I still own the land right around the mill and dam, about an acre and a half, so you don't have to worry about getting permission from the property owner."

"I wish we'd go back to baptizing in the creek, too," Minnie Ree concurred.

"Well, you found a preacher that'll be glad to do it," Cassie commented. With a laugh, she added, "One hundred percent of my experience at baptizing has been in Salyers Creek below the dam at Bailey's Mill. I've got a picture Miss Addie gave me of a baptismal service there back in the 1920s, when the mill and the covered bridge were still there. Looks like about twenty-five people lined up, standing in the water, waiting to be baptized. I'd love to have that many to baptize all at once, and do it in the creek."

"It's been about three years since we had anybody to baptize," Josie spoke up. "It's sad to have to admit that. I remember the big baptismal services there. There were probably twenty or more baptized the same time that J. T. and I were baptized. I remember several of the churches around here baptizing at the mill—our church, Freeman Valley Baptist, Old Mount Moriah Primitive Baptist, County Line Baptist, and one of the black churches, Moses Chapel Baptist. If the Methodists had somebody who wanted to be baptized by immersion, they'd go there too. I can remember Shady Grove Methodist and Freeman Valley Methodist baptizing there. I remember several times that there'd be two churches baptizing there the same day. If another church was there when we got there, we'd just mingle with them, watch their people being baptized, and when they finished, we'd baptize the ones we had awaiting baptism and they'd stay to see our folks baptized. Never will forget one time, I think it was about 1940, I know it was after J. T. and I got married and not long before the war, old Preacher Bates was our pastor at the time. We came down to the mill for a baptism and Moses Chapel was just finishing up a baptismal service. They'd baptized about half a dozen people. My cousin Bill Nestor, big man, well over six feet tall and about three hundred pounds, was being baptized. Preacher Bates was a small-built man, short and probably didn't weigh a hundred and thirty pounds, close to eighty years old, and had back problems. The pastor at Moses Chapel, Preacher Carter, was a giant of a man, bigger than Bill, made two of Preacher Bates with change left over. He had the biggest hands I've ever seen on a man. He looked at ol' Bill and looked at Preacher Bates, and said in his big deep booming voice, 'Looks like you need some help, Reverend.' He waded back in and helped Preacher Bates baptize Bill and all the rest we had being baptized that day. People would come from all around when any of the churches had baptism. I've seen people who just came to watch fall under conviction, start weeping, call on the Lord to save them, and be baptized right then and there. I'd love to see it like that again."

"Funny thing," Minnie Ree observed. "The ones who are gonna have a dying duck fit over us calling a woman pastor aren't winning the whole county to Jesus either. They'd rather be sticking their noses in what other churches are doing instead of trying to bring people to the Lord or offering to help the churches that are struggling. I listened to way too much of this 'men have to be in charge just because they're men and women have to sit down and shut up just because they're women' foolishness, and I've had my fill of it. If I hadn't been in this church all of my life and if I hadn't been kin to nearly everybody in the church, I would've been ready to drive into Harrington and go to Harrington Baptist. Henry and I've been talking about doing that anyway. Now that Bobby Simpson's gone and we're looking at calling Sister Cassie, I think we'll stick around. The association'll kick us out next, the way they did Harrington Baptist, but that's okay. It's ironic when you stop to think about it. Peyton's Chapel and Harrington have connections way back. I'm the unofficial historian here. A lot of preachers came out of this church years ago. Peyton's Chapel is one of the churches that helped constitute Harrington Baptist. Helped start Freeman Valley, too. The first four pastors at Harrington—John Beckett, Phillip Nestor, E. L. B. Hamilton, and Bartholomew Lang—all were ordained at Peyton's Chapel, all of them are buried here. All of them served Freeman Valley at one time or another, too. I remember Preacher Lang from when I was a little girl; he was an old man when I knew him, lived well up into his nineties, last surviving Civil War soldier in Mintz County. Snow white hair and beard, all the children loved him, the way he took on over all of them and knew all of their names. Addie knew every pastor who ever served Harrington Baptist Church. Those first four were all kin to her one way or another. So, we helped Harrington get started. Now it's Harrington's turn to send us a fine young preacher to help us get back on our feet."

"Thanks," Cassie responded. "I knew about the connection between the two churches. Miss Addie told me. And now it's coming full circle with me coming from Harrington Baptist to Peyton's Chapel. I wonder if that means that you'll have four consecutive pastors from Harrington."

"That'd be all right by me if they're like you," Minnie Ree laughed.

"I don't care if Floyd Williams is my nephew," Henry added, speaking to whoever was in hearing range. "Floyd's got no business stirring up trouble in the association, trying to tell Harrington who they can license to preach or trying to tell us who we can invite to preach for us. He gets all upset about a woman preacher, but he don't say a word about a preacher who beats his wife. He knew full well what kind of man Bobby Simpson was, knew about all the trouble he'd had with the law in Phillips County and how he treated his wife, and he flat-out lied and told us what a good preacher he was and how good a pastor he'd be for us. I don't care how good a preacher he is if he's mean to his wife and mean to everybody else. To tell you the truth, I wad'n all that impressed with his preaching. If what a preacher's saying's not a message from God, him sayin' it louder and jumpin' up and down and workin' up a sweat don't make it any better. The young lady we heard this morning is a whole lot better preacher. She preached the gospel, didn't talk down to us, talked to us like she thinks we love Jesus and have good sense, whole different attitude from what we've been used to. She set out to do us some good, and she did. I told J. T. and Arnie when we called Bobby Simpson that I had an uneasy feeling about anybody Floyd Williams recommended. Ol' Floyd made the mistake of calling me after he didn't get anywhere talking to J. T., telling me, 'Uncle Henry, we'll have lots of trouble in the association if y'all go ahead and let that girl preach.' I told him what I thought about him and Bobby Simpson, told him I can't help being kin to him, and he'd best go ahead and get ready to make whatever trouble he was gonna make in the association, 'cause the young lady was going to preach, and if she done all right we might just call her as pastor. Told him any young lady who loves the Lord and loves us would be an improvement over him or Bobby Simpson. 'Fraid I wad'n real nice to him, Minnie Ree said she'd never heard me use that tone of voice or slam a receiver down like that in all the fifty-eight years we've been married. Mama and Daddy tried their best to talk my sister out of marryin' Malvern Williams, glad she finally wised up and left him. Did'n none of us have much use for him or any of the Klan boys 'round here. Floyd reminds me too much of his daddy Malvern, that man was mean as a snake, don't ask me what the association was thinking when they picked his son who's just like him as moderator. There's a different breed of preachers takin' over the associa-tion the last few years. Some of them are just plain mean, and there's a bunch of them who worry too much about keeping other churches in line. I don't much care if they do kick us out."

"Hey, Preacher," the obviously pregnant young woman said as she hugged Cassie like she had known her all of her life, "my name's Lindsey Harper, J. T. and Josie's granddaughter. So glad your friend Mary Grace sat with me in church. She's sweet. I enjoyed meeting her and talking with her. Wish my husband could've been here. He wanted to come, but he had to work today. He works with the sheriff's department in Mintz County. He's supposed to be off next Sunday. The dark-headed four-year-old, who's all over J. T. and Josie, is our daughter Susanna. She inherited her Papa Bailey's jet-black hair. Unfortunately, she knows how cute she is, and she thinks her Papa Bailey hung the moon and stars in the sky."

"Pleasure to meet you. Susanna's beautiful, and I love that name. Do you know if you're going to be having a boy or a girl?"

"It's a boy. Jed Bailey Harper, gonna call him J. B. It feels good to be here, Preacher. You don't know how good. I haven't been to church in a while. We quit not long after they called the last pastor. We visited a few other churches, but we really haven't been going anywhere to amount to anything. I don't know how to say it, don't want to go into it, but suffice to say the last pastor here gave me the creeps. When I heard about your unpleasant run-in with him at the cemetery, I said, 'Yep, that's the Bobby Simpson I know.' My husband and I will vote in favor of calling you."

Cassie and Mary Grace were among the last to leave Peyton's Chapel. It was a little after 2:30 p.m. when Cassie parked the OGM in the driveway behind her father's red Silverado. Jerry was talking on the phone when they went in, and Cassie heard enough of her father's side of the conversation to figure out that he was talking with Brother Mike. "Here she is, Preacher," Jerry said into the phone, "talk to her and tell her what you told me."

"Hey," Cassie greeted Mike. "Like to have never gotten away from Peyton's Chapel. Mary Grace and I were about the last ones to leave. We had a good morning, everybody wanted to talk with me."

"I know it went well," Mike told Cassie. "I was just telling your dad that Mr. Bailey, the deacon chairman at Peyton's Chapel, called me as soon as he got home, told me that they had asked you to preach the next two Sundays and then they were going to vote Sunday, November 1, on calling you as pastor. He wanted to give me a heads up to be thinking about when we could ordain you. Said they'd send the formal request after the church votes on you, but he said unless he got completely blindsided and things went a lot different than he expected, he felt sure the church would vote to call you."

"I'm still trying to process this, Brother Mike. I thought I'd just be filling in for them a couple of Sundays until they got somebody. Until they got somebody, you know, male. When Mr. Bailey announced to the church that they were going to vote on calling me as pastor, you could've knocked me over with a feather. I told him in front of the church that I had no idea that they would consider calling me, I just thought I'd get to preach a Sunday or two until they found somebody. He laughed, gave me a hug, and said, 'We found somebody.'

"That's good," Mike commented. "I dated a half dozen other girls before I met Karen. I don't have anything bad to say about any of the others, just didn't connect with them the way I did with Karen. After the first date with Karen, I knew I didn't need to look any further. She'd tell you it was the same way for her. I think that's pretty much how Peyton's Chapel operates. Little country church doesn't over think things and make them more complicated than they need to be. Mr. Bailey said you delivered the goods with your preaching, said you were way better than what they've been used to hearing, and he expects you to get even better as you get more experience. He told me that he realizes that Peyton's Chapel may never be a big church, and he's starting to realize that the church needs to think beyond just paying the bills and keeping the doors open, needs to think past next Sunday, and focus on doing what it is able to that bigger churches can't or won't do. He said that one thing Peyton's Chapel can do is give young preachers a place to get started off on the right foot. He said if God calls a young woman to preach—which, in your case he obviously did, there needs to be some little church that'll help her and encourage her. He said there was more enthusiasm in the church today than he's seen in years. The church hasn't had a baptism in three years. You telling the church about baptizing Mary Grace at Bailey's Mill got all of the older ones talking over dinner about the big baptisms they used to have there, and he said they're already talking about having a work day out at the mill, clear the place off, put down gravel and fix it so more cars can park there, fix the road in there a little better, so they can start baptizing there again. He thinks they're going to need a baptizing place again. I asked him if we could make that a joint work day with our church. He said they could use the help. I told him I thought that would be a good way to celebrate the historic connection between the two churches and a further way, in addition to the ordination service, to give our blessing on you becoming their pastor. We might even do some baptizing out there in the summer. Of course, the work day out at

Bailey's Mill will give your dad and Darrell Brinson an excuse to fire up those monster grills."

"Yeah, the King of the Grill will be all for that. Wow, this is happening so fast, it's scary," Cassie commented. "I've gone from not knowing whether I'd ever be ordained to the prospect of being ordained when I'm barely nineteen and in my first year at Mercer."

"Speaking of Mercer," Mike observed, "it's interesting that you're looking at your first pastorate and ordination at nineteen. I did some reading about ol' Jesse Mercer here awhile back. He was called to his first church and ordained at nineteen. I'm going to call Heather tonight to see what her availability is, when she can come down. I know you'll want her to have a part in your ordination, and I know she'll want to do it. If all goes like I think it will and they call you, I'm thinking about November 22. Heather's husband teaches, and they'll probably have a fall break the week of Thanksgiving. Of course I know you're out of school that week, too."

"I'm expecting a call from Heather," Cassie responded, "let me tell her first, then you can talk to her about the logistics."

Cassie had barely hung up the phone and joined Mary Grace in packing up for the drive back to Macon when she heard the phone ring again. Her mom caught it on the first ring. "Cassie, hon, phone's for you. It's Heather, wants to know how it went this morning. I told her it went well, I'll let you give her more specifics."

Cassie took the phone eagerly. "Hey, Heather! Good to hear from you, been looking forward to talking with you. How was church this morning up at Clear Springs?"

"Good. I think I told you we have two services on Sunday morning now, it was either do that or build a new sanctuary, both services are about eighty percent capacity, and the early service is reaching some people we weren't reaching before. Wouldn't trade places with any preacher I know. So much for me and Clear Springs. I'm calling to find out about you and Peyton's Chapel."

"It went well this morning," Cassie began. "Had a lot more people than they're used to having. There were about twenty of my family and friends there, along with some members who hadn't been coming for a while. About sixty or sixty-five people where they've been used to having about twenty on a good Sunday. I told you about my friend Coretta and how beautifully she sings. I can't wait for you to meet her and hear her sing. Sweet person. Dead-on perfect pitch, accurate as a tuning fork. No accompaniment. She sang 'How Sweet the Name of Jesus Sounds,' magnificent old hymn by John Newton, same guy who wrote 'Amazing Grace.' You could've heard a pin drop. Let's just say I know how Graham feels, getting to preach right after Bev Shea sings."

"That's how it is here when Tycina Nichols is back home visiting family. She sings whenever she's here. She's sung all over the world, and she brings that concert hall voice to this little country church. I'll never forget her singing at Wallace Coggins' funeral. She thought the world of Wallace."

"Heather, you won't believe what I did. I've got this grungy old pair of sneakers I keep in the car, mostly for when I stop at Bailey's Mill so I won't scuff up my good shoes. Mary Grace and I left the house early this morning, stopped to pray at my holy place on our way to church. While Coretta was singing, right before I got up to preach, too late to do anything about it, I just happened to look down and saw that I still had those old sneakers on."

"And, of course, they promptly took you out and stoned you to death for not wearing proper shoes to preach in?"

"We had a good laugh about it, and I went ahead and preached."

"And they've got something they can tease you about to keep you humble and keep you real," Heather commented. "That's good. You need that, to keep you from exalting yourself above measure, as Paul says over there in II Corinthians."

"Heather, I thought at the most I'd get to preach for them a Sunday or two while they look for another preacher. After I preached, J. T. Bailey, the chairman of deacons asked me right there in front of the whole church if I'd come back and preach the next two Sundays and then let them vote on calling me as pastor. That possibility wasn't even on my radar screen."

"Wow, Cass, that's great!" Heather exclaimed. "I was thinking the same thing as you, that you'd probably get to supply a Sunday or two, and that we'd just be thankful for any opportunities you get to preach. With you being a couple of weeks past your nineteenth birthday, I figured that was the best we could hope for. I can relate to that. Mike asked me to fill in for him the Sunday he preached for the pastor search committee from Harrington. I never had any idea that it would amount to anything more than just filling in, never even occurred to me that they'd consider calling me. It went well, so Mike asked me to fill in again the Sunday he preached the trial sermon at Harrington. Next thing I knew, they had called me as pastor and ordained me. Been here about eight years now, baptized ninety-seven people, and gained a husband and two kids since I've been here. It all started with filling in for Mike one Sunday."

"Not ready to acquire a husband and kids, but I'm excited about this, Heather," Cassie acknowledged, "excited, but scared, too. I'm barely nineteen years old. I've still got a lot to learn. I still live at home with my parents when I'm not at school during the week. I still need my late-night talks with Mom, and I still cuddle up on the couch with my dad and watch cartoons on Saturday mornings before anybody else gets up just like I did when I was six years old. Most of these people have been Christians longer than I've been alive. Preaching once in a while is one thing, preaching Sunday after Sunday to the same people and always having something worthwhile to say is a whole different animal. Then there's this whole issue of me carrying a full load at Mercer on top of preparing a sermon every week and trying to cram in a pastoral visit on Saturday or on Sunday before I go back to Macon. You know how competitive I am..."

"I do, Cass, and you're right, this will be a big thing to take on in addition to carrying a full load at Mercer. You'll burn yourself out and have a nervous breakdown if you try to do it all. The good news is that neither God nor the church expects you to do it all. Probably every pastor Peyton's Chapel ever had has been somebody who was either a student or worked a full-time job or had a business. These people are accustomed to doing most of the day-to-day ministry and some of them are very good at it. Let them do it. The whole ministry belongs to the whole church. That's the way Clear Springs was when I came here, it's still that way and I'm not trying to change it. That's a healthier model anyway, encourages people to develop and exercise their gifts. I'm not going to try to fix something that's not broken. Wallace Coggins, long as he lived, visited the sick and homebound, visited people in the hospital, he was good at it and loved to do it. We've got others who've taken up the slack since Wallace died. This church makes me look better than I am. They still like to tease me about both of our children being born on Sunday morning, Wallace at 10:25 a.m. and Olivia at 11:41 a.m., one during Sunday School and one during worship."

"I can see Peyton's Chapel doing that for me. There are some very capable people in the church, even if they're getting some age on them, they're still active and involved for now. The deacon chairman, J. T. Bailey, is eighty but doesn't look it. He started out working as a truck mechanic for the State Highway Department before he went in the service in World War II, went to school on the GI Bill after the war, and retired as an engineer with the State Highway Department. Minnie Ree Lane, teaches the adult Sunday School class, is a retired high school history teacher, did really well teaching the lesson this morning. I totally forgot that some of the people in the class have grandchildren older than I am. She doesn't lecture. We had some lively discussion about the lesson, and they really put Mary Grace at ease. She brought up a couple of good questions, they welcomed her questions and didn't make her feel stupid because she's a new Christian who doesn't know much about the Bible. Mrs. Lane hugged Mary Grace after Sunday School and told her that she enjoys teaching the Bible a lot more when she has new Christians in the class who are full of questions. I paid as much attention to how they treated Mary Grace as I did to how they treated me."

"This is a good church, Cass. Maybe better than you thought going into this. If they call you, you'll have an opportunity to grow and learn that not many women get."

"As for the 'if' I don't think there is one. I think it's 'when' instead of 'if.' I just got off the phone with Mike. He said that Mr. Bailey had already called him as soon as he got home from church, told him how well things went and that he expected the church to call me, said he wanted to give him a heads up to be looking at dates to plan the ordination service. Mike said he'd call you tonight because he knew that I would want you to have a part in my ordination."

"Wouldn't miss it, Cass. This'll be my first time to have a part in ordaining a preacher. I think Clear Springs will loan me to Harrington one Sunday for that. Best time for us would be the Sunday before Thanksgiving, November 22. Joel's got that whole week off, Wallace has the week off from school, and we were going to go down that week to see Joel's folks at Bremen. I'll call Ashley Orr, see if she'd like to preach that Sunday. Her family joined Clear Springs about two years ago. Good folks. Ashley's the same age as you, we just licensed her about six months ago. If Peyton's Chapel calls you and it works for everybody else, we're on for November 22."

As Cassie made the turn onto Bailey's Mill Road at Pulliam's Store/ Gloryland Way Missionary Baptist Church, Mary Grace commented, "I wonder how they reacted when they found our sign."

"Don't know. I'm like you, Mary Grace, I wonder whether they got the pun."

"Speaking of getting it," Mary Grace observed, "I'm going to eventually be going home and telling my parents about all of this, becoming a Christian, you baptizing me, me going to hear you preach and actually enjoying being in church and getting something out of the sermon. I need you to pray that they'll get it, at least accept that that's who I am now and who I plan to be from now on."

"I'm one step ahead of you," Cassie commented. "Already been thinking and praying along those lines."

They rode in silence for a long time, maybe a half hour, before Mary Grace broke the silence with a single word, "Surreal."

"Hmmm?" Cassie asked, a bit startled.

"I'm talking about everything from Thursday evening up to the present moment," Mary Grace clarified. "It's surreal."

"Yeah, I agree, except it goes back to Saturday a week ago when I got the news that Miss Addie died. Everything since then has been surreal."

Chapter 15

"It sure is good to see all of you here at Peyton's Chapel this morning," J. T. began. "Sister Cassie McWhorter has preached three consecutive Sundays. We've made tapes of her sermons from the past two Sundays available to our homebound members, and she's taken the time the past two Saturdays to go with Josie and me to meet our members who are not able to get out and come to church. Let me just say we thoroughly enjoyed that time with her. We've done our best to give every member of the church an opportunity to meet Sister Cassie and hear her preach. She's brought three fine messages. Speaking on behalf of the deacons, we realize that we'll most likely get voted out of the association if we call this young woman as our pastor. Harrington Baptist Church was voted out of the association after they licensed her to preach. Be that as it may, the deacons of this church are convinced that God has called Sister McWhorter to preach, and that he has led us to her and her to us. It all came about on account of Addie's funeral. You might say Addie recommended her to us. We believe that one of the best things this church can do is offer her an opportunity to gain some experience, further develop her gifts, and do what she's called to do. We believe that this will be beneficial for the church and for her. We unanimously recommend that Peyton's Chapel Baptist Church call Sister Cassie McWhorter as pastor effective immediately, and that our clerk send a letter to Harrington Baptist Church asking them to ordain her as a minister of the gospel. Sister Cassie, if you'll wait back in one of the Sunday School rooms while we vote, we'll come and get you directly. We've provided paper ballots and pencils, and we're ready to vote. Only members of Peyton's Chapel Baptist Church may vote, but we want every member to vote prayerfully and thoughtfully. We've collected the ballots of our homebound members in plain sealed envelopes to be counted at the same time as the rest of the ballots. Please mark "Yes" if you're in favor of calling Sister Cassie as pastor and asking Harrington Baptist Church to ordain her. If you're opposed, vote "No." After you mark your ballot, fold it in half, and put it in the offering plate when it comes by. I'll ask Henry and Minnie Ree to pass the offering plates around to collect the ballots. As soon as they're collected, our deacons will count them and report to the church and to Sister Cassie. Myrtle, if you'll come up to the piano after you mark your ballot, let's sing *Leaning on the Everlasting Arms* while we collect and count the ballots."

Mary Grace joined Cassie in going back to one of the Sunday School rooms to await the verdict. "You okay, Cass?" Mary Grace broke the silence as she put an arm around Cassie and gave her a gentle hug.

"Yeah, but my heart's pounding so hard I can hear it, surprised you don't hear it. I'm just anxious to know how this is gonna turn out."

"Me, too, Cass."

"I've got that nagging fear that the vote won't go well, that there won't be enough votes to call me or the vote'll be so badly divided I wouldn't touch it with a ten-foot pole."

"However it comes out, the anxiety'll be over pretty soon, shouldn't take long to count the ballots, seeing it's either 'Yes' or 'No,' they can't vote 'Maybe,'" Mary Grace observed. "By the way, you had another good sermon today. This is coming from someone who never would've pictured herself listening to a preacher. You make a lot of sense. You'll be good for this little church. I hope they vote to call you. I think they will. They're crazy if they don't."

"Thanks," Cassie said as she dabbed tears from her eyes and reciprocated Mary Grace's hug. "You've helped me more than you realize. Wish I felt as confident as you do." Cassie and Mary Grace could hear the congregation singing the last stanza of *Leaning on the Everlasting Arms*, and Cassie almost unconsciously joined in singing with them,

What have I to dread, what have I to fear, Leaning on
    the everlasting arms?
I have blessed peace with my Lord so near, Leaning on
    the everlasting arms!
Leaning on Jesus, leaning on Jesus, Safe and secure from
    all alarms,
Leaning on Jesus, leaning on Jesus, Leaning on the ever-
    lasting arms.

"I like that song, what it says," Mary Grace commented. "I don't think I've ever heard it before. You've probably been hearing it all of your life, but it's new to me. Reminds me of that night I broke down and cried, pretty much spilled my guts, and you just pulled me close and held me until I realized that you weren't the only one holding me. So, I really do like that song. That poor piano needs tuning something awful, though, if it's not beyond tuning."

Mary Grace had just gotten those words out when they heard J. T.'s voice sounding cheerful, calling down the hallway, "Preacher! Mary Grace! Come out, come out, wherever you are!" J. T. was smiling as Cassie and Mary Grace met him in the hallway. "It's good, don't worry. We voted to call you. Y'all come on out in the sanctuary, you can hear the results the same time the church does." Mary Grace took a seat on the front pew as J. T. motioned for Cassie to follow him up to the pulpit. "You might as well get used to standing behind this pulpit, Preacher. It's yours. The votes've been counted. Fifty-seven members voted, almost our entire resident membership. The total was fifty-five in favor, and two opposed. That's ninety-six and a half percent, well above the seventy-five percent that our bylaws require to call a pastor. The church has voted to call Sister Cassie McWhorter to be our pastor and ask Harrington Baptist Church to ordain her to the gospel ministry. Preacher, will you accept the call to be our pastor?"

"I accept," Cassie responded, a bit surprised at the strength of her own voice. "I am so amazed that this is really happening, thought I'd just fill in a Sunday or two and that would be it and I'd be grateful for that, but yes, I accept."

"I've already spoken with the pastor of Harrington Baptist Church, Brother Mike Westover, let him know to be thinking about when they could ordain Sister Cassie. Our church clerk will follow up with a letter to Harrington Baptist Church calling for Sister Cassie's ordination. In a minute I'll ask our new pastor to pronounce the benediction," J. T. announced, "but first, does anybody have anything to say for the good of the church?"

Mary Grace stood and faced the congregation. "Other than weddings and a couple of funerals, I think I've been to church maybe five or six times in my whole life. That's counting the three Sundays I've been here. This is all new to me and I've got so much to learn, but I know I believe in Jesus and want to follow him. Cassie's already baptized me. Y'all've made me feel welcome and accepted, just like Cassie and her family have. I won't be able to be here every Sunday, have to go up to Elberton and see my folks once in a while, but I'd like to join this church if I can."

J. T. was beaming and had tears trickling down his face as he motioned for Mary Grace to come and stand beside him. "You certainly can, Mary Grace." Turning to the congregation, he continued, "Sister Mary Grace Tillison comes this morning to be received on statement of her Christian experience and baptism. What's the pleasure of the church?"

"Move we receive her," Myrtle Hill spoke in the strong, confident voice of a veteran high school teacher.

"Second," Arnie Peyton called out.

"All in favor, say 'Aye,'" J. T. announced. After a strong chorus of 'Ayes,' he asked, "All opposed, same sign. Sounds unanimous to me, amen?"

As the 'amens' echoed in the 150-year-old sanctuary, Daniel and Coretta Groves stepped out into the aisle, came down to where Cassie was standing in front of the communion table, and hugged her. Daniel spoke to Cassie loudly enough for everyone to hear, taking full advantage of the superb acoustics of an old building with a fourteen-foot arched ceiling and wide-plank heart pine floors. "Preacher, Coretta and I would like to join this church by letter."

Cassie and Coretta had talked at the cookout at Cassie's home, and they had exchanged some e-mails, talking about the frustration she and Daniel felt with dividing their time between two churches and arriving at their decision to join Peyton's Chapel if the church called Cassie. Still, Cassie had not expected them to do it the same day the church voted to call her. Daniel addressed the congregation, "Coretta and I have been married a little over two years now, and we're expecting our first child. Since we've been married, we've divided our time and giving between Coretta's home church and mine. We love both churches and have the highest respect for both pastors. We've found it impossible to choose between the two. I don't want to ask Coretta to leave the church she grew up in to join Harrington Baptist. She doesn't want to ask me to leave the church I grew up in to join Greater New Hope. Cassie's call to be the pastor of this church is an answer to prayer for both of us. Now that you've called Cassie, instead of choosing between our home churches, we want to join this church together, do all we can to build up this church and encourage and help our dear friend Cassie McWhorter. We offer ourselves to you to help this church and help our pastor any way we can."

J. T. had sat down on the front pew. Addressing Cassie, he said, "You're the pastor now. You go ahead and present them to the church."

"Let's hope I do this right," Cassie laughed. "First, let me say thank you, Daniel and Coretta, for the gracious way in which you've offered yourselves to support me and support this church. As Daddy would say, this time and once more will make twice that I've done this. Daniel comes to us on promise of a letter from Harrington Baptist Church. Coretta comes on promise of a letter from Greater New Hope Progressive Missionary Baptist Church. What's the pleasure of the church?"

"Movewereceive'em," J. T. rolled it out as though it were all one word.

"Second," Arnie called out.

"All in favor, say 'Aye,'" Cassie instructed. After a chorus of 'ayes,' she continued, "All opposed, same sign." After a moment's pause, she continued, "I hear no opposition. Daniel and Coretta, welcome to Peyton's Chapel. Our church clerk will request your letters. Who's our clerk?"

"I am," Josie Bailey called out.

"You can send the request for Daniel's letter in the same envelope with the request for my ordination," Cassie laughed. "Save a stamp. Address it to my mom, Elaine McWhorter. She's the church clerk at Harrington."

"And my aunt Bessie Hammondtree's the clerk at Greater New Hope," Coretta added. "Her address is 334 Florida Avenue in Harrington."

After Daniel and Coretta sat down on the front pew beside Mary Grace and J. T., Cassie continued, "I look forward to being your pastor. I'm a full-time student at Mercer, living on campus during the week, so you'll continue to do a lot of the day-to-day work of ministry, as you've done for many years, and that's a good thing. That's not a problem we need to fix. My pastor, Mike Westover, likes to remind us that the whole ministry belongs to the whole church. You're a better church than you've given yourselves credit for being, a lot better than you've been told you were. You're not a big church, but you're a courageous church, strong enough to swim against the current. You believed in me and my calling to preach the gospel. You invited me to preach in spite of threats and intimidation, and now, you've called me to be your pastor. Any consequences we may face for that decision, we will face together. God is at work for good in all of this. Today, November 1, is All Saints Day, a good time to remember that we're surrounded by a great cloud of witnesses like Miss Addie who've gone on before us, cheering us on." Looking heavenward, Cassie called out, "Happy All Saints Day, Miss Addie! Thanks for recommending me to Peyton's Chapel!" Looking back at the congregation, she continued, "And now for our benediction: The God of hope fill you with all joy and peace in believing, that you may abound in hope by the power of the Holy Spirit. Amen."

One thing about those old wide-plank heart pine floors in the sanctuary at Peyton's Chapel, they acted as a sounding board not only for the preacher's voice but also for footsteps. One could not sneak in late and not be noticed. Cassie was aware of the woman who came in about five minutes after the service started, trying to be inconspicuous, slipping in during the first hymn and taking a place on the back pew, positioning herself to make a stealth exit during the benediction. Cassie had not seen her the previous two Sundays. She was a slender woman wearing a plain cotton dress, perhaps in her mid-fifties, although it was hard to tell, with chestnut brown hair turning gray and pulled straight back in a tight pony tail. One could tell that she had been a very pretty woman before life became so hard for her. When Cassie got up to preach, the woman was no longer sitting alone. Myrtle Hill noticed her, went back, greeted her with a hug, and sat down beside her. The woman, whoever she was, seemed to have been relieved of her anxiety. When Cassie got up to preach, the woman appeared more at ease and less poised for a hasty exit. She listened intently to the sermon. When Cassie pronounced the amen at the end of the benediction, the woman could not have escaped if she had wanted to, being tightly surrounded by people waiting their turn to greet her and give her a hug.

"Preacher," Myrtle Hill began the introduction, "I want you to meet Ruth Ann Simpson, our former pastor's wife…"

As Ruth Ann hugged Cassie, a warm smile came across her tear-streaked face as she added with a laugh, "Soon-to-be former pastor's former wife. Bobby'd explode if he knew I was here this morning listening to you. He'd sure enough explode if he knew I voted in favor of calling you. I moved out last weekend, staying right now with our daughter and son-in-law. They live on Bailey's Mill Road right after you cross the Phillips County line. My son-in-law told Bobby he'd have him locked up if he set foot on their property. When Bobby got himself locked up for going off on you at the cemetery, and the deacons told him he'd preached here for the last time, I told him I'd slept with him for the last time and he'd blown up on me for the last time. I told him he'd torn me away from churches and people I love for the last time. I filed for divorce last week. Honey, I feel so bad about the way Bobby went off on you at the cemetery. Bad thing about it, he doesn't think he did anything wrong." Hugging Cassie again, she added, "I'm sorry. I really am."

"Please don't apologize for something somebody else did," Cassie said as she reciprocated the hug. "It's not your fault. Nobody holds that against you. You and Bobby are two different people. I'm really thankful you came to church today, and I hope you'll be back. I look forward to getting to know you better."

"Thanks, Cassie. Don't worry, I'll be back. This is a good church. You're the first woman I ever heard preach, and you brought a fine message. It's refreshing to hear a sermon that's meant to encourage people and help them instead of beating them up and ripping them apart."

"Preacher Conway over at Greater New Hope says that his prayer every time he gets up to preach, is 'Lord, let me do these people some good.' I've made that my prayer, too," Cassie responded. Hugging Ruth Ann again, Cassie added, "I look forward to being your pastor."

Josie Bailey was waiting her turn after Cassie to hug Ruth Ann, and Josie invited her and Myrtle Hill to join them for lunch. "Nothin' but plain country cooking, but we got plenty of it. Got a beef roast cooking in the crock pot, all I've got to do is warm up the vegetables to go with it and brown the rolls. Be a pleasure to have y'all join us."

Ruth Ann and Myrtle accepted Josie's invitation, and Cassie took her place in the narrow entrance foyer—not really big enough to be called a narthex, and most Baptists would not know to call it that anyway—greeting the line of people waiting to speak to her. It was about 12:30 p.m. when Cassie shook the last hand and received the last hug. "As soon as we stop by the house to tell my folks how the vote came out," Cassie said to Mary Grace as she headed the OGM back toward Harrington, "we'll head on over to Mike and Karen's. They've invited us for lunch. Ted and Brenda Coleman and their daughter Molly are coming, too. Ted's the editor of our local paper. He must have felt pretty confident about things at Peyton's Chapel. Ted always does a nice write up when one of the local churches calls a new pastor. He told Mike that if he could talk with me today before we head back to Macon, he could get the write up in this week's paper. Ted knows Bob Ballance, the editor at *Baptists Today*. He's going to send the write up to him, too. Mike said there wasn't much use in sending it to *The Christian Index*. He figures the *Index* will wait and do a nice write up when we get booted out of the association, make the association look like the last brave defenders of the Alamo, standing against the invading hordes of women preachers."

"So there's nobody like a bishop or anything who can tell Peyton's Chapel they can't call a woman pastor, but Baptists still have ways to tighten the screws and ostracize people and churches who don't toe the line?" Mary Grace asked.

"You got it," Cassie responded.

"Come on in the house," Mike greeted Cassie and Mary Grace as he held the storm door open and hugged both of them. "Already heard the good news. J. T. called me; the phone was ringing when we came in the door from church. Glad we're planning an ordination service instead of another funeral. I've already e-mailed Heather and told her to be getting ready to do the charge to the candidate. Mary Grace, let me introduce you to the cast of characters here. This is our older daughter, Asalee, our younger daughter, Deborah Estelle, and you've met Karen. This is Ted Coleman, he's the editor of our local paper, his wife Brenda, who teaches fourth grade at Miss Addie's School and serves as chair of our deacons, and their daughter Molly."

"Pleased to meet all of you," Mary Grace responded. "I told them at church we all need to wear name tags 'til I learn the cast of characters."

"Wouldn't be a bad idea," Brenda concurred. "I do that with my kids the first couple of days of school. I hate to call a child by the wrong name."

"Everything's just about ready to put on the table," Karen spoke up. "Y'all have a seat in the living room, make yourselves comfortable, while Mike and the girls take everything up and put it on the table. Just waiting for the rolls to brown, those are Mike's homemade yeast rolls you smell."

"Well, Preacher," Ted spoke to Cassie as he picked up a pricey Nikon camera from the top of the piano. "While we're waiting, let's get some good pictures of you and pick one for the newspaper. I brought some lights from my studio, got them set up over here. That ivory color on the wall gives us a nice neutral background and good contrast with what you're wearing, makes a good black and white image that'll reproduce well in the paper. For a new pastor photo, I want to take the classic preacher pose, standing, holding your Bible in your right hand."

"I'll have to go get my Bible out of the car," Cassie replied.

"Just use my dad's, it's on top of the piano," Asalee offered.

Ted set up the lights, had Cassie stand tall in classic preacher pose with borrowed Bible, made minor adjustments, and took a half-dozen shots. "J. T. asked me to give them a nice write up like I always do when one of the local churches calls a new pastor. Told him we had it covered. Okay, Cass. Look at these pictures, see which one you think is best for the paper."

"Let's go with this one," Cassie suggested.

"That's the one I hoped you'd pick. I think it's your best shot," Ted agreed. "I brought you a copy of the write up for the paper. I went ahead and got it ready, assuming they would call you. I just need to get a good quote from you to finish it. See what you think."

Cassie picked up the typed text of the article and began reading,

Historic Church Calls First Woman Pastor

The oldest Baptist Church in Mintz County, Peyton's Chapel Baptist Church, established in 1846, has called Rev. Cassie E. McWhorter as pastor. Rev. McWhorter, a freshman ministerial student at Mercer University, is the first woman to serve as pastor of a Baptist Church in Mintz County. Rev. McWhorter is a 1998 graduate of Harrington High School, where she was class valedictorian. She is the daughter of Jerry and Elaine Whitmire McWhorter of Harrington. Rev. McWhorter assumed her pastoral duties on November 1. J. T. Bailey, chairman of deacons at Peyton's Chapel, told the *Courier*, "We are blessed to have this gifted young woman as our pastor. We invite everyone to come, meet our new pastor, and hear her preach."

Rev. Mike Westover, pastor of Harrington Baptist Church, told the *Courier*, "Cassie was the first person I baptized after I became pastor of Harrington Baptist Church in 1990. I've watched her grow up, mature in her faith, and discover her gifts for ministry. It will be an honor to preside at her ordination."

Rev. Westover noted a historic connection between the two churches, "The first four pastors of Harrington Baptist Church were ordained by Peyton's Chapel. It is now our privilege to ordain a fine young minister to serve Peyton's Chapel."

"Now," Ted told Cassie, "I just need to get a good quote from you to finish the article."

"And you'll have to get it after we eat, or get it over dinner, Ted," Brenda spoke up. "I'm starving in a pile. We're ready to eat with you or without you."

After Karen said grace over the meal and everyone helped their plates, Mary Grace commented, "Everything's delicious. Thanks for inviting us."

"You're welcome," Karen replied. "Mike and I have enjoyed getting to know you."

"Mary Grace joined Peyton's Chapel this morning," Cassie added. "So did Daniel and Coretta."

"That's great," Mike commented. "I knew that Dan and Coretta were going to. They've talked to me about the frustration they felt splitting their time between two churches, and they saw this as a positive solution. They look forward to being there to support and encourage you. Mary Grace, you got yourself a good church and a good pastor."

"And Mary Grace, Dan, and Coretta are all going to be good for Peyton's Chapel," Cassie observed. "Myrtle Hill out at Peyton's Chapel, retired high school history teacher, knows how to teach, loves to teach, and it shows, as good an adult Bible teacher as I've had the pleasure of hearing, has really taken a liking to Mary Grace. Mary Grace has asked some good questions in Sunday School, helped stimulate some discussion. Mrs. Hill likes that. First thing the church did after they got rid of that clown Brother Bobby was to bring the men and women back together into one class. Brother Bobby couldn't stand the thought of a woman teaching men. Dan and Coretta were at Sunday School this morning. They jumped right into the discussion. Of course, everybody at Peyton's Chapel loves to hear Coretta sing. That old building has great acoustics; they don't really need a sound system. Don't know if it was pure luck or if the guys who built it knew what they were doing, but they got the acoustics right. Glad they've resisted the urge to carpet over those beautiful old heart pine floors. Coretta sang 'Children of the Heavenly

King' this morning. Wish you could've heard how her voice filled that place! Already told her she's singing at my ordination. Sweet person as well as a powerful singer. Speaking of sweet people, Brother Bobby's soon-to-be ex- wife was at church this morning, Ruth Ann Simpson's her name. She told me Jack Kinnebrew was representing her, and I told her that her lawyer was my uncle and he'd treat her right. She slipped in a few minutes late after the service started, sat on the back row like she was going to sneak out during the benediction. She didn't know how people would react to her being there. Myrtle Hill went back and sat with her. She didn't get a chance to make a hasty exit, I think every person there hugged her and told her how happy they were to see her. The Baileys took her and Myrtle home with them for dinner."

"That's good," Karen responded. "It speaks well of the church. They don't blame her for her husband being crazy. Glad she got out before he killed her."

"I told Mom when we stopped by the house to tell the folks how the vote came out. She said that she couldn't tell me before because of attorney-client confidentiality, but since Ruth Ann told me, she said she typed up the petition last week. Uncle Jack filed it in with the clerk in Phillips County on Wednesday. Ruth Ann was willing to walk away with nothing but her clothes and her old '78 Malibu. Uncle Jack told her no way was Bobby Simpson getting off that light after the way he treated her all these years. Uncle Jack can be gruff sounding, and he normally doesn't show much emotion, but when that guy in Harrington stabbed his wife to death about two years ago, it really shook him up. She'd been in to see Uncle Jack about two weeks before that, husband sweet-talked her into coming back, so she called off the divorce. Not long after that, she was dead, just twenty- four years old, stabbed right through the heart while she was holding their baby. Mom said it was the only time she's ever seen Uncle Jack cry. Since then, he's really tried to help women in dangerous situations with crazy men, works with them regardless of their financial situation. Mom said that she and Dad remembered Ruth Ann from high school. She was about two years ahead of them. Glad the church is there for her. She doesn't have much family. Dad said that Ruth Ann was an only child, parents were about forty when she was born, both of them worked in the hosiery mill, so they didn't have much, and they're both dead now. Mom said that when Ruth Ann came in the office, it was the first time she'd seen her since high school. She saw Mom's name sign on her desk, put two and two together, and said, 'You're Cassie McWhorter's mother, aren't you? You were Elaine Whitmire before you married.' Mom said she was. Ruth Ann started crying and apologizing to Mom for the way Bobby Simpson acted toward me. Mom told her that nobody blamed her for the way Bobby acted and nobody expected her to control his behavior. She thanked her and said she was tired of apologizing for his behavior, that's why she was divorcing him. Mom said she talked her into going back to church at Peyton's Chapel."

"Glad she did," Karen commented, "and glad she came to Peyton's Chapel."

"No doubt about her coming back," Cassie continued. "You would've thought she was a celebrity, somebody famous, the way the church welcomed her. She told me she was going to try to get her daughter, son-in-law, and grandchildren to come with her next Sunday, but it won't be easy. Said that Bobby turned their daughter against church altogether. Jennifer got married four days after her eighteenth birthday, she and her boyfriend eloped, said if she ever got away from her daddy she'd never set foot inside a church building again as long as she lived, and so far she hasn't. Ruth Ann told me that her son-in-law's a good guy, always been a hard worker and good to Jennifer and their kids. Ronnie's a mechanic on big trucks, works for Harding Concrete, been there about twenty years. He's got a shop at their house, works on their cars and does a little mechanic work on the side for extra cash. He's kept Ruth Ann's old car going. Ronnie doesn't have any animosity toward the church, he just didn't grow up in the church and it's never been a part of his life. Ruth Ann thinks the world of her son-in-law. He has no use for Bobby, never did. After Ruth Ann left Bobby, Ronnie told Bobby if he ever had any thoughts of coming around his house to start trouble, he'd better call 911 before he started over there, tell them to send the law and an ambulance. So I think she's safe over there."

"Daddy," Asalee called out. "It's for you. Preacher Heather up in Virginia."

"Hey, Heather," Mike answered the phone. "You timed it just right. We just finished dinner and sat down in the living room. Looks like we need to plan that ordination service on November 22. Here's Preacher McWhorter. I'll let her tell you all about it."

"Hey, Cass," Heather's voice on the phone greeted Cassie. "Sounds like it went well this morning. So they voted to call you?"

"Yeah, they did," Cassie responded. "The vote was 55–2, most of the resident members voted. I couldn't believe it was that strong a vote. The former pastor — the one that assaulted me at the cemetery when we buried Miss Addie — his soon-to-be ex-wife slipped in about five minutes after the service started this morning. I think she was afraid of how she'd be received, but it turns out she didn't have anything to worry about. The people were lined up to hug her after the service and tell her how glad they were to see her. She told me how much she enjoyed my preaching and said she voted in favor of calling me, assured me she'd be back. She's going to try to get her daughter, son-in-law, and grandchildren to come to church with her. That'll be a challenge, she said, because her daughter is totally turned off of church on account of her daddy."

"Wow. That's sad," Heather commented. "I've found as a woman in ministry that some women who've been abused are able to trust me. I've been able to have some conversations that a male pastor would probably never be able to have. We've got at least four women coming to Clear Springs now who used to be in abusive relationships. One of our deacons is a preacher's daughter who used to say she never wanted to see the inside of a church again. I'll always get teary-eyed when we sing,

> Down in the human heart, Crushed by the tempter
> Feelings lie buried that grace can restore.
> Touched by a loving heart, wakened by kindness,
> Chords that were broken will vibrate once more.

Lots of stories I associate with that song. Anyway, let's talk about you and an ordination service. Mike said I'm the only preacher he's helped ordain so far, and I told him that's one more than I've done, so you get to be my first. What part do you want me to do?"

"I want you to do the charge to the candidate. Mike's going to charge the church. My friend Coretta's going to sing. Mom's doing the invocation. Daddy's doing the ordination prayer. Four scripture readings, going to ask my sister, my brother, Mary Grace, and Aaron Stewart to do those. Aaron's our police chief here, deacon at Greater New Hope. He and Daddy have been friends for years. Aaron's the one who arrested Brother Bobby when he assaulted me at the cemetery."

"Well, you know I'll be honored to have whatever part you want me to have," Heather replied. "So, if you don't mind a sentimental teary-eyed preacher doing the charge to the candidate and at least one good hug during the laying on of hands, I'm ready. We'll leave on Friday, November 20, as soon as Joel gets home. He's off and Wallace is out of school all of that next week for Thanksgiving. We were planning to go see Joel's folks at Bremen for the holiday anyway, so we'll just plan on coming down a few days earlier. Mike said we'd do the ordination council at 6:00 p.m. on Saturday and the ordination Sunday afternoon at 3:00 p.m. Joel and the kids and I will plan to be in church with you at Peyton's Chapel on Sunday morning." "Great," Cassie responded, "You want to preach that morning?"

"I'd be glad to, Cass, you know I love to preach, but I don't get too many chances to hear someone other than myself. I've never had a chance to hear you, so you plan on preaching and let me sit and listen for a change."

"Okay, Heather. As long as you promise to go easy on me at the ordination council," Cassie laughed.

"Don't worry, Little Sister. As long as you can tell us where Cain got his wife, name all the kings of Israel and Judah in chronological order and pronounce their names correctly, clarify what Paul meant by that reference to baptism for the dead in I Corinthians 15, and settle once and for all the question of who wrote Hebrews, you'll be fine."

Chapter 16

Mike normally took Mondays off, and he'd planned to go over and help Tommy Sheridan with the wiring on his '46 Chevy pickup, at least run the starter, alternator, and ignition circuits so they could crank it and hear it run. Mike had assembled the 350 Chevy engine after his father's shop, Westover Automotive Machine Shop over at Denham, did the machine work on the block, heads, and crank. Tommy could afford the parts to build it right. Mike had not built him a racing engine by any means, but it would be a sweet runner that could move that little truck along at a quicker pace than the old 216 babbit pounder six ever did. He and Tommy both wanted to get the essential circuits wired so they could take it to the end of the driveway and back under its own power. Under the watchful eye of Grady Westover, Mike had assembled his first engine, a slant six Dodge, when he was thirteen. There was something about the first time firing up an engine that he built that excited him as much as it did back then. Grady told him one time that he figured he'd put several thousand engines together over the past fifty-odd years, the first one being a flathead Ford he put together under his father's watchful eye when he was about twelve or thirteen. Grady said it still excited him to hear one that he put together fire up for the first time. Mike told Tommy that once they fired it off, he'd set the timing by ear, then if Tommy wanted to, he'd be welcome to try out his brand new top-of-the-line shiny chrome Snap-On timing light to see that he already had it dead on the money, eight degrees advanced. After helping Tommy on his truck, he needed to mulch the last of the leaves from the pecan tree in the back yard. Karen had already left for her job at the middle school and dropped the girls off at school on her way. Mike was in his coveralls, ready to go over to Tommy's when the phone rang.

"Hey, Preacher," Mike recognized the familiar voice of Tommy Sheridan. "Sure as I think I've got the day off, somebody up and dies. Got to go with Daniel to the VA hospital in Atlanta to pick up a body directly. Mr. Oliver Pate, ninety-eight years old, last World War I vet in Mintz County, good old man, member of our church. He was my Sunday School teacher when I was a kid. Looks like it'll be after lunch before we get a chance to do anything on the truck, if we get to at all."

"Alright, just holler at me when you get back from Atlanta. Call the cell. I'll be outside doing some yard work if the rain holds off. Peyton's Chapel called Cassie as pastor yesterday, so we've got to plan an ordination service. This'll only be the second one I've done, but it's lots more fun than planning funerals. The first preacher I helped ordain is coming down from Virginia to help us ordain Cassie."

"Great! Tell Cassie congratulations if you see her and talk to her before I do. Harrington Methodist was on its last leg, down to about seventy people on a good Sunday, when Eleanor Basden became our pastor. We considered anybody who wad'n retired young adults. Eleanor did a good job, real good preacher, saw a lot of growth while she was with us. We've got us another good one now, Janice Hall, she's been with us since the conference played musical chairs in July. She's still learning her way around, but she's good. Excellent preacher. Her husband's a state trooper, good guy. Hope they get to stay with us a while."

"I've met Janice," Mike commented. "Enjoyed talking with her, haven't had the opportunity to hear her preach, but I've heard good things about her. I can tell just from conversations with her that she's got a pastor's heart, loves the Lord, and loves people. Enthusiasm is contagious, so is despondency, and she's spreading enthusiasm. Loves what she does, and it shows."

"You got that right, Preacher. I think she's going to be good for the church. I'll holler at you when we get back. Dan's gonna prepare the body, I'm just riding up there with him to bring Mr. Pate back to the funeral home. Only bad thing about being a funeral director in a small town, you end up buryin' a lot of good friends and people you've known all of your life. Dan said he appreciated me preparing Miss Addie, said he'd take care of Mr. Pate so I wouldn't have to." With his trademark horse-whinny laugh, Tommy added, "You be seein' about Miss Karen's honey-do list while I'm gone. If you run out of stuff to do or it sets in to rainin'"fore I get back and you want to go ahead'n be working on the truck, you got a key to my garage and you know your way around in there."

"Better than you do, Tommy." Mike never missed a chance to get in a friendly dig at Tommy about his lack of mechanical expertise. He had no sooner hung up from talking with Tommy when the phone rang again.

"Preacher Westover, good morning. Josie Bailey here."

"Hey, Mrs. Bailey, good morning, good to hear from you. I heard that y'all called a new pastor out at Peyton's Chapel. You got a good 'un this time. Cassie's got a sharp mind, a tender heart, and a pure love for Jesus. Proud to say I helped her daddy baptize her, look forward to helping ordain her."

"We're excited about it, too," Josie concurred. "J. T.'s needing something from the hardware store, probably just an excuse to run to town and shoot the bull with some of his old cronies, can't imagine any kind of bolt or screw that he doesn't already have some of in one of those coffee cans out in his shop, so I told him I'd ride into town with him. J. T. can go for a loaf of bread and be gone half a day because he ran into somebody and got to talking. I got the request for Daniel Groves' letter and the request for Preacher McWhorter's ordination in my purse, if it's okay I'll drop them by the church while we're out."

"That'll be great. I'll meet y'all over at the church directly and put on a pot of coffee for us." Mike hastily traded the coveralls for a shirt, slacks, and decent shoes, and petted Wallace the Dog on his way out the door. Normally Mike would walk or ride his bike the short distance to the church, but it looked like it might rain before the morning was over, so he drove this time. About the time the coffee finished perking, he heard the door open at the end of the hall. "Hey, Mr. and Mrs. Bailey, y'all come on in. Welcome to Harrington Baptist Church, I'm Mike Westover."

"We met you briefly at Addie's funeral and before that at some of the associational meetings," J. T. responded, "didn't really get a chance to talk with you then, so I appreciate you meeting us this morning. Since you made coffee, we ran by York's Bakery for some donuts. Help yourself. I told Josie I believe Addie's funeral was the best one I've ever been to. If I thought mine'd be that good, I'd want to have it before I die so I can attend and enjoy it. Everybody that had a part in it was really good, music was wonderful, never heard better music or better messages, and I've been to a lot of funerals. Addie deserved that if anybody ever did. After a life like hers, all you can say is 'Thank you, Lord.' Addie had already done more good than most people do in a lifetime, then to top it all, last thing she did, she put us in touch with a fine young preacher."

"Such a different attitude, a kinder and more humble spirit than what we've been used to," Josie commented. "I wrote down something she said Sunday was a week ago: 'Study your own Bible, do your own thinking and your own praying. Don't follow me if I'm not following Jesus. If you see I'm about to walk off a cliff, try to stop me. At least don't follow me off the cliff.' She's a good preacher, especially to be as young as she is with no more experience than she has."

"She is," Mike concurred. "Gracious spirit, no doubt about her having the calling and the gift, but she knows the gift has to be developed. She's got about the same amount of preaching experience I had when Clear Springs up at Ledford, Virginia, called me. I value what I received at Mid-Atlantic Seminary, but Clear Springs Baptist Church taught me as much as the seminary did, taught me things you can only learn in a local church. I'm glad Cassie's getting this opportunity. She'll learn and grow, and she'll come at her religion studies at Mercer and her seminary education later on with some good pastoral experience. Very few women get to sign up for Country Church 101. They don't offer that course in seminary."

"We're blessed to have her," J. T. replied. "I hate to speak ill of anyone, but Peyton's Chapel couldn't've stood much more of Bobby Simpson. Makes me think of that old country song, 'Thank God and

Greyhound He's Gone,' except it was the Mintz County Sheriff instead of Greyhound that hauled him off. Main thing is we got shed of him. It wasn't just him going off on Preacher McWhorter at the cemetery. That was the straw that broke the camel's back. I guess that's what it took for us to put our foot down and say enough is enough. Deacons tried to talk to him, reason with him, every time we did he'd quote I Chronicles 16:22, 'Touch not mine anointed, and do my prophets no harm.' He applied that to himself, never got so tired of one preacher quoting one passage of scripture in all my life, took it to mean that nobody had any right to disagree with him or question anything he said. If you disagreed with him, you were arguing with God and you probably had'n been saved."

"He had the sweetest wife, though," Josie spoke up. "Bobby Simpson didn't have enough sense to realize what a good wife he had. The way he treated her in public, I hate to think how he treated her when nobody else was around. It's sad to see couples separate and divorce, but sometimes it's the best thing. God didn't mean for anybody to live with what that poor woman lived with. I've been blessed these past fifty-nine years to live with somebody who's kind, considerate, and reasonable. J. T.'s easy to please. I told her I couldn't've put up with what she put up with as long as she did. We had the best time with her and Myrtle Hill over't our house yesterday after church. Saw a side of her I'd never seen as long as she was with Brother Bobby. First time I ever heard her laugh was yesterday at our house. She always walked on eggshells around him, afraid to crack a smile, let alone laugh. She may be sore from laughing so hard yesterday. I told her how much I enjoyed hearing her laugh, told her she's a pretty woman when she holds her head up and smiles."

"I told her what the Harrington police chief said to Brother Bobby at the cemetery," J. T. continued. "He said 'there's a fine line between acting stupid and breaking the law, and you just had to cross it.' That was pretty bad, him blowing up like that and attacking Preacher McWhorter with the Harrington police chief all dressed up in his uniform standing about ten feet from him. Don't know what went through his mind, I reckon he expected Chief Stewart to stand there like a wooden Indian while he attacked Preacher McWhorter. He sure did have a surprised look on his face when Chief Stewart and Preacher Jennings shoved him down on the hood of that hearse and put the handcuffs on him."

"Reminds me of a guy I heard about in my former pastorate up in Virginia," Mike commented. "This was before my time, back when Logan Clark was pastor, but people still talked about it. Guy lost his temper over something in a church business meeting, pitched a tantrum like a three-year-old, went stomping out of the church, got in his truck, slammed the door so hard the glass shattered, and tore out of the church parking lot slinging gravel every which way, square in front of a state trooper. Trooper had to lock it down to keep from hitting him. Carol Richardson said that trooper was still skidding when the blue lights came on."

"Sounds like the Lord had that trooper and the Harrington police chief in the right place at the right time," Josie laughed as she sipped her coffee. "Here's the request for Daniel Groves' letter. I've been clerk at Peyton's Chapel thirty-one years, I've sent and received plenty of letters for church membership, but this is the first time I've ever done a request to ordain a preacher. We're just a little country church, don't have any church letterhead. I just typed it up on plain paper, worded it the best I knew how."

Mike took the letter that Josie handed him, typed on an old manual typewriter, the e's and o's blacked in and some of the capital letters flying just a hair above the line, and read it,

4501 Peyton's Chapel Rd.
Harrington, Ga. 30199
November 1, 1998

Rev. Mike Westover, Pastor
Harrington Baptist Church
630 Peyton St.
Harrington, Ga. 30199

Dear Rev. Westover:

   Peyton's Chapel Baptist Church voted today to call Rev. Cassie McWhorter, a member of Harrington Baptist Church, as pastor. Peyton's Chapel Baptist Church asks that Harrington Baptist Church ordain Rev. McWhorter to the gospel ministry as soon as possible.
   Please let us know if this request meets with the approval of Harrington Baptist Church and, if so, when Rev. McWhorter can be ordained.

Sincerely,

Josie P. Bailey

Josie P. Bailey, Church Clerk

"Looks good to me. I've been to a total of two ordination services for preachers, and that includes my own. When Heather Simmons was called as pastor at Clear Springs, her home church wouldn't ordain her because she was a woman. Pastor said no woman'd be ordained while he was pastor, didn't even present it to the church. We ordained her at Clear Springs, didn't bother us a bit that her home church at McMillan, Tennessee, wouldn't ordain her. It just meant that we got to do it. It turned out to be a bigger celebration than homecoming and decoration day, and we're talking about a country church that knows how to do homecoming and decoration day. Bunch of folks from her home church came up to Clear Springs for the ordination service, ended up with a new church started at McMillan because of that. She got to preside over constituting the new church in McMillan. Helen's coming in around 10:00 a.m. to put the newsletter together, run it, and take it to the post office. I'm writing her a note now to put in the newsletter that y'all called Cassie and that we'll vote on the request to ordain her at the close of the service this Sunday. Cassie's mom is our clerk. I'll put your letter and the request for Daniel's transfer of membership in her box so she can pick them up when she comes to church Wednesday night. Brenda Coleman, she's the one who did the invocation at Miss Addie's funeral, is the chair of our deacon group. She teaches at Miss Addie's School. I'll call her this evening when she gets home, let her know we got the request. She'll call the other deacons, let them know, and the deacons can recommend that we approve the request and give me the go-ahead to call an ordination council. Heather Simmons Moore is pastor at Clear Springs Baptist Church up at Ledford, Virginia, the church I served when I was a seminary student. She followed me there eight years ago. She's still there, and the church is doing well. Heather preached a revival here in '91 and has preached here a couple of other times. She and Cassie have gotten close, so Cassie wants Heather to have a part in her ordination. I've already talked with Heather, we're looking at her and her family coming down on November 22 and doing the ordination then, assuming the church votes to go forward with ordaining Cassie, which I expect it will."

"Won't be easy to round up an ordination council around here," J. T. opined. "Not a lot of preachers around here who go along with ordaining women."

"Or nineteen-year-olds. Not to mention nineteen-year-old women. Already thought about that," Mike commented. "Of course, our deacons and the deacons from Peyton's Chapel are invited. Heather will be on the council. Bob McKnight, served as interim here before I came, will do it."

"Brother Bob's a good man," Josie concurred. "We've known him forty years or more. He filled in for us several years back when we were without a pastor. Good preacher."

"I thought Bob's calls for interim work and pulpit supply would dry up after we got kicked out of the association, since he's a member here," Mike observed, "but ol' Bob's seventy-nine years old and still preaching just about every Sunday. Stays as busy as he ever did. I hardly ever get to see him and Susan because he's always preaching somewhere. Good man, very kind and gracious. His wife Susan's kin to Cassie. Bob McKnight's usually the first one they call when a church is in turmoil. He's been filling in at Alabama Road while their pastor's been recovering from heart surgery. Soon as he finishes there, he's going to be interim at Harmony. Church split, pastor left, and took about half of the church with him."

"Yeah, heard about that," J. T. commented. "The ones that split off from Harmony started a new church in the old Pulliam's Store building. Gloryland Way, the name suggests they think they're going to heaven but the folks they split off from are not. People are gonna call it Pulliam's Store no matter what the sign says."

"I saw the church sign on the old store building the day we buried Miss Addie," Mike commented. "Figured it was a split off of some other church. Sign out front lists all the things they're against. In Cassie's honor, they added, 'No Women Preachers.' Since we're not in the association any more, I'm out of the loop, don't hear as much gossip as I used to, which is a good thing. I didn't know where they came from. Hate to hear of any church splitting, but it's really bad when it's one named Harmony. Anyway, talking about an ordination council, Henry Conway at Greater New Hope will be there if he can. So will Brad Terry, the new guy out at Taylor's Crossroads. I've been impressed with Brad. He's young, twenty-four years old, first pastorate. Raised down at LaGrange, works on computers for a living, engaged to a nurse who works at Pine Ridge Assisted Living. First time I met him was at the meeting when we got kicked out of the association for licensing Cassie. He spoke against the motion to kick us out, said Taylor's Crossroads intended to remain in fellowship with Harrington Baptist Church no matter what the association did, then asked me right there in front of the whole meeting if I'd come over and preach a revival at Taylor's Crossroads. I did, back in May. Our Sacred Harp Singers came over and sang one night, and Coretta sang one night. Really enjoyed being over there."

"I remember that," Josie reminisced. "We were at the meeting. All of our messengers, 'cept Brother Bobby, voted against the motion to kick y'all out. So we'll still be friends with y'all and Taylor's Crossroads after we get kicked out."

"Yeah," J. T. added. "I thought Brother Bobby was gonna have a stroke or heart attack. He was revved up so tight I thought he was about to put a rod through the side of the block, all because we didn't vote the way he did. I guess we're next in line to get kicked out of the association, then Taylor's Crossroads will be next after us. We'll be in good company when we get kicked out. Don't think I'll miss the association that much. Used to enjoy it back when it was about promoting missions, fellowship among the churches, and churches helping each other out, now it seems to be more about keeping everybody in line. I'm all for helping other churches, don't care anything about trying to control them."

Mike enjoyed visiting with J. T. and Josie as a slow drizzling rain moved in. He was still talking and sipping coffee with them when Helen Walters came in to put the finishing touches on the newsletter, print it, and take it to the post office. "Helen," Mike greeted her, "there's a little coffee left in the pot if your want some, and we've got some good donuts here from York's. They make the best ones. I'd like for you to meet J. T. and Josie Bailey from out at Peyton's Chapel, where we buried Miss

Addie and where Cassie's been preaching the last few weeks. J. T. and Josie, this is Helen Walters, our church secretary. Her husband, everybody called him Doc, was a dentist here for years."

After J. T. and Josie exchanged pleasantries with Helen and told her that Doc had been their dentist for years before he retired, Mike continued, "They just voted to call Cassie as their pastor yesterday. Josie's the church clerk at Peyton's Chapel, just brought us the request for Cassie's ordination. I put a sticky note on your computer screen, need to put the announcement in the newsletter that the church will vote on the request at the close of the service Sunday morning.

"She certainly is young to be ordained and be a pastor," Helen commented icily.

"She is," Josie acknowledged, "but we had a fifty-six-year-old man as pastor who was mean as a snake and didn't have the sense God gave a billy goat, so you never know. Sister Cassie is kind and tender-hearted, knows her Bible, good preacher, seems to have a lot more sense about her than Brother Bobby did. Brother Bobby needs to stick to running a backhoe and putting in septic tanks. God's called this young lady to be a pastor. She'll be good for us. Our attendance has been up the Sundays that she's been with us, and she's brought a good message every time, lot better than what'd we'd been hearing. I think we'll be good for her, too. Some things they can't teach a preacher in college or seminary, so we signed her up for Country Church 101."

Helen logged onto her computer and pulled up the file for this week's newsletter. She deleted some filler artwork to make room and typed in:

> **Congratulations** to Cassie McWhorter, who was called last Sunday as pastor of Peyton's Chapel Baptist Church.

> **Called Business Meeting** immediately following Sunday morning worship on November 8 to vote on a request from Peyton's Chapel Baptist Church to ordain Cassie McWhorter to the Gospel Ministry. The deacons will recommend that we approve the request.

The overcast skies and slow, steady drizzle continued, ruling out the possibility of any yard work today, so Mike went home, told Wallace the Dog to go back to sleep, changed back into his coveralls, and headed the faded blue Ford Fairmount wagon over to Tommy's place. Tommy's black S-10 was still at the funeral home when Mike passed by there, so Tommy and Daniel were not back from Atlanta yet. Mike unlocked Tommy's garage and switched on the lights. Harold Mabry had gotten all the body work straight as an arrow before he laid a slick paint job on Tommy's truck. He painted it back the original colors, dark green cab and bed with black fenders and running boards. This was going to be one nice old truck, with the looks of a restored original and the ability to run with highway traffic all day long. Mike breathed a sigh of relief when he saw the box from Ron Francis Wire Works unopened on the workbench. "Wait'll I get there before you start pulling wires out and looking at them," Mike had told Tommy last week when he called to say that the wiring kit had arrived. With Tommy a safe distance away, Mike opened the box and took inventory of the contents. Everything was there. Mike had cleared Tommy to set the battery in the battery tray and fasten it down, mount the alternator, and mount the starter. Mike crawled under the truck with a 9/16" socket and breaker bar to be sure Tommy had the starter bolts snugged up tight. He had also cleared Tommy to run a ground strap from the engine block to the firewall and another from the engine block to the frame. After he made sure the ground straps were in place, Mike confirmed that Tommy had the fan belt tight enough to keep it from slipping but not tight enough to burn up the bearings in the alternator and water pump. Mike took the wiring panel out of the box, held it in position, and marked the spot to drill for two #8 sheet metal screws to hold it in place. Even if Tommy didn't know what to do with half the tools he had, he at least had them and had them organized. Mike found a fully charged cordless drill and a 1/8" bit, drilled the holes, and mounted the panel to the inside of the firewall. He found the new battery cables Tommy bought lying on top of the engine. He ran the shorter one from the negative terminal of the battery to an intake manifold bolt at the back of the engine. It really didn't matter which of the basic circuits he wired first, all had to be done before they could crank it. He retrieved the bag with the starter wiring, jacked up the right front corner of the truck, and put a jack stand under it. Tommy had gone and bought one of those really nice creepers at Advance, being like a kid in a candy store at that place, but Mike preferred a big sheet of cardboard for crawling under a car. "Poor man's creeper," he explained to Tommy. "Cheaper, and you don't have to jack it up as high to get under it." Mike tore open the bag with the starter wiring and slid under on the passenger side on his poor man's creeper. He could do this in his sleep. Mike made short work of connecting the starter, ignition, and charging circuits and mounting the ignition switch in the dash. He bundled everything neatly with zip ties. Just as Mike connected the positive cable to the battery, he heard Tommy pull up, get out of his truck, and open the door of the shop. "Come in out of the rain, Tommy, before your undertaker suit gets wet, and I'll be sure to tell everybody you have the sense to come in out of the rain. Let me grab a distributor wrench. You get in this thing and fire it up so I can time it for you. I'll time it by ear, put it dead on the money, and then I'm gone to the house to start supper before Karen and the girls get home. Some other time, I'll show you how to use that pretty timing light you bought so you can see I've already got it timed right and you don't need to fiddle with it."

"Preacher Man," the familiar voice of Tommy Sheridan greeted Mike on Saturday morning just as he was fixing to put the biscuits in the oven. "Don't worry, nobody's dead and I had'n messed anything up on the truck. Stopped by Food World while ago and picked up some coffee to have at the funeral home. Saw a flyer on the bulletin board at Food World announcing the start of a new radio program on the Harrington station, comes on in about ten minutes. I grabbed the flyer off the board 'fore anybody else saw it. It's the True to the Word Radio Ministry with Brother Bobby Simpson, sponsored by Simpson's Septic Tank and Backhoe Service. I don't think I told you he came by the funeral home the first of last week, asking for the funeral home to help sponsor him on the radio. Mr. Webster leaves that kind of thing up to me since he halfway retired and made me manager of the funeral home. Now, you know me, I'm all for anybody that's preaching the word and telling people about the Good Lord. We've underwritten Harrington Methodist's broadcast of the Sunday morning service for twenty years or more, and we've helped sponsor Greater New Hope Baptist and Preacher Conway for about four or five years now. I love to listen to Preacher Conway, good man and he's always got a good message. We're glad to help support them, and we don't ask either one to mention the funeral home on the air. We support them because the Lord's given us the means to do it, and we like to give back to the community by supporting good ministries. We don't do it to drum up business for the funeral home. People are already dying to do business with us."

"Bad pun, Tommy."

"Yeah, I know, Preacher. Anyway, I told Bobby Simpson we wouldn't give him a dime. He got all pitiful, said 'Brother Tommy, you've known me close to twenty years,' and I told him, 'Yeah, I have, and that's why I'm not going to help pay for you to be on the radio. I'm not going to support a preacher who treats his wife worse'n a dog and assaults another preacher at the cemetery.' Told him the only sponsorship we'd give him would be the day his obituary's on The Obituary Column of the Air. So anyway, Preacher, you might want to tune in just to see what he has to say."

Mike clicked on the radio in the kitchen to the local AM station, where he and Karen kept it mostly to listen to The Obituary Column of the Air and The Swap Shop on Saturday mornings. Precisely at 8:30 a.m., the recording of children singing "The B-I-B-L-E, yes that's the book for me, I stand alone on the word of God..." followed by Bill Bailey's voiceover, "A good Saturday morning to everybody! It's time for the True to the Word Radio Ministry with our friend Brother Bobby Simpson, brought to you by Simpson Septic Tank and Backhoe Service, the folks to call for all your septic tank and backhoe needs in Phillips and Mintz Counties."

"Thank you, Brother Bill, and hello to all of our friends out there in radio land, 'specially the sick and the shut-ins. God bless you, Amen! This is your old friend and neighbor Brother Bobby Simpson, bringin' you a message that's true to the word of God, Amen, 'cause we're livin' in perilous times. Like the apostle Paul wrote over there in II Timothy the fourth chapter verses three and four, 'For the time will come when they will not endure sound doctrine, but after their own lusts shall they heap to themselves teachers, having itching ears, and they shall turn away their ears from the truth, and shall be turned to fables.' People today don't care no more what the word of God says, I'm talkin' about people in the churches, people that're 'sposed to be saved, they don't care what the Bible says, they're gonna do what they want to do, Amen? Over there in Romans chapter one verse twenty-six, Paul says, 'For this cause God gave them up unto vile affections; for even their women did change the natural use into that which is against nature.' 'Course now, we don't expect them liberal United Methodists to follow the word of God on much of anything, don't surprise me much that they got 'em another woman preacher, Amen, but now we got supposed to be a Baptist church in Mintz County that's done gone and called not just a woman but a nineteen-year-old girl that ain't even married! Standin' up in front of people and preachin' ain't the natural use of a woman. It's against nature, Amen? Brother Paul tells us over there in I Corinthians fourteen and verse thirty-four, 'Let the women keep sil...'" The radio went silent for a moment before the voice of Bill Bailey came back on saying, "Ladies and gentlemen, we are experiencing technical difficulties. Please enjoy some good gospel music while we resolve the problem and return to our regularly scheduled programming as soon as possible." Mike couldn't help but notice that the return to regularly scheduled programming occurred precisely at 8:45 a.m. when the next program started.

Mike was putting breakfast on the table when Tommy called again. "Hey Preacher, just so you know, I called my buddy Gerald over't the radio station to find out what kind of technical difficulties they had right when Brother Bobby was getting 'revved up. He said their technical problem was a preacher with a screw loose. Bill shut him off. Said the only rule the station enforces on religious programs is no slandering other churches and preachers. He said it's fine for Brother Bobby to say he's against women preachers, but they're not gonna let him slander the

Methodists, Peyton's Chapel Baptist, or Cassie. Brother Bobby won't be back on the air in Harrington."

At the close of the invitation on Sunday morning, Mike announced, "Everybody please be seated for a moment before the benediction. As we announced in the newsletter you received this week and in today's bulletin, we are called into a brief business meeting to consider a request from one of our sister churches, Peyton's Chapel Baptist Church. I recognize the chair of our deacon group, Sister Brenda Coleman, to present the recommendation from the deacons concerning this request."

"Thank you, Brother Mike. The last time this church ordained a minister of the gospel was in 1934 when we ordained Brother Emory Baxter to serve Freeman Valley Baptist Church. Miss Addie was the last person left who remembered him." With a laugh, Brenda commented, "Our deacons agree it's high time we ordained another one." Tears were starting to trickle down her face as she continued, "As most of you know, Peyton's Chapel Baptist Church, the oldest Baptist church in Mintz County, has called one of our own, Cassie McWhorter, to be their pastor. The first four pastors who served Harrington Baptist Church were ordained by Peyton's Chapel. We need to return the favor and ordain a good one for Peyton's Chapel. Brother Mike, I'm glad you put this box of Kleenex up here," Brenda's voice broke with emotion. "You know me. You knew I'd need it. I told you I couldn't get through this without getting all teary-eyed, thinking about Miss Addie preaching the glory down that Sunday eight years ago when Cassie was baptized. A year ago, at the beginning of her senior year in high school, Cassie preached her first sermon and we licensed her to preach. Now we've received a request from Peyton's Chapel to ordain Sister Cassie McWhorter to the gospel ministry. I have spoken with all of our active deacons, and we unanimously recommend that our pastor be authorized to convene an ordination council and schedule a service for the purpose of ordaining Sister Cassie McWhorter as a minister of the gospel."

"Thank you, Brenda. You have heard the recommendation from our deacons. No second is needed on a recommendation that comes from the deacons. Is there any question or discussion regarding the recommendation?" After waiting a couple of seconds, Mike continued, "All in favor, say 'Aye.'" Following a strong chorus of 'Ayes,' he asked, "All opposed to the recommendation, say 'No.'" Mike held his breath momentarily and breathed a sigh of relief when nobody said 'No.' "The motion carries. Jerry and Elaine, I'm sure you'll let Cass know. I will go ahead and convene the ordination council on Saturday, November 21, and we will plan to ordain Cassie on Sunday, November 22."

Chapter 17

"Cassie," Mary Grace broke the silence as she turned out the light over her bed on Wednesday night. "I've been enjoying these weekends with your family and the church, but I've got to get back up to Elberton and see my folks. Eventually. You know I've been putting it off. You know I came here to Mercer instead of UGA so I'd be further from all the craziness at home, but I'm gonna catch hell from Mother and Daddy if I don't show up and help them play happy family for the day on Thanksgiving."

"Yeah," Cassie acknowledged. "You do. I mean you eventually have to go home to your family."

"It's easier to go home to yours," Mary Grace responded. "I mean, I love my family, but I like yours better. I'm so comfortable with your folks, the 'Mr. and Mrs. McWhorter' thing didn't make it through the first hour at your house. Then there's the church. Everybody at Peyton's Chapel treats me like I was born there. Of course, there's no way I'd miss your ordination. I'm honored that you asked me to read one of the Bible readings."

"And I'm honored that you said 'yes' when I asked you. It means as much to me as having Heather come down from Virginia to preach. Every bit as much."

"Thanks, Cass. I've read over the passage you asked me to read so many times because it's important to me to read it well. I think I could just about recite it from memory. So, Friday evening, I'll drive my car and follow you down to Harrington, stay with your folks through Sunday, be there for church and your ordination. Monday morning, I'll plan to head on up to Elberton. I don't know how many days Dad is taking off for Thanksgiving. He might work through Wednesday or he might take off the whole week. Won't be too bad if he works through Wednesday and doesn't get to start drinking 'til Wednesday night. Thursday'll be bad. All of Dad's family is getting together at my uncle's place in Athens. We'll eat, the ball games will come on, all the guys and about half the women will get sloppy stupid drunk and somebody will start an argument. That, or Dad'll be sure when he's half drunk and has an audience to slap me on the butt in front of everybody and tell me how hot I look and how Daddy's little girl's all grown up now, and he'll say I'd probably make real good tips if I worked at Hooters or something stupid along those lines, and he'll act like I ought to be flattered by him saying stuff like that. If it gets too crazy at home, I'll couch surf with friends like I did in high school, or I'll spend a couple of nights up at Royston with my grandparents. Definitely plan to spend Saturday night with them, go to church with them on Sunday. Surprise the living daylights out of them, but they'll be delighted. By the time I get through Thanksgiving, I'll be needing to go to church to pray for forgiveness for some of the things I've said to my parents and some of my dad's kinfolks. It's a lot easier to keep from cussing when I'm not around them. You'd learn to cuss if you were around them."

"Can't say that's a skill I want to acquire," Cassie commented. "You have cut back on the cussing, not that you ever did that much around me."

"I really don't like it," Mary Grace acknowledged, "but it was normal conversation at home. It's easy to fall into talking that way, but I've always found it more pleasant to be around people who don't drop F-bombs all over the place and don't think 'damn' is God's last name. That's probably one reason we've gotten along well from the get-go this semester. I do slip up sometimes because it was just so normal in my family. I'm glad nobody at Peyton's Chapel had a cow when I said 'damn' in Sunday School a couple of weeks ago. I didn't realize I'd done it until you kidded me about it on the way home. Nobody at church reacted at all, didn't even raise an eyebrow."

"The people at Peyton's Chapel pretty much love you the way you are, so that didn't surprise me. I'm glad you're going to spend some time with your grandparents," Cassie commented. "I'm pretty close to Grandma and Grandpa McWhorter. They go to the Church of God in Harrington. Daddy grew up in the Church of God, joined Harrington Baptist when he and my mom got married. I miss Granny Whitmire. We were close. She died when I was in the tenth grade. I barely remember Papa Whitmire. I think I was maybe four or five when he died. So enjoy your grandparents while you can. I'm sure they'll be glad to have you stay with them some and go to church with them on Sunday. You've got some people up that way who'll downplay your Christian commitment, won't think it's any big deal, they just don't get it, or they'll think it's just a phase you're going through that you'll get over. You've got some like your dad who may be hostile to your faith. Just remember you've got some who get it. There will always be the scoffers and the ones who don't see what the big deal is, but you know that you had a very real encounter with a very real God. God will always give you some who believe your testimony."

"That scripture you showed me in Romans 8, I've got it marked and highlighted in my Bible, the one that says that 'nothing shall separate us from the love of God which is in Christ Jesus our Lord,' that and the new song I learned at Peyton's Chapel, I know it's not new to you but it is to me, the one that goes 'What have I to dread, what have I to fear / Leaning on the everlasting arms, / I have blessed peace with my Lord so near, Leaning on the everlasting arms,' that's helped me a lot. The anticipation of going to see my grandparents, spending some time with them, going to church with them, has really started to overshadow the dread of dealing with my dad and his side of the family. My grandparents on my mom's side are really sweet people, though my dad despises them, makes fun of them, calls them 'the Hicks from the sticks' and puts them down as religious nuts. He's tried to drive a wedge between mom and her parents. Actually more than tried, he succeeded. Last time I went to church with Nanny and Papa Hicks, I was a little bitty squirt, no more than six or seven years old. I remember that I liked Sunday School and church the few times I got to go with them, and I tried to get Mother and Daddy to go to church and take me, but they never would. Those few times with Nanny and Papa were the only acquaintance I had with church before I started going with you to Peyton's Chapel. I met the pastor of Nanny and Papa's church when we had the fiftieth wedding anniversary reception a few weeks ago. He seems like a nice guy, and the people I met from their church were really cordial. I'm just so used to Peyton's Chapel and your preaching that it's gonna feel weird to go anywhere else and hear anybody else preach. I don't know if I could go by myself, but I'll be okay going with my grandparents. It's gonna feel odd to see a fifty-year-old man behind the pulpit. You're the only preacher I've heard more than once, so a nineteen-year-old woman preacher is the norm for me."

"When you're with your grandparents and visiting their church," Cassie observed, "You'll be among people who won't look at you like you're speaking Swahili when you talk about becoming a Christian, being baptized, and joining the church. Of course, they might give you that 'Are you speaking Swahili, Hon?' look if you tell them you helped ordain your roommate the Sunday before, or if you tell them that your pastor is a nineteen-year-old girl who baptized you in Salyers Creek before she was ordained."

"I'm not going to get into the thing about women preachers yet, don't know how Nanny and Papa feel about that. I know it's not some-thing they're used to. Just gonna tell them that I've gone home with you the past few weekends, tell them that you led me to the Lord, and I've started going to church with you and I've been baptized and joined the church, all of which is true. We'll get to the rest of the story, the part about you being my pastor and the one who baptized me, and the whole ordination thing, all in due time.

"Probably a good idea, at least for now," Cassie concurred. "I know Miss Addie said 'If Moses had waited until everybody was ready, the chil-dren of Israel would still be in Egypt,' but sometimes you have to give people information in installments. Give them the most important infor-mation first, then when they've had a chance to be happy about that, you can tell them the rest. Let them be glad that you're saved, baptized, and involved in a good church. Let them take you to their church and brag on you. Then, maybe over Sunday dinner, mention the woman preacher roommate part. Timing's everything," Cassie added with a laugh. "Don't tell them while they have food in their mouths, so you don't have to do the Heimlich thing on them."

"I'm really not too worried about Nanny and Papa," Mary Grace observed. "Even if they're not for women preachers, it's like J. T. out at Peyton's Chapel, it was just something they hadn't thought much about 'til they heard you at Miss Addie's funeral. They'll be so glad that I'm saved and trying to follow Jesus that nothing else will really matter that much. They'll probably be like, if a woman preacher led Mary Grace to Jesus, maybe women preachers are not such a bad thing. Just pray for me when I tell my parents. Mom'll be okay with it. She grew up in church. I think she's still a member of the church where my grandparents go. I can't remember her ever going to church in my lifetime, unless you count weddings and funerals, but she'll probably say 'that's nice' or something. She won't oppose me being a Christian and going to church. She'll respect my decision and my faith, she'll be like that's fine for me even if it's not her cup of tea. Dad didn't grow up going to church. He'll give me a hard time about it. He'll come up with something to do or somewhere to go on Sunday morning to conflict with me going to church, and he'll give me a hard time like I'm a traitor to the family when I insist on going to church. Knowing him, that's probably how he got Mom away from church. Dad has a real negative attitude toward religion in general, makes fun of churches and preachers, and loves to get on his rant about how all the people who go to church are hypocrites and phonies. Sometimes when he's drinking, he'll turn on some of the more flamboyant TV preachers, the ones who are obvious charlatans and always begging for money, watch them just for entertainment and make fun of them and the people who are stupid enough to follow them and send them money. He'll use that to say all preachers are just in it to separate people from their money."

"You can tell him Peyton's Chapel pays me $75 a week," Cassie suggested. "Gonna take me a while to get rich at that rate. Don't think I'll trade the Old Gray Mare for a Lexus any time soon. As for flashy jewelry, the necklace with the little gold cross pendant that belonged to Miss Addie that I wear every time I preach, my Harrington High School class ring, and my grandmother Whitmire's Bulova watch are about it. I'm too tall to find many dresses that fit me in the stores, got some nice tailor-made dresses because I've got a mom who's really good with the sewing machine, knows how to fit me, and loves to sew."

"Then," Mary Grace continued, "When Dad gets good and pickled, he'll wax philosophical on us and want to know how come there's so much pain and suffering in the world if there's a good God who cares about people, and I don't have a real good answer for that."

"Put that ball back in his court," Cassie suggested. "Bear with me and the basketball metaphors here. Ask him how he explains all the goodness, kindness, generosity, mercy, and compassion in this world."

"Good point. I'll remember that, Cass. Thanks. I guess I've been like a plant in a greenhouse with this whole religion and faith thing."

"Interesting analogy," Cassie commented. "Tell me what you mean by that."

"In a greenhouse, you create conditions that are perfect for the plant to grow, but the question is, can the plant survive outside the controlled conditions of the greenhouse? So far, I've been like a plant in a greenhouse, surrounded by people who support my decision to become a Christian—the church, all of your family and friends in Harrington, the Baptist Campus Ministry here at Mercer."

"Oh yeah," Cassie injected. "I meant to tell you. I've talked to probably half a dozen people we know from BCM who are coming down to Harrington Sunday to go to church at Peyton's Chapel and be at my ordination Sunday afternoon. I e-mailed Coretta and let her know they're coming. She e-mailed me back and said to tell them they're all welcome to come Saturday and spend the night with her and Daniel, said they'd put pallets on the floor or whatever they needed to do. Bob Ballance, the editor of *Baptists Today*, is coming, too. He's interim pastor of a church up at Cartersville, but he's got somebody to cover for him this Sunday so he can come down and help with my ordination. His wife is a minister, too. They're both coming. They've been friends with Ted and Brenda Coleman for years, so they're staying with the Colemans. Bob's going to do a feature about me and Peyton's Chapel for *Baptists Today*."

"That's great. Back to my greenhouse analogy, I'm surrounded by all these people who support me becoming a Christian. On top of all of that, my pastor is my roommate, or my roommate is my pastor, however you want to describe that, so it's been pretty easy so far for me to be a Christian. I've been surrounded by people who understand and support me. There may be hypocrites and phonies in the church somewhere, but the ones I've met so far seem to be the real deal. Not to say that some of them might not disappoint me somewhere down the road, but they haven't yet. I don't think it'd shatter my faith if some of them did, because nobody's perfect and nobody gets it right all the time. I'm not perfect, so I don't expect anybody else to be. What I'm worried about is how I'll respond to people in my family who just don't get it or they'll put me down or ridicule me or bring up questions I don't have answers for or act like I've gone off the deep end and joined some cult when I talk about my faith."

"I'm glad you brought that up," Cassie observed. "You don't know it, but you're helping me with my sermon. I'm going to be nervous as a cat having all these preachers in the congregation. I know Heather, don't know Bob other than from reading what he writes in *Baptists Today* and hearing the Colemans talk about him. I'd be honored to have Heather or Bob or Bob's wife preach, Lord knows they're all better preachers than I am, but they all said they want to hear me, so I'm going to preach from the thirteenth chapter of Acts, where the church at Antioch sends Saul and Barnabas out on their first missionary journey. Since you're going up to see your folks at Elberton on Monday, I want to tie that into the sermon. Peyton's Chapel is going to send you on your first missionary journey. When you go to see your folks, you will go as an emissary of

Peyton's Chapel Baptist Church. We'll have your back in prayer. So will Saint Addie." With a yawn, Cassie added, "Good night, Mary Grace. Give all your worries to the Lord and go to sleep."

"Good night, Cass."

Cassie was drifting off to sleep when she heard Mary Grace softly whisper, "Saint Addie, pray for us."

"Brother Mike, I hope I didn't get ahead of myself." Mike recognized Rhonda Brinson's voice on the phone. "But you know Miss Addie liked to say that it's easier to get forgiveness than permission, so she just waited and got forgiveness after the fact. So, if I shouldn't have done what I did, forgive me."

"Sounds serious, Rhonda. What'd you do, choke the living daylights out of some parent for mistreating their kids?"

"No, nothing like that, Brother Mike. You know it's against DFCS policy for us to strangle parents no matter how much they need it or deserve it. Policy doesn't allow us to use the 'he needed killing' defense. Unfortunate in a way, because it would save the state a ton of money. They can appeal termination of parental rights. There's no appealing a death certificate. But no, no strangled parents, nothing like that."

"So what did you do, Rhonda?" Mike asked.

"Invited another preacher to be on Cassie's ordination council."

"You did? Who?"

"Don't know if you've heard of Ruby Welsh Wilkins," Rhonda answered. "She lives a little ways over the Alabama line at Wadley, Alabama. First woman to pastor a Baptist church in Alabama, served Antioch Baptist Church at Wadley from 1971 to 1984."

"Heard of her." Mike responded. "Don't know her.

"Well, I do, Brother Mike. I was born and raised at Wadley. I've known her all my life. Sweet lady. She's like family to me. I was half grown, probably eleven or twelve years old, before I realized I wasn't kin to her. I still call her Aunt Ruby like I always did. That's what Davis and Laura call her, too. They love her. My daddy was in the used car business about forty years, and Aunt Ruby's husband, Uncle Millard, owned a body shop. He did a lot of work for Daddy, fixing dents and dings and touching up paint on cars before Daddy put them on the lot to sell. As far back as I can remember, I used to go with Daddy to take cars over there and pick them up. Soon as I turned sixteen and got my driver's license, Daddy had me taking cars over there and picking them up for him. I told Aunt Ruby about Cassie when we licensed her to preach. I told her how well Cassie did with Miss Addie's funeral and told her that she was preaching out at Peyton's Chapel. She's been wanting to meet her, give her a hug, and hear her preach. As soon as I found out we were ordaining Cassie this weekend, I called Aunt Ruby and told her if she wanted to come up and be on the ordination council, go to Peyton's Chapel on Sunday morning and hear Cassie preach, and be here for the ordination service, I'd run down there Saturday morning, get her, and bring her up here. She can stay with us, and I'll take her back Sunday night. She was delighted when I asked her, said she'd love to come. She's so eager to meet Cassie, and I know she'll be an encouragement to her. If you liked Miss Addie, you'll be impressed with Aunt Ruby."

"You're forgiven," Mike laughed. "I would've given permission if you'd asked. I know Cassie'll be delighted to meet Ruby, and I look forward to meeting her, too. We've got a good group of preachers for the council. Bob Ballance, editor of *Baptists Today*, Bob's wife Catherine, Henry Conway from Greater New Hope, Brad Terry from Taylor's Crossroads, Bob McKnight who was interim pastor here before I came, Heather Simmons Moore, your Aunt Ruby, and me. That's eight, plus our deacons and the deacons from Peyton's Chapel. Give me Ruby's number. I'll call her and tell her that we're honored that she's coming."

Cassie didn't set an alarm clock when she went to bed Friday night. She was tired from an intense week of school the last week before the Thanksgiving break and the drive in from Macon. She and Mary Grace had talked late into the night about the anxieties they both felt, Cassie about facing her ordination council and Mary Grace about facing her parents. It was straight-up-and-down 6:00 a.m. when Cassie was awakened by the aroma of fine Colombian coffee and the gurgling sounds of the big coffee urn. She yawned and stretched as she walked to the bathroom, leaving Mary Grace sound asleep, ran a cold wet washcloth over her face, and made her way toward the aroma and sound of coffee. She took one of the big mugs on the counter, poured it a third full with milk, topped it off with coffee, and stirred in a spoonful of sugar before cuddling up with her father on the big overstuffed sofa in the den. The newscaster on CNN kept droning on about something, but neither Jerry nor Cassie was paying any attention to him.

"Hey, Preacher Girl. Sleep good last night?" Jerry asked as he gave Cassie a gentle hug.

"Kind of wound up, Daddy Longlegs," Cassie replied. "Talked with Mary Grace 'til I drifted off about 1:30 a.m., slept fine while I slept, but woke up sooner than I meant to. Part excitement and part nerves when it comes to the ordination council this evening. Tell me it's going to be okay. I mean, it'll be bad if the council splits down the middle over whether to ordain me. I have this recurring nightmare about everybody showing up for the ordination tomorrow afternoon and Brother Mike has to announce, "Sorry folks, the council yesterday evening decided this girl's not ready for 11:00 a.m. Sunday prime time.""

"Don't think you've got anything to worry about, Cass," Jerry spoke reassuringly. "I had all of those same worries when I was ordained as a deacon, your mom did too when she was ordained, especially since she was the first woman that Harrington ordained. Brenda Coleman was already ordained by the church they came from in Macon. Don't know which one of us was worse. It turned out to not be bad for either of us. I don't know all of the people who are going to be on your council, but I don't think there'll be anybody who wants to shoot you down. You don't have to have all the answers. In my case, that was a good thing, because I sure didn't, and I was only six years older than you are when I was ordained as a deacon. And don't forget that your mom and I are going to be there, so if anybody tries to trip you up, Daddy Longlegs'll beat 'em up for you—after your mom scratches their eyeballs out, of course."

As Jerry laughed and pulled Cassie close for another reassuring hug, Cassie reached across him, snatched the remote from the sofa arm, switched the TV to the Cartoon Network, and stuffed the remote down between the sofa cushions. "Got your 'mote, Daddy Longlegs!" Cassie exclaimed gleefully as she resumed sipping her little girl pretend coffee while watching the antics of Road Runner and Wile E. Coyote.

"So what're you preaching on Sunday morning?" Jerry asked.

"Thirteenth chapter of Acts, where the church at Antioch commissions Saul and Barnabas for their first missionary journey. I'd already planned to preach from that text since I'm being ordained that day. Mary Grace is leaving Monday morning to go up and spend Thanksgiving week with her family up at Elberton. You know she's been real anxious about going up there, hasn't been home since the weekend Miss Addie died, says she loves her family but likes ours a lot better. Mary Grace hasn't told her family yet about becoming a Christian, being baptized, and joining Peyton's Chapel, and she's pretty anxious about how they'll react. She says her mom'll probably be like 'that's nice,' it'll be like no big deal to her, while her dad and his whole side of the family that's getting together at her uncle's house for Thanksgiving dinner will ridicule her and put her down, especially when they get some alcohol in them, treat her like she's joined the Moonies or the Hare Krishnas or something. We've had several late-night conversations about it, and I know she's talked about it with Chris Fuller at Baptist Campus Ministry. Anyway, back to Peyton's Chapel and Acts thirteen. We can't control how Mary Grace's family treats her, but two things we can do—we can pray for the Holy Spirit to prepare them to hear what she has to say, and we can throw all of our support behind her as she goes, let her know that we've got her back in prayer. Peyton's Chapel is doing a missionary commissioning Sunday morning. We're going to surround Mary Grace, lay hands on her, and send her on her first missionary journey to Elberton as a representative of Peyton's Chapel Baptist Church."

"That's great," Jerry commented. "I like that idea a lot. Looks like all of the McWhorters'll be at Peyton's Chapel Sunday morning. I want to be part of that, and I know your mom will, too. She and Mary Grace have gotten really close."

"Glad y'all will be there. It'll mean a lot to her," Cassie concurred. "Might ought to stock up on Kleenex. Won't be a dry eye in the house."

"By the way, been meaning to tell you," Jerry said, "On a somewhat related subject, I talked to my sign painter buddy, John, up at Hansonville Monday morning. Come to find out, some of his wife's people are buried at Peyton's Chapel. Long story short, I mentioned to him that the Peyton's Chapel sign out on Bailey's Mill Road is looking kind of weathered, and we need a sign board with your name on it. Told him that freshly painted sign board saying 'Rev. Cassie McWhorter, Pastor' is going to make the sign above it look even more weathered, so he said he'd donate a whole new sign to go out there where you turn to go to the church and a sign board with your name to go on the sign in front of the church. I called Mr. Bailey out at Peyton's Chapel. He and a couple of guys from the church are meeting John out there this morning to put up the signs."

"I think you know everybody in Mintz and Phillips Counties, Daddy Longlegs," Cassie commented. "Couldn't get by with anything when I was a kid 'cause I knew you had so many eyes and ears out there. If I did anything bad, the news about it would get home before I did. Kind of limiting back then, comes in handy now for getting favors done."

"Not many I don't know," Jerry acknowledged, "though I've met some I didn't know before out at Peyton's Chapel. I was acquainted with J. T. years ago, before he retired, back when he was still working as an engineer with the State Highway Department, hadn't seen him since he retired, that's been about fifteen years ago, never knew back then that our paths would cross again. J. T.'s all right. You've got a lot of good people in that little church."

"We do," Cassie agreed. "And it's been picking up a little every Sunday. The Sunday they voted to call me, Ruth Ann Simpson was there. The next Sunday, Ruth Ann was back and had her two grandchildren with her. The grandchildren are eight and eleven, first time they'd ever been to Sunday School or church. This past Sunday, Ruth Ann and the grandchildren were back, and they had the children's mother, Ruth Ann's daughter Jennifer, with them. Jennifer's the one who said she'd never set foot in church again once she got out from under her daddy's roof. Never say 'never,' I guess. Seemed like she enjoyed being there, said she'd be back."

"Speaking of good people doing favors for us, don't know if your mom told you last night. We've got a bunch of folks fixing dinner at the church for you and everybody on the ordination council. Rhonda Brinson got the ball rolling on that, Josie Bailey called the preacher and said Peyton's Chapel wanted to fix dinner, so Brother Mike told Josie to call Rhonda and combine their efforts. So, if you smell smoke when you go outside, it'll probably be ol' Darrell with his grill fired up. Now, he ain't the King of the Grill, that'd be me, but I got to admit he's pretty good. The boy can cook some fine pork barbeque. We're supposed to eat at 5:00 and start the inquisition at 6:00. While we're there, Daniel and Coretta have invited Karen and the girls and Mary Grace to hang out with them."

"What about the Little Brat? You gonna leave him here, leave him to his own devices?" Cassie asked.

"Oh, no, nothing like that," Jerry spoke reassuringly. "You know he's got a girlfriend. He's sweet on Amanda Hall, the Methodist preacher's daughter. They're both fifteen, not old enough to really date, but her folks have invited him over for the evening. Between the Methodist preacher and her husband who's a state trooper, he ought to be pretty well supervised. By the way— mentioning Rhonda Brinson—she invited another preacher to your ordination council."

"She did? Who?"

"She just referred to her as Aunt Ruby, said she lives over't Wadley, Alabama, where Rhonda's from. Said her Aunt Ruby was close to eighty years old, and she was the first woman to pastor a Baptist church in Alabama."

"Oh, wow!" Cassie exclaimed. "I've heard of her, read about her. Always wanted to meet her. Ruby. Wadley, Alabama. First woman to pastor a Baptist church in Alabama. That's got to be Ruby Welsh Wilkins. She's coming to help with my ordination?"

"Yep. Rhonda's going down there to get her and bring her up here this morning."

Chapter 18

Cassie was accustomed to driving herself everywhere, so she felt like a little kid when she rode with her parents. When he drove, Jerry put the seat all the way back; when Elaine drove she put it up under the dash. Cassie, being long-legged like her dad, sat behind her mom to have legroom. Mary Grace, being much shorter, sat behind Jerry. As they dropped Mary Grace off at Daniel and Coretta's house, she reached over, gave Cassie a hug, and told her, "Relax. It's going to be good. I'm praying for you. Remember Miss Addie."

"I appreciate your prayers. Can't think of anybody I'd rather have praying for me," Cassie replied. "And I think Miss Addie is in on this."

"You look good," Elaine spoke reassuringly as she reached across the back of the seat and took Cassie's hand as Jerry turned the car into the Harrington Baptist Church parking lot. "I like that dress on you. Looks good if I did make it. Emily did a nice job on your hair. Try not to be too worried. You're going to do well. We're so proud of you."

"Thanks, Mom."

Jerry parked next to the Brinsons' two-tone blue Chevy Astro van, put it in park, turned off the ignition, and released the seat belt buckle. "Cassie, before we go in, would you let your mom and me just hold you a minute and let me pray for you?"

"I'd like that very much," Cassie said as she leaned forward into the embrace of her parents who were reaching over the back of the seat to put their arms around her.

"Heavenly Father," Jerry began praying, his voice breaking with emotion. "Thank you for Cassie. Lord, I remember the first time I held her in the delivery room at the hospital in Carrollton, I knew then that you had good things in store for her, and I knew we were going to raise her to love you and follow you. I remember when I stood in the baptistery with her and brother Mike and helped put her under the water, I knew she was on the right track. And now, here she is about to be ordained as a minister of the gospel. I thank you, Lord, for all the people who helped Elaine and me guide her in your way, the good people you brought into her life, especially Miss Addie and Preacher Simmons. Lord, I remember how scared I was when Cassie told us you were calling her to preach. I was scared because I know how some people are about women preachers. I knew she'd face a lot of opposition, and I didn't want her to get hurt. Lord, I had to face my fears and trust you more. Thank you, Lord, for bringing us to this place, getting ready to ordain Cassie for the work you've called her to do. Take away her fears and worries, help her realize that every member of this council is praying for her and no one wants to trip her up. Thank you for every member of this council. Help Cassie remember this night for the rest of her life as a time when you were close beside her. Guide us tonight so that all we say and do may bring honor to your name. In Jesus' precious name, Amen."

"Amen," Cassie and Elaine concurred.

"The guest of honor has arrived!" Mike announced as Cassie and her parents came into the fellowship hall. Two long tables were covered with a fine spread of food, starting with Darrell Brinson's pork barbeque and a selection of his homemade sauces ranging from 'child-mild' to 'guaranteed to clean out your arteries,' along with several big packages of buns. Then there was Cole slaw, potato salad, baked beans, fried chicken, an array of vegetables, and a choice of a half-dozen or more desserts. Cassie remembered Mike saying that the round tables were among the best investments the church ever made, because nobody sits at the head of a round table, and it's easier to engage in conversation with more people. Cassie had just spotted Heather and gotten a hug from her when Mike announced, "Hope y'all are hungry. Looks like the food's ready and everybody we're expecting is here. I want to thank those from our church and Peyton's Chapel who prepared lots of good food for us this evening and got here early to have everything ready for us. Let's go ahead and have the blessing and fix our plates so we'll have plenty of time to eat and visit with each other before we start the ordination council at 6:00 p.m. I'll ask Reverend Henry Conway, pastor of the Greater New Hope Progressive Missionary Baptist Church, to give the blessing for our meal." Conway was known for his ability to segue seamlessly from praying into preaching, falling into the rhythm of call and response, but he must have wanted a hot meal, so he didn't do it this time. He gave thanks for the food and for those who prepared it. He prayed for bodies to be nourished by the food and for minds and spirits to be nourished by the conversations around the table. He prayed for Cassie and the ordination council to be guided by the Holy Spirit. He asked it all in Jesus' name and built up to a mighty crescendo, saying, "and all of God's people said, 'Amen!'"

As the chorus of 'amens' reverberated in the fellowship hall, Cassie felt someone touch her elbow gently to get her attention. She turned to find herself towering over a petite woman with silver gray hair and a warm smile. Had the woman been wearing high heels, she might have topped five feet. Cassie's extended right hand was enveloped by the woman's two small arthritic hands as she introduced herself, "So you must be Cassie! I'm Ruby Wilkins. I've heard a lot about you from Rhonda and her family, been looking forward to meeting you. I was so excited when Rhonda called and asked me if I wanted to come up here for your ordination. I told her I didn't drive that far from home, she said she knew that and she was coming to get me and bring me up here."

"Wow," Cassie exclaimed, "do you have any idea how long I have known about you and wanted to meet you? And here I am speaking face-to-face with you! I read about you when I was in the ninth grade and I've wanted to meet you ever since."

"Well, your wish has been granted," Ruby laughed. "You've met me. Such as I am, here I am. I've wanted to meet you every bit as much as you've wanted to meet me. I feel like I already know you from all that Rhonda and her family have told me about you. I read about this church getting voted out of the association after they licensed you, saw that in *Baptists Today*, and Rhonda sent me the write up about it in the Harrington paper. Antioch got booted out after they called me in 1971. Rhonda told me about Miss Addie, told me what a fine job you did with her funeral, and how that led to you being called as pastor at Peyton's Chapel. Rhonda's precious. I love her like one of my own. She still calls me Aunt Ruby like she did when she was a little girl. She said she was shocked to find out when she got older that she wasn't really kin to me."

"Ruby Welsh Wilkins!" Heather exclaimed when she overheard the conversation between Ruby and Cassie, "I've read about you, too! I was so excited when I found out you were going to be here! I'm Heather Simmons Moore, pastor of Clear Springs Baptist Church at Ledford, Virginia."

"Pleased to meet you, Heather," Ruby replied as she reciprocated Heather's hug. "I am just as happy to meet you as you are to meet me. I never thought I was anybody special. I never thought that I was doing anything more than my duty, just a simple act of obedience. God called, I answered. He led, I followed."

"And your simple act of obedience to God helped clear the path for so many more who came after you," Heather commented. "You are somebody special, and I'm honored to be in your presence. You answered God's call when others did not."

"Yeah," Cassie quipped as she gave Ruby a hug, "Ruby the Baptist, making a way through the wilderness!"

"Now y'all just hold that pose right there, look at the camera, and smile," the man with the camera spoke up as he took aim at the three laughing, hugging women. "This picture's going in *Baptists Today*." After he clicked the camera, he continued, "Ruby, Cassie, Heather, I'm pleased to meet you all. I'm Bob Ballance, editor of *Baptists Today*, and this is my wife Catherine, who is also an ordained minister. Catherine, as soon as we eat, I want to get a picture of you with Ruby, Heather, and Cassie."

"So how was the trip down here, Heather?" Cassie asked when they sat down at the table.

"Good. Joel drove all the way, and the kids travel well. As long as Wallace has some books to look at and some cassettes of music he likes, he's good. Riding makes both of them sleepy. Wallace napped a lot, and about the only times Olivia woke up were when she was hungry or needed changing. We got into Bremen about noon. Joel and the kids'll be with me tomorrow for church at Peyton's Chapel and the ordination service. I left them all up at Bremen so Nanny and Pop-Pop can work on spoiling those grandkids. I think Joel's folks may follow us down to Harrington in the morning. They'd never thought much about a woman being a preacher until Joel started dating me. They've been members of the same church close to forty years. Joel's dad was a deacon for years, rotated off and hasn't been asked to serve again. They both sing in the choir. She used to be W. M. U. director. They've felt ostracized ever since Joel and I got married. Apparently the church's opposition to women preachers extends to people who are related to one by marriage. I've been blessed with a sweet husband and great in-laws. They've accepted me and love me like their own. Won't meet any finer Christian people anywhere, but some people in their church have shunned them since their son married that woman preacher."

"They'll be welcome at Peyton's Chapel," Cassie commented.

"And they'd probably join if they lived close enough,"

Heather acknowledged. "They sure have enjoyed the times they've been up to visit us at Clear Springs, so I'm sure they'll enjoy being at

Peyton's Chapel. They'll be complimentary about your preaching as they have been about mine. After the first time Joel's dad heard me preach, he hugged me and said, 'Now I see why some of these preacher boys are so against women preachers. They're jealous because you can preach better than they can.' This afternoon at their house, before I came down here, I was kicked back in the recliner nursing Olivia. Joel's mom told me, 'I love having you as our daughter-in-law and the mother of our grandchildren. I wish we could have you as our pastor.'"

As they continued eating, Catherine commented to Heather, "I love the names you chose for your children. Is there a story behind those names?"

"There is," Heather replied. "Wallace, our oldest, is Wallace Coggins Moore, named for Wallace Coggins, who was one of our deacons when I first became pastor at Clear Springs. Eighty-six years old, but one of the most progressive-thinking men I've ever known. He was so kind, helpful, and encouraging when I was starting my ministry at Clear Springs. He died on Christmas day my first year at Clear Springs. Olivia is Olivia Gladys Moore, named for two special people, Preacher Olivia Harris and my Granny Becker. Preacher Olivia was older when God called her to preach. No opportunities for her to preach anywhere, so she went out and started a church, Bluejay Street Baptist Church, in the poorest section of town, not far from the campus of Graves College, where I did my undergraduate work. I preached my first sermon at Bluejay Street when I was eighteen. The first funeral I conducted was Olivia's. My Granny Becker and I were very close. She was the first person I told that God was calling me to preach, and she offered the ordination prayer when I was ordained at Clear Springs. My home church in McMillan, Tennessee, wouldn't ordain me, so the ones from McMillan who came up for my ordination ended up starting a new church, Providence Baptist Church in McMillan. Granny was the driving force behind starting that church. She helped ordain me, and I got to make a trip down to McMillan to help ordain her as a deacon and constitute the new church. Then, about two years ago, I conducted her funeral."

"Those are some great names for your children to live up to," Bob commented between bites of Darrell Brinson's pork barbeque.

"I can't wait to see your kids, I mean children," Cassie corrected herself. "As soon as I said it, I could hear Miss Addie saying, 'kids are baby goats, and I have seen no young goats. I've taught many children with varying degrees of success, but I could never teach a goat anything. I'm sure you mean children.' So, yeah, I'm eager to see your *children*. I know Wallace has grown so much since the last time I saw him, and I've only seen pictures of Olivia."

"I've really enjoyed all of this good food," Ruby commented. "Living by myself, I don't cook a lot unless I have company. Heather, your friend Olivia sounds a lot like me. I was in my late twenties, married, with small children at home when the Lord called me to preach. I didn't know God could call a woman to preach until he called me. I was fifty-two when I became pastor of Antioch Baptist Church, served the church thirteen years. Only reason I gave it up, my husband had Alzheimer's, got to where somebody had to be right there with him all the time. I took care of him until he died. I loved being pastor at Antioch, still miss preaching every Sunday. I still get called to conduct funerals pretty often. Sometimes it's someone I've known a long time. Sometimes the funeral home calls me when the family doesn't know a minister to call because they know I'll help out if I can. Cassie, you don't know how happy it made me when Rhonda called and asked me if I'd like to help ordain you. I'm seventy-nine years old, so I expect to be with the Lord before too many more years, but you'll still have my signature on your ordination certificate after I've passed on." At ten minutes before six, everyone had finished eating. The conversations around the table were good, and Cassie was beginning to feel relaxed and confident. No one was in a hurry to get up from the tables when Mike announced, "Thanks again to all of you who prepared and served this excellent dinner. We welcome all of you who have come here tonight to help with Cassie's ordination. We'll move to the choir room for the ordination council in about ten minutes. If you go through this door, it's down the hallway on your right. Rest rooms are on your right before you get to the choir room."

The council would have been little more than a continuation of the dinner table conversations, with people hugging Cassie and telling her she didn't have anything to worry about, if Mike had not called it to order a couple of minutes past six o'clock. After a brief opening prayer, Mike announced, "I love being a minister of the gospel and being the pastor of this church. One of the best things about that is getting to be a close observer of the work of God in the lives of some fascinating people. One of those fascinating people, Cassie McWhorter, is the reason we're here tonight. Cassie was ten years old when I became the pastor of this church in June of 1990. She was the first one I baptized as pastor of this church. Her father and I baptized her just before her eleventh birthday. Starting when she was about fifteen, she and I had many conversations that led up to her preaching her first sermon and being licensed at the beginning of her senior year in high school. She is now a student at Mercer University, preparing herself for the work God called her to do. I am still amazed by the turn of events that led to her being called as pastor of Peyton's Chapel Baptist Church. I could be ready to sign off on her ordination right now. I really don't have any unanswered questions about this young woman. When we leave here tonight, my hope is that those of you who have not known Cassie as long and as well as I have will have your questions answered and that you will be as confident as I am that we should proceed with her ordination. The first thing we need to do is elect someone from among us to take minutes of this council and present the report of the council to the church tomorrow afternoon. The floor is open for nominations."

"Brother Mike," Catherine Ballance spoke up, "I'd like to nominate Sister Ruby Welsh Wilkins."

"Second," Bob McKnight called out in his God-speaking-from-heaven voice.

"Are there any other nominations?" After a brief pause, Mike continued, "I hear no other nominations." Handing Ruby a legal pad and a pen, Mike said, "Ruby, you are elected by acclamation to take the minutes of this council and present the council's report to the church."

"I'm honored," Ruby responded. "I'll be glad to do that."

"This is only my second time to preside over a minister's ordination council," Mike observed. "The only other preacher I've helped ordain, Heather Simmons Moore, is here with us tonight. She followed me as pastor of Clear Springs Baptist Church at Ledford, Virginia. I'll begin with the first question. Once Cassie responds to that question, the floor is open for you to ask whatever questions you wish to ask." Turning to Cassie, Mike continued, "Cassie, for the benefit of those who haven't known you as long and as well as I have, tell us how you came to faith in Christ and your experience of being called to preach."

"Brother Mike," Cassie began, "the way you worded the question makes it easy for me, because you know that those are not two separate things for me. It's like pancake batter—I know all of the ingredients that are in it, but once they're mixed together, there's no more separating them, it's just pancake batter. Becoming a believer in and follower of Jesus and being called to preach are ingredients in my Christian experience, but the ingredients are so mixed together that I cannot separate them. I experienced a call to follow Jesus and be obedient to him. That call led to preaching, and it led to be becoming pastor of Peyton's Chapel Baptist Church.

"My spiritual birth is like my physical birth," Cassie continued. "I know my mom gave birth to me on October 2, 1979 at Tanner Medical Center in Carrollton, but I don't remember it. I don't remember the beginning of my spiritual life for the same reason—I was so young when it started. I don't remember when I first heard of Jesus and his love for me. I've known about Jesus as far back as I can remember knowing anything. I began learning to pray around the time I learned to talk. Some of my earliest memories are of my parents reading me Bible stories and praying with me. I could quote the twenty-third Psalm and John 3:16 before I started first grade. I grew up with parents who loved me very much, I knew they loved God and that there was a connection between their love for God and the way they loved each other and loved me. The church has always been a part of my life, a part that I loved.

"Just a few weeks ago, I had the honor of having a part in the funeral of a very special person God brought into my life. Mrs. Addie Jane Peyton Aldridge—everybody knew her as 'Miss Addie.' Miss Addie lived to be a hundred and one years old. She was my best friend as far back as I can remember. I always sat with her in church while my parents were in the choir. She lived three doors down from us, and I used to ride my bike over to her house and visit with her a lot from the time I was elementary school age. I would tell her about my day at school, and she told me stories about going to a one-room school when she was a child and then teaching in a one-room school. She talked about Jesus and about her faith, as freely and naturally as she talked about anything else. She told me about being baptized in the creek out at Bailey's Mill when she was eleven years old.

"So," Cassie recounted, "as far back as I can remember I've known that Jesus loved me and gave himself for me, and I've known the Lord as a real presence in my life. When I was about nine or ten, I began to think more about how I ought to respond to one who already loved me and was already a part of my life. I had learned more about what baptism means and why it's important. I had talked with Mom and Dad and with Miss Addie a lot about it. Not long after Brother Mike became our pastor, he and his family had Sunday dinner with my family. I talked with Brother Mike after dinner about why I wanted to be baptized. That night, in the evening service, I went forward and made my public profession of faith. Not long after that, Daddy and Brother Mike baptized me. Just before I was baptized, Miss Addie gave me this necklace with the gold cross pendant that I'm wearing tonight. Her parents gave it to her the Sunday she was baptized in 1908. It had been her most cherished possession for eighty-two years, and she gave it to me. Now, it is my most cherished possession. I wear it every time I preach. Brother Mike asked Miss Addie to tell her faith story just before my baptism. He will tell you that turned into one of the best sermons ever preached in Harrington Baptist Church. I remember one thing Miss Addie said that has stuck with me: 'Cassie, when you come to the hard decisions in life, remember your baptism. Close your eyes and feel the water, and you'll know what you need to do.'

"So," Cassie explained, "my call to preach, like my baptism, is really just a matter of responding in love to the one who first loved me. It's a matter of recognizing that God has given me the ability to be an effective communicator and a deep desire to tell people about Jesus. Not long after I was baptized, Brother Mike invited Heather Simmons, Heather Simmons Moore she is now, to preach a revival at Harrington. She became the second woman I heard preach, counting Miss Addie's sermon the day of my baptism. Heather, you were amazing! I got to see a woman who does the same thing Brother Mike does Sunday after Sunday and does it well, the very thing I wanted to do more than I'd ever wanted to do anything. Heather and I became pen pals. She wrote me letters and told me about how she heard and responded to God's call. Heather, I still have every one of those letters you wrote me in a binder at home. You don't know how many times I've read and re-read those letters you wrote to me when I was twelve, thirteen, fourteen years old. Even though I'm a lot taller than you now, it still feels good for you to call me Little Sister. When I was fifteen, Miss Addie became the first person I told that God had called me to preach. She was ninety-seven at the time. When I told her that, she said she'd known it a long time, and she'd been praying that I would tell her before she died. She said the reason the Lord let her live so long was so she could be there to tell me that I wasn't crazy for thinking God was calling me to preach. When I told her, and when I wrote and told Heather, they both told me that I should tell my parents and Brother Mike. I did, and they have believed in me, trusted me, and encouraged me.

"At the beginning of my senior year in high school, Brother Mike led the church to affirm my calling by licensing me to preach, even though it meant that this church was expelled from the Mintz County Baptist Association. This church that helped lead me to Christ, nurtured me, and taught me how to live as a follower of Jesus tells me that I'm not the only one who thinks God's calling me to preach. Now, another church, Peyton's Chapel is telling me they think so, too, and they want me to be their pastor. My roommate and friend Mary Grace Tillison will be reading scripture at my ordination service. God gave me the privilege of leading her to faith in Christ, and she affirmed my calling by asking me to baptize her out at Bailey's Mill where Miss Addie was baptized in 1908. So, long story short, I just started following Jesus, and this is where the journey led, to me being here tonight in front of this council. I plan to keep following. It'll be interesting to see where the journey leads."

"So far, Sister McWhorter," Henry Conway quipped, "you're doing better than I did with my council. I was just twenty years old with a half-dozen sermons under my belt when Moses Chapel called me back in 1956. I used to think God only called men to preach, but the Lord already showed me I was wrong when Sister Eleanor Basden became the pastor of the Methodist church in Harrington. She was a powerful preacher, and the Lord blessed her ministry there. I see the same Spirit at work in you that I saw in her, so all of my questions were answered before I got here."

"Cassie," Bob Ballance asked, "tell us about your plans to continue your education for Christian ministry."

"I'm currently in my first year as a religion major at Mercer," Cassie replied, "and there are many reasons I'm glad I chose Mercer. I plan to finish my undergraduate degree there and then go on to seminary to work toward a Master of Divinity with a focus in pastoral ministry. I'm undecided about where I will go to seminary. The one thing I am sure of is that the pastorate, local church ministry, is where my heart is. I love people and getting to observe God at work in them, and I love preaching. I got to be with my friend and roommate, Mary Grace, when she began believing in and following Jesus, and Mary Grace asked me to baptize her, so I did, and I know I love being in baptismal water with new believers. So, pastoral ministry is what I see myself doing, and that's the direction I'll go with my seminary education. Last summer, I met Dr. Molly Marshall from Central Baptist Seminary in Kansas City and got to talk with her at length. Central is a very attractive option, but since I've been at Mercer, I've learned more about McAfee in Atlanta, met a couple of McAfee professors who've visited the Baptist Campus Ministry at Mercer and talked with them, so I don't know. Those are not the only good options. I intend to pursue seminary education, I just don't know where. I'm only in my first year at Mercer, so I have time to make my decision about seminary. What I can tell you is that I am in this for the long haul. I love what God has called me to do, and this is what I plan to do with my life. I intend to prepare myself well."

"Cassie," Heather asked, "Do you want to marry and have children, and if you do, how do you see yourself balancing marriage and parenthood with ministry?"

"Heather," Cassie began, "I'm glad you're the one who brought up that question. That question is probably not asked of many male candidates for ordination, and no doubt some would raise the demands of marriage and parenting as an argument against women being ordained and serving as pastors. It's a question that would be equally appropriate for a male candidate. First of all, I'm called to be a minister of the gospel. This is something I must do in order to be obedient to God. Marrying and becoming a parent is a choice, not something I must do. Having said that, it's something I want to do and probably will do, just not something I want to do right now. I'm not saying this just because my parents are here, but I have seen up close how good marriage can be. I want to have the kind of marriage my parents have. I'm not ready to be married at this point in my life, and I am not romantically involved with anyone. My call to ministry is a part of who I am. A man who can't accept that can't accept me. I broke up with two guys I dated in high school because they were freaked out when I told them that I plan to be a pastor. Heather, you found and married a good man who loves the Lord, loves you, and supports your work as a pastor. That's what I want to do. I want to build a marriage on the mutual submission principle of Ephesians 5:21 as my parents have done and as you and Joel have done. When I meet the right man and the time is right, I have some good examples to follow about how to do ministry. Clear Springs seems to be doing well with a pastor who is married and the mother of small children."

"Well, Cassie," Brad Terry spoke up, "I had a couple of questions prepared, but you've already answered them to my satisfaction before I had the chance to ask them, so the only other question I've got for you is, 'Will you come and preach a revival for us at Taylor's Crossroads when you're out of school for spring break?'"

"You're on!" Cassie laughed. "I'd love to. I'll get with you on the dates."

"Cassie," Bob McKnight spoke up. "A lot of people interpret I Corinthians 14:34-35 and I Timothy 2:12-15 to prohibit women from preaching and prohibit women from teaching men. You obviously take the Bible very seriously, so how do you deal with those scriptures? You know you're going to get those passages thrown in your face."

"I'm glad to respond to that, Brother Bob," Cassie began thoughtfully. "The first time I remember reading those passages, I felt like somebody had hit me in the face with a baseball bat. I've known since I was eleven years old that God was calling me to preach. Brother Mike helped me a lot in sorting out those passages. As to the I Corinthians passage, Paul had received a letter or perhaps several letters from the church in Corinth. From the beginning of chapter seven onward, he's answering that letter or letters. Those verses in I Corinthians 14 are not Paul's position. He's quoting what people in Corinth had written to him. He quotes what they said in verses 34-35 and then refutes it in verses 36-40. It can't be Paul's position because it contradicts what Paul wrote in chapter eleven. Also, the appeal to 'the law' ought to raise a red flag.

Paul doesn't impose Jewish law on non-Jewish Christian churches, and the 'law' that is cited is not the law of Moses but Jewish rabbinical law, what Jesus called 'the tradition of the elders.' As for the I Timothy passage, one needs to know as much as possible about what was going on in Ephesus when Paul wrote that. Paul was dealing with a specific group of women there who were influenced by some of the Greek religions that had a big presence in Ephesus. They were blending elements of Greek mythology with the creation stories in Genesis. You might say that Eve didn't recognize herself after the makeover she got in Ephesus. It really helped me to read a book that Brother Mike loaned me by Richard Kroeger and Catherine Clark Kroeger titled *I Suffer Not a Woman...* It sheds light on the religious climate in Ephesus and the nature of what this particular group of women was teaching. Paul was addressing a particular group of women who were teaching a distortion of the gospel, not all women in all times and places. So, the short answer is that neither of those passages has anything to do with the place of women in the church today."

"You're right, Cassie," Bob Ballance commented, "but you know there are some people who are not going to listen to any of that. They won't hear anything you have to say because you are a woman, and some of them'll be mean to you."

"Tell me about it," Cassie laughed. "I had an unpleasant run-in with one of them in the cemetery at Peyton's Chapel the day of Miss Addie's funeral. Otherwise, I never would've been invited to preach at Peyton's Chapel and we wouldn't be having this ordination council, would we?" As the laughter died down, Cassie added, "My God got the last laugh on that one. So, yeah, I've got a testimony about how my God can wade right into the middle of mean and ugly to bring about something good. There are some who won't hear me because I'm a woman, but there are some who will hear me for the same reason."

"And some people are going to say you're too young to be ordained and be a pastor," Bob McKnight added. "Just tell them you're the same age Jesse Mercer was when he was ordained. Speaking as a Mercer alumnus,

I think ol' Brother Jesse did all right." With a laugh, he added, "Besides, you won't always be this young. Ask me how I know that."

"Miss Addie told me that, when she was young, her hair was the same color as mine." Cassie commented. "Then she laughed and told me that when I get old, my hair'll be the color of hers."

"Brother Mike," Ruby spoke up. Despite her soft voice and diminutive size, a hush fell over the room when she spoke. "Most of us'll have words of encouragement and fatherly or motherly advice for Cassie, but I think we're in agreement about ordaining her. I'd like to make a motion that we present a favorable report to the church and proceed with Cassie's ordination."

Before Mike could ask for a second, he heard a chorus of voices give it. "We have a motion by Sister Ruby Welsh Wilkins with many seconds. All in favor say 'Aye,'" he asked. Following a solid 'Aye' from the whole council, he continued, "Any opposed, say 'No.'" After waiting through a couple of seconds of silence, Mike announced. "That sounds unanimous to me."

It was about 7:30 p.m. when Mike declared the council adjourned and called on Deacon J. T. Bailey from Peyton's Chapel to dismiss them with a word of prayer. J. T.'s prayer was full of joy and gratitude but concise and to the point. Still, it was more than an hour later when she got the last hug, the last word of counsel and blessing, and folded her long legs to get into the back seat of her parents' Buick Century.

"You did good, Cassie," Jerry commented as Cassie closed the car door.

"You really did," Elaine concurred. "Proud of you."

"I felt pretty much at ease once we got into it," Cassie responded. "I'm glad we had the informal time with the meal before we got into the actual council. I wasn't worried about the ones I knew, and that gave me a chance to meet and get acquainted with the ones I didn't know. I was comfortable with all of them by the time we got started with the council."

"And you pretty well passed muster with all of them over dinner, so they'd made their minds up about you before we got started with the council," Jerry observed as they pulled up in Daniel and Coretta's driveway to pick up Mary Grace.

"Hey, Girl, you're smiling!" Coretta exclaimed as she opened the door to Cassie. "It must have gone okay."

"It did," Cassie acknowledged.

"We were praying for you," Coretta replied. "You know Daniel and I like to play board games, so I had Scrabble, Clue, Monopoly, you name it ready thinking everybody might want to do that, but after we ate and cleared the table, we tried to get into Clue, but everybody was kind of half-hearted about the game. Asalee looked over at Karen and said, 'Mom, I think we need to be praying for Cassie,' so that's what we did, a lot of praying and a lot of talking about what was happening over at the church and why."

"I appreciate it," Cassie commented. "It helped. I could tell people were praying for me. I thought I'd be nervous but I wasn't. Glad we had the meal before the council, since that gave me a chance to get acquainted with the ones I didn't know before we got started. Daddy said he thought everybody made their minds up about me over dinner before we got into the council."

"Karen and the girls left about five minutes ago," Mary Grace spoke up. "You just missed them. I really enjoyed getting to know them better. Asalee and Deborah Estelle are sweet kids."

"Just so you know, Preacher Woman," Daniel said as he hugged Cassie, "you have opened a can of worms."

"Well, that can be a good thing," Cassie laughed. "I heard Jennifer Thurston say at the Women in Ministry conference last summer that she tried to open at least one can of worms in each sermon. So what can of worms did I open?"

"Deborah Estelle was full of questions about what was going on over at the church," Daniel answered. "Karen answered her questions and that just raised more questions. Asalee told what she remembered about Heather's ordination at Clear Springs, and we could tell that made a big impression on her because she remembered a lot considering how young she was at the time. Anyway, just as we were about to congratulate ourselves on how well we had explained ordination to an eight-year-old, Deborah Estelle asked Karen, "Momma, when am I gonna get ordinated?"

Chapter 19

"Sleep good, Preacher?" Jerry asked as Cassie fixed her coffee before snuggling up with him on the sofa.

"I did once I went to sleep. My mind was racing when I went to bed, not worried about anything, just processing all of it, the ordination council, thinking about all these folks coming to Peyton's Chapel this morning to hear me, including four preachers, all of them better than I am, and then the ordination service. I got pretty comfortable with everybody over dinner last night, and then the council went well, so I'm not nervous about them hearing me preach, just excited about them being there."

"From what I gathered last night," Jerry commented, "they're all excited about hearing you."

"I know they are," Cassie acknowledged, "and that makes me feel good. Daddy, I remember reading about Ruby when I was in the ninth grade, and wishing I could meet her. Come to find out, we live three doors down from somebody who's known her as far back as she can remember. I was in awe getting to meet her, and she said that she'd heard about me and she was as excited about meeting me as I was about meeting her. That was a bigger deal for me than it would be to meet President Clinton or some celebrity. Bob Ballance promised me an 8" x 10" of that picture he took last night of me, Ruby, Heather, and Catherine laughing and hugging each other. So, I wasn't worried or anything, just wound up because last night was so good. Mary Grace and I talked 'til after midnight, just winding down. She's nervous and excited about what we're doing for her this morning at Peyton's Chapel before she goes up to Elberton to see her folks. I told Ruby, Heather, Bob, and Catherine about it—they all love the idea of what we're doing for Mary Grace, turning that dreaded trip back to Elberton to see her folks into her first missionary journey. They're excited about coming to Peyton's Chapel and being a part of that as well as my ordination this afternoon."

"That's a really good idea that you came up with," Jerry commented. "You know your mom and I love Mary Grace. She's been like family ever since the first time you brought her home with you, so we're excited about what you're doing for her. Of course, that first meeting was kind of memorable, what with her hair being sopping wet from you baptizing her. I introduced myself to her, and said, 'Hey, Mary Grace, I'm Jerry, Cassie's dad, sorry I smell like charcoal, and by the way, your hair's soaking wet like you just got baptized or something,' and you said, 'Daddy, that's kind of what happened.'"

"You don't have the TV on CNN," Cassie observed.

"CNN and prayer don't go together all that well," Jerry replied. "I woke up early, read over the Sunday School lesson again, then I've just been thinking and praying about all that's happening today. You ready for some breakfast?"

"I don't want much, Daddy. I think I'll just eat a bowl of cereal and a banana this morning. I'm not real hungry, and my church is fixing lunch for us and all of the ones coming in from out of town for my ordination," Cassie said as she got the milk out of the refrigerator and checked out the cereal options in the pantry.

"Darrell Brinson's covering Sunday School at Harrington for me this morning. Daniel and Coretta are picking up Preacher Wilkins and bringing her with them to Peyton's Chapel," Jerry outlined the logistics for the morning. "If Mary Grace wants to sleep a little longer and you need some time at your holy place, you can go on when you're ready and she can ride with us."

"That'll work. It's according to when she wakes up. I'm going to go ahead and eat a bite, then take a shower and get ready. If she's ready and wants to go early with me, she can, or she can ride with y'all. You know I want to go early and spend some time at Bailey's Mill and Miss Addie's grave. I know I can pray anywhere, but those places are holy ground for me. I do feel the need to pray more than usual this morning."

It was about five minutes after eight when Cassie headed the OGM north out of Harrington and made the slight right onto Bailey's Mill Road at Pulliam's Store/ Gloryland Way Missionary Baptist Church (Independent – Fundamental – Premillennial – KJV Bible – No Women Preachers). It felt strange to be making the drive alone, but Mary Grace showed no sign of life until Cassie was getting her dress and shoes out of the bedroom closet. Mary Grace told her to go on and she would ride with Cassie's folks. Cassie was actually glad that it worked out that way, as she felt the need to be alone at her holy places this morning. Just before the Salyers Creek bridge, she put on her left turn signal, waited for an oncoming car, and then made the left onto the narrow dirt road leading into the clearing up near the foundation of the mill. She parked the car, shut off the ignition, and reached behind her seat to get the grungy old sneakers and the green and white Harrington Hornets stadium cushion.

Cassie did not pay much attention to the white Ford Ranger that had been behind her all the way from Harrington. As far as she knew, it was just someone who happened to be going the same direction at the same time. She didn't notice exactly when the truck fell in behind the OGM, but it was before she was out of the Harrington city limits. It was behind her as she went north out of town toward Hansonville. When she bore right onto Bailey's Mill Road, so did the white Ranger. When she put on her left turn signal and stopped to wait for the oncoming car before making the left onto the little dirt road leading down to the mill, the truck slowed almost to a stop behind her. The driver of the truck was far enough behind her that he didn't have to stop completely. Cassie made her turn, and the Ranger continued straight ahead.

The white Ranger did continue straight after Cassie turned, but it did not go very far, perhaps only to the next driveway, before turning around and coming back. Cassie had walked perhaps a hundred feet from her car, down toward the creek, walking slowly, filling her lungs with the exhilaratingly crisp, cool morning air and the mist that hung in the air as she got down closer to the water, down to the rock outcropping where she usually sat to think and pray. She didn't know why she had brought her purse, as she normally left it locked in the car when she came here, but she put it down along with the stadium cushion on the rock outcropping. This morning's sermon was prepared, and she felt no need to go over it right now, but she intensely felt the need to meet the one Robert McCheyne called "the one whom my soul loves." Instead of her sermon text for this morning, she opened her Bible to Psalm 62. She had just begun reading the words she had read in this place countless times, words that she associated with this place, words that she had long ago committed to memory, "For God alone my soul waits in silence, From him comes my salvation. He alone is my rock and my salvation. My fortress; I shall never be shaken," when she heard another vehicle coming down the dirt road into the clearing.

Probably somebody just coming out here to fish, she thought. She usually had the place to herself, but once in a while somebody else would already be there or arrive after her. The ones who came to fish never bothered the tall, slender auburn-haired girl sitting on the rocks reading her Bible. Sometimes they spoke, sometimes they didn't. They shared her desire for silence, even if not for the same reason. Besides, Cassie never felt completely alone here, so it had never occurred to her to be afraid. Here, as at Peyton's Chapel, where she laid her open Bible every Sunday on a pulpit used by preachers who died a hundred years before she was born, Cassie was intensely aware of what the author of Hebrews called "a great cloud of witnesses." The witnesses who came for Miss Addie's baptism in 1908 were all around, as were the people in that photograph that Miss Addie gave her that was taken here back in the 1920s. There had been no shortage of witnesses for Mary Grace's baptism a few weeks ago. Mary Grace commented on it herself several days afterward, a keen awareness that she and Cassie were not the only ones there when Cassie baptized her. Cassie showed Mary Grace the scripture about the great cloud of witnesses and the picture Miss Addie gave her of the baptism at Bailey's Mill seventy-five years ago, and Mary Grace realized how public her profession of faith and baptism had been.

Cassie felt the first tinge of fear when the vehicle she heard came into view. It was the same white Ranger that had been behind her all the way from Harrington. He had gone straight on after Cassie turned, but obviously he turned around and came back. Cassie had laughed at her mom for buying her the little can of pepper spray after her run-in with Brother Bobby at the cemetery, but now she was reaching in her purse to get it. The white Ranger pulled up beside her car and stopped. Cassie was aware of her heart pounding as she stood up, put down her Bible, and tightly gripped the can of pepper spray. Brother Mike had given her a copy of Bruggemann's little book, *Praying the Psalms,* for her sixteenth birthday, and she devoured it. She didn't know how many times she had re-read it, enough times for the binding to be loose, enough times that she had to use a rubber band to hold it together. Cassie had learned to draw from the rich treasury of the Psalms when she prayed. The opening words of Psalm 54 came to her mind, "Save me, O God, by your name, and vindicate me by your might. Hear my prayer, O God, give ear to the words of my mouth, For the insolent have risen against me, the ruthless seek my life, they do not set God before them." Those words became her prayer as she recognized the lone occupant getting out of the white Ranger.

Floyd Williams, pastor at Freeman Valley and moderator of the Mintz County Baptist Association (Cassie wondered whether all of that was on his driver's license), was around the age of Cassie's parents. He managed to be both tall and pudgy, about six feet tall but looking as though he had been melted and poured into his suit. The redness of his face gave him the appearance of a heart attack or stroke looking for a place to happen. Cassie cringed at the thought of having to do CPR on him. When she took the Red Cross class, she had envisioned herself resuscitating someone less obnoxious. It would be awful tempting not to intervene and just let him go on to Glory or wherever.

"Miss McWhorter," Floyd addressed her as he approached. "I'm not going to hurt you. I ain't crazy like Brother Bobby. I just want to talk with you. What are you doing here?"

"I was about to ask you the same question, Floyd. We agree that Bobby Simpson is crazy, but I can't think of a blessed thing we need to talk about," Cassie responded firmly. "As for why I'm here, I often come here to think, pray, and just be alone with God. I don't recall inviting you to join me. J. T. and Josie Bailey own this property, and they're fine with me coming here whenever I want."

"Well, I suppose you could say the Lord invited me to join you," Floyd shot back sarcastically. "I'm just tryin' to make sense of why you're doin' what you're doin'. I just want to help you, try to show you the error of your ways, 'fore you cause any more trouble in the association than you already have."

"First of all, Floyd, don't come any closer to me unless you want a face full of pepper spray," Cassie warned. "You might have a hard time driving yourself over to Freeman Valley after that. I don't recall causing any trouble in the association, best I remember, you're the one who did that. Now you want to know why I'm reading my Bible, thinking, praying, and seeking time alone with God? That's what I was doing when you interrupted me. I know you're against women preachers, but you're even against a woman reading her Bible, thinking, and praying? You're afraid of where that might lead if a woman thinks, prays, and reads her Bible without supervision?"

"No," Floyd shot back, the note of irritation at Cassie's perceived insolence apparent in his voice, "and put down that damn pepper spray for God's sake!"

"I'll put it down when you get back in your truck and leave here," Cassie retorted. "There is nothing you and I need to talk about."

"Miss McWhorter," Floyd's voice softened into a more condescending tone. "I just want to talk to you, help you see the error of your ways, help you get back in the will of God. I wanna know why you're trying to do something God don't call women to do. Pretty as you are, you need to think about finding yourself a nice Christian young man, maybe even find yourself a fine young preacher boy, get married, take care of your husband and have some babies instead of tryin' to get yourself ordained and tryin' to preach and pastor a church."

"Floyd," Cassie responded thoughtfully, "Maybe you and I are not dealing with the same God here. My God can do things yours can't. You've got your little god all figured out, what he can and can't do. My God's full of surprises, way beyond what I can wrap my mind around. Floyd, you're smarter than your god! You've trained your little god to hate the same people you do. What other tricks have you taught him? You don't have much of a god, Floyd."

"Miss McWhorter, honey..." Floyd spoke with feigned tenderness as he stepped closer to Cassie. "I don't hate you, but I hate what you're doin' 'cause it's somethin' God hates."

"I'm not your honey, Floyd. I've warned you once. No more warnings. One more step toward me and you get a face full of pepper spray and a kick where it hurts."

"Ohhhh, I seeee," Floyd sneered. "You ain't satisfied with bein' a woman like God made you. You wanna take over a man's role."

"I'm perfectly happy being a woman," Cassie spoke icily. "I have no desire whatsoever to be a man. I don't need to be a man to preach the gospel, never saw how that would be any real advantage."

"You done went off to that lib'ral school and got it in your head that it's okay, fine and dandy, for men to have sex with men and women to have sex with women. The Bible says, at least the King James Version does, 'For this cause God gave them up unto vile affections: for even their women did change the natural use into that which is against nature.' Just about everybody in Mintz County's seen you and that girl you run around with all the time. Just addin' two and two there."

"Floyd, you idiot! You're talking about Mary Grace? You just added two and two and got nine, so you flunk first grade math. She's my roommate at Mercer. We are friends. She's about the closest friend I've had since Miss Addie died, but we're not sleeping together, not that it's any of your business, but we're not. I got to lead Mary Grace to the Lord, and she asked me to baptize her. I baptized her a few weeks ago here where Miss Addie was baptized."

"I'm just addin' it up, Miss McWhorter. You don't like bein' a woman 'cause you're steppin' outta your place, takin' over a man's role pastorin' a church and baptizin' people. And you expect me to believe you run around with that girl all the time and they ain't nothin' goin' on between y'all? You just think you like it with another woman 'cause you ain't never been with a man to know how good it is..." With those words, Floyd stepped toward Cassie. As he raised his right hand toward her, Cassie didn't know whether he meant to put his hands on her or just take the pepper spray away from her, and she didn't wait to find out. She felt a white-hot rage that she had only felt one other time in her life, at the cemetery when Bobby Simpson tried to snatch her Bible out of her hands and grabbed her breast instead. At the very instant Floyd's hand clamped down on her right wrist, Cassie aimed for his eyes, mashed down hard on the nozzle, and emptied the little canister in his face. Blinded, with his face, eyes, and throat on fire, gasping for breath, Floyd involuntarily released his grip on Cassie's wrist. He stumbled backwards, putting his hands to his face to rub his eyes, which only exacerbated the burning. Cassie kicked high and hard, harder than she'd ever kicked a soccer ball. She didn't lose her balance this time, and the toe of her shoe hit its mark. Floyd let out a yelp as he doubled over in pain and fell backward.

Cassie quickly grabbed up her Bible, purse, and stadium cushion and made her way back up to her car. She put the things in her car and looked back to see Floyd still writhing on the ground, moaning and crying. She hadn't killed the fool, only put him out of commission temporarily, long enough to give herself time to get away. She put her things in the OGM and noticed that Floyd had left the keys to his truck in the switch. She opened the passenger side door of Floyd's truck and snatched his keys, got in her car, belted herself in, raced the engine, and tore out of the clearing, up the little stretch of dirt road, and back out onto Bailey's Mill Road. She was closer to Peyton's Chapel than she was to home, so she headed that direction. She began shaking and weeping as she came down from the adrenalin surge, realized how fast she was going, and watched the speedometer needle fall from 80 to 75 to 70 to 65 to 60. Cassie braked hard to make the turn onto Peyton's Chapel Road. A quarter mile or so later, she braked hard again to aim the OGM between the mill-stones that were on each side of J. T. and Josie's driveway. She slid to a stop on the gravel behind J. T.'s truck, shoved it into park, turned off the ignition, released the seat belt and opened the door. When she swung her legs out and put her feet on the ground, her legs were as limp as cooked spaghetti, and she could not get up out of the car. She fell back against the seat back, feet on the ground, half in and half out of the car, sobbing uncontrollably.

J. T. and Josie came running out of the house to see what was wrong, and as they did, a beat-up, muddy green Ford F-150 4x4 with big over-sized mud grip tires pulled up behind Cassie's car. Cassie didn't really know how she made it to the safety of J. T. and Josie's house without wrecking. She was blinded by her tears, but she recognized Josie's embrace pulling her close, and inviting her to bury her face against her shoulder. Josie whispered soothingly, "It's okay, Preacher. You're safe. Nobody's going to hurt you here." She felt J. T.'s gentle hand on her shoulder and heard him speak softly, "Somebody tried to hurt you, didn't they, Preacher? You've got a big bruise on your wrist, looks like somebody grabbed it when you were trying to defend yourself."

Cassie regained her composure enough to lift her face from Josie's shoulder. She took slow deep breaths and felt her heart slowing to a more normal pace and the strength returning to her legs. "We need to call 911, get the law and paramedics to go out to the mill and check on Floyd Williams," Cassie explained breathlessly. "I left home early this morn-ing. Mary Grace is coming with Mom and Dad. I stopped at the mill to have some time at my holy place. Didn't realize Floyd had been behind me all the way from Harrington. After I turned to go down to the mill, he waited long enough for me to get out of the car and then he pulled in after me. Had to leave him on the ground in a lot of pain after I gave him a face full of pepper spray and kicked him in the groin for putting his hands on me. Of course, I know the law'll want to talk to me, too. I didn't know how long it'd take for the pepper spray to wear off, and I saw the keys to his truck in the switch. I grabbed them so he couldn't take off after me. I'll give Floyd's keys to the deputy to give back to him."

Cassie recognized the large bearded man in camo coveralls as Ronnie Wofford, Ruth Ann Simpson's son-in-law. He didn't come to church, but he brought Ruth Ann and picked her up last Sunday because he was doing some work on her car that morning. "I was goin' down to the store to get me a pack of Red Man and I met you drivin' like a bat outta Hell, recognized your car, that ol' Citation kinda stands out, 'specially when it's flyin' low to the ground, knowed somethin' was wrong, so I turned around, tried to catch up with you," Ronnie explained his presence. "Seen you turn toward the church, did'n think you's gonna make that turn, that lil' car was all over the place. You like to'a turned it over. I come on down, 'spectin' to find you upside down in a ditch, seen your car in J. T. and Josie's driveway." Ronnie extended his hands, large powerful hands permanently stained by oil and grease. Cassie's hands looked like a little child's when Ronnie took hold of them to help her to her feet. He could not have been more gentle. Pulling against him was like pulling against a big oak tree. Cassie could have made it on her own, but it was comforting to have Ronnie walking close beside her, his right arm around her waist, steadying her, knowing that he could easily pick her up and carry her like a little child if it came right down to it. "You gon' be all right, Preacher. Kinda glad to see ol' Floyd get what he had comin' to him, 'specially nice that he got it from a woman preacher. The two biggest jackasses I ever seen were preachers, him and my father-in-law, two peas in a pod, never cared to hear what either one of 'em had to say. Generally speakin', I respect preachers, just not them two. You ain't like them. My mother-in-law loves you to death. My wife used to say she'd never set foot in church again if she ever got away from her daddy, but her'n the kids're getting ready for church this mornin'."

J. T. held the screen door open, and Ronnie brought Cassie on into the living room and eased her down into the recliner. As Josie wrapped some ice cubes in a washcloth and applied the cold compress to Cassie's bruised wrist, J. T. was on the phone with the 911 operator. After he hung up, J. T. told Cassie, "I called your folks before I called 911, let them know what happened, told them you were safe at our house. They're on their way. Then I called 911. They're sending the law and the paramedics out to check on Floyd, and they're going to come and talk with you, take a statement about what happened and get Floyd's keys. That was some good thinking, Preacher, taking Floyd's keys."

"I saw the keys in the switch when I was getting back in my car," Cassie responded, "and I said, 'Thank you, Lord!' because I didn't know how long it would take for the pepper spray to wear off, and I didn't want him trying to follow me. I'll let the sheriff take his keys back to him. He'll need to go back home and change suits before he heads out to Freeman Valley. He got kinda dirty rolling around on the ground, and he lost his breakfast all over himself when I kicked him."

"Serves him right," J. T. commented. "It's 9:00 a.m. now. If you're okay, Preacher, Josie and I are going to finish getting ready for church. I've already been up there and turned the heat on to knock the chill off. If Arnie and Ruth or Henry and Minnie Ree get there before we do, they can unlock."

"Go ahead," Cassie replied. "I'm all right. I just need to run a wash-cloth over my face and redo my makeup."

"Anything else I can do for you, Preacher?" Ronnie asked. "My wife and kids are at home getting ready for Sunday School and church. If the roof won't cave in on me, I think I'm gon' go home, get cleaned up, and go with them."

"I'm good, Ronnie, and I'll look forward to seeing you in church," Cassie responded. "I really appreciate you checking on me and stopping to help me. There is one small thing you can do for me before you go that would mean a lot to me."

"What's that, Preacher?"

"There's J. T.'s Bible on the coffee table. The Psalms are just about in the middle of the Bible. Would you be so kind as to read Psalm 124 to me? I know it by heart, but I'd like to listen while you read it."

"I ain't done much Bible readin' in my life, Preacher, don't know much about it," Ronnie answered apologetically, "but if you want me to, I'll give it my best shot." He picked up J. T.'s well-worn Bible, handling it gently and reverently, opened it to the middle, and found his way to Psalm 124. Cassie closed her eyes and listened as Ronnie read the familiar words. His voice began to break with emotion, and tears were streaming down his face as he read and Cassie mouthed the words along with him, "Blessed be the Lord, who hath not given us as a prey to their teeth. Our soul is escaped as a bird out of the snare of the fowlers, the snare is broken, and we are escaped. Our help is in the name of the Lord, who made heaven and earth."

"Thank you, Ronnie," Cassie responded as she stood to hug him. "You read it beautifully. That helped me a lot."

"You're welcome, Preacher, glad I could help you," Ronnie replied. "I'm gonna head on to the house and get ready for church. Look forward to hearing you preach."

It was about 9:15 a.m., about five minutes after Ronnie left, when the Mintz County Sheriff patrol car pulled into the driveway. Cassie recognized the youthful-looking deputy as Jason Bradshaw. He was in his early twenties but looked about fifteen or sixteen. His younger sister

Katie was in Cassie's graduating class. Cassie and Katie had run track and played basketball together. "Hey, Jason. Thanks for coming out."

"You're welcome, Cass. Heard you were preaching at Peyton's Chapel. That's great. Wish I didn't have to work. I'd come and hear you. You all right?"

"Yeah, he just shook me up and scared me more than anything. Got to redo my makeup before church. Got a pretty big bruise on my wrist where he grabbed me."

"Want me to call EMS to check you over and make sure you're okay?"

"No, Jason. No need for that. I'm all right. Josie put some ice on it. That helped."

"Well, let me take a good picture of that bruise for evidence," Jason replied as he took out a small digital camera. "Pull your sleeve up. Here, put your arm on this white sofa cushion, that'll help the bruise stand out in the photo." Cassie cooperated with Jason's request, and he took three or four pictures of the bruising on her arm.

"I didn't kill Floyd or anything, did I?" Cassie asked hesitantly.

"No, but he wouldn't've looked any worse if you had," Jason answered. "I've seen dead people who looked better, 'cept Floyd was up and walking around, rantin' and ravin', when we got there. He'd been on his knees down by the creek splashing water on his face, trying to wash away the pepper spray. Don't think the dry cleaners can save that suit. He refused any help from EMS, said he needed to get back home and change clothes before Sunday School starts at 10:00 a.m., and he was having a dying duck fit 'cause he couldn't find the keys to his truck."

"Right here, Jason," Cassie replied as she handed him Floyd's keys. "Didn't know how long it'd take for the pepper spray and the pain from that kick to the groin to wear off, and didn't want him trying to come after me."

"Good thinking," Jason commented as he took the keys. "Now tell me what happened. I've known you since you were a little kid. You and my little sister've been friends since elementary school. Can't recall many incidents of you stomping the living daylights out of obnoxious fifty-something preachers. You nailed him good with the pepper spray and just about made a soprano out of him, so I figured you had a good reason. I'm thinking he probably had it coming to him and this is an open-and-shut case of self- defense."

Cassie related the sequence of events to Jason, starting with Floyd's white Ranger being behind her all the way out from Harrington. She explained that she often came to Bailey's Mill to find the solitude to meditate and pray, and that she really didn't pay that much attention to the truck behind her because it continued straight on after she turned off. Cassie told Jason that Floyd waited for her to have time to get down to the clearing at the mill and get out of the car before he turned around and came back, and that she didn't know who it was until he pulled up beside her car and got out of the truck. She told him that it really creeped her out that he approached her in such an isolated place and insisted that he just wanted to talk with her about why she was doing what she was doing. Cassie said that she took the pepper spray out of her purse because she was afraid and didn't know what Floyd's intentions were. "But my gut feeling was that he was up to no good and not just there to have a conversation. He was acting weird. I didn't know if he meant to attack me, rape me, kill me, or what. On the day I'm supposed to be ordained, he starts out about why I want to preach and be ordained, and he's like he just wants to help me see the error of my ways and get back in the will of God, and I need to forget all of that, get married and have some babies. Then he starts saying I must not be content with being a woman because I want to take over a man's place. Then he accuses me of being in a lesbian relationship with Mary Grace—Mary Grace is my roommate at Mercer, really good friend who comes home with me a lot on weekends. I can assure you, I'm attracted to guys, and I'm not doing anything like that with Mary Grace. So anyway, I keep warning Floyd not to come any closer or I'll spray him. I told him I'd put down the pepper spray when he got back in his truck and left. The last thing he said to me was that I just think I like doing it with another woman because I've never been with a man to know how good it is. When he said that, he took another step closer and grabbed my arm. That's when I let him have it with the pepper spray and then I kicked him."

"Sounds like you had reason to believe you were in imminent danger," Jason commented, "and Floyd Williams had better be thankful you only had pepper spray instead of a gun." Jason looked up from his clipboard when he and Cassie heard the sound of a car coming down Peyton's Chapel Road way too fast. They looked up and saw the maroon Buick Century belonging to Cassie's parents. Jerry braked hard and laid down some rubber making the turn into J. T. and Josie's driveway. As Jerry, Elaine, Mary Grace, and the Little Brat piled out of the car, they were visibly relieved to see Cassie in one piece, standing on the porch talking with Jason, and glad to see that the sheriff's deputy was someone they knew. Jason stepped back to make way for the rush of people eager to hug Cassie, hold her close, and express their gratitude that she was alive and safe. J. T. and Josie came out on the porch about the time Cassie was surrounded by the embrace of four weeping people. Elaine peeled off from the group hug to hug Jason, J. T., and Josie and thank them for their kindness to her daughter.

"I'm all right," Cassie reassured everybody. "Worst scare I ever had, didn't know if I'd live to tell about it and see y'all again, but it's over. I just need to fix my makeup and head on to church. I'll be in better shape once I see everybody and get all of my hugs. Y'all need to give Ronnie Wofford a hug when you see him. He stopped to help me, too. He's at home getting ready to come to church."

"You had a pretty bad scare, Preacher," J. T. observed. "If you don't feel up to preaching, it's all right. We're going to have a bunch of preachers with us this morning. You can still go to church and get your hugs."

"Thanks, J. T.," Cassie replied, "but I'll be all right. I'm excited about commissioning Mary Grace for her first missionary journey, and I need to do it for Ronnie. He felt the need to change his plans and come to church after what happened this morning, and I want him to hear me. I think I'll be in better shape if I go ahead and preach than I will be if I sit it out and get somebody else to fill in at the last minute."

"Cassie," Jason asked, "do you want to press charges against Floyd? We can do stalking, terroristic threats and acts, and simple battery."

"Do I have to decide that right now?" Cassie asked.

"No, you can come in tomorrow morning, see the magistrate, and take out warrants, if you want to do it that way."

"Either way, you need to press charges," Elaine told Cassie.

"Mom," Cassie protested. "Let me shift gears, focus on church this morning and the ordination service this afternoon, then I'll think about that."

"All right," Jason responded. "At the very least, you need to get a restraining order against him, so we'll have grounds to arrest him if he comes anywhere around you. I'll take Floyd's keys back to him, take my time, read him the riot act when I get there. I don't care if he's late for church. Let him explain that."

"Just let me get in the bathroom and fix my makeup," Cassie asked.

"Help yourself," Josie responded. "We're going to go on to church, just lock the door and pull it to when you're ready to leave."

"If y'all want to go on," Mary Grace suggested, "I'll stay with Cassie and ride with her." After everyone else was out of hearing range, Mary Grace commented, "Wow, Cass. You whooped Floyd's ass."

Cassie broke out laughing. "Not the exact language I'd use, but, yeah, I can see this in *Baptists Today*. 'Cassie McWhorter, nineteen-year-old pastor of Peyton's Chapel Baptist Church near Harrington, Georgia, whooped associational bully Floyd Williams, pastor of Freeman Valley Baptist Church and moderator of the Mintz County Baptist Association. Sources within the association told *Baptists Today* that Williams had it coming and that it's about time somebody gave him an attitude adjustment. Pastor McWhorter attributed the victory to the Lord and Saint Addie.'"

Chapter 20

"Today got off to a rough start, as most of you heard about during Sunday School or between Sunday School and worship," Cassie began her sermon. "It was a frightening experience, but the Lord brought me through it, and I'm okay. I'm thankful for the people God had on duty to help me — J. T. and Josie, Ronnie Wofford, my parents, my brother Anthony, Mary Grace, and Deputy Jason Bradshaw with the Mintz County Sheriff's Department. I love Peyton's Chapel Baptist Church! This is such a good place, and I look forward to being here every Sunday, but it felt especially good to arrive here this morning. You know how to make me feel loved. I'm a hugger anyway, but you need to know how much God ministered comfort, grace, and strength to me this morning through your hugs. Even the little children who hug me around the knees ministered to me! I don't think I could've preached today without the ministry of good hugs. Today will take its place alongside the day of my baptism, the day I had a part in Miss Addie's home going celebration, and the day I baptized Mary Grace as one of the most significant days in my Christian experience. This afternoon, we'll have a special service at Harrington Baptist Church. Starting at 2:30 p.m., Coretta, Jenny Latham, and the Sacred Harp Singers of Harrington Baptist Church will present a mini-concert for those who arrive early. When the ordination service starts at 3:00 p.m., some of the people who know me best and love me most will read scripture, offer prayers, sing, or play the piano. When I was in the ninth grade, I read about Ruby Welsh Wilkins, the first woman to pastor a Baptist church in Alabama, and wished that I could meet her. Little did I know that our friends Rhonda and Darrell Brinson, who bought Miss Addie's house, know Ruby well. Rhonda grew up in Wadley, Alabama. She's known her as far back as she can remember!

Rhonda was half grown before she realized she wasn't really kin to her Aunt Ruby. When she heard that I was going to be ordained, she invited Ruby to come up for the weekend and help ordain me. I'm delighted to have Ruby here this morning. She will present the report of the ordination council this afternoon. Ruby, I'm gonna go ahead and let the cat out of the bag — I passed my ordination council!"

As the laughter died down, Cassie continued, "Mike Westover, my pastor since I was ten years old, the one who baptized me, will deliver the charge to the church. He and I have been having conversations about my call to pastoral ministry since I was fifteen. He took me seriously. I could not have had a more supportive and encouraging pastor to help me explore my calling. I have benefited from his wisdom. He has loaned and given me good books. Today, my pastor becomes my colleague and my fellow minister of the gospel. He will continue to be one of my mentors, and we'll have lots of 'now what do I do?' conversations. Brother Mike never set any limits on my response to the claim of Jesus Christ on my life. When I told him that God was calling me to preach, he said, 'Well, Cassie, that's what we get for baptizing you.' He gave me the gifts of time, encouragement, listening, and gentle guidance. He introduced me to one who has become another dear friend and mentor, Heather Simmons Moore, pastor of the Clear Springs Baptist Church at Ledford, Virginia. Brother Mike was the pastor there during his time at Mid-Atlantic Seminary. He invited Heather to preach at Clear Springs the Sunday he preached for the pastor search committee from Harrington. When Harrington called Brother Mike, Clear Springs called Heather. Heather and I have something in common — both of us thought we'd get to fill in a Sunday or two and ended up being called as pastor. Heather's been at Clear Springs a little over eight years now. The church is thriving, and Heather has gained a good husband and two delightful children in that time.

"I first met Heather when Brother Mike asked her to preach a revival at Harrington. It did me so much good to see a woman doing what God was calling me to do, and doing it well. Heather, I was not quite twelve years old when you preached that revival. When you got up to preach at the first service of that revival, something deep in my soul shouted, 'Yes!' Heather is here this morning along with her husband Joel, their children Wallace and Olivia, and Joel's parents who live up at Bremen. She will deliver the charge to the candidate this afternoon.

"Following the charge to the candidate, I will kneel before the congregation for the ancient ritual of the laying on of hands. The laying on of hands will not be limited to those who have been ordained, because so many of you who have never been ordained have precious gifts and powerful blessings to impart to me. For some of you, the laying on of hands will turn into a tearful embrace. When we finish, my hair will be all out of place and my makeup will be streaked with tears, and I couldn't care less. You can take my picture like that if you want to! You'll offer your words of encouragement and blessing, but I'll recognize many of you by the touch of your hands before you say a word. You'll challenge me to aim for excellence in ministry as Paul did with Timothy when he exhorted him to 'stir up the gift that is in you through the laying on of my hands.'

"The gifts given to me by God and by the people of God are not given *to* me, they are given *through* me to the body of Christ for the benefit of others. The gifts of God and the gifts of God's people are meant to be shared. My dear friend Miss Addie is with the Lord now, but the gifts God gave through her to me and to others continue to bear fruit. In Ephesians 4, Paul tells us that God gave some to the church to be pastors and teachers 'to equip the saints for the work of ministry, for building up the body of Christ.' The end result of this gifting is that the saints — that's the church, that's all of us — are equipped for the work of ministry, and the body of Christ is stronger and healthier. These precious gifts can't be paid back, they are to be paid forward, invested in others. The ministry is not just the work of ordained ministers, it's the work of the church, the work of all of God's people — as you all demonstrated when you took care of me after my ordeal earlier this morning. This morning taught me that all of us are both ministers and recipients of ministry. God will not allow me to minister to you without accepting your acts of ministry to me. The whole ministry belongs to the whole church! No act of Christian ministry is scripturally restricted to the holder of a particular office in the church or to those who have been formally ordained. The church in New Testament times had a formal procedure for licensing people to exercise their gifts in ministry — they called it 'baptism.' One of the strengths of this church is that, with pastors who worked a full-time job during the week and now with a pastor who is a full-time student at Mercer, you're already accustomed to doing much of the day-to-day work of ministry. That's the healthiest pattern for doing church. It would be even if I lived next door to the church and worked here every day. The worst heresy in the history of the Christian church is the idea that the clergy do the work of ministry and the laity merely support the work of ministry. Breaking down that wall between clergy and laity defined our Baptist forebears as much as immersion baptism.

"The laying on of hands has traditionally been associated with ordination, but it should not be restricted to that occasion. What we have in Acts 13 is probably not ordination with a capital O, but setting Saul and Barnabas apart for a specific assignment. They were already gifted people. They were already using their gifts to build up the church in Antioch. They would've continued to be an asset to the church in Antioch if they'd stayed there, but God called them, stirred up in them the desire to undertake a journey, preaching the gospel, encouraging and teaching new believers, and forming believing communities. They were emissaries of God! They could've gone out in obedience to God without any human endorsement of their effort. They could have, but they didn't, and it's a good thing they didn't, because the same God who spoke to them also spoke to the people in the church at Antioch. When God speaks to you, he'll give you somebody who will believe your testimony and tell you that you're not crazy for thinking that God spoke to you. Miss Addie was the first person I told that God was calling me to preach. I was fifteen and she was ninety-seven. She said she already knew, said the Lord told her that a long time ago, and she'd been praying that I'd get around to telling her before she died. She said the reason the Lord let her live so long was so she could be there to tell me I wasn't crazy for thinking God was calling me to preach! We need other believers to help us discern the will of God, to keep us from going off on tangents. I'm very clear in my own mind that I want to make Christian ministry my life's work. This afternoon at 3:00 p.m., at the church that nurtured me from cradle roll onward, helped lead me to faith in Christ, and encouraged me to grow in Christ and develop my gifts, a whole bunch of brothers and sisters are coming together to say two things: First, 'we agree with you that this is what you need to do with your life;' and Second, 'we want to have an investment in what God is doing through you.' The Holy Spirit helped the church realize that they needed to have an investment in this missionary undertaking. God sent Barnabas and Saul as his emissaries, but it was important for the church in Antioch to also send them as their emissaries also. What we see here in Acts 13 benefited the church at Antioch as much as it benefited Saul and Barnabas. I pray that my ordination this afternoon will benefit Harrington Baptist Church, this church, and the other churches represented as much as it benefits me. What we're about to do for Mary Grace this morning will benefit Peyton's Chapel Baptist Church as much as it benefits her.

"You've heard Mary Grace's faith story. She and God gave me the privilege of baptizing her, and you received her as a member of this church. Mary Grace didn't have the advantage of growing up in a Christian home. Her parents are not yet believers. Mary Grace has not been back home to her family since she began believing in and following Jesus, and quite frankly, she has been dreading it, expecting her family will be less than enthusiastic about her Christian commitment. Here with my family and with this church, among people who share her faith and support her commitment to live as a follower of Jesus — this is the most comfortable place for her to be, just as Antioch was the most comfortable place for Saul and Barnabas. Saul and Barnabas were perfectly happy in Antioch. They would've had much easier lives and would've encountered far less resistance if they'd stayed there. The folks at Antioch would've been happy for them to stay. They were loved and appreciated there. Nobody was trying to run them off. We all need those comfortable places, places where we are loved, wanted, and appreciated, places where we can get a good hug any time we need one, and nobody wants to run us off. As Mary Grace's church family, you've accomplished much by loving and accepting her, teaching her, and encouraging her. What you've done has been reinforced by the Baptist Campus Ministry at Mercer. What my family has done, what this church has done, and what the Baptist Campus Ministry has done have helped to prepare Mary Grace for what comes next.

"The church at Antioch did not send out turkeys. They didn't send their problem people down the road to be somebody else's problem. They sent out two of their best. They wanted to make a good investment in the spread of the gospel. That's what we're doing. Peyton's Chapel is not sending out a turkey. We're not sending a problem person down the road to be somebody else's problem. Mary Grace, you're a blessing, not a problem, and you've been good for this church." After a solid chorus of 'amens,' Cassie continued, "We're sending one of our best. Mary Grace is young in the faith, but she's strong and growing. She's warm and genuine, with a pure love for Jesus. She'll represent us and represent the Lord Jesus Christ well. Sending her as our emissary, our missionary to Elberton, our missionary to her family, is a solid investment in the spread of the gospel.

"I told Mary Grace that I couldn't guarantee that her parents and extended family would all respect and accept her Christian commitment, let alone guarantee that they would all become believers. I told her what we could do is turn that dreaded trip to Elberton and the Thanksgiving holidays with her family into her first missionary journey. I told her that she could go there, not just as Mary Grace Tillison, but as an official representative of Peyton's Chapel Baptist Church and of Christ himself who sends all of us who believe in him into this world as his ambassadors. I told her that the Holy Spirit would bear witness with her spirit that she is a child of God! I told her I could guarantee that we'd have her back in prayer, and I told her about the ancient ritual of the laying on of hands and the significance of it.

"I told Mary Grace that we'd have a packed house today because that great cloud of witnesses would be here! A couple of days after I baptized Mary Grace out at Bailey's Mill, she commented to me, 'You know, Cass, it felt like we weren't the only ones out there when you baptized me.' I showed her the picture Miss Addie gave me that I have as the screen saver on my computer, of the big baptismal service out at Bailey's Mill back in the 1920s, and I showed her the scripture in Hebrews 12 about the great cloud of witnesses. Mary Grace realized just how public her profession of faith and baptism had been! So this is a good time for me to welcome the great cloud of witnesses. Mary Grace, they were coming to my ordination anyway, so it was no problem for them to show up here! This afternoon when I'm ordained, I'll feel the hands of Miss Addie, Heather's friend Preacher Olivia, my Grandma and Grandpa Whitmire, and so many others. Mary Grace, you may feel them, too, because it's not just this church that is invested in this, it's all the saints of all the ages! Mary Grace, please come and kneel before the congregation. Sister Ruby Welsh Wilkins is going to offer a prayer of blessing for your missionary journey, and then we will lay our hands on you..."

Cassie had just finished greeting everyone after the service and was about to make her way back to the fellowship hall when she saw the Mintz County Sheriff patrol car pull up into the church parking lot. She had a sudden sick feeling in the pit of her stomach when she saw Jason Bradshaw get out of the car and walk toward her. "What's the matter, Jason?" Cassie asked when he got closer. "Are you here to arrest me?"

"No, Cassie. Nothing like that. Relax, you're not in any trouble. I just came to tell you before you heard some other way. You don't need to worry about pressing charges against Floyd or getting a restraining order against him."

"What are you getting at, Jason?"

"Floyd's dead, so I'd say he's dealing with God right about now. Heart attack just as he was starting his sermon this morning at Freeman Valley."

"Oh my God!" was all that Cassie could get out. "I knew I heard sirens while I was preaching, sounded like they went by on Freeman Valley Road."

"Yeah," Jason added, "the first one you heard was mine. I got the call at 11:30 a.m. I was close by, hit the lights and siren and got there in two minutes, got there before EMS. People said he was red as a beet and acted short of breath when he got up to preach. Said he'd just started his sermon when he gasped and grabbed at his chest. Then his eyes rolled back and he slumped to the floor. When I got there, he'd done turned plumb gray, wasn't breathing and didn't have a pulse. He was dead when he hit the floor. I started CPR, worked on him 'til EMS got there with a defibrillator. They used the jumper cables on him three or four times, never could get a pulse, pulled the sheet over him and took him to the hospital to get him pronounced dead."

"Tommy Sheridan just texted me," Daniel Groves spoke up. "He was just coming out of church at Harrington Methodist when he got the call from the funeral home answering service. He and his son who helps us part-time have gone to the hospital to pick up the body."

"Need to tell Henry and Minnie Ree," Cassie told Jason. "Floyd is Henry's nephew. Floyd's mother is Henry's sister. They're back in the fellowship hall putting food on the table."

"And you might as well stay and eat with us," Coretta added. "We fixed dinner for all the ones who came from out of town for Cassie's ordination, got plenty of food and you'd be welcome."

"Well, I was gonna hit the drive-through at McDonald's directly," Jason replied. "I'm starting to get hungry. Thanks for the invitation. I'll take you up on it. Sounds a lot better than another burger and fries. Gonna be a world-wide salt shortage one of these days 'cause McDonald's put it all on the fries."

"Amen on that, Jason. I can't eat 'em. Way too salty for me. Come on back with us and get some real food," Cassie told Jason. "I'll introduce you to Henry and Minnie Ree, and you can tell them about Floyd. I really feel bad about this. I didn't mean to kill him."

"You didn't kill him, Cassie."

"I know I didn't. He did it to himself, getting all worked up the way he did. Thought he was gonna do the Fred Sanford thing on me this morning out at Bailey's Mill, have the big one right before my eyes. Glad it was you instead of me doing CPR on him. Still, I feel bad about it. Feel bad for his wife and kids and his mama." Cassie spotted Henry and Minnie Ree in the fellowship hall and motioned them over to where she was standing with Jason. "Henry, Minnie Ree, want you to meet Jason Bradshaw. He graduated from Harrington High School a few years ahead of me. His sister Katie was in my graduating class. Jason needs to tell you something."

"Mr. and Mrs. Lane," Jason began awkwardly, searching for the right words, "I told the preacher she didn't need to worry about whether to press charges against Floyd or get a restraining order against him..."

"Because he's dead?" Henry asked searchingly.

"Yes, sir. Had a massive heart attack just as he was starting his sermon. I was close by when the call came over the radio. I was there in two minutes, did CPR on him until EMS got there and took over. They had a defibrillator, did everything they could for him, but he didn't make it. I'm sorry."

Minnie Ree moved closer to Henry and put her arm around him as he absorbed the news of his nephew's sudden death. "Was Floyd's mama, Sue Ellen, there? Does she already know?" Henry asked.

"Yes, sir. She was in church, in fact she said she told him he didn't look good before church started, but Floyd insisted he was all right. She saw us working on him, trying to resuscitate him, saw them pull the sheet over him and take him out. She went home with her daughter-in-law Joanie, Floyd's wife."

"She's in good hands with Joanie," Henry observed. "Joanie's a good woman, she's Ruth Peyton's niece. Floyd would've been meaner than he was if it hadn't been for her. It was always easier to stomach Floyd if she was with him. I appreciate you and the EMS guys doing all you could. We need to go over and see Sue Ellen and Joanie before we go to the ordination service, but we might as well take time to eat. Minnie Ree's diabetic, needs to eat right and eat on time. We'll have plenty of time to eat and go by and see Sue Ellen before we go to the preacher's ordination. Can't say that this surprises me. I remember what J. T. said about Floyd when Harrington Baptist got voted out of the association."

"What did he say?" Jason asked.

"He said that one of these days Floyd was gonna rev himself up too tight and put a rod through the side of the block." Turning to Cassie, Henry added, "Preacher, you don't need to blame yourself for killing Floyd. If he hadn't got his self all worked up over our woman preacher, he'd a got his self worked up over something some other church in the association did. Revved his self up too tight and slung a rod. He did this to his self."

"Thanks for this morning," Mary Grace broke the silence as Cassie made the turn onto Tennessee Avenue toward Floyd Williams' house. "I feel a lot less anxious about going back to Elberton tomorrow morning."

"You're welcome," Cassie responded. "I feel pretty anxious about right now, going to see Floyd's wife and mother. I'd really planned on just relaxing at home until time for the ordination service. Now I understand your situation a lot better — needing to go somewhere, dreading it, not knowing how I'm going to be received. They might hug my neck or they might slap me cross eyed, accuse me of killing him, and ask me how I dare to show my face. But I am a pastor, and this is what pastors do. I need to do this, regardless of how they receive me."

"Henry and Minnie Ree and Arnie and Ruth will be there," Mary Grace commented as Cassie parked the car at the curb in front of Floyd's house. "I don't think they'll show out too bad with them there. Good, Henry and Minnie Ree are already here. I see their car."

"And that's Arnie and Ruth pulling up behind us," Cassie observed. "Glad I've got backup going into this one. Saint Addie, pray for us. You know how Floyd was. Lord knows you tried to teach him better."

"Amen," Mary Grace concurred as they got out of the car. Arnie and Ruth flanked them as they walked toward the house.

"Sure is sweet of y'all to come over here," Ruth commented as Arnie opened the storm door for them. Joanie got up from the couch and hugged Ruth and Arnie as Ruth made the introductions. "Joanie, I want you to meet our pastor, Cassie McWhorter, and her roommate at Mercer, Mary Grace Tillison."

Joanie, her face tear-streaked and her eyes red from crying, hugged Cassie. "Thank you for coming."

Mary Grace, led by the Spirit, stepped in close to tightly embrace both Joanie and Cassie as Cassie prayed aloud, "Father of mercies and God of all comfort, be very near to your child and my sister Joanie, care tenderly for her, and surround her with your peace and comfort. In Jesus' strong name, Amen."

"Amen," Joanie responded. "Thank you, Preacher. Thank you, Mary Grace." Henry and Minnie Ree went back to the bedroom where Sue Ellen was lying down. Joanie sat down on the couch, with Cassie and Mary Grace on one side of her, Ruth on the other, and Arnie sat down in the armchair on the other side of the room. "Preacher," she continued as she caressed Cassie's right hand in her hands, "I'm so glad you and Mary Grace came. Please don't blame yourself for this. And, since Floyd's not here to hear me say it, I've heard good things about you. God bless you as you are ordained today." Joanie and Cassie embraced, and Joanie added,

"Don't be too surprised if me and Mama Sue Ellen show up at Peyton's Chapel one Sunday to hear you preach."

"You'd be welcome," Cassie responded. "Bobby Simpson's soon-to-be ex-wife is there every Sunday. Her daughter, son-in-law, and grandchildren were there today."

"That's how I heard about you," Joanie laughed through her tears. "Ruth Ann's my cousin, and we both work in the lunchroom at Miss Addie's School. I sure am proud to hear that Ronnie and Jennifer and their kids came to church today. Jennifer got turned off of church on account of her daddy, and Ronnie didn't grow up going to church, but they're good people."

"They really enjoyed being there," Mary Grace commented. "You could tell. Everybody hugged them and made them feel welcome. Ronnie said they were all coming to Cassie's ordination, said they wouldn't miss it for the world."

"If it wad'n for our son and daughter being on their way here, and needing to look after Sue Ellen, and people from our church coming by," Joanie explained, "I'd be there, too. Wish I could be there."

"Joanie," Arnie spoke up, "Harrington Baptist is recording the service. They got the machine that duplicates cassette tapes, pastor at Harrington told us he would make us some copies and to let him know if we wanted more, so I'll make sure you get one."

"Thanks, Arnie," Joanie responded. "I'll look forward to hearing it, and I sure will be praying for the service."

"And Joanie," Cassie added, "we'll feel your presence anyway. There really is such a thing as being present in spirit when we cannot be present in person. You have that gift. I've already been blessed by the touch of your hands."

"Thank you for coming by," Joanie responded. "It's right at 2:30 p.m. now, and I know y'all have to head on to the church for the ordination service, but do come back when you can stay longer."

Cassie and Mary Grace answered her with a hug and a promise to return.

"Welcome to Harrington Baptist Church!" Mike began his introductory remarks. "This is a joyful occasion for us as we ordain Sister Cassie McWhorter to the gospel ministry. We welcome Peyton's Chapel Baptist Church, where Cassie serves as pastor. Most of the members of Peyton's Chapel are here today. We celebrate the historic connection between this church and Peyton's Chapel. Peyton's Chapel, the oldest Baptist church in Mintz County, helped establish this church and ordained its first four pastors. Peyton's Chapel, we owe you one! It's about time we sent you a pastor, and we're giving you a good one! We have a dozen or more churches represented here today, and we're glad all of you are here to be a part of this celebration. Cassie was ten years old when I became the pastor of this church. She is the first one I baptized here. It has been a pleasure to watch her grow up, to be her pastor, and to observe the work of God in her. I look forward to being her fellow minister and colleague.

"As we join in prayer this afternoon, let us remember the Freeman Valley Baptist Church and the family of their pastor, Brother Floyd Williams, who collapsed and died as he was beginning his sermon this morning. Cassie's mother, Deacon Elaine McWhorter, comes now to lead us in prayer..."

Elaine's voice was breaking with emotion as she concluded her prayer and sat down on the front pew between Jerry and Cassie. Jerry gave her a gentle hug, and Cassie whispered, "Here, Mom," as she tenderly massaged her mom's shoulders and handed her one of the boxes of Kleenex that Karen Westover had distributed. Elaine had barely dried her tears when Eric Latham asked the congregation to stand and join in singing the two hymns Cassie had requested, "I Love to Tell the Story" and "He

Leadeth Me, O Blessed Thought." Anyone with the least reluctance to sing was lifted to his feet and compelled to join in as Jenny unleashed the full power of the big Baldwin grand piano.

A hush came over the congregation as the tiny gray-haired woman stepped up to the pulpit. "I am honored to be here today," Ruby Wilkins began, "and I want to thank Rhonda Brinson for bringing me up to Harrington to have a part in this service. I've known Rhonda since she was a little girl, and I love her like one of my own. I met Cassie for the first time yesterday evening. It's been a pleasure for me to get to meet her and hear the story of God's work in her life." With self-effacing humor, Ruby continued, "Cassie told me that she was excited to finally get to meet me, told me that she had read about me when she was in the ninth grade, and I told her, 'Well, you've met me. Such as I am, here I am.' I told her that Rhonda and her family have been telling me about her, and I read in *Baptists Today* about this church being kicked out of the association for licensing her, so I was just as excited to meet her. Just being a member of Cassie's ordination council would've been an honor in itself. To my great surprise, I was chosen as the spokesperson for the council! The names of the ministers who were on the ordination council are listed in your bulletin. These ministers, along with the deacons of this church and Peyton's Chapel Baptist Church, questioned Cassie about her Christian experience, her call to preach the gospel, and her doctrinal views. The members of the council who already knew her had all of their questions answered before they arrived last night. Those of us who were meeting her for the first time had all of our questions answered as we talked with her over dinner and in the council meeting. It's my honor and pleasure to report to you that the council voted unanimously to proceed with the ordination of this good minister of the gospel, Sister Cassie McWhorter. Thanks be to God, and thank you for giving me this privilege."

It occurred to Cassie that she really needed to stop referring to her brother Anthony as the Little Brat, but she quickly dismissed that thought. He would think she was upset with him if she ever called him by his proper name. Today, he was reading scripture in church for the first time. He had been terrified at the thought of doing that, but he agreed to do it today for his sister. If he was nervous, it didn't show. He read the account of Isaiah's call in Isaiah 6 in a strong, clear voice. The reading ended with the words Cassie had offered when she was fifteen as her own response to the one who called her, "Here am I, send me." Cassie was impressed that the Little Brat had even put on a suit and tie for the occasion. When he finished, he sat down on the second pew next to his girlfriend Amanda and her Methodist preacher mama. Cassie turned around, gave him a quick hug, and whispered, "Love you, Little Brat."

As Aaron Stewart came to the pulpit to read the sixteenth Psalm, the image of Bobby Simpson spread-eagled on the hood of the hearse and Aaron clicking the handcuffs on him flashed before Cassie's mind. She had known Aaron and Latisha Stewart all of her life and knew their children. She remembered how quickly Aaron intervened when Bobby Simpson put his hands on her. She recalled the good lesson that Aaron taught her at the cemetery the day that Miss Addie was buried, that there are some things she could not control. "It's not up to you whether to press charges against Bobby Simpson," Aaron had told her that day. "I saw what went down, and I'm charging him." Cassie loved the sixteenth Psalm, and it had even greater significance as Aaron Stewart read the familiar words, "The Lord is the portion of mine inheritance and of my cup; thou maintainest my lot. The lines are fallen to me in pleasant places, yea, I have a goodly heritage... Thou wilt show me the path of life, in thy presence is fullness of joy, at thy right hand there are pleasures forevermore."

Coretta began singing the familiar words that she and Cassie had both learned from Miss Addie, "There is an unseen hand to me, that leads in ways I cannot see..." Coretta began without accompaniment, perfectly on pitch, and Jenny joined in, weaving a light, delicately improvised piano accompaniment around Coretta's powerful voice. When she finished, she stopped to give Cassie a quick hug before sitting down next to Daniel.

It had taken Cassie's sister Emily a while to get to the place where she could bless Cassie's calling to ministry. She had always been the more practical of the two McWhorter girls, while Cassie had always been the idealistic one. She used to roll her eyes when Cassie talked about being called to preach, always reminding Cassie that she had to be able to make a living, and that there just aren't many Baptist churches in the south willing to consider women as pastors. She had urged Cassie to accept the way it is and find some other way to serve the Lord. The night before Emily's wedding, she and Cassie had talked until almost 3:00 a.m. The conversation had started out as girl talk, full of laughter, teasing, and silliness, until Emily turned the conversation in the direction of a Last Desperate Effort to talk some sense into her kid sister. Emily's words, "I know you mean well, but..." had stung painfully. Emily and Jacob came the Sunday night that Cassie preached her first sermon, and they came to Miss Addie's funeral. The Saturday night before the funeral, when Jacob and Emily took her out to eat and buy a new outfit for the funeral, Emily had said, "Cass, I love you and I need to apologize to you," and they had embraced each other. In the weeks since that conversation, Emily had talked and e-mailed back and forth with her about the painful ostracism they were experiencing in their church in Carrollton because her sister was about to be ordained as a Baptist minister. Emily sought Cassie's advice, not only as a sister, but as a pastor. She and Jacob had been in church at Peyton's Chapel this morning, and they told her after the service that they felt more welcome there than they had felt in their church in a long time, and they wished that Peyton's Chapel were closer to Carrollton. Hot tears trickled down Emily's face as she read the gospel lesson, and both sisters gave thanks for forgiveness, mutual understanding, and the healing of their relationship.

"This is only the second time I've done this," Mike began the charge to the church. "Heather Simmons Moore followed me as pastor of Clear Springs Baptist Church at Ledford, Virginia. I had the pleasure of helping ordain her. She's here today, and she will deliver the charge to the candidate. My assignment is to deliver the charge to the church. The first thing I would say to our friends from Peyton's Chapel is *identify and cele-brate your strengths.* When a church is small and struggling, with an aging membership, it's easy for the church to overlook some of its strengths. When Cassie and I debriefed after her first Sunday preaching at Peyton's Chapel, she told me, 'Brother Mike, I love these people. They are so much better than they think they are! Half of them are kin to Miss Addie, so there's probably some kind of genetic basis for it.' You nailed it, Cass! You are right. Peyton's Chapel, you embody the spirit of Miss Addie! Miss Addie was the first person Cassie told about her call to preach. Miss Addie, ninety-seven at the time, encouraged a fifteen-year-old girl and told her that she was not crazy for thinking she was called to preach. In that same spirit, Peyton's Chapel gave a nineteen-year-old young woman the opportunity to preach, and that speaks volumes. That alone says that you are an exceptional church. You took a risk! Instead of bemoaning the fact that you can't afford a full-time pastor, you recognized an opportu-nity to help a young minister just getting started — a young minister most churches wouldn't touch with a ten-foot pole because she happens to be a woman. I have been nothing short of astounded at Cassie's preach-ing gift. Never will forget, just over a year ago, when she preached her first sermon — at least the first public one, she'd been preaching to the rocks, the trees, and the great cloud of witnesses out at Bailey's Mill. I'm embarrassed to admit it, but my expectations were low. I wasn't expecting her to do any better than I did my first time, and she hit it out of the ball park, solid message and powerful delivery — and she's gotten better since then! You heard Cassie for the first time at Miss Addie's funeral. You saw grace under pressure when Cassie was assaulted at the cemetery that day. You found yourselves without a pastor, and you saw the obvious solution that God put in front of your eyes. You heard her prayerfully and gladly, and you were not disappointed. You discerned the work of God in her life. You realized that she could be good for you and you could be good for her, and you took the bold step of calling her as your pastor. You'll probably be voted out of the Mintz County Association for that, just as we got voted out after we licensed her to preach, but you're going to be too wrapped up in revival to worry too much about that. I remember what my friend Heather Simmons said after her church was voted out of the association for calling her as pastor. She said, 'All who want to be a part of what God is doing at Clear Springs are welcome. Those who don't like what God is doing at Clear Springs can go sulk in the corner until they get over it.' Peyton's Chapel has so many strengths — a rich heritage, a willingness to take risks, gifted lay leaders, and a gracious, nurturing environment that helps people come to faith in Christ and helps them grow in grace.

"The next thing I would say to Peyton's Chapel is this, *Remember that ministry is a two-way street.* Countless times as a pastor, I've gone to encourage or comfort someone else, and they encouraged me and strengthened my faith. Remember that in your relationship with your pastor. There will be times that she'll be discouraged or frustrated or overwhelmed, and you'll need to care for her soul even as she cares for yours. Cassie tells me that you've already been doing that and doing it well. May you and your pastor have the kind of relationship in which each strengthens the other and each brings out the best in the other.

"The final word I would say to you is, *Embrace the future that God offers you.* You have been discouraged, struggling even to believe that there is a future. But now, I am already seeing a renewal of hope among you. You're starting to see people who've never been in church and people who haven't been in a long time. This morning, you commissioned Mary Grace Tillison for her first missionary journey — going back to Elberton to bear witness to her parents and family of her new life in Christ. I leave you with the words of the prophet Jeremiah: "For surely I know the plans I have for you," says the Lord, "plans for your welfare and not for harm, to give you a future with hope." Thanks be to God! Amen!

Mike sat down, and Cassie looked over at Mary Grace, whispered, "Your turn," and squeezed Mary Grace's hand gently before she got up to read the epistle lesson.

"I am blessed," Mary Grace began, prefacing the scripture reading, "to have Cassie McWhorter as my pastor, my roommate at Mercer, and my friend. Cassie led me to faith in Christ and baptized me. Cassie, I love you as my sister in Christ, and it is an honor for me to participate in your ordination. Hear the word of the Lord, the apostle Peter writing to young ministers, 'Now as an elder myself and a witness of the sufferings of Christ, as well as one who shares in the glory to be revealed, I exhort the elders among you to tend the flock of God that is in your charge, exercising the oversight, not under compulsion but willingly, as God would have you do it — nor for sordid gain but eagerly. Do not lord it over those in your charge, but be examples to the flock. And when the chief shepherd appears, you will receive the crown of glory that never fades away.' This is the word of the Lord. Thanks be to God."

Wallace Moore was sitting with his dad and Grandpa Moore two pews behind Cassie, while Grandma Moore held Olivia. As Heather stepped up to the pulpit, he leaned forward and whispered to Amanda and her Methodist preacher mama, loud enough for everybody to hear, "That's my mama up there. She preaches good."

"Thanks for the intro, Wallace!" Heather laughed along with everyone else. "It's good to know that my son has confidence in my preaching ability. I have long felt sure that this day would come, when we would ordain Cassie to the gospel ministry. It came sooner than I expected! I met Cassie for the first time eight years ago when I preached a revival here at Harrington. Cassie made an indelible impression on me even then. Cassie, I knew God was up to something good with you. The evening I had dinner with your family, you had more questions for me than my ordination council did. Your parents may have wished you weren't so full of questions, but I loved every minute of it." As Heather took a folded letter from between the pages of her Bible and held it aloft, she continued, "I still cherish the letter you wrote to me, thanking me for coming to Harrington and preaching. I want to incorporate in my charge to you the letter you wrote when you were not quite twelve years old. You wrote,

Dear Preacher Heather,

Thank you for coming to preach the revival at my church. I enjoyed your sermons, and I especially enjoyed you eating dinner with us at our house.

You are the first woman preacher I ever heard. I am glad that God calls girls to preach, too. I know I asked a lot of questions. Thank you for listening and answering my questions and telling me about God calling you to preach. I just got baptized last summer. I love Jesus and like learning more about him. I am going to pray for you every day, and I hope you can come back to Harrington again.

Your Friend,
Cassie McWhorter

"Well, Cass, here I am back in Harrington, here to help ordain the little girl who wrote that letter. The apostle Peter's words about being an example to the flock and leading by example apply to any minister, but they are especially relevant to you as a woman in ministry. Especially among Baptists, we women who preach and do pastoral ministry are a small minority. I've been at Clear Springs long enough that some of the children may not know that God can also call men to preach. Claude Bradley up in Virginia is a neighboring pastor and dear friend of mine. Someone asked Claude one time whether he believed in women preachers. Claude said that not only did he believe in them, he'd actually seen one! He said he'd not only seen one — talking about me here — he'd had her come to his church and preach a revival. That was a good meetin' over at Coley's Station Baptist Church! Cassie, you're the first woman preacher that some people ever saw. I would say to anyone beginning in ministry, stay close to the Lord and live what you preach. That basic advice is infinitely more important for you as a woman called to be a pastor.

"I realized that when I was down here eight years ago to preach the revival. I noticed how closely you and other young girls paid attention when I was preaching. I realized that I was on holy ground at your house, listening to your thoughts and questions, especially one that you asked: 'How did you know that God wanted you to be a preacher?' I found myself on holy ground again last summer at the Women in Ministry conference. We shared a room, I was eight months pregnant with Olivia, having to elevate my feet to bring down the swelling in my ankles, and we had some good, long late-night talks. You showed me a letter that you kept folded and tucked in the pages of your Bible. It was the letter I wrote, answering the letter from you that I just read. It made me realize that I am a role model whether I want to be or not. Cassie, as women called to ministry, you and I do all of the things that all faithful ministers of the gospel do, and we also do something else. For the girls and women who hear us preach and see us doing the day-to-day work of ministry, we define what is possible. God gave me the privilege of doing that for you. Then, when you were in the ninth grade, you read about Ruby Welsh Wilkins, the first woman pastor of a Baptist church in Alabama. Even before you met her for the first time last night, Ruby helped you see what is possible. Ruby, I'm so glad you're here. I've enjoyed meeting and talking with you, and I'd like for us to stay in touch. May you be known henceforth and forevermore as 'Ruby the Baptist,' preparing a way through the wilderness for women called to ministry, helping girls and women know that God can, in fact, call women. I'm thankful that Cassie finally got to meet you! Cassie, boys and men called to ministry have an abundance of role models, ranging from excellent to, shall we say, not quite so good. Girls and women have fewer role models. Many girls and young women have the gifts and the ability to be excellent ministers, but they have never heard a woman preach, and they are in churches that tell them they can't be hearing God right because God doesn't call women to preach. I can't overemphasize how important it is for the few of us women who do pastoral ministry to be people of faith, good students of the scriptures, people of prayer, people of integrity, and live what we preach. Cassie, when I was out at Peyton's Chapel this morning, I couldn't help but notice the three little girls who hugged you around the knees, and a girl who looked to be about eleven or twelve who was hanging on every word when you were preaching. I met two women who had pretty much given up on church who came back because of you. For their sake, the way you shepherd the flock of God is critically important.

"Cassie, I love your awareness of the great cloud of witnesses, those who were in Christ before us. My awareness of the great cloud of witnesses grew when the two women for whom my daughter is named — Preacher Olivia Harris and my Granny Gladys Becker, and the man for whom my son is named, Wallace Coggins, and other saints dear to me went to be with the Lord. They imparted powerful blessings to me, as your friend Miss Addie did to you. You are only nineteen, but the spirit that was in Miss Addie dwells in you. She was a blessing to me even though I only got to spend a little time with her when I preached the revival here. She invested her life and soul in you. She preached the glory down the Sunday you were baptized. When you were fifteen, she told you that you weren't crazy for thinking God was calling you to preach — just like Granny Becker did for me. Every Sunday, you lay your open Bible on a pulpit used by preachers who died a hundred years before you were born. You are the heir of a great heritage, and you are perpetually surrounded by a great cloud of witnesses who are your biggest fans!

"Cassie, you are about to receive a gift through the laying on of our hands. By the grace of God, we have power to bless you. We will lay hands on your head because God has obviously laid hands on your heart. Receive God's gift and our gifts, use the gifts well for the good of the body of Christ. As you receive the gifts, pay them forward. Thanks be to God. Amen."

As Cassie stood and walked over to the kneeling bench, her eyes surveyed the congregation. She noticed that Jason Bradshaw, still in uniform, had slipped in and sat down next to Ronnie Wofford and his family.

Chapter 21

"You be careful driving up to Elberton," Elaine said as she, Jerry, and Cassie hugged Mary Grace in the driveway before she got in her car.

"I will," Mary Grace responded. "And thanks for everything. I love you guys."

"We love you, too," Jerry replied. "Give us a call when you get there, let us know you made it."

"Don't worry, Daddy Longlegs, I will, and thanks for checking my car over for me."

Mary Grace's car was just over three years old and had less than 20,000 miles on the odometer, nonetheless Jerry had gone over it with a fine-toothed comb, checking belts, hoses, wiper blades, tire pressure, and fluids before she got on the road. Finding her windshield washer reservoir a tad low, he had topped it off from the jug he kept under the workbench in the garage.

"Cass, you've got my e-mail address," Mary Grace winked at Cassie. "I must hear all about your hot date with Jason Bradshaw."

"Don't worry, you will," Cassie shot back, "if you call going out to eat after the viewing for Floyd Williams a hot date."

Elaine had the whole week of Thanksgiving off. Howard Ellis was spending the whole week in the Bahamas, and Jack Kinnebrew said he'd take care of getting the mail and checking phone messages for the law firm. Jerry had meant to be off, too, but five minutes before Mary Grace left, he got a call about a break in one of Harrington's almost century-old water mains over on Tennessee Avenue. He complained to whoever would listen that the city was putting in new water mains eight feet at a time. The Little Brat had school through Wednesday. Cassie welcomed the opportunity to enjoy a leisurely day at home with her mom. Jerry, always up by 5:00 a.m., had a good fire in the wood heater in the den and the big coffee urn going by the time everybody else got up. Cassie got a couple more pieces of well-seasoned hickory from the woodpile and brought them in before she poured herself another cup of coffee and settled down in the den. She picked up the beautifully framed certificate and read,

> This certifies that, upon the recommendation and request of Peyton's Chapel Baptist Church, and after satisfactory examination by us with regard to her Christian experience, call to ministry, and doctrinal views, Cassie Elise McWhorter was joyfully and pub-licly set apart and ordained to the work of the Gospel Ministry by Harrington Baptist Church at Harrington, Georgia, on the 22nd day of November, 1998.

Cassie read the signatures, Michael G. Westover, moderator of the council; Ruby Welsh Wilkins, clerk of the council; both of her parents, Heather, and nineteen others.

Then, she picked up what Mary Grace had dubbed her "twenty-pound ordination Bible," as in, "Now if you have a run-in with somebody like Brother Bobby or ol' Floyd, you can whack 'em upside the head with that twenty-pound ordination Bible" — *The New Oxford Annotated Bible*, with the Apocryphal/Deuterocanonical Books, New Revised Standard Version. Her name, "Rev. Cassie E. McWhorter," was embossed on the cover in gold leaf, and the flyleaf was inscribed in

Myrtle Hill's elegant hand, "This Bible is presented to our pastor, Rev. Cassie Elise McWhorter, on the occasion of her ordination to the Gospel Ministry, by Peyton's Chapel Baptist Church at Harrington, Georgia, November 22, 1998." Lastly, Cassie picked up the long flat rectangular box containing the beautiful white linen pulpit stole, a gift from the Little Brat's girlfriend's Methodist preacher mama and her family. Cassie read the card again,

> Dear Cassie,
>
> Blessings as you are ordained today to the Gospel Ministry. Our prayer is that many will be led to Christ and that many will be strengthened in the faith through your ministry. May the weight of this stole around your shoulders remind you of the hands laid upon you at your ordination and the Spirit of the Living God that is upon you.
>
> —Janice, Grover, and Amanda Hall

"I love your stole, Cassie," Elaine commented as she sat down close to her daughter and felt the soft, smooth fabric. "Stand up and try it on."

"Over my pajamas and housecoat?" Cassie asked as she stood and her mom draped the stole over her shoulders and evened up the ends.

"I know it'll look better with your Sunday dresses," Elaine acknowledged, "I just wanted to see it on you. It's beautiful." As she embraced Cassie, she added, "and so are you."

"Thanks, Mom."

"You surprised me taking a date to the funeral home tonight," Elaine stated matter-of-factly.

"I was surprised when Jason asked me at the reception after the ordination service yesterday," Cassie laughed, "and I'm not sure it's a date with a capital D. He was so sweet and thoughtful about it, I couldn't say no. He said he knew it was going to be awkward to go and pay my respects, me being a woman preacher and knowing how Floyd felt about that along with feeling sort of like I killed him, told me he was off tonight and if it'd help make it less awkward for me, he'd like to go with me and take me out to dinner afterward. Viewing's from 6:00 p.m. to 9:00 p.m., he's picking me up at 6:00 p.m."

"Jason's a nice young man. Your dad and I have known his dad since elementary school. And of course, you graduated with his sister. The Bradshaws are good people. They're all members at Alabama Road. Bob McKnight filled in there while their pastor was recovering from heart surgery. I assume Jason's a member there, too."

"He is, Mom. He speaks well of Bob and Aunt Susan. He couldn't have been nicer or more helpful to me yesterday morning after that run-in with Floyd. I'm not ready for a serious relationship, but..."

"There's nothing wrong with going out with a really nice guy," Elaine finished her daughter's sentence.

Daniel Groves was standing in the lobby of Webster Funeral Home when Jason and Cassie arrived. The funeral home was crowded with two viewings taking place, and Daniel was stationed in the lobby to direct people to the right place. "Hey, Preacher," Daniel greeted Cassie with a hug, and as he extended a hand to shake hands with Jason, continued, "and your friend here is..."

"Jason Bradshaw," Jason introduced himself. "My sister Katie graduated with Cassie."

"Daniel married Coretta Brinkley. She teaches kindergarten at Miss Addie's School. Daniel's dad owns the Chevy dealership and his mom has Red Carpet Realty. Coretta's folks own Brinkley's Garage. Daniel and Coretta are members at Peyton's Chapel. I've known them just about all of my life," Cassie explained to Jason. Turning to Daniel, Cassie added, "Jason works with the Sheriff's Department. He's the one who responded yesterday morning after my run-in with Floyd out at Bailey's Mill. Then he got the call about Floyd's heart attack, got there first and did CPR on him until EMS got there."

"Not just saying it 'cause she's standing here," Daniel commented to Jason, "we love Cassie, so blessed to have her as our pastor." The line of people coming into the funeral home was backing up, so Daniel had to cut it short. "The viewing for Reverend Williams is in Parlor A."

Jason's hand rested lightly on Cassie's shoulder as she signed the guest book, "Rev. Cassie McWhorter, Pastor, Peyton's Chapel Baptist Church," then Jason signed under her. She picked up one of the cards with the obituary and funeral arrangements before they took their place in line. On the front, under the praying hands design, she read "Rev. Floyd Malvern Williams, born March 19, 1947, entered eternal rest November 22, 1998." The funeral would be tomorrow at 1:00 p.m. at Freeman Valley Baptist Church with Rev. Bobby Simpson and Rev. Milford Braswell officiating. Deacons of Freeman Valley Baptist Church would be the pallbearers, and all ordained ministers are asked to be honorary pallbearers. Jason, who was looking on as Cassie read, commented, "Looks like you can be an honorary pallbearer if you want to be. I go on duty at 3:00 p.m. tomorrow. Don't know if you plan to go to the funeral or if you plan to sit with the preachers. If you want to go, I can come in uniform, take you to the funeral, and take you home on my way to work. Won't have time to go the cemetery, but I can go with you to the funeral."

"Don't think I'll go to the funeral," Cassie replied, "though it's sweet of you to offer to go with me. I could enjoy hanging out with you for a while tomorrow. We could go up to the rec, shoot some hoops or something. We don't have to plan anything elaborate. I couldn't stomach

Bobby Simpson even for a funeral. I'm here tonight for the folks in my church who are kin to him or his wife, and I'm here for her. I feel pretty sure that 'all ordained ministers' thing doesn't really mean *all* ordained ministers. That's Bobby Simpson, short bald-headed guy in the green suit with the brown tie, no woman to match up his clothes for him, standing at the foot of the casket. He creeps me out. He's court-ordered not to have contact with me. Do me a favor Jason, just stay between me and Bobby Simpson."

"You got it, Cassie," Jason whispered as he moved to her right side and put a reassuring hand on her shoulder. They managed to arrive in front of the casket without acknowledging Bobby Simpson, who was tied up talking to somebody neither of them knew. As they looked down on Floyd's lifeless form, Cassie breathed a silent prayer of thanks that he had waited until he got to church to do the Fred Sanford thing instead of doing it on her at Bailey's Mill like she thought he was going to after she pepper-sprayed him and kicked him in the groin. She had halfway expected him to have the big one last year at the annual meeting of the Mintz County Baptist Association when Harrington got booted out for licensing her to preach. Miss Addie had been one of the messengers to the association when Harrington got kicked out. Cassie picked her up from Pine Crest Assisted Living and took her back afterward. Miss Addie told Cassie on the way home that she hated to admit it, but she had taught Floyd and his father Malvern. Cassie told Miss Addie that she should ponder how many of her former students turned out well, and that she should not blame herself for Malvern and Floyd turning out the way they did. Cassie knew that Miss Addie would tell her now, "If I don't blame myself for how he turned out, you shouldn't blame yourself for killing him." Besides, as Miss Addie noted, one seldom heard of people her age dying. It was mostly younger people like Floyd.

Jason's gentle touch on her shoulder told Cassie that she had lingered at Floyd's casket longer than she meant to. They moved on, and Cassie spoke to Joanie, who was seated a few feet past the head of the casket. Joanie introduced her to her son and daughter as "Preacher McWhorter, the new pastor at Peyton's Chapel." They were cordial to her and accepted her expressions of condolence, so they didn't blame her for killing Floyd either. They knew that, if their father had not gotten himself worked up over the woman preacher in the association, he would've revved himself up too tight over something that some other church did.

Most of the regular Sunday morning crowd at Peyton's Chapel was at the funeral home. Jason knew a fair number of people Cassie didn't know, and she knew some that he didn't know, so they were constantly introducing each other. She introduced him as "my friend Jason Bradshaw," and he introduced her as "my friend Cassie McWhorter, pastor of Peyton's Chapel Baptist Church."

"Preacher, come here," Myrtle Hill beckoned. "I want you to meet my granddaughter, Marcie Hill. She's the girls' basketball coach at Hansonville. She and her roommate brought me over here because I don't drive at night if I can help it."

"I know you, Cassie McWhorter!" Marcie exclaimed as she reached up to hug Cassie. "You're the reason my girls lost to Harrington three years in a row. You had no mercy on us! Believe me, Granny Myrt, I know this girl! She was a holy terror on the basketball court and she's your pastor now?"

"She is," Myrtle acknowledged with a laugh, "and she's good. Just ordained yesterday. You ought to come and hear her one Sunday."

"Don't be surprised if I do, Granny," Marcie retorted. Cassie noticed another thirty- something woman with short-cropped hair standing a foot or so behind Marcie. When Myrtle turned to speak to someone else and left Cassie and Jason with Marcie, Marcie introduced the woman standing just behind her, "Cassie, Jason, this is my partner, Connie Harmon..."

"So where would you like to eat?" Jason asked as he closed the driver's door on his Toyota pickup.

"I'd say The Lonesome Whistle, but they're closed Sunday and Monday," Cassie replied. "What've you got in mind?"

"How does Mexican sound? I've heard the new Mexican place that just opened a few weeks ago in Hansonville is pretty good."

"Sounds good to me. I'm starting to get hungry. Let's check it out." Jason headed north out of town onto the Hansonville Highway, and it was a while, after they passed Pulliam's Store/Gloryland Way Missionary Baptist Church, before Cassie said anything else. "I'm glad you were with me at the funeral home, Jason. It would have been a lot harder without you. And I noticed that you really seemed to enjoy introducing me to people as 'Cassie McWhorter, pastor of Peyton's Chapel Baptist Church,' like that was all on my birth certificate and driver's license."

"Well, I do enjoy introducing you. I'm proud to be seen with you," Jason commented.

"You're the first guy I've gone out with who wasn't put off by me being a preacher. I didn't date a lot in high school, couple of guys I did go out with suddenly acted like I had three heads when I mentioned that I plan to go to seminary and be a pastor."

"Well, I sort of knew that going into it, since I asked you out at the reception after your ordination service. Not like it was a well-kept secret or anything. Besides, that's a good thing as far as I'm concerned. Next time I get a Sunday off, I want to come and hear you preach."

"You'd be welcome. Start a lot of gossip about 'Preacher's got a boyfriend,' but I'm okay with that. That is, if I'm still there after Marcie and

Connie show up together for church. I may have the shortest pastorate in the history of the church and be forever remembered as 'the one who invited the lesbian couple to church.' That may be what I'm remembered for more so than being the first woman pastor."

Jason pondered all of that for a minute before he spoke. "So what were you supposed to do, tell them they can't come to church when the sign in front of the church and the one out on Bailey's Mill Road plainly says 'everyone welcome'?"

"I did the only thing I could do, Jason. I'm not eager to get into controversy, but I'm gonna do what I believe Jesus would do. I know it's what Miss Addie would do. Much as I love Peyton's Chapel and hope I can stay there until I finish Mercer and go to seminary, if they fire me for inviting Marcie and Connie to church, so be it."

"They're not going to fire you, Cass. They'll have to figure out what to do with Marcie and Connie, but I don't think they'll throw you out over it. Besides, Marcie's grandmother's in the church, been there forever."

"You're probably right. Myrt's been there since the beginning of time," Cassie acknowledged. "But I noticed that she referred to Connie as Marcie's roommate, like they were just sharing an apartment to save money, like that's all there was to it, like they hadn't been together eight years."

"She knows, Cass," Jason responded thoughtfully. "She'd have to be dumber than a rock not to know, she just feels like she has to act like she doesn't know, because she loves her granddaughter no matter what, and she loves Connie more than she can admit, so the big question for her is what to call Connie."

"I don't know how this is all going to look when the dust settles," Cassie was searching for the right words. "I like guys. You, especially. Funny thing, when I had my run-in with Floyd out at the mill, he insinuated that I was in a lesbian relationship with Mary Grace, my roommate at Mercer. Now, I love Mary Grace like a sister, and she's the same way about me, hope we can be friends for the rest of our lives, but she's attracted to guys, too, and we have no desire to be in bed with each other.

I don't understand how a woman can be sexually attracted to another woman or how a guy can be attracted to another guy that way, but I don't need to understand it to accept Marcie and Connie..."

"I don't remember making a choice to like girls," Jason commented. "I just started really noticing girls when I was eleven or twelve. Nobody had to tell me not to feel attracted to other guys, because I couldn't be if I wanted to."

"And you think it's the same for Marcie and Connie?" Cassie probed.

"Yeah, I think so. I'm like you. I don't understand it, but there are a lot of things I don't understand. I don't have to understand it to accept them and treat them right. They're not evil people. It's not like Marcie's trying to convince all of the girls on her basketball team to become lesbians..."

"And its not like we're thinking of the people in our lives who persuaded us to become heterosexual," Cassie commented. "Maybe I'm too tenderhearted, but it broke my heart when they talked about their church situation, going to different churches for the whole eight years they've been together, because they can't find a church where they can go together."

"So Marcie volunteers with the youth group at First Baptist in Hansonville. Connie, who grew up in Freeman Valley Baptist Church, works with the children's choir at First Methodist in Hansonville," Jason observed, "and everybody pretends they don't know."

"Right," Cassie continued the thought, "and the only people harmed are two adults who love the Lord and each other and wish they could go to church together."

"That was good," Cassie commented as they walked from the restaurant to the truck.

"It was," Jason agreed, "but the best part was being with you. Even if the food hadn't been good, I would've still enjoyed being with you. I like you better than any of the other girls I've gone out with. I can't believe we talked about some of the stuff we talked about on a first date."

"I feel the same way. And I'm all for going up to the rec and shooting some hoops in the morning." With a sinister laugh, Cassie added, "Just remember what Marcie said. I show no mercy on the basketball court." As Jason was about to pull out of the restaurant parking lot, Cassie spoke up. "Turn right, Jason. Let's go around by Bailey's Mill Road."

Once he made the turn onto Bailey's Mill Road, there was little traffic. Jason drove slowly with his left hand, and Cassie welcomed his right arm around her shoulders. As they approached the bridge at Bailey's Mill, Cassie broke the silence, "You know where the little dirt road is that goes down into the clearing down by the mill?"

Jason answered Cassie's question with a gentle squeeze of Cassie's shoulder before slowing almost to a stop, clicking his headlights on bright to make sure he didn't miss it, and making the turn onto the dirt road. "Daddy and I used to come out here to fish above the dam. Never parked here with a girl before."

"And I've never parked here with a guy, either. Here, or anywhere else for that matter. Jason, I guess this sounds kinda strange, and I know Floyd's dead and can't bother me any more, but this is my holy place, where I like to come to think and pray. It's where my friend Miss Addie was baptized in 1908 when she was eleven years old, and it's where I baptized Mary Grace a few weeks ago. It's not just that Floyd scared me to death yesterday morning, it's like he desecrated my holy place. I need my first time back here to be with somebody who makes me feel safe." Cassie unbuckled her seat belt and slid over into Jason's waiting embrace. "Just hold me, Jason." Jason held her close, and she rested her head on his shoulder. They sat like that probably half an hour before Jason kissed her lightly, gently on her forehead. In response, Cassie lifted her head from Jason's shoulder, and their lips met in a long, passionate kiss that left them both out of breath. As she caught her breath, Cassie broke out laughing.

"What's so funny, Cass?" Jason was genuinely puzzled.

"I just realized something. Jason, don't take this personally, but I can't believe I just kissed the lips that did mouth-to-mouth on Floyd Williams."

"Yeah, you did, Cass. Kissing you kinda helped me get that image out of my mind."

It was about 11:00 p.m. when Jason brought Cassie home. The porch light was on. "I can't believe a date to go to a viewing at the funeral home turned out this good," Cassie commented as they walked together toward the front door. "We're definitely on for tomorrow morning before you have to go to work. Pick me up about 9:00 a.m. I'll fix us a picnic lunch. We can go up to the rec, shoot some hoops, chase each other around the track, then we'll go to the park and eat our lunch.

"Sounds good."

"Just remember one thing, Jason." "What's that?"

"I'm very competitive and very fast. No mercy on the track or the basketball court." They exchanged another hug and kiss. As she opened the door, Cassie added, "Come on in, say 'Hi' to my folks before we say good night.

Cassie logged on to her mom's computer to check her e-mail. There were two new messages. The first was from the Little Brat's girlfriend's Methodist preacher Mama, sending her the order of service for the community Thanksgiving service tomorrow night at the Methodist church. Reverend Conway from Greater New Hope was preaching. Cassie had one of the scripture readings, from the ninety-second Psalm, and she would wear that beautiful white linen pulpit stole for the first time. She printed out the order of service that Janet sent her, then clicked on the second message, the one from Mary Grace.

> Hey, Cassie,
>
> Got here a little after 12:00 p.m.. Dad's working out of town until Wednesday. Mom took me to lunch at Chili's, and we had a good talk. I told her that I am following Jesus now and told her about you baptizing me and you getting called as pastor at Peyton's Chapel and me joining the church. I told her I hope she and dad can accept that, because that's who I am and it's not going to change. I told her I wish she and Dad would trust Jesus and start following him too, but at the very least I hope they can accept my decision and respect my faith. Mom cried, said she was happy for me, and we need to talk some more tonight. Pray!
>
> How was your date with Jason?
>
> Love you,
> Mary Grace

Cassie clicked Reply and typed,

Hey, Mary Grace,

Got your back in prayer, as does our friend Saint Addie. Praying that a really good long conversation with your mom is going on as I type this.

The date with Jason was so good. He's light years ahead of any of the other guys I've gone out with. He has to go on duty at 3:00 p.m. tomorrow, but we're planning to get out tomorrow morning, go up to the rec, shoot some hoops and chase each other around the track, then take a picnic lunch out to the park. He's so kind and considerate, and that's important to me. I can see myself getting serious with him.

I'll call you tomorrow night after we get home from the community Thanksgiving service. Not sure what time that will be. Preacher Conway from Greater New Hope's the preacher. Love to hear him, but he can get wound up, especially if the congregation gets into the rhythm of it with him.

Hugs,
Cassie

As the McWhorters came within sight of their home on their way back from the Thanksgiving service, Elaine was the first to notice the Mintz County Sheriff's Department patrol car sitting in their driveway, awaiting their return. "Jerry, hon, there's a Sheriff's car at our house."

"What in the world?" Jerry asked no one in particular as he pulled up in the driveway, shoved it in park, and turned off the ignition.

"Oh my God, NOOOOO!" Cassie screamed as she recognized Tamika Barrentine getting out of the patrol car. "Something bad's happened to Jason!"

Anthony instinctively embraced his sister as she wept uncontrollably. All of the strength drained out of her body. He and Jerry took Cassie's arms around their shoulders in a two-man carry, took her into the living room, and sat her on the sofa. Jerry sat on one side of her, Elaine on the other, holding her tightly as Tamika knelt in front of her and took both of Cassie's hands in hers. "Reverend," Tamika began, her voice breaking with emotion, "I'm sorry to have to be the one to tell you this, but I didn't want you to hear about it some other way..."

"No! No! No!" Cassie screamed, her whole body convulsing violently as Jerry and Elaine struggled to hold her.

"We lost one of our officers in the line of duty tonight," Tamika continued. "It was Jason." With those words, Cassie fell forward onto Tamika. The two women embraced and wept together.

"Anthony, call Brother Mike and let him know," Jerry spoke in the commanding tone of voice he rarely used. "And call the Baileys out at Peyton's Chapel, get the word to the church. They're in the phone book, listed as J. T. Bailey on Peyton's Chapel Road. Hurry, Son."

When Tamika was able to speak again, she said, "Sheriff Holland, Chief Deputy Wells, and Reverend McKnight have gone to be with Jason's family. They sent me over to break the news to you, Reverend. We all been teasin' Jason about havin' a girlfriend," a smile broke across Tamika's tear-streaked face. "ever since he came in Tuesday talkin' about you and what a good time the two of you had together. That boy was head over heels in love if anybody ever was. He couldn't stop talking about you, how pretty and sweet you are, and how much he enjoyed being with you. We wad'n gonna have you findin' out some other way."

"What happened?" Cassie managed to get out the words, her voice hoarse, almost gone, from screaming her lungs out when she first heard the news.

"Routine traffic stop out on Hansonville Highway, about a mile past where Bailey's Mill Road turns off, radioed in that he was pulling him over for one of his taillights being out, had his dashboard camera turned on, so we got the whole incident on film. Jason pulled the guy over, got out of his patrol car, and walked up to the car to ask for his license, registration, and insurance. Got up to the driver's window, guy stuck a gun out the window, shot him and killed him, and took off. Silver Lexus, Fulton County tag. Ran the tag, came up stolen from up at Alpharetta. Trooper Hall, the Methodist preacher's husband, was the first one on the scene. He topped the hill and saw Jason's car on the side of the road idling, blue lights flashing, Jason lying on the edge of the pavement. Trooper Hall radioed for EMS and backup and secured the crime scene. Jason was barely alive when Trooper Hall got to him, unconscious, shallow breathing, weak pulse. They tried to life flight him to Grady but he died before the helicopter could take off. I'm sorry, Reverend. You know he's with the Lord."

"I know, and I don't want him with the Lord. I want him with me." Cassie broke down sobbing again. "Mom, call Mary Grace for me, let her know," Cassie tried to compose herself and gain a modicum of control over the situation. "Her number's in my little book on my dresser." As soon as she got those words out, her eyes met her father's, and she collapsed against him, weeping uncontrollably again. "Hold me, Daddy. Just hold me."

Jerry held Cassie tightly, rubbed her back, and gently stroked her hair. "I can hold you all night long if you need me to," Jerry whispered softly.

Cassie didn't know how long it had been when she lifted her head up from her father's shoulder and saw herself surrounded by J. T. and Josie, Ronnie Wofford, Myrtle Hill with Marcie and Connie because Myrtle didn't drive after dark, Brother Mike and Karen, Daniel and Coretta, and the Little Brat's girlfriend Amanda and her Methodist preacher mama and state trooper daddy. She heard Trooper Hall telling Tamika that Hansonville Police and Fire Department and the Phillips County Sheriff's Department had shut down the highway and one of the Hansonville officers shot and killed the suspect. Maybe her grief was making her see things, but she caught a fleeting glimpse of Miss Addie just before her mom handed her the phone to talk to Mary Grace.

Chapter 22

Cassie woke up on Thursday morning, Thanksgiving Day, in her bed in her room, not knowing how she got there. Everything from the time they spotted the Sheriff's Department car waiting for them when they came home from the community Thanksgiving service last night until now was all a blur. She did not know what she had dreamed and what was real, but she knew nothing was as it should be. Jason was dead, or was that a bad dream? She didn't know, she only knew that she felt more completely drained than she had ever felt. Mary Grace was supposed to be in Elberton with her family, but there she was over on the other bed, still in her clothes, asleep on top of the cover, with the crocheted afghan that Granny McWhorter made spread over her. Her mom was halfway asleep in the rocking chair pulled over close beside her bed.

"What time is it, Mom? How did I get in here? And when did Mary Grace get here?"

"It's 8:40 a.m., Cassie. About midnight, Marcie suggested we all, everybody that was here, form a circle around you and Tamika to pray for you. As many of us as could, laid our hands on one or both of you. Marcie prayed for you, Jason's family, Tamika, and all of the law enforcement people, prayed the sweetest prayer. After that, you hugged everybody and said you wanted to go to bed. Your daddy and Anthony walked you to your room. Then I came in here, helped you change into your night-gown, and tucked you in like I used to when you were little. I lay down beside you and held you until you were asleep. Then I just sat here in the rocking chair beside your bed the rest of the night. Mary Grace got here about thirty minutes ago."

"She must have gotten on the road about 5:00 a.m.," Cassie responded, the bewilderment audible in her voice. "It's a good three hours from Elberton to Harrington any way you go."

Elaine kept her voice down, trying not to wake Mary Grace. "I talked to her last night after she talked to you. She told me then that she was going to try to get on the road about 8:00 a.m. Like I said, she showed up here about the time she'd planned to leave Elberton. Said she couldn't sleep, tossed and turned all night, so she decided about 4:00 a.m. to go ahead and get up, get ready, and come on down. Ronnie and Jennifer Wofford got here about the same time, pulled in right behind Mary Grace. They're in the kitchen cooking breakfast for all of us. Emily and Jacob just called, and said they'd be here about 10:30."

Mary Grace yawned, sat up in bed, and stretched. "Not too bad a drive, not much traffic this early on a holiday. I had that little Ford Contour rolling once I got on I-20, blasting the music pretty loud to stay awake."

As Mary Grace came over and sat down on the side of her bed, Cassie sat up and hugged her. "Thanks for coming, Mary Grace. You didn't have to do this. You're missing your family's Thanksgiving."

"The annual drunkenfest? I hated being around drunk relatives telling me how hot I look even before I was a Christian, so I'd already decided to skip that trip over to Athens to Uncle Wilson's. Besides, I can do more good here. Dad went off the chain last night when Mom stood up to him and told him she was skipping drunkenfest this year because she was tired of everybody getting drunk and stupid, told him she volunteered to help cook and serve Thanksgiving dinner at the domestic violence shelter this year. Dad'll have to sleep over at Uncle Wilson's tonight to sober up enough to drive himself home if he gets pickled like he usually does. Some time around midnight, he ended up apologizing to Mom for getting that upset and said he'd be okay going by himself. That was a first, him apologizing to Mom, and he was understanding about me needing to come and be with you. He doesn't get the whole religion and faith thing, but he didn't put me down because of it, and he understands how close you and I have become. Like I told him, you've become my sister, and you're going through the hardest thing you've ever had to face, and I'm going to be with you. He said to express his condolences to you and Jason's family and said he'd be thinking about you, guess that's as close as he comes to praying."

"Closer than he has been," Cassie commented. "It's progress, probably as good as I can do right now. I'm glad other people can pray for me right now 'cause I don't feel much like praying."

"I've been praying for you," Mary Grace responded. "A bunch of people have. Including Saint Addie. And you know the passage in Romans 8 you're always quoting to me about how the Spirit intercedes for us with groanings too deep for words. Not knowing what to say is not a problem when you're dealing with one who knows you better than anyone else and loves you more than anyone else."

"Yeah," Cassie acknowledged, "thanks for being such a good listener and quoting my own sermon material back to me. You're right about Saint Addie, too. Deborah Estelle, Mike and Karen's younger one, was right when she said that, if we forgot Miss Addie, we might forget Jesus and God. Mary Grace, I trust you a lot to tell you this, trust you not to think I'm losing it, and I know grief can mess with your mind, but Miss Addie was here last night along with all of the other people who came when they heard about Jason. I only caught a fleeting glimpse of her, no more than a fraction of a second, but I saw her, don't know whether anybody else saw her or not and I'm afraid to ask because they'll think I'm hallucinating."

"Maybe," Mary Grace observed, "they saw her, too, and they're all afraid to say it because they all think they're the only one and people will think they're crazy. Besides," Mary Grace laughed, "you know that great cloud of witnesses you like to talk about. There's something to that. Out at Bailey's Mill when you baptized me, I sensed their presence so real it made the hair stand up on the back of my neck. Maybe the great cloud of witnesses elected Saint Addie to represent them all last night."

Cassie answered Mary Grace with a silent hug before she swung her feet off the bed and made her way to the bathroom. She had never felt this weak with a stomach virus or the flu. Maybe this was what a bad hangover felt like. If so, she was sure she never wanted to have one. She looked in the mirror, and saw that all of the color was drained out of her face. Her eyes were red and bloodshot from crying. Her voice sounded like a three-pack-a-day smoker from screaming last night when she heard the news about Jason, yet she was ready to scream away what voice she had left if it would do any good. Tamika Barrentine's words kept replaying in her mind, "We lost one of our officers in the line of duty tonight. It was Jason." Especially those last three words, "It was Jason." She could not stop the tape, and it played over and over. "It was Jason. It was Jason."

Cassie turned the shower on as hot as she could stand it. The hot water cascading over her body felt good, and she stayed in as long as the hot water lasted, but nothing felt as good as Jason's arms around her. The most they'd done was hold each other close and kiss, but that had felt so good. She had felt safe and loved with him. She replayed the two dates they'd had. He had been so considerate at the funeral home, and he had proposed taking her to the funeral home to help her get through an awkward situation. On their first date, they had intelligent conversation about a touchy subject, neither of them knowing what the other's thinking was before they got into the conversation. It had been her idea for them to park at Bailey's Mill. He could have taken advantage of her and tried to go further than she was ready to go, but he didn't. He understood when she told him that Floyd had not only made her feel violated, but he had desecrated her holy place. Now, the place of Miss Addie's and Mary Grace's baptism and her place of prayer and meditation was reconsecrated as the place where they had held each other close for the first time, the place of their first kiss, and the place where he first told her that he loved her. Tuesday morning had been so much fun. Jason was pretty good at straight-by-the-rules basketball, and that's how they started out, but it had not taken long for them to get silly with her doing all of the crazy Harlem Globetrotters show-off moves that Coach Sawyer never would let her do in regulation play. The temperature was in the upper sixties that day, and they had raced each other around the track until they were hot and sweaty. They were about the same height, and they had embraced so tightly that they could feel each other's hearts pounding. The kisses didn't do anything to slow their hearts down. Cassie had gone to sleep Tuesday night thinking about Jason, and she had the whole future worked out. She dreamed about a wedding at Peyton's Chapel, being in bed with Jason, making love with him, and a baby bump on her otherwise slender form. Until she saw Tamika's patrol car in the driveway Wednesday night, she could see all of those things happening in due time. She aimed the shower head straight at her face, but it was not enough to wash away the tears pouring down her face because none of those dreams would be realized.

Now the tears of grief were turning into tears of rage, and for the first time in her life, four days after she was ordained to preach the gospel, she really hoped someone was burning in hell forever. The rage she felt now was infinitely beyond the rage she had felt toward Bobby Simpson or Floyd Williams. She didn't know his name or have an idea of what his face looked like, but she hated the sonofabitch who killed Jason. There, she had said it. Sonofabitch. That was the only name he needed or deserved. She said it over and over. Sonofabitch. She wanted to hug and thank the Hansonville officer who shot and killed him. She would tell him, "Thank you for killing Sonofabitch and sending him to hell for me." Cassie had never fired a gun in her life, and the object of her hate was already dead, but she wished she could take Jason's .357 Magnum and fire every last round into him just for good measure. Yet, she knew that discharging every round from Jason's service weapon would not begin to discharge the intense hatred she felt. Still, she wished for that as intensely as she wished that Jason could hold her again. Sonofabitch might be dead, but he wasn't dead enough to suit her. He wasn't a tenth as dead as she wanted him to be. She wanted her mom to scratch his eyeballs out, her daddy to beat him to a bloody pulp, then she wanted to empty every last round from Jason's .357 Magnum into him. She realized the absurdity of that.

Dead, she reminded herself, is an absolute adjective, one that does not take degrees of comparison, no dead, deader, or deadest. Jason was dead and Sonofabitch was dead, the just and the unjust, the loved and the despised, the one who deserved to live and the one who deserved to die, equally dead, neither of them less dead nor more dead than the other. Nothing she could do would make Jason less dead or Sonofabitch more dead, and she, full of all her grief, rage, and burning hatred, was supposed to get through the rest of this week with Jason's funeral, preach Sunday at Peyton's Chapel, and resume classes at Mercer on Monday. She was doing good, damn good as Mary Grace would say, just to put one foot in front of the other.

God was next in line for Cassie's rage. She tried to pray and couldn't because she was just too angry to say anything to God right now. Jason had to be in court yesterday morning, so they didn't get to spend the morning together. She used the time to work on Sunday's sermon. Then she prayed for Jason before he went on duty, prayed for God to watch over him and keep him safe. Was that such a big assignment for God, to watch over one Mintz County deputy patrolling the Hansonville highway from Harrington to the Phillips County line? Tamika said this was the first time the Mintz County Sheriff's Department had lost an officer in the line of duty. All God had to do was make the gun malfunction, make the bullet miss its mark, or at the very least stop Jason from dying until they could get him to a trauma facility and into surgery. As far as Cassie could tell, God had not done a blessed thing to intervene and take care of Jason. She wondered whether she would get zapped if she told God that he fumbled the ball big time on this one and that he had done a poor job of protecting Jason. She didn't much care if she did get zapped. She thought it might even be a blessed relief. One big zap, then she would see Jason, Miss Addie, and Grandma and Grandpa Whitmire again. This sounded like a pretty good proposition, about the most merciful thing God could do right now.

Next in line was Jason himself, dead because he was a little too conscientious about doing his job. It must have been a slow night, because he pulled the creep over for a stupid burned-out taillight, for God's sake! They had two extra officers working Wednesday night into Thursday morning because they expected to round up some drunk drivers. Jason told Cassie that it had gotten so that the night before Thanksgiving was nearly as bad as New Year's Eve and early New Year's Day for drunk drivers. It was really just a courtesy stop about the taillight, because the driver probably didn't know it was out. Jason had anticipated an uneventful stop, because he didn't ask for a backup. License, registration, and insurance would be in order, he would write a courtesy warning about the taillight, and the guy would promise to fix it as soon as he could get to the auto parts store to get another bulb. Jason would be pleasant and courteous, and he would tell him to be careful and have a happy Thanksgiving, and they would both be on their way. The fatal shot tore into Jason before he could say, "Good evening, sir." If Jason had been less vigilant, he would still be alive, and they would have been spending time with each other's families today. If Jason had noticed the burned-out taillight and decided the guy probably knew and just hadn't had a chance to fix it, he would still be alive and their plans for today would still be on. Jason was twenty-two years old, three years older than Cassie, and he had gone to work for the department in May, straight out of the police academy. Cassie had gone out with him twice, just enough to know that she liked him a lot and wanted the relationship to continue. He had called her Wednesday afternoon before he went on duty, they had talked about Thanksgiving plans, and his last words to her had been, "You are beautiful. I love you." Now, he was dead. None of the stuff that she dreamed about was going to happen. She would never feel his arms around her again. The kiss he gave her when he brought her home Tuesday was the last time their lips would touch. All she would have left would be memories and another grave to visit.

Cassie toweled herself dry, put on her robe, and went back to her room to get dressed. One foot in front of the other. Keep moving. The aromas of breakfast cooking and coffee perking met her in the hallway along with the cacophony of voices — her parents, Mary Grace, Jennifer and Ronnie, the Little Brat and his girlfriend. She put on jeans and a Harrington Hornets sweatshirt, bedroom slippers, and brushed her hair straight back and fixed it in a pony tail. One foot in front of the other, keep moving. A lifeless, "Hey, everybody," was all she could manage to say to the people she encountered in the den and kitchen. She managed that only because of the manners drilled into her early on.

Ronnie was wearing the same camo coveralls he had on early Sunday morning. He gave her a hug and said, "We love you, Preacher. So glad you're our pastor. We're gonna get you through this somehow."

Cassie heard herself say, "Thank you," and then felt herself being released from Ronnie's embrace into Jennifer's, and from Jennifer's into Amanda's, and from Amanda's into the Little Brat's. She heard herself say, "I love you, Little Brat," before she slumped onto the sofa beside her Daddy Longlegs, felt herself drawn into his embrace, and felt his hand gently rubbing her back and shoulders.

Jennifer was surprised on Sunday when Ronnie came in and announced that he was going to church with her and the children and his mother-in-law. He had gone with them to the ordination service, and he had told her he was going to start going to church every Sunday. Still, she was as surprised as anybody when Ronnie said he wanted to say grace before they ate breakfast. He looked like a grizzly bear in camo coveralls, but he was a kind, tenderhearted man. Ronnie gave thanks for the food. He prayed for God to comfort Sister Cassie and her family, all of Jason's family and friends, and all of the law enforcement people who worked with him. He gave thanks for the love that was just starting to grow between Jason and Sister Cassie. He confessed that he didn't understand why Jason had to be taken away so young. He told the Lord, "We're gonna keep trustin' you when we don't understand, 'cause you're all we got, Lord." He gave thanks that Jason was in the Lord's presence. He prayed, "Lord, help Sister Cassie realize how much you love her, how much we love her, how good she has been for our church, and how much we need her," and he asked it all in Jesus' name, Amen.

Over breakfast, Jennifer told Cassie that she'd been trying to teach their children about the Lord even though they hadn't been going to church, and she reckoned Ronnie had been paying attention, too. After they started going to church with their grandmother, ten-year-old Gordon and eight-year-old Amelia started asking questions about being baptized and joining the church. Sunday night, Ronnie told her that there was still a whole lot he didn't know about the Bible, but he knew enough to know that he needed to be baptized and start going to church and living for the Lord, and he wanted to be baptized at the same time as their children. Ronnie told Cassie that he wanted to do that anyway seeing as how Jesus died for him and it was the right thing to do. He said he needed to do that because he didn't want Gordon to see him sitting at home or working in the shop while they went to church and get the idea that the Lord and the church were just for women, children, and old people. Ronnie said he could listen to her preaching because she wasn't like his father-in-law or Floyd Williams, and he could handle being baptized at Bailey's Mill in December because he'd been in colder water than that trout fishing, but Cassie said she was sure that they could use the baptistery at Harrington Baptist on a Sunday afternoon. Ronnie said he'd be all right with that since the kids might think the water at the mill was too cold. Cassie told Ronnie that her dad had helped Brother Mike baptize her, so she would baptize him first and then he could help her baptize Gordon and Amelia. Ronnie said he knew he'd get all teary-eyed helping baptize his children, and Cassie told him that she and the whole church would just get teary-eyed with him and that would be fine. For a brief few minutes, Cassie was able to feel some joy breaking into her grief. The first prayer she was able to offer since last night was a silent one giving thanks for Ronnie's salvation as evidenced by the depth of his kindness and compassion and his desire to do all that is right and pleasing to God.

Jennifer and Ronnie were cleaning up after breakfast, and Cassie was sitting in the den with Mary Grace, the Little Brat, and Amanda when the phone rang. Elaine answered it, and Cassie caught on that she was talking to Gary Bradshaw, Jason's father. "She's right here, Gary. I'll get her for you."

Cassie took the phone from her mom. "Hey, Mr. Bradshaw."

"Hey, Preacher," he responded. "And please call us Gary and Donna."

"If you'll just call me Cassie," Cassie replied.

"Cassie," Gary began, searching for words, his voice breaking with emotion, "I just want to say Donna and I love you because Jason loved you. I know y'all just went out for the first time Monday night, but I never saw a boy so love-struck in all my life. You're all he talked about since he came home Sunday night and told us he'd asked you out. 'Course, we knew you 'cause you and Katie ran around together in high school and played basketball together, and I grew up and went to school with your mom and dad."

"Jason was different from any of the other boys I've dated," Cassie began, dabbing tears from her eyes with a Kleenex. "I've never felt more comfortable with a guy. Y'all did something right raising Jason. Some of the guys I dated in high school looked at me like I had three heads when I said I was called to be a preacher and a pastor. Jason wasn't like that. He came straight from work, still in uniform, to be at my ordination service and asked me out right after the service, so he was okay with me being a preacher. He was so thoughtful and considerate. We had serious, intelligent conversation on our first date, and we had so much fun, laughed until we hurt, horsing around at the rec. I had him laughing so hard he couldn't see straight when I did some of my Harlem Globetrotters show-off stuff with the basketball. He was supposed to be off this Sunday, and he was planning to come to Peyton's Chapel to hear me preach. So, thank you for raising Jason to be the way he was."

"We're proud of the way he turned out, though we can't take all the credit for it," Gary acknowledged as he fought back tears. "We want you to know that we'll always love you and you'll always be welcome in our home because of the happiness you gave our son. We're supposed to go to the funeral home at 3:00 p.m. to make the arrangements, and we'd like for you to go with us if you will."

"Sure, anything I can do to help you..." Cassie responded.

"One thing, we want you and your family to sit with our family. There's going to be a huge crowd, a lot more than will be able to get into the church. We just got a call from Governor Miller about thirty minutes ago, expressing his condolences, and telling us that he and his wife are coming to the service, and there'll be law enforcement agencies from all over Georgia and Alabama represented. Sheriff Holland and Chief Deputy Wells are doing everything they can for us. Sheriff Holland is coming at 2:45 p.m. to take us to the funeral home."

"I'll meet you over there. 3:00 p.m."

Emily and Jacob were already planning to bring some of the food and help put dinner on the table. They tried to get Elaine to rest and let them take care of all of it since she'd been up all night, but she couldn't sit still, and Mary Grace couldn't either, so both of them were in the middle of all of the dinner preparations, too. Amanda and the Little Brat were deputized to set the table. Jerry and Cassie had the den to themselves. The TV was on ESPN, but it was mostly background noise. Cassie was snuggled up close to her father, head resting on his shoulder, drifting in and out of restless sleep. At 1:00 p.m., Mary Grace came in the den and announced that everything was on the table and they were ready to eat. Jacob said grace, and Cassie went through the motions, putting small portions on her plate and picking at her food. Conversation at the table was subdued. After they ate, Emily went with Cassie to her room to fix her hair for her before she went to the funeral home. Cassie chose the dress Elaine made for her to wear when she preached her first sermon. As she was putting the finishing touches on her makeup, Mary Grace stuck her head in and announced, "I'm ready when you are. I know you could drive yourself, but I'm parked behind you and I'd have to move my car anyway, so I'll take you to the funeral home. I just want to do something for you."

Mary Grace turned into the parking lot of Webster Funeral Home right behind the unmarked dark blue Ford Crown Victoria with its blue lights visible across the top of the windshield and the bottom of the back window. Cassie saw Bob McKnight and Tommy Sheridan standing on the porch watching for everybody to arrive. Mary Grace pulled in beside the Crown Vic. Sheriff Holland and another officer got out of the car and opened the back doors for Gary, Donna, and Katie Bradshaw. Tommy came quickly down the steps to open the passenger side door of Mary Grace's car for Cassie, and he gently took her hand as she stepped out of the car. Cassie was drawn into a long, silent, tearful group hug with Jason's parents and sister. When she was able to come up for air, Cassie said, "I want you to meet Mary Grace Tillison. She started out just being my roommate at Mercer, then she became my friend, and then my sister. She's the first one I baptized." The introduction was answered with another group hug that drew Mary Grace in as well before they made their way up the steps where Sheriff Holland and the other officer, in uniform with black ribbons across their badges, held the double doors open for the Bradshaws, Cassie, and Mary Grace.

"First," Tommy Sheridan began, "I want to express to you the condolences of Mr. and Mrs. Webster and all of us here at Webster Funeral Home. Deputy Bradshaw was a fine young man, and this is a great loss for all of Mintz County. We at Webster Funeral Home are honored to serve your family during this time. This will be the first time our funeral home has handled a service for an officer killed in the line of duty. My son, Tommy Junior, has gone with Daniel Groves to pick up the body from the crime lab, and they should be back about 5:00 p.m. so we can prepare the body tonight."

Gary Bradshaw sat stoically, biting his lip and holding his sobbing wife, with Bob McKnight's hand on his shoulder, as Tommy moved the discussion to the question of whether to have an open or closed casket, since Jason had been shot in the face. Katie broke down, and Cassie moved in beside her and held her close as she wept. "You don't have to make that decision right now," Tommy spoke softly. "Daniel is really good at the restorative work. He can prepare him for a private family viewing tomorrow morning. You can decide then whether you want the casket open for the public viewing. Of course, the casket will be draped with the American flag, as is fitting for an officer who died in the line of duty."

Sheriff Holland spoke up and said that law enforcement would be providing transportation for Jason's family and Cassie's family for the viewing tomorrow and the funeral on Saturday, adding, "Of course, officers will be stationed to watch your homes while you are at the viewing and the service. There are a hundred and fifty-nine counties in Georgia, and I expect most of them will be represented, along with the state patrol and no telling how many municipalities, plus we'll probably have some from Alabama, since we're this close to the state line. Some of the other jurisdictions will help us and Harrington city shut down the roads and control intersections along the route of the procession and provide security on your homes while you're at the viewing and the service. There will probably be three to four hundred law enforcement vehicles in the procession."

Cassie felt numb as she listened to the plans taking shape. The private family viewing would be at 11:30 a.m. tomorrow, and Jason would lie in state from noon until 9:00 p.m., with the family there from 2:00 p.m. to 4:00 p.m. and 6:00 p.m. to 9:00 p.m. Two Mintz County deputies would be stationed, one at each end of the casket, throughout the viewing. The funeral would be Saturday at 1:00 p.m. at Alabama Road

Baptist Church, with burial at Woodland Memorial Gardens. It would be a long service, and all of the Atlanta television stations would have reporters and camera people there. Sheriff Holland would give the eulogy, and Governor Miller would have some remarks. There would be congregational singing, and Bob McKnight would bring the message. Donna said that she'd like it if someone could sing "Precious Lord, Take My Hand," and Tommy said he'd call Coretta because he'd never heard anybody sing it better. "Cassie," Donna spoke up, "we'd be honored if you would have the invocation at the church and the committal at the graveside."

"I'll do it for you and for Jason," Cassie responded, choking back tears as Katie squeezed her hand and Mary Grace put an arm around her shoulders. "I'll get through it somehow."

"It'll mean a lot to us," Gary responded, "and I think Jason would be pleased."

"The Fulton County Sheriff's Department's sending their honor guard," Sheriff Holland added. "They'll do the rifle salute. There's a quartet of Cedartown city officers coming. They're going to sing 'God Be With You 'Til We Meet Again' at the graveside. My department will provide the pallbearers, and I'll present the flag from the casket to Mr. and Mrs. Bradshaw."

The Bradshaws asked Cassie and Mary Grace to go with them when Tommy took them back to the selection room to look at caskets and vaults. Cassie had never been in this part of the funeral home before, and it felt bizarre to see twenty-one caskets — she counted them, all price ranges, painted steel in various thicknesses and finishes, stainless steel, bronze, and woods ranging from pine to solid cherry, sealing and non-sealing models, all arranged like so many sofas at Markham's Furniture Store. With Katie's and Mary Grace's arms around her, Cassie watched silently as Gary laid one of Jason's uniform shirts in first one casket, then another, and another, before he and Donna made their selection. Then there were those little scale-model vaults, like the caskets, offered in a variety of prices, materials, and finishes. Tommy talked about them all, the merits and features of each, and he told them that Woodlands

Memorial Gardens required a vault on all burials, but he did not try to sell them on the most expensive models.

As Mary Grace drove back to the house from the funeral home, Cassie noticed the flags at city hall, the police station, the fire department, the Mintz County Courthouse, the sheriff's department and jail, the post office, the Veterans Memorial, the American Legion, and the library, all at half staff. Then, they passed the Church of God, where the sign out front read, "In Memory of Dep. Jason Bradshaw MCSD 1976-1998." Cassie wept as the harsh reality hit her as hard as it did last night.

Cassie was sitting in the den in her pajamas and chenille robe, with the reading lamp aimed at her open Bible and the legal pad on which she had made some notes when Jerry came through a couple of minutes before 5:00 a.m. on his way to the kitchen to start the coffee. He was startled to see her and detoured over to give her a gentle hug and a kiss on the forehead. "Love you, Cassie. Good morning. Trouble sleeping?"

"I slept in fits and spurts. Mostly watched Mary Grace sleep. Love you, too, Daddy. I don't know what time I got up, didn't look at the clock, been up a while, an hour or two I guess. Figured I might as well work on my sermon for Sunday. I can't just preach what I was planning to preach like nothing happened. Still using the same scripture readings since Peyton's Chapel always has communion on fifth Sundays and it's the first Sunday in Advent."

"I'll get some coffee going for us. You know J. T. told you Wednesday night not to worry about preaching this Sunday if you're not up to it, said y'all could have a good service just singing, praying, and having the Lord's Supper. Not only that, Ronnie and his two children are coming as candidates for baptism, and Jennifer's moving her membership from Freeman Valley to Peyton's Chapel."

"And Marcie and Connie are coming to church," Cassie finished Jerry's sentence. "Together. Not sure how the church is going to handle that. Marcie's Myrtle Hill's granddaughter, so that helps. Daddy, this is harder than when Miss Addie died. I loved her; you know how close we were. I miss her, and I'd give anything if I could talk with her right now, especially about Marcie and Connie, but she was a hundred and one years old and I didn't expect her to be around another fifty or sixty years. Losing Jason is harder, hardest thing I've ever had to face, first time I've ever been knocked down to where I couldn't pray. That was terrifying, worse than the time I got the breath knocked out of me two years ago when we were playing Centralhatchee, and I thought I was gonna die right there on that gym floor because I couldn't breathe. Praying used to come easily for me, and then to be down where I couldn't pray, and I was so afraid I'd never be able to pray again. Guess you could say I got the prayer knocked out of me."

As Jerry sat down beside Cassie and pulled her close, he continued the thread, "and the folks at Peyton's Chapel need to hear you say that, because most of them are a lot older than you, and they've had the prayer knocked out of them. They've been afraid they'd never be able to pray again, been afraid they'd never feel the Lord close to them again. They need to hear you say that, because they've come through that. You're preaching to the people who pretty much picked you up, brought you to the Lord, and laid you at his feet."

"So, you're saying you think I need to preach Sunday?"

"No, Cassie. That's your call, not for me to tell you what to do. It'll be okay and the church will understand and everything'll be all right if you don't, but if you do, I think you'll be glad you did." Jerry fixed himself a cup of real coffee and fixed his daughter a cup of little girl pretend coffee and brought it to her. "What I'm saying is that the folks at Peyton's Chapel are not going to be shocked to discover that you don't feel the Lord close all the time, or that you feel like you've been run over by a freight train after you lose someone you love, or that you don't know how God is going to get you through this time. Honey, they've had to look up to see the bottom, too. You are heart broken, struggling to believe, struggling to pray, questioning why God didn't do something to keep Jason from dying. You're in a good place to know Jesus as 'a man of sorrows, acquainted with grief,' who cried out, 'My God, My God, why have you forsaken me?' I'm not saying you need to preach this Sunday, but I think you know you've got to preach your way through this valley."

"And if I fall flat on my face?"

"They'll see that you're human, which they already know, no great surprise there. You'll be about the most prayed-for preacher that ever got behind a pulpit. You know that II Corinthians passage you quote so much, 'we have this treasure in earthen vessels, that the surpassing greatness of the power may be of God and not from ourselves.' That means that God will stand by his word even if the preacher falls flat on her face."

Cassie was fighting back tears as she hugged Jerry and said, "Thanks, Daddy Longlegs. I needed to hear that. Kind of providential that it's the first Sunday in Advent, and I'm looking forward to introducing my little country church to the Christian calendar. Advent's all about recognizing how broken we are and preparing to receive the Messiah."

"And it'll be your first time to lead a communion service, since Peyton's Chapel always does it on fifth Sundays," Jerry noted.

"Oh yeah!" Cassie's voice and expression perked up, "I was gonna tell you. J. T. told me last Sunday that we really need four people to help serve communion and we only have three deacons, and it didn't seem right to him to only have men serving communion especially since we have a woman pastor, so he asked Ruth Ann Simpson to help serve communion."

"I'm glad he did that," Jerry commented. "Ruth Ann's a good person. It'll mean a lot to her to get to do it, and if Brother Bobby finds out about it, it may finish him off. Don't know when that turkey's supposed to go to trial on all the charges he racked up the day of Miss Addie's funeral."

"It'll happen when it happens, I guess. Maybe he'll act stupid and get himself some more charges by then," Cassie yawned and took a long sip of her coffee. "I'm just glad Ruth Ann's not living with his craziness any more. Don't know how she lived with him as long as she did. Besides, Brother Bobby's trial is too far off for me to think about. I'm trying to get through today and tomorrow, make it through Jason's funeral and burial, to get to Sunday. Today and tomorrow is the wilderness. Sunday's the Promised Land. I've been looking forward to leading my first communion service ever since I've been at Peyton's Chapel. I just didn't know I'd be coming to the table needing to take communion more than I've ever needed to, craving it more than I ever have. God, I need to hear somebody say, 'The body of Christ broken for you, the blood of Christ shed for you,' and Ruth Ann'll be the one saying those words to me. J. T. asked Ruth Ann to serve me."

"And," Jerry added, "you'll be receiving communion from somebody else who had to go through a long, dark valley to get to the table."

Chapter 23

While she was cooking breakfast, Elaine turned on the kitchen radio that stayed tuned to the local AM station that you can't pick up more than ten miles from town, just in time to hear the recording of the Hammond organ with too much vibrato playing "Sweet Hour of Prayer." As the bad organ music was turned down, Bill Bailey's voiceover began, "Welcome to *The Obituary Column of the Air*, brought to you by the courteous professional staff of Webster Funeral Home in Harrington, neighbors serving neighbors in times of sorrow since 1938. In today's announcements, Deputy Jason Evans Bradshaw, age 22, of Harrington, passed away Wednesday evening November 25, the first Mintz County Sheriff's Department officer killed in the line of duty. Deputy Bradshaw was born April 11, 1976, in Carrollton, son of Mr. and Mrs. Gary Bradshaw. A 1994 graduate of Harrington High School, Deputy Bradshaw began working with the Sheriff's Department following his graduation from the police academy in May of this year. Deputy Bradshaw is survived by his parents, one sister, Miss Katie Bradshaw, grandparents, Mr. and Mrs. Homer Bradshaw and Mr. and Mrs. Lawrence Evans, a special friend, Reverend Cassie McWhorter, all of Harrington, numerous aunts, uncles, and cousins, and his colleagues in law enforcement. Deputy Bradshaw will lie in state today from noon until 9:00 p.m. at Webster Funeral Home, with the family receiving friends from 2:00 p.m. to 5:00 p.m. and 7:00 p.m. to 9:00 p.m. Deputy Bradshaw was a member of Alabama Road Baptist Church, where funeral services will be conducted tomorrow at 1:00 p.m. with Reverend Cassie McWhorter and Reverend Bob McKnight officiating, with a eulogy by Sheriff Wayne Holland and remarks by Governor Zell Miller. Mintz County Sheriff's Department deputies will serve as pallbearers. Law enforcement officers from throughout Georgia and Alabama will be honorary pallbearers. Officers from other counties and municipalities in Georgia will assist local law enforcement with security and traffic control. Interment will follow at Woodlands Memorial Gardens with Reverend Cassie McWhorter, the Fulton County Sheriff's Department Honor Guard, and the Cedartown Police Department Quartet conducting graveside rites. Webster Funeral Home has charge of arrangements for Deputy Jason Evans Bradshaw." Elaine turned the radio off, really not knowing why she had turned it on, since the announcement didn't tell her anything she didn't already know.

"Honey, go knock on the door and let Cassie and Mary Grace know breakfast is ready," Elaine spoke to Jerry. "I think both of them slept well, didn't hear either of them up during the night."

"Not like either one of them to crash as early as they did last night," Jerry concurred. "Something to be said for exhaustion. They were both out like a light around 8:30. Cassie got up early, drank some coffee and talked with me a while, then she went back to bed right before you got up. I'll call them." Jerry rapped his knuckles on Cassie's bedroom door. "Cass! Mary Grace! Mom's got our breakfast ready." As he returned to the kitchen, he saw that Anthony had the table set. He heard the girls yawning and walking stiffly to the bathroom before making their way to the dining room.

"Hey, Daddy Longlegs, Hey Little Brat, Hey Mamalaine," Mary Grace yawned as she hugged people in the order she came to them. She had long since contracted Mama Elaine to Mamalaine. "Oh good, the big coffee pot," she observed as she filled a mug with Jerry's rich steamy brew. "You've got me hooked on this stuff. I wasn't a big coffee drinker 'til I started hanging out here with Cassie."

"Mary Grace, you may be a Tillison, but you drink your coffee like a McWhorter," Jerry observed. "I think you're kin to us somewhere back there, we just had'n traced back far enough to figure it out. In all seriousness, we love you like one of our own, and we appreciate you coming down here to help Cassie through this time."

"She's my sister," Mary Grace replied. "My heart breaks for her right now. I couldn't stand not to be with her. Considering what she's done for me, it's a privilege to do anything I can for her. Same goes for all of you. I consider you family. You too, Little Brat."

"Can't believe I slept this long," Cassie yawned as she made her way toward the gurgling sounds and aroma of the coffee urn.

"I'm glad you did," Elaine responded. "It's going to be a long day with the viewing, seeing and speaking to so many people. You'll be glad you got the extra sleep. Wednesday night, when Marcie prayed for you and Tamika before you went to bed, she prayed that you'd get restful sleep."

"Have to tell her she got her prayer answered," Cassie commented. "I usually sleep well, but I think that's the longest and hardest I've ever slept. Speaking of Marcie, I hope it's not going to be a problem if they come to church together Sunday."

"Cassie," Anthony surprised everyone when he jumped into the conversation, "it wasn't a problem when they were here with Marcie's grandmother Wednesday night. Mrs. Hill loves her granddaughter no matter what. She really loves Connie, too, when it comes right down to it."

"Mom! Dad!" Cassie's voice registered a note of surprise. "The Little Brat can talk! He can even make complete sentences!" Turning to her brother, she continued, "I hope you're right. Jason and I talked about the same thing when we went up to Hansonville Monday night after the viewing for Floyd Williams. Can't believe the serious stuff we talked about on a first date. I felt so comfortable with him, never felt that comfortable with anybody else I've dated. You just said the same thing Jason said when we talked about Marcie and Connie being at the funeral home together and bringing Myrtle because she doesn't drive at night. Jason said they won't understand how a woman could be attracted to another woman that way, and I said I didn't either, told him that I like guys, him especially. I told him that Mary Grace and I are very close as friends, more like sisters, but not like that. Jason said they might not understand it, but they don't have to understand it to accept them for who they are, love them, and treat them right. He said they'd be grateful that Myrtle has somebody who looks after her and helps her the way they do."

After Jerry said grace over breakfast, Elaine picked up the thread, "I can't believe I'm hearing myself say this, but Jason was right about Marcie and Connie, Cass. If Myrtle needed help at 3:00 a.m., Marcie and Connie would be right there. It's like I heard you say in one of your sermons, 'Every time I start to think I've got God and his ways figured out, he throws me a curve ball.' This may be one of God's famous curve balls. I know it is for me. Now, if you'd asked the people at Peyton's Chapel, Myrtle included, if they were okay with same-sex relationships, they'd say 'No,' but Myrtle's already carved out an exception for Marcie and Connie because they're family and they're good to her. After Wednesday night, seeing how the Lord worked through Marcie, how she was led by the Spirit, gathering everybody in close around you and Tamika, and hearing the prayer she prayed, you can tell she's not talking to a stranger when she prays. I'm still trying to process that. I've always believed that, you know, a woman sleeping with another woman was wrong, and I still can't say I'm comfortable with it, but God worked through her last night whether I'm comfortable with it or not. Like Brother Mike said the other Sunday, our comfort level is not God's top priority. Maybe — and it's hard for me to say it, but maybe Marcie and Connie belong together the same way your dad and I do."

"I agree," Jerry commented. "Honey, you remember Miss Holman and Miss Orr, who taught at Harrington Elementary when we were kids, Miss Holman taught first grade and Miss Orr taught fifth. We thought they were two hundred years old when we had them. They were both good teachers, Miss Addie thought the world of both of them. I had them both and you had Miss Orr in fifth grade. They lived together over on Carolina Avenue as far back as I can remember, lived there 'til Miss Orr died and Miss Holman went in the nursing home. Just had one car, an old airplane-nose '51 Studebaker just like the one Fozzie drove in *The Muppet Movie*. Might've been the same car for all I know, always wondered what happened to that ol' Stude. It sat under the shed behind their house after Miss Orr died 'til Miss Holman went in the nursing home, then it was gone and the house was up for sale. Every time I saw that car go down the road, they were both in it. Miss Orr was always the one driving. She was real short, drove looking through the steering wheel and never topped thirty miles per hour. If you were behind them, you couldn't even see the top of her head. It looked like the car was going down the road without a driver. Both of them went to the Methodist church. As far as we knew when we were kids, they were just two old maid teachers. We knew they lived together, but we didn't give it any thought, didn't know anything about sex or that there was such a thing as a lesbian when we were that age. If our parents knew, and I'm sure they did, they acted like they didn't. We don't know, don't need to know, what they did in the privacy of their home. I do know, when Miss Holman died, they buried her next to Miss Orr and they've got a double marker with both of their names, Julia Orr and Bessie Holman, just like a married couple. Whatever they did while they were living didn't hurt anybody else, sure not hurting anybody else for them to be buried next to each other. It's not like they had some disease you could catch just from being around them. They were both good Christian people and good teachers. It's different when you talk about actual people instead of hypothetical problems."

"Yeah, it is," Mary Grace acknowledged. "Talking about Marcie and Connie or talking about Miss Orr and Miss Holman feels different from talking about lesbians. Like you said about Miss Orr and Miss Holman, you never thought about them being lesbians."

"Cass," Jerry continued, "if you'd asked most of the people at Peyton's Chapel if they'd consider a woman preacher before they met and heard you, they'd've said 'No.' When they met you and heard you, it was a whole different ball game. It wasn't about women preachers any more, it was about you. They didn't vote on women preachers, they voted on Cassie McWhorter. Women preachers don't have a name and a face, you do. You've got that red dress, but you don't have the horns, tail, and pitchfork to go with it, and you can preach. Even more important than that, you love them, and it shows. Wouldn't matter how well you could preach if you didn't love them. Same thing with Marcie and Connie. It's not about accepting lesbians, it's about accepting Marcie and Connie. Marcie is Myrtle's granddaughter, and she knows God and knows how to pray. The ones from Peyton's Chapel who were here Wednesday night saw how the Lord worked through her. They've got enough sense to see when God's working and accept it for what it is. You don't go telling God he can't work through this person or that person, 'cause God's gonna say, 'Stand back and watch me.'"

"Cass," Elaine added, "you know I'm pretty old school and traditional. If you'd asked me twenty years ago if I thought it was okay and if I thought our church would accept a black person and a white person married to each other, I'd've said 'No' to both, but I had to adjust my thinking on account of Daniel and Coretta. Those two belong together as much as your dad and I do. Couldn't imagine either one of them being married to anybody else. You can tell they love each other and like being married to each other. Our church accepted them because it wasn't about black and white, it was about Daniel and Coretta. Looks like Peyton's Chapel has accepted them, too."

"Oh, yeah," Mary Grace spoke up. "Peyton's Chapel loves Daniel and Coretta. It's like they haven't even thought about Coretta being black, she's just Coretta and they love her and love to hear her sing. They're all excited about her being pregnant. The church is looking forward to that baby as much as Daniel and Coretta are. All of the women at church pat her belly and ask about the baby every time they hug her. Ruth Peyton's already said it's gonna be a girl, don't know how she knows, but I'm told she has a good track record when it comes to predicting the sex of the baby. That baby's gonna get passed around like an offering plate. Peyton's Chapel accepts people for who they are. At least, that's how they've been with me. I'm the girl who asks the off-the-wall questions in Sunday School, and it's like they look forward to my questions about as much as they look forward to hearing Coretta sing and hearing Cassie preach.

Nobody got upset when I slipped up and said 'damn' in Sunday School, it was in context and I don't even think they noticed. They've accepted me. They'll accept Marcie and Connie."

The phone rang as they were clearing the table after breakfast. Elaine answered it. It was Sheriff Holland, calling to tell them that Aaron Stewart and Sheriff Gentry from Phillips County would be there at 11:15 a.m. to take them to the private viewing for the family. A Troup County deputy would be coming to guard their house while they were gone. The Fraternal Order of Police lodge was serving lunch for the Bradshaw and McWhorter families at Harrington United Methodist Church. Uncle Lease's Barbeque, The Lonesome Whistle Cafe, and York's Bakery were all sending food.

Jerry and Elaine rode with Sheriff Gentry. Cassie, Mary Grace, Anthony, and Amanda rode with Aaron. They pulled up behind Sheriff Holland's car at the funeral home. Another Mintz County deputy pulled up behind them with Jason's grandfather and grandmother Bradshaw, and a Harrington officer pulled up behind him with Jason's grandfather and grandmother Evans. Chief Deputy Wells and another Mintz County deputy, black ribbons across their badges, opened the car doors for Gary, Donna, and Katie Bradshaw, then snapped to attention and saluted as they got out of the car. Tamika Barrentine and a Phillips County deputy extended the same courtesy to Cassie, Mary Grace, Anthony, and Amanda. A Carroll County deputy and a Harris County deputy did like-wise for Jerry and Elaine. A Columbus-Muscogee County deputy and a Heard County deputy did those honors for the Bradshaw grandparents. Deputies from Meriwether and Talbot counties took care of the Evans grandparents. Amanda's Georgia state trooper father and an Alabama trooper held the double doors of the funeral home open as the phalanx of officers escorted them into the funeral home where they were met by Tommy Sheridan, Daniel Groves, and Bob and Susan McKnight.

"If we're all here," Tommy announced, "Reverend McKnight will offer a word of prayer, and then Daniel and I will take you back to the chapel for the private viewing for the family." After Bob prayed, they all followed Tommy and Daniel into the chapel and up to the open casket. After a long silence punctuated by muffled sobs, Tommy asked, "Do you want us to have an open or closed casket?" Daniel had done a good job with the restorative work on Jason's face. It helped that he remembered Jason from school and had a good portrait of him for reference. Still, it was apparent that he had to use a heavy application of cosmetics to conceal where the bullet tore into Jason's face.

"What do you think?" Donna asked Gary.

"It's up to you, honey. He'll have the flag draping his casket..."

"Because of the amount of restorative work involved," Tommy explained, "if you choose an open casket, I'd recommend using a veil."

Turning to Cassie and Katie, Donna asked, "What do y'all think?"

"Like Dad said, he'll have the flag over his casket," Katie said, implying her opinion without coming right out and saying it. "We've got that big ten by thirteen portrait of him in his uniform that he had made for your birthday. If the funeral home has an easel, we could display that picture..."

"We have easels," Tommy spoke up, "about a dozen of them. Displaying pictures won't be a problem."

"You are family, too, Cassie," Donna choked back tears as she put her arm around her. "We love you because Jason loved you. You made him so happy. What do you think?"

"I'll support whatever decision you make," Cassie responded as she reciprocated Donna's hug and tenderly caressed Jason's hands for the last time. "Sounds like you're leaning toward having the casket closed. I think that'd be best."

"Close the casket, Tommy," Donna managed to get the words out before she buried her face against her husband's chest and wept. Tommy closed the casket, and he and Daniel spread the flag before rolling the casket out to the parlor. Chief Deputy Wells and Tamika Barrentine followed. They were the first of eighteen officers who would stand sentry, two at a time in one-hour shifts, one at each end of the casket, during the viewing. All of the Harrington city officers, state troopers from the Villa Rica and Lagrange posts, two GBI agents, and some officers from neighboring counties were signed up to stand sentry by the casket all through the night and up until the hour of the funeral. Daniel said that he and Coretta were going to spend the night at the funeral home, and the doors would be open all night for on-duty law enforcement, EMS, and firefighters who wanted to stop by and pay their respects.

The Little Brat's girlfriend's Methodist preacher mama said grace over the big spread of food. Before she started fixing her plate, Donna Bradshaw asked whether someone was going to fix plates and take them to the officers guarding their homes. Junior Harwell, retired from the Georgia State Patrol and then retired again as police chief in Harrington, was a member at Harrington Methodist. He assured Donna that they already thought of that. He said they had plenty of carryout boxes, and he and his wife would fix plates for them and deliver them.

With their blue lights flashing, Sheriff Holland, Sheriff Gentry, Chief Stewart, and the officers transporting Jason's grandparents drove slowly from the Methodist church to Webster Funeral Home and brought the families around to the staff entrance at the back of the building. The line of people waiting to pay their respects was out the door and spilling out onto the front lawn of the funeral home. The funeral home parking lot was full, with many more parked on the street or nearby at Harrington Presbyterian Church and Greater New Hope Progressive Missionary Baptist Church. Daniel showed them all the staff lounge and told them that they could make themselves at home there any time if they needed to take a break from greeting people.

It seemed like everyone Cassie knew from Peyton's Chapel and Harrington Baptist was there. Marcie and Connie brought Myrtle Hill to the afternoon viewing, and they told Cassie that they were both coming to church Sunday at Peyton's Chapel with Granny Myrt. Connie told Cassie that she could only try to imagine how difficult it would be for her to preach Sunday, and she and Marcie wanted to support her with their presence as well as their prayers. The Bradshaws were perpetually introducing Cassie and her family to people from Alabama Road Baptist Church. As Donna repeatedly introduced Cassie, she progressed from introducing her as "Jason's friend" to "Jason' girlfriend" to "Jason's fiancée," and she seemed to delight in telling people that Cassie was the pastor of Peyton's Chapel Baptist Church and that Jason had fallen head over heels in love with her. Cassie made a similar progression as she introduced Mary Grace, from "my roommate at Mercer" to "my friend who is like a sister to me" to "my sister." Cassie remembered seeing Eric and

Jenny Latham and their children at the viewing, and Jenny told her that she would be playing the piano for the service since Jason's mother was the pianist at Alabama Road.

Cassie barely remembered coming home from the funeral home last night and falling into bed exhausted. At 3:45 a.m., she was as awake as she would ever be, so she got up and ran a warm wet washcloth over her face before she turned on the reading lamp beside the big overstuffed sofa in the den, wrapped herself up with the afghan that Granny McWhorter made, and picked up her Bible, pen, and note pad. It felt good to be able to pray again, as good as her breath coming back after she got it knocked out of her when they played Centralhatchee a couple of years ago. She was grateful to Brother Mike for putting her onto the observance of the Christian calendar and following the Revised Common Lectionary. He told Cassie that he had followed the lectionary for years without telling the church what he was doing. He said that it kept him balanced in his preaching, forced him to deal with difficult passages of scripture, and saved him a lot of time spent staring at a blank sheet of paper.

Cassie had thrown away the sermon she had begun preparing for Sunday because it was written at the happiest time of her life. She had experienced her greatest happiness and her most devastating sorrow within the space of three days. She had looked forward to the good-natured kidding about having a boyfriend. It would give them something other than the shoes to kid her about. Now, she was starting over. All she had was a blank page with the four lectionary readings listed at the top. Jeremiah 33:14-16. Psalm 25:1-10. First Thessalonians 3:9-13. Luke 21:25-36. Her mind was darting back and forth between four things, the invocation at Jason's funeral, Jason's committal, Sunday's sermon, and communion on Sunday. The first prayer she prayed was that she would be able to focus on one thing at a time. She read the lectionary readings, and her thoughts began to flow freely. The first thought she wrote down was, "The season of Advent always begins, not with looking back to Jesus' birth in Bethlehem, his coming in history, but with looking forward to his coming at the end of history." By the time Jerry got up at 5:00 a.m. to start the coffee, she had filled six pages of the legal pad, and she had realized how interconnected her four seemingly disparate tasks were.

Jerry stopped on his way to the coffee pot, sat down beside Cassie, and pulled her close to himself. As he held her with her head resting on his shoulder, he began gently massaging the back of her neck the way he did when she was little. It was several minutes before either of them broke the silence. "You're going to put me to sleep, Daddy Longlegs. It always did make me sleepy for you to massage the back of my neck. Feels good, but I can't let myself go back to sleep. I woke up about fifteen 'til four, decided to go ahead and get up, make good use of the time. By the way, Daddy, thanks for what you said to me yesterday morning. I'm quoting you in my sermon on Sunday."

"What did I say that was that good?" Jerry asked.

"You said that it was my call as to whether I should try to preach this Sunday, but that I am going to have to preach my way through this valley. You reminded me that I preach every Sunday to people who've had the prayer knocked out of them at one time or another, and they've wondered whether they'd ever be able to pray again or feel the Lord close to them again. You said the church would understand if I felt like I couldn't preach this Sunday, but if I decided to go ahead and preach, I'd be glad that I did."

"You will be able to preach and preach well," Jerry responded as he gently kissed Cassie's forehead. "You just won't be able to preach as though the events of the past few days didn't happen. I'm gonna start a pot of coffee for us." As he was starting the coffee, Jerry continued, "Your mom had an e-mail from Emily when we got in last night. She said that she's coming about 9:00 a.m. to help you, your mom, and Mary Grace with your hair. Aaron Stewart and Tamika Barrentine are taking us to the funeral. Sheriff Holland said a Polk County officer would be coming to watch our house while we're gone. Our church is doing lunch for the families today. Aaron and Tamika are picking us up for lunch at 11:30 a.m."

"Too early to call them now," Cassie began, "but I really want to call Heather and Ruby Wilkins before the funeral. Can't believe I haven't already called them to let them know what's going on. Ruby made sure after the ordination service that I had her address and phone number, said she wanted me to stay in touch with her."

"Call them," Jerry responded. "That's why we got that flat-rate long distance plan. Just remember the time difference. It's an hour earlier in Alabama. It'll help you to talk to both of them, and it'll be good to know that they're praying for you. I just thought of something else, Cass."

"What's that, Daddy?"

"If Brother Bobby shows up and acts a fool at the cemetery today, Aaron'll have lots of help taking him down."

Before they got back in Tamika's patrol car after lunch at Harrington Baptist, Mary Grace helped Cassie drape her pulpit stole over her shoulders and even up the ends. "You look nice," Mary Grace commented. "Emily did a good job on your hair. I like the way she did mine, too." Mary Grace noticed the necklace that Cassie received from Miss Addie on the day of her baptism. She held the small delicate cross between her thumb and index finger as she added, "You're going to get through this. Remember Saint Addie has your back. She and I are both praying for you."

Sheriff Holland, Chief Deputy Wells, Aaron, and Tamika had their blue lights flashing as they drove the families to Alabama Road Baptist Church. At each intersection, officers were stationed to hold traffic and move them through. Cassie saw officers from Rome, Rockmart, Aragon, Dallas, Hiram, Dalton, Chatsworth, Cave Spring, Macon, Atlanta, Athens, Cartersville, Tallapoosa, Bremen, and Buchanan switch on their blue lights as they approached, pull their cars into position to block the cross streets, get out, stand at attention, and salute as they passed. The small procession grew in length as each officer they passed got back in his patrol car and fell in behind them. As they got closer to the church, both sides of the road for half a mile in either direction from the church were lined with patrol cars from all over Georgia and Alabama. Cassie had lived in Georgia all of her life, and she didn't know where some of these counties and towns were — Echols County, Ware County, Peach County, Jeff Davis County, Union County, Powder Springs, Grovetown, Waleska, Dade County, White County, Coffee County, Baker County, Colquitt County, Blackshear, and Temple were only a few of the ones that Cassie could not have pinpointed on a map of Georgia. When they arrived at the church, deputies were stationed to open their car doors for them and escort them into the church. A Douglas County deputy and a Paulding County deputy did the honors for Cassie, Mary Grace, Anthony, and Amanda. The Webster Funeral Home hearse was in position with police motorcycles from Atlanta, Savannah, Rome, and Albany parked two on each side. The lawn of the church was a sea of law enforcement officers in uniform with black ribbons across their badges. Last night at the funeral home, Cassie had met Brandon Holloway, the Hansonville officer who shot and killed Jason's murderer. He was a young man, not much older than Jason. She had hugged him and thanked him for coming, but she sensed that he wanted no accolades because he simply did what he had to do, something he had hoped he would never have to do. He took no pleasure in killing anyone, but he realized that he was alive only because the suspect shot at him and missed, and he returned fire and didn't miss. He wanted nothing more than to be one of the many officers paying his respects to a fallen colleague and expressing his sympathy to the family as he pondered how close he came to being another fallen officer. Cassie saw him and made eye contact with him as they made their way into the church. It was as Brandon wished. He was one of many, all with black ribbons across their badges, lining both sides of the sidewalk, snapping to attention and saluting as the family passed by.

Cassie moved ahead of the family to join Bob McKnight in the foyer of the church. "Hey, Preacher," Bob whispered as he gave her a gentle hug. "We're going to get through this." Jason's flag-draped casket was in front of the pulpit where the communion table was supposed to be, and the aisle looked to be about a mile long. Precisely at 1:00 p.m., Bob shouted in his booming God-speaking-from-heaven voice, "Blessed are the dead who die in the Lord from henceforth. Yea, saith the Spirit, for they rest from their labors and their works do follow after them." As soon as he spoke those words, Jenny Latham lifted the congregation to its feet with her loud, majestic arrangement of "All Hail the Power of Jesus' Name." Cassie and Bob passed between Jason's casket and Governor and Mrs. Miller as they made their way up to the pulpit. In addition to the governor, his wife, and their security detail, the front pew was occupied by Sheriff Holland, Chief Deputy Wells, Coretta, and the quartet of Cedartown officers. Cassie and Bob remained standing as the family and the Mintz County officers took their seats.

Tommy and Daniel asked the congregation to be seated, and Cassie stepped up to the pulpit. As she looked out on the congregation and made eye contact with the governor, Sheriff Holland, all of the law enforcement people, and Jason's family, she felt surprisingly calm, and her voice was strong and clear as she quoted the familiar words from II Corinthians, "Grace to you and peace from God our Father and the Lord Jesus Christ. Blessed be the God and Father of our Lord Jesus Christ, the Father of mercies and God of all consolation, who consoles us in all our affliction, so that we may be able to console those who are in any affliction with the consolation with which we ourselves are consoled by God."

Cassie made an almost seamless transition from the words of scripture to the words of her prayer.

The quartet of Cedartown officers sang "I'll Meet You in the Morning," and they sang it well. They sang it up to tempo, all four officers sang and harmonized well, and their diction was good. When the congregation at Grandpa and Grandma McWhorter's church sang it, their diction was not so good, and "meet you" sounded like "me chew." Then, they sang "Jesus, Hold My Hand" and invited the congregation to join with them in singing "In the Sweet By and By." The packed sanctuary with people singing four-part harmony sounded really good. Cassie didn't try to hold back the tears flowing freely down her face as she harmonized the alto part with them and thought about meeting Jason along with Miss Addie and Granny and Granddaddy Whitmire on that beautiful shore.

Sheriff Holland, who was also a member of Alabama Road Baptist Church, had been in law enforcement about forty years and was in his second term as sheriff of Mintz County. He was fighting back tears as he began his eulogy, talking about knowing Jason from the day he was born, encouraging his interest in law enforcement, recommending him to the police academy and hiring him to work for the department when he graduated back in May. He talked about his department being small enough for everybody to know everybody, so that it was news through the whole department when Jason started dating Preacher McWhorter. Turning to Cassie, he said, "Preacher, even though Jason had just started dating you, he was very much in love with you. He delighted in you, and you were the source of much happiness for him." He said that Jason's death was a death in the family for him and his whole department. He praised Jason's work ethic, integrity, easygoing manner, and his Christian faith. He pledged his prayerful support to the family, adding, "That includes you, too, Preacher McWhorter." He expressed appreciation for all of the support his department had received from other counties and municipalities and from the State Patrol, and paused to hug Cassie before returning to his seat.

The governor's remarks were brief and apropos, but he had not known Jason, and he probably had to look at the map to find Mintz County, so he could only speak in generalities about the dangers officers face every day, never knowing when the most routine traffic stop for a burned-out taillight might turn out deadly. He commended Trooper Hall for coming to the aid of Deputy Bradshaw and the outstanding work of all of the emergency medical personnel from Mintz County and the Life Flight helicopter for doing all they could for him. He recognized the Hansonville Police and Fire Departments and the Phillips County Sheriff's Department for their quick action to set up a roadblock and stop the one who killed Deputy Bradshaw. He expressed his personal sympathy and the sympathy of the people of Georgia to Deputy Bradshaw's family, friends, and law enforcement colleagues.

Governor Miller sat down, and Coretta came up to sing. A hush came over the congregation as she unleashed the full power of her voice on "Precious Lord, Take My Hand." She didn't need a microphone any more than she needed the piano to keep her on pitch, but she liked having Jenny on the piano today because Jenny was good at improvisation and she knew how to accompany a singer. Coretta began unaccompanied, perfectly on pitch, and Jenny eased in unobtrusively, weaving a light, delicate accompaniment around Coretta's voice.

Bob McKnight's presence was comforting and reassuring before he said anything. He was still a vigorous, active man at seventy-nine, and he brought fifty-five years of pastoral experience to the task before him today. He used the story in John 11 where Martha said to Jesus, "Lord, if you had been here, my brother would not have died." He said that Martha came right out and said what most of us are thinking. He acknowledged struggling with the questions himself and said that most of his efforts at prayer the past few days had started out "Lord, if only..." and "Lord, why..." He said that, while he didn't have all of the answers to his own questions, let alone anyone else's, he was sure of several things. He said that the Bible makes no promise that God will answer all questions but it does promise that God himself will wipe away the tears of those who trust in him. He was sure that Jason's death was not the will of God or something needed to accomplish God's purpose. God's will was not done by a murderer. The will of God, he said, was done by the law enforcement and emergency medical services personnel who rushed to Jason's aid and did everything they could for him. The will of God, he said, was done by the Hansonville police and fire departments and the Phillips County Sheriff's Department who stopped Jason's killer. The will of God continues to be done, he said, by all who show kindness and compassion to Jason's grieving family, friends, and law enforcement colleagues. Bob talked about Jason's secure hope in Jesus Christ and the promise of the resurrection, and he talked about the family that gave him life, nurtured him, taught him the way of the Lord, and brought him to faith in the Lord Jesus Christ. He spoke of the duty of Christian people to care for their own and to fulfill the law of Christ by bearing one another's burdens. Turning to Cassie, Bob said, "Cassie, you ministered today not in spite of your sorrow but in the strength of your sorrow. I am pleased that my signature is on your ordination certificate and that I am among those who laid hands on you this past Sunday." Then he quoted the great benediction from the epistle of Jude, "Now unto him who is able to keep you from falling, and to make you stand without blemish in the presence of his glory with rejoicing, to the only God our Savior, through Jesus Christ our Lord, be glory, majesty, power, and authority, before all time and now and forever. Amen."

As Bob sat down, Coretta came back to the pulpit and sang unaccompanied,

> Take the name of Jesus with you,
> Child of sorrow and of woe.
> It will joy and comfort give you,
> Take it then where'er you go.
> Precious name, Oh how sweet,
> Hope of earth and joy of Heaven!

Precious name, Oh how sweet,

Hope of earth and joy of Heaven!

Tommy Sheridan announced that the service would be concluded at the graveside, and Cassie and Bob walked ahead of the casket out to the waiting hearse. As the procession got underway, two state troopers driving side by side led the way, and Daniel drove the hearse down the middle of the road with two motorcycle patrolmen riding on each side of him. When they reached Woodlands Memorial Gardens, deputies from Rockdale and Banks counties were pulled across the road with their lights flashing, holding back traffic as they made the left turn.

Cassie stepped out of Tamika's patrol car and paused for hugs from her parents, Mary Grace, the Little Brat, and Amanda before taking her place at the back of the hearse. The honor guard from the Fulton County Sheriff's Department was in position, five men with vintage '03 Springfield bolt-action rifles, standing at parade rest. "Officers who are serving as pallbearers," Daniel announced, please take your places four on each side and take the handles of the casket as I pull it out. Reverend McWhorter will walk ahead of us to the gravesite, and I will help you position the casket on the lowering device." The cemetery had a cart designed to easily roll a casket across the smooth terrain, but it was important to Jason's colleagues to bear the weight of his body. When the Bradshaw and McWhorter families were seated under the tent, Cassie took her place at the head of the casket and did the committal. When she concluded her prayer at the end of the committal service, Sheriff Holland and Chief Deputy Wells folded the flag from Jason's casket. Sheriff Holland, with tears streaming freely down his face, presented Gary and Donna Bradshaw with the flag that had draped their son's casket. Tommy Sheridan gave the agreed-upon hand signal to the squad leader of the honor guard. The squad leader barked out the orders, and he and the other members of the honor guard fired three rounds in perfect unison. The quartet of Cedartown officers sang "God Be With You 'Til We Meet

Again." The eight officers who had borne Jason's body kept their vigil along with Daniel and Tommy until the grave was closed.

Chapter 24

Cassie set the clock for 6:00 a.m. to give herself time to go over her sermon again before time to get ready for church, but she was awake an hour earlier. Jerry was just starting the coffee when she made her way toward the kitchen, and she got a hug and a good neck massage from him before settling down at her mom's computer to check her e-mail and finding two new messages. The first message she had was from Heather,

Hey, Cass —

Up early as usual to nurse my little Olivia and making good use of the time for prayer and meditation. I'm thankful that you called me yesterday so Joel and I could pray for you while the funeral was going on. We got the word out to the Clear Springs folks and had a prayer chain going for you. I'm glad you talked to Ruby, too. She is precious! I just met her last Saturday and I feel like I've known her forever. She gave me her address and phone number, and I look forward to staying in touch with her. Our mail came right after we talked, and I had the sweetest note from her telling me how much she enjoyed meeting me and helping ordain you.

I am sorry for what you're going through with Jason's death. I only got to meet him briefly at the reception after your ordination. It sounds like you were attracted to him for the same reasons I was attracted to Joel — he was kind and considerate, you could have serious, intelligent conversation with him, you could laugh and have fun with him, and he was okay with your calling to be a pastor. I give thanks for the love that was starting to grow between you and Jason, even as I weep and ask why it had to be cut short. You paid me a very high compliment when you said that I knew how to give hugs from four hundred miles away. You are hugged and prayed for today as you preach and as you lead your first communion service on this first Sunday in Advent. Clear Springs will be praying for you today and in the days ahead. Call me or e-mail me when you can. So glad I could visit Peyton's Chapel and help ordain you. Joel's parents said they'd join Peyton's Chapel in a heartbeat if they lived closer.

Love you, Little Sister!
Heather

The second message was from Ted Coleman,

Cassie,

I want to commend you for how well you did with your part in Jason's service yesterday. I talked with Governor Miller and Sheriff Holland at the cemetery, and they both commented on how well you did. I did a little bragging, told them I was your Sunday School teacher when you were in high school. I told them that Brenda was your fourth grade teacher and taught you in Sunday School when you were younger. Cassie, I can only try to imagine how hard these past few days have been for you. Brenda and I are praying for you today as you preach, as you lead your first communion service at Peyton's Chapel, and this coming week as you go back to school. As you go back to Mercer, please don't try to shoulder your burden alone or act like the past few days didn't happen. You have a good roommate who understands and cares. She is new to the faith, but she knows the Lord and knows how to pray. You're already connected with Baptist Campus Ministry, so let the BCM folks know what you've been through. Remember that Brenda and I are Mercer alumni, so we know nearly everybody at Mercer and a lot of other good people in Macon. Brenda and I continue to pray for you daily. You have our e-mail and phone number. Please stay in touch.

Grace and peace,
Ted

They had all been so tired when they got home from the funeral yesterday, and they ended up talking a while with the Polk County deputy who had watched their house while they were gone. Elaine got the mail out of the box and put it on the end table close to the front door without really looking at it. Cassie picked it up and shuffled through it. There was the water bill, several pieces of junk mail, and then there were two letters, old-fashioned honest-to-goodness hand-written letters. Both were addressed in the same small, neat, precise script. They were from Ruby, one addressed to Cassie and one addressed to Mary Grace. Before she opened hers, Cassie knew that this letter would become a cherished keepsake, tucked between the pages of her Bible along with the graduation card from Miss Addie and the letter she received from Heather when she was eleven going on twelve. She opened it carefully and unfolded it, and the first thing she saw was the signature. She began laughing, the first good laugh she'd had in days. Ruby had signed it "Ruby the Baptist." That gentle touch of humor was a timely, much-needed grace gift this morning.

"What's so funny, Cass?" Jerry was puzzled by the sound of Cassie's laughter.

"I just picked up yesterday's mail. It was on the end table by the door. Two letters from Ruby Wilkins, one for me and one for Mary Grace. I just read mine. You know Heather and I were carrying on foolishness with her when we had the ordination council, nicknamed her Ruby the Baptist because she made a way through the wilderness for other women preachers. She signed her letter "Ruby the Baptist." I'm going to keep this forever!"

Woodlands Memorial Gardens is on the Hansonville highway, on your left, about a mile before you get to where Bailey's Mill Road bears off to the right at Pulliam's Store/Gloryland Way Missionary Baptist Church, so Cassie knew that she would be stopping to visit Jason's grave on her way to church. She was just thankful that she would be making the turn onto Bailey's Mill Road, so she would not be passing the place where Jason was killed. There were three stops on this morning's itinerary before church. She was glad that Mary Grace would be with her to keep her from lingering too long at Jason's grave, her holy place at Bailey's Mill, or Miss Addie's grave. Jerry started flipping pancakes and grilling sausage links as soon as everybody was up. Mary Grace volunteered to say the blessing over breakfast, and Cassie had more appetite than she thought she would have. It was 8:45 a.m. when she and Mary Grace left for church.

"I like the red dress on you," Mary Grace commented as Cassie drove north out of town on MLK Boulevard, which most people still call Monument Avenue. "Your pulpit stole is going to look nice with it."

"Thanks," Cassie responded, "I just hope I can get through the service without losing it and breaking down." As she spoke, she put on her left signal, slowed down, and made the turn into Woodlands Memorial Gardens.

"And if you don't make it through the service without losing it and breaking down," Mary Grace probed, "what will the consequences be?"

"Well, I don't guess there would be any consequences," Cassie answered thoughtfully, "unless you count a lot of hugs and a lot of people crying with me and praying for me."

As she and Cassie got out of the OGM and walked toward Jason's grave, Mary Grace put her arm around Cassie's waist. "Exactly," she commented on Cassie's response to her question. "You're looking at the same consequences I got the week after Miss Addie's funeral when my façade cracked. I broke down and cried, and you pulled me close, held me, and prayed for me until I realized that you weren't the only one holding me. If you break down, it'll just be the same thing on a bigger scale, more people to hug you, cry with you, and pray for you. And we'll hold you until you know somebody else is holding you, too."

They stood silently for a couple of minutes at Jason's grave before Mary Grace broke the silence. "The great cloud of witnesses, Cass. They're all around us. Including Saint Jason and Saint Addie. They're praying for us, and they're cheering for us. Remember when you ran track and played basketball, hearing the people in the stands go crazy, yelling and whooping it up for you?"

Cassie hugged Mary Grace and, with tears streaming down her face, replied softly, "Yeah, I remember." They got back in the car, and Cassie drove on to their holy place at Bailey's Mill. As she turned onto the narrow dirt road and pulled up into the clearing near the ruins of the mill, Cassie commented, "Mary Grace, the last time I was here was with Jason. The time before that was last Sunday morning when I had that nasty run-in with Floyd Williams. Only time I ever parked with a guy was when Jason and I came here Monday night, must've been about 10:00 p.m. It was my idea. I told him how Floyd not only made me feel violated, but he desecrated my holy place. He understood and, for the longest, just held me close and made me feel safe and loved, and then we kissed. That was it. We re-consecrated what Floyd desecrated."

"And that was beautiful," Mary Grace commented. "This place is holy because of what has happened here. We both remember Miss Addie's baptism and mine, and the first time you baptized someone, and now your time alone with Jason and your first kiss. Before you showed me the passage that talks about the great cloud of witnesses, I sensed *something* when I came here the first time and you baptized me. It's like Faulkner said, 'The past is not dead. It is not even past.' That's why you and I can remember something that happened here more than seventy years before we were born. It's why I can remember Miss Addie, too, even though I never met her."

"I think I just figured out something," Cassie said after several minutes of silence.

"What's that?"

"I'm thinking of a line from an old hymn that Miss Addie liked to quote,

> Eternity with all its years
> Stands present in Thy view.
> To Thee, there's nothing old appears,
> Great God, there's nothing new!

That says what I'm trying to get at, Mary Grace. Past, present, and future is all the same to God."

"So what is it that you figured out?" Mary Grace asked.

"We don't become part of the great cloud of witnesses when we die. We are a part of it now, and as far as God is concerned, we've always been a part of it. We can remember Miss Addie's baptism because we were in the great cloud of witnesses. Or, I should say, we *are* in the great cloud of witnesses. The passage in Hebrews 12 doesn't say the cloud of witnesses looks down on us like somebody way up in the nosebleed section at a stadium peering through binoculars to see the action down on the field. It says we are surrounded by them. They're with us on the field where the action is. They're not just spectators who cheer when we make a good play. They're in the game with us whether we're winning or getting trampled."

"So," Mary Grace questioned, "you do remember Miss Addie being at your house Wednesday night when you got the news about Jason, and you're saying they're all going to show up for church at Peyton's Chapel this morning?"

"Yeah, I think so," Cassie responded as she bent over at the edge of the creek, scooped up a double-handful of Baptist holy water, and let it drip slowly through her fingers, "and it's 9:20, so we'd best be heading on toward Peyton's Chapel if we want to have some time at Miss Addie's grave."

Cassie usually had the radio on in the car, but it never occurred to her to turn it on this morning. She and Mary Grace rode in silence from Bailey's Mill to Peyton's Chapel. When they got to the church, Arnie Peyton's truck was in the parking lot. He and Ruth had come early to unlock the building, turn on the heat, and be there to greet the first arrivals for Sunday School. Cassie drove on through the church parking lot onto the road that winds up the hill through the cemetery, up to the top of the hill where she parked as close as she could get to the Peyton-Aldridge plot. They got out and walked over to the still-mounded grave. "Saint Addie, pray for us," Mary Grace broke the silence. "You too, Saint Jason. We need all the help we can get."

Cassie hugged Mary Grace the way you hug your sister and added, "Saint Mary Grace, pray for us." Mary Grace prayed, and Cassie said, "Thank you, Saint Mary Grace, and Saint Addie, and Saint Jason. Saints before us, saints among us, and saints yet unborn, saints all around us, thank you. I'm going to be all right this morning."

"Just remember to change your shoes when we get back to the car, Cass," Mary Grace suggested. "Won't matter much in the great eternal scheme of things, and I don't think the great cloud of witnesses will care, but the grungy Bailey's Mill shoes don't really go that well with the red dress."

Marcie and Connie sat with Granny Myrt, who was in her usual place, about halfway back on the piano side, right behind Arnie and Ruth Peyton. Most of the congregation had been at Webster Funeral Home twice within the past week, on Monday night for Floyd Williams and again Friday night for Jason, so the ones who didn't already know them both met them there. Ronnie Wofford was there with all of his family, the first time that Cassie had seen him in anything other than the camo coveralls. Today, the grizzly bear wore new-looking blue jeans and a flannel shirt. He told Cassie before the service that his whole family would be joining Peyton's Chapel today. Jennifer would be joining by transfer from Freeman Valley, and he and their two children would be coming as candidates for baptism. Jason's parents and sister were there, just visiting for the day, taking a Sunday off from Alabama Road because they wanted to hear Cassie and thank Peyton's Chapel for their kindness to their family. Cassie recognized the Bradshaws during the announcement time. They thanked the church and Cassie for all of their expressions of kindness and caring and said that they wanted to buy the church a new piano in memory of Jason.

Cassie teared up a couple of times but made it through her sermon better than she thought she would and began the transition into the communion service. "We come now to the Lord's table," she began as Ruth Ann Simpson took the other end of the white linen cloth covering the table and helped Cassie fold it and set it aside. "All who love the Lord Jesus Christ, who look to him alone for the forgiveness of their sins, and desire to live a life pleasing to him are welcome to partake. We welcome those who were in Christ before us and our brothers and sisters from around the world who are spiritually present with us at this table. We welcome brothers and sisters who are visiting with us today to the Lord's table."

Cassie had noticed the fifty-something woman who came in a few minutes after the service began and sat down on the back pew. Mary Grace had moved over and was sitting with her. Cassie had barely gotten out the words about welcoming brothers and sisters who were visiting when the woman stood up. "Reverend..."

"Yes," Cassie responded, startled and wondering what this stranger was going to say.

"My name is Pearlie Harkins. I got up early this morning and decided to drive down here not knowing how I'd be received. You don't know me, but I buried my son yesterday, too." Choking back tears, she continued, "I loved my son, hated the stuff he done, but I loved him. He wad'n raised no such way. That was my son that shot and killed Deputy Bradshaw Wednesday night..."

Donna Bradshaw was sobbing as she got up and walked back to where Pearlie was standing. Gary, Katie, Ronnie, and Cassie followed closely, not knowing what she was going to say or do, thinking they might have to pull Donna off of Pearlie, but Donna embraced her, and they wept together. A holy, tearful silence came over the congregation as Donna and Pearlie comforted each other, bore each other's burden, and fulfilled the law of Christ. Gary broke the silence. "Pearlie," he said, "Come and sit with us."

As Pearlie took her seat with the Bradshaw family on the same pew with Granny Myrt, Marcie, and Connie, Cassie resumed her place at the communion table. Her voice was breaking with emotion as she said,

"This is my first time leading a communion service, and I need to receive communion more than I ever have. We all come to the table needing to forgive and be forgiven. We all come, needing the nourishment offered at this table. We all come, needing the fellowship of those who gather at the table with us." Cassie surveyed the congregation and, through her tears caught a glimpse of Miss Addie, Jason, and Grandma and Grandpa Whitmire seated among them. As she broke the loaf of bread in half and put it on the two trays to be served, she said, "The body of Christ, broken for us, for all of us, every blessed one of us," and as she poured the grape juice from the small pitcher into the one unfilled individual cup, she said, "The blood of Christ shed for us, for all of us, every blessed one of us. Amen."

CPSIA information can be obtained
at www.ICGtesting.com
Printed in the USA
BVHW091728080722
641661BV00011B/386